The Fractured Hues of White Light

ALSO BY LAURA J. W. RYAN

Dusty Waters: A Ghost Story

The Fractured Hues of White Light

A NOVEL

Laura J. W. Ryan

FIELD STONE PRESS

Field Stone Press
2970 Lafayette Road
Lafayette, NY 13084
onemind@twcny.rr.com

First Edition 2010

09 10 11 12 13 14   6 5 4 3 2 1

EAN-13 9780982491645

This novel is a work of fiction—really, cross my heart, 'n hope to die,
I made it all up—therefore, any resemblance to people, places, events, paintings,
facts of life, and perhaps a few figments of imagination are purely coincidental.

The Fractured Hues of White Light
was designed and composed in 10/15' Sabon
by Fred Wellner (onemind@twcny.rr.com).

This book is for those who love the written word, and for those who still prefer to hold a book in their hand while sipping from a cup of hot tea...or a tall glass of Guinness. It's a beautiful thing.

LAURA J. W. RYAN is a writer and an artist, she lives in an old farmhouse on a windswept hilltop in Upstate New York with her husband, their son, five cats, and one dog named Max. For more information about the author, please visit: http://upstategirl-laurajwryan.blogspot.com/ where she discusses the creative life and inspiration, writes essays, posts writing in progress, photographs, and artwork.

"It is the first vision that counts. The artist has only to remain true to his dream, and it will possess his work in such a manner that it will resemble the work of no other man— for no two visions are alike...Imitation is not inspiration, and inspiration only can give birth to a work of art."

—ALBERT PINKHAM RYDER.

The Fractured Hues of White Light

Samantha's Wedding

"...until death do you part?"

"I do," I said with meek shyness, the words spoken barely above a whisper. At least, I think I said it—though I can never be too sure—*I better check*. My gaze went roaming beyond the veil for a sneak-peek at Preston; he is smiling at me with so much pride, he might pop his shirt buttons. Then I slyly checked Judge Nadine Ardyce who had just made the inquiry regarding my promise that required me to answer, *"I do"*. To my relief, she's still tying up the loose ends—uninterrupted by a *Sammy disaster*, so it seems I actually articulated the proper reply loud enough to be heard. *Whew!* I'm glad that I didn't fuck it up, I said what was required of me, and no one had to groan, *"Oh Sammy, why can't you just blah blahblah-blahblah blah."*

With a soft sigh, I dropped my veiled gaze to stare at our joined hands; Preston's large, too perfect hands are damp with nervous energy as they gripped my small ones so tight that it nearly hurt. I wiggled my fingers just a little to ask for relief, but he didn't loosen his grip, almost as if he was afraid I'd float away if he did anything to relieve my discomfort. Giving up, I struggled to remain quiet—*to be good*—my overwrought mind wandered along with my gaze away from the intertwined pale pink flesh to look out the window just past Judge Nadine's left arm. The imperfect old glass with the undulations and bubbles soothed me, I loved the way it distorted the daylight, turning the landscape beyond into pale blue-green abstract expressions.

"You may kiss the bride," Judge Nadine pronounced loudly; my stray attention returned to silence. It seemed everyone sucked all the air from the room. *What happened? Are we done?*

Preston raised my veil before I was ready for it; although I twitched, I stayed calm because I knew he wasn't going to hurt me, this is what he's supposed to do because we rehearsed it yesterday. *What a happy man, he's just so happy today*—I don't think I've ever seen him smile so much as I have today; his thin, strangely pale pink lips drawn back from those perfectly white teeth, smiling—*oh, happy day!* His smile is contagious, so I smiled back. With the puffy illusion netting finally off my face, he bent forward and pressed that wide grin on my mouth. I relaxed just like I have practiced since I first let him kiss me, trying so hard—*sohardsohard*—so hard to be good as gold. I'll just let him kiss me—he likes to kiss me.

Then there was applause—*how weird, why are people clapping?* I didn't expect this. Are they clapping because I didn't fuck it up or are they just happy for us? Turning around, I nearly screamed—*don't clap, stop it!* But I didn't, I held my anxious tongue, and refrained from picking up my lace and hauling ass—*I'm blowing this popcorn stand*—*I'm outta here, I want out of this dress*—*I want*—*I wantiwantiwantiwant*—*I want peace and quiet.*

Smiling to disguise my unsettled guts, I focused my attention toward the window again, the wavy glass calmed me; I took a deep breath and sighed. Two tears dropped onto my cheeks.

People are surrounding us, laughing and smiling—Whitley, Helena, and Sylvester—they took turns hugging me. Sylvester caught my tears in a hanky that he pulled from his pocket—he understood—*he knew*—he knows me better than anyone in the whole wide world. He said nothing as he dabbed away my emotions with tender discretion and tucked them in his pocket once he was sure he got them all.

I smiled. *Oh, happy day.*

༄

Oh, happy day, how much longer does this have to go on? They had promised that it wouldn't take too long, but it has dragged out beyond my patience. There has been too much happening in this one day—way too much! I need a little time alone to wrap my mind around it. Thankfully, in spite of everything that could confuse me or *set me off*, I'm having a *good* day—I am grateful for this good day, for everyone's sake, not just my own. But it is also a bad day, because I'm so tired—being so tired makes me feel out of sorts, I can easily tip-over into being *bad*. Although, I suppose I am being bad right now because I'm hiding in Guthrie's old bedroom—*I really, really, really hope no one comes looking for me.* I just want to be alone; I haven't been alone since the last time I peed about an hour ago, and that was a fleeting moment of privacy while I sat with my fancy accoutrements bunched up around my waist, hoping that I didn't dip any trailing lace or puffy illusion netting into the toilet bowl. It was also a frustrating moment because I was feeling rushed—rushed by Helena's plaintive voice pleading, *"Hurry up, Sammy, the photographer doesn't have all day."* So, my finicky bladder held its breath until she went away. I just wanted five minutes alone to do my business and relax—*Is that a lot to ask?* For now, I just want to be quiet—I need another five or perhaps ten minutes alone. It is just too loud with all of those voices talking at once—and the laughter is just too much to bear. The noise makes me feel so confused, I just want to scream, but that would be *bad*—that would be embarrassing—so I won't scream; I'll be good—*I'll be good as gold.*

Good as gold. My mother, Lenore, had always put my *goodness* in those terms, although my tantrums were always a factor to reckon with, she appreciated my efforts when I tried hard to be good when circumstances cast the expectation for an emotional detonation. How absurd, here I am today, a grown woman still worried about being *good*. A normal young woman *"pitching a fit"* would be accused of being *"on the rag"*, or to have the predisposition toward bad behavior due to a certain heritage. I do try very hard, but there are days when *"Sammy, you should know better"* doesn't work out so well, especially when I'm over-tired I tend to lapse into *bad* on purpose. Why not? I figure no one knows the difference, they just say that I'm having one of my *episodes*, so I'm not considered liable when I really do go off the deep end. If anything, I'm consistent when I'm being weird.

My being autistic was just an obstacle that my family worked around; often their over-protectiveness set up the circumstances that would trip me up and ruin a good day. But without them, I would never have come so far. With the diligent help of Lenore and Whitley, Guthrie and Helena, and then Sylvester, I learned what I needed to do to behave accordingly. They all took turns talking to me, reasoning with me, explaining to me: *"We don't understand what you want when you throw things or scream—look at me and say what you want—say what you mean—come on, Sammy, you know the words."*

To this day I still laugh at my misinterpretation when the doctor diagnosed me as *autistic*—I thought he said *"artistic"*—so I laughed and cried out, *"I draw just like my Daddy!"* But no one laughed with me; my mother cried, my father became indignant, and the doctor defensive. As my gaze rolled over the adult reactions—*their faces so grim, not funny*—I became confused because I didn't know what they were talking about—*about me, so serious*—and decided that I needed to adjust my response to reflect theirs—*I need to be quiet—be seen not heard.* With a cartoon character's flair for the dramatic, I mimed turning the key to my lips and flipping it over my shoulder just like Guthrie had taught me at Christmastime. Then my pencil went about the business of drawing—after all, I am *artistic.* But *little picture's* have ears—and my eyes didn't miss a thing, especially the emotions that sparkled in my mother's tear-filled eyes. My fixation with the emotional landscape of faces was always the quirky discrepancy of my being autistic—my drawings documented with intricate detail the people I loved best of all. The doctor thought this very unusual—puzzling, yet unique, he called me *"special."*

"We are not going to institutionalize her!" Lenore had shrieked horrified by the doctor's suggestion to send me away to a *special* place where children like me can go for *special* treatment. She sat cuddling me in her lap, sobbing into my hair—crying, crying, crying. I didn't cry—didn't want to cry, partly because I didn't really understand what the fuss was about, and partly because I was too busy doodling in my pad of paper—*she was interrupting me.* My mother, so young, she was not much older than I am now when she learned the news about my mental misfortune; she seemed so wounded by it, as if it were her fault that I was born defective.

My father, Whitley, already an old man in his sixties, sat beside her with his craggy face furrowed into a profound sadness; then he rose to his full height—*he looked like a giant to me back then when I was so small*—and he scooped me up into his arms. *"Give it whatever name you want, Doc—*

she's just different—she doesn't need to be institutionalized," he shrugged; it was a gesture of defiance in the face of the doctor. *"There's only one place this child is goin'—that's home,"* he drawled, his accent is a mellow blend of New England burr and Mid-West twang, his voice low and powerful—yet gentle. Lenore always said he sounded so *sexy* even when he's giving someone a piece of his mind. It was peculiar how he seemed so accepting of my disability, almost as if he knew all along. Lenore always complained that he is such a narcissist—so he didn't see anything wrong with me at all, because he thought I was being *normal*—just like him. Like father, like daughter, the nut didn't fall too far from the old oak tree.

"We'll work something out as a family—how hard can it be?" he said to calm Lenore with his rare paternal assertiveness. Whitley always had the finesse to know when to go with the flow; he knew that if he overreacted Lenore would have imploded on the spot. It would have been *ugly* all over the doctor's office. The doctor should have been grateful that my father diffused the *Mom Bomb* and prevented her verbal flailing from spewing into the waiting room full of patients. My mother—the lioness protecting her cub—there was no one fiercer in the whole wide world. No, I knew they wouldn't send me away, I trusted that my family would look out for me. And so, cocooned in my bedroom with the shades drawn against the setting sun of that summer day just after my third birthday, I felt safe, and I went to sleep without a quibble or a tear—*I was good as gold today and I'm special.*

Being autistic seemed like a rare thing back then—back then was when I was three. Treatments were not like they are today—today a kid with autism isn't so rare, and it has become known as a *"spectrum disorder"*—I fall within the high-functioning category. With an IQ of 132, I was considered more fortunate than the other afflicted poor souls, but not by much since I spent my time making scribbles, obsessively organizing my crayons by color, or lining up the salt n' pepper shakers, the creamer, and sugar bowl on the kitchen table in a special way. *Oh, boy, I'd pitch a fit if things weren't right!* My quiet, withdrawn behavior worried them the most, but I'm not as oblivious as they thought—I was all too aware. I was a sponge—I absorbed my entire world that was contained within our old Gloucester house with its twisty, narrow stairs, wavy glass windows, and pointed gables. And I soaked up the sounds and smells of Good Harbor Beach down the road where we go to play on the endless summer days that turned my skin brown as a berry. This special place in my world filled my mind with a treasure trove of colors, shapes, and textures—*I'd organize all of the stones on the beach if they'd let me.*

My remaining home was a success in spite of the doctor's predicted odds against it; after years of careful edification, my independence within the confines of our house seemed guaranteed by the time I was a teenager. Working around the obstacle of my autism created a fixed routine; I get up at the same time every morning and follow a pattern of life structured around time, and time meant clocks; time meant alarms, buzzers, chimes, bells, and for a special amusement, there is a cuckoo clock in the studio where I spend most of my time. Along with the signals of time, there are several notes posted as reminders such as, *"When the cuckoo sings twelve times, it's time for Sammy to have lunch."* This is how I have been programmed toward achieving normal behavior—toward independence—in other words, so I don't need someone watching me every minute. *Well, who knows what I might do otherwise! Oh, the imagined disasters that must have run through their collective heads—it had to be frightening.*

It was my mother, Lenore, who made sure that I knew how to tell time. She implemented the routines because she was there teaching me every day during those crucial early years; cutting the groove into which I function as close to normal as I can get. If only she were here to see how I turned out— that I remembered her repetitive lessons. Lenore died when I was six. I never forgot her. Everyone says that I look like her—or act like her, I'm reminded of that all the time. It really stinks that she died—I really do miss her. I loved how she'd play silent games with me at the kitchen table; the silverware, the sugar bowl, and creamer were my favorite characters. She talked to me all the time and I'd respond to her with my blunt honesty, making her laugh through her gloomy tears that would pop up like unpredictable summer storms; her emotional upheaval was often intense. She always said that I made her happy. My making her laugh was the best gift I could give her—I try to remember her laughing rather than crying. Unfortunately, I can't forget her unhappiness. She was a constant source of frustration for Whitley, and even for the patient Guthrie. Whitley would often take a potentially deadly chance to tease her *"You're so beautiful when you're mad!"* and he'd also say things like *"It's that Latin blood that makes you so hot-tempered!"* as if to blame her ethnicity for making her so high-strung. *"Shut up, you!"* She'd laugh, and smack him on the shoulder, smirking; a fleeting happiness, her deep dimples in bloom. As I got older, I wondered if there was something more to her unhappiness—something that had nothing to do with her being Italian—there was something in her core that wasn't right—something unsettled—dissatisfied. Guthrie always rolled his eyes and said it was *"a woman thing."* Maybe so, but during my recent musings about my mother, I'm inclined to think it was *a Lenore thing* just like I have my quirky *Sammy things* that drive people bat shit.

It seemed my being *different* became problematic outside of home, but my desire to move freely insisted upon my learning how to manage, and after lots of practice with my various guardians accompanying me, my movements weaving through the outside world became uneventful—I can ride my bike to the beach or into town to shop. As an adult, I am able to take the train to Boston unescorted to meet Helena and Sylvester for lunch at the university. I can go shopping at the mall, I can go to the Kramer Gallery to meet with Will and Marie about my commissions, or I can go to the museum to contemplate such wonders like the *Nine Dragon Scroll*. Overall, I try to live a normal life. When I'm having a good day, I'm very independent—but then I have days in which I can't find my ass with both hands and a flashlight. Good and bad, it's so random one day from the next, but I don't believe I'm different from anyone else—you don't need to be autistic to have a bad day.

Helena has ass-up-head syndrome and no one has institutionalized her yet.

Yet, in spite of this training and practice, there is no getting around that I am different from everyone else, all because I *suffer* from autism. But do I really *suffer?* I don't know any better, so how can anyone say that *I am suffering?* It's the people around me who seem to be suffering; I'm fine with it—*they* can't stand it when I *pitch a fit* or *become impossible*, or when I'm *being a pain in the ass*, but they love me anyway. If they didn't, they would have put me away in one of those special places for retards and forgot about me a long time ago.

Whitley and Helena still treat me like a child, yet they expect me to be an adult. Their ever-present concern for my well-being has taken root over years of worry about my future. They make decisions for me all the time, and when they do ask for my opinion, it is presented in a curious way that seems to offer me no choice, and they are disturbed that I don't always agree with their consensus—I often have to remind them of my practiced autonomy. God forbid I may have an opinion exclusively my own.

Would you like to get married someday and have children? Whitley had asked me about six months ago. *Do I?* At the time, I couldn't give him an answer, but he pestered me enough about it that I agreed it might be a nice thing to do someday. This idea of marrying me off came about because Whitley is getting old, he is almost ninety—I guess he's very old. He's afraid of dying; he's afraid of leaving me alone without someone to build my frames—or to manage my life. Whitley says that we can't expect Helena to take on the responsibility because she has a life of her own with Sylvester, and her job teaching at the university, and she travels a lot to do research. Truth of the matter is I wouldn't trust Helena to manage the contents of her purse. It was Whitley's opinion that a spouse would be a built-in caretaker, someone always there; someone who loves me for who I am—someone who understands what I am.

"So, is that a good reason to have some unsuspecting man marry me?" I had asked him at the time. "*Most men are unsuspecting to begin with—we don't know what we're getting into—it's a charade until after the wedding, then the gloves come off and the battle of the sexes begins in the bedroom,*" he said with a hearty chuckle.

I guess he should know—he's had enough wives.

Once I made it known that I would consider getting married, Whitley wasted no time introducing me to Preston Ackerman with the hope that the eligible bachelor would court me. He said that Preston would make a *good catch* for me because he is the type of man who has a good head for *this sort of thing*—he meant managing—being an administrator that's what he does best. I first met Preston at Whitley's Retrospective exhibition; a show co-curated by Helena and Sylvester to celebrate the distinguished professor's retirement from the university.

Whitley was in his glory on that day; he dove into the crowded gallery, talking to everyone, shaking hands, and tooting his horn. Helena and Sylvester kept me company as we strolled through the gallery, starting with the early paintings and drawings from his late modernist phase that looked vaguely cubistic. Then we viewed the bulk of the show covering his more familiar abstract expressionist era, which was a bounty of free-flowing lines suggesting figures in fields of color bleeding and blending into vague landscapes like views of the Earth from outer space. And finally, his recent *I don't give a fuck about hoity-toity art movements—I'll paint whatever I damn well please* period in which realism denotes without a doubt that a figure is a figure and a landscape is a landscape; his recent work from the *Salt Island* series are so lush with color they're visually refreshing.

As we walked together, Sylvester quietly engaged me with attentive bits of conversation; a clever tactic that he has learned to keep me *calm* in situations such as this day spent in a crowded gallery. Helena remained elegantly aloof as she walked slightly apart from us. I sensed that they had been arguing again—well, she had been nagging him all day, and I marveled over how he let her rude comments trickle off him like water from duck feathers. Their relationship as a couple has had ups and downs these last nine years because it seems like Helena is never satisfied with anything Sylvester has done; she does nothing but complain—*the poor man.* She's a bigger pain in the ass than I am on the worst end of one of my bad days—*it's no wonder Shep screwed around behind her back, no man is going to put up with some woman bitching at him night and day.* In spite of her obnoxiousness, Sylvester has stuck by her like a loyal dog; he is as patient with her as she is mean to him. He's such a good man; perhaps she likes it that she can bully him, and he takes it with the forgiving grace of practice because he loves her, and has practiced that love for as long as I've known him. I know that he loves her, he told me so once a very long time ago, way before they finally got together. When I offered to tell her for him, he frantically made me swear not to, so I pretended to forget—I never forgot anything, even when I tried.

I felt uncomfortable that day in the gallery, but it wasn't their disharmony making me feel uncomfortable—it was my clothes. I didn't want to wear a dress, but Helena had made me. I hated this particular dress because the satin fabric smothers my skin, it always makes me sweaty, and I could smell my armpits starting to stink in spite of the deodorant that I slathered on before getting dressed. Throughout the last hour, I was struggling not to scream, a long day has potential to go south, especially when I'm tired, sweaty, stinky, and by this point, my feet hurt, and my itchy pantyhose had gotten twisted during my last visit to the ladies room; I'm so awkward already, pantyhose just make me ten times worse. *I am not normal, why does Helena insist that I should dress as if I am?* Lenore was sensible; she always dressed me in boy clothes—jeans and overalls, t-shirts and sweatshirts; the less fuss, the less muss. Sylvester seemed aware of my chronic discomfort and kept me hydrated with punch and lots of ice cubes to suck on. Helena kept scolding him because I had been to the bathroom four times already, but he ignored her criticism with selective hearing; it seems he's gotten good at that—*I have taught him well.*

I am always grateful for Sylvester's steady 'being there', I had clung to his arm on that day because I was terrified by the pressing crowd; whenever he felt the tension perking under my skin he would lead me to a clearer section of floor space where I could regain my composure. No sooner did our little trio settle in a place where I could breathe with ease, Whitley's shaggy white head appeared above the milling crowd; a path of humanity stepped aside to let him through, and in his wake came Preston as if he were in tow.

Our father is always showing off *"my girls"* to acquaintances because we are his pride and joy (when Lenore was alive, she was included in the Girls Club too). It always amazes me how many people he knows. Most of them humor him because they love him; some kiss his ass because he may be in a position to give them something they want, and then some have that bored demeanor of bland tolerance. As Helena and I appraised the newcomer with a connoisseur's interest, it appeared as if this young, self-important man possessed the attributes of the latter. Preston is young, yet older than I am, on the side of thirty-five closer to forty. He stood tall with broad, powerful shoulders; his ice-blue eyes sparkled with keen brightness from their centered position on his ruddy face; immaculately groomed, he sported short blond hair that seemed tailored to fit his chickpea-shaped head.

"My-my, ain't he pretty?" Helena nudged me. After absorbing her comment, I only shrugged with a non-committal motion, muttered: *"He's more Saxon than Anglo."* and rolled my eyes, sending my gaze to ponder Sylves-

ter's profile as he politely shook hands with the newcomer. His tolerance baffles me, he's either gotten good at ignoring Helena's glances over the fence at greener pastures or he just doesn't care if she window shops—or is he really as *ob-liv-i-ous* as Helena claims? Returning my gaze to Preston Ackerman, I noticed a slight resemblance to her ex-husband Neil Shepherdson, otherwise known as *Shep*—physically, Shep was Helena's ideal man; Sylvester's understated male refinement would be considered *puny* in comparison—considering her laundry list of faults she's found in him, it baffles me that she has tolerated Sylvester for all these years.

"Preston, you haven't met my youngest daughter, Samantha," Whitley exclaimed, pulling me away from Sylvester's comfortable presence, and I immediately crumpled into a less confident posture in spite of Whitley's reassuring arm around my shoulders. Because strangers make me feel uncomfortable, I place my trust in the people who know me to help me through my awkwardness during introductions.

"Ah, the other celebrity of the Ryder family," Preston acknowledged with a broad grin as he narrowed his focus on me; I let him take my hand in both of his very soft, warm hands. "I've heard so much about you from Whitley—I feel as if I know you already—I am honored to meet you at last," he said, pouring on the schmooze-charm. Feeling pressured to reply, I made a grunt of acknowledgement, pasted on a practiced smile, and nodded as I mumbled, *"Pleased to meet you."* and immediately forgot his name. Names are elusive fiends, it's as if a brain-fart blows them away—I have such a stupid head—but I never forget faces.

During past introductions to strangers, most of them have treated me like a novelty freak, or regarded me with pity; then there are the ones who have acted as if shaking hands with me might give them what I have. But Preston was different, he was very gracious and attentive, and made every effort to draw me out as he cross-examined me about of all things—*me*. He also possessed an aggressiveness that initially made me feel unsure of his intentions, but his charisma offered a nimble reassurance that offset my uncertainty. I didn't know what to think of him, he kept coming back like a bad penny—*seeking me out*, and grinning from ear to ear every time he saw me from across the room. Each time he made a beeline for me, Sylvester would lean over and whisper into my ear as if to warn me *"There he is— back again."*

By the end of the reception, I had started to connect his name and face. I also remembered his hands; they were curious, soft hands—*office hands*—there was not a nick or callous on them; the skin was perfectly pink and cream in color—they looked pretty as far as color goes. *What does he do?* I wondered. *He can't be an artist with hands like that.* Even Sylvester, the office-bound scholar and professor of art history, has signs of his dabblings with life; in fact, on this particular day, I noticed that the back of Sylvester's hand sported a nasty scratch courtesy of his cat, Daisy. When I examined the wound with concern, he had laughed, *"I got what I deserved."* I laughed too because Sylvester doesn't laugh much; I always loved the way the corners of his eyes crinkle whenever he smiles.

When Preston Ackerman with his too perfect hands reappeared at my side again, I inquired about what he thought of Whitley's work; the new dean of the school of art acquired a tickled-pink blush as if my attention pleased him.

"Most of it I don't get, so I have a knee-jerk reaction to dislike it—but who am I to judge? I can't draw anything more than a stick figure, but that doesn't matter—I have a great deal of respect for talented people," he floundered, and then looked at me with curious eyes. *"Yours is an unusual talent—so technically perfect. I would like to come see your studio some day,"* he had said with the most charming smile—boyish—I suppose smitten.

This roundabout request usually means a person wants me to paint something. I figured he carried a photograph of some unobtainable art historical relic that he coveted ever since he was a boy, perhaps something that inspired him to become the dean of an art school, and now he wants to frame it in a gaudy gilded frame to hang in his office like a prized trophy. He looks like the sort of guy who'd want the mysterious Jan van Eyck painting *Portrait of Giovanni Arnolfini and his Wife* in his office—or maybe at home in the living room over the fireplace. After a prolonged awkward silence in which it seemed like the cat had caught my tongue, Whitley broke in on my behalf to extend an invitation to Preston to come to our house for dinner.

❧

Preston didn't want to commission anything, he wanted to see me, and he even brought flowers. Although it was a very nice gesture, I didn't feel right about accepting them; I thought it was weird that he gave me a dozen red roses because he doesn't know me that well. Helena made a bigger fuss over them as if to make up for my lack of enthusiasm.

Helena and Sylvester joined us for dinner as per our normal routine. My sister kicked me under the table a few times to remind me that I have company to attend to, which only made me withdraw from him more. Sylvester sat opposite her, engaging me in a kitty-corner conversation; I suspected that my oldest, dearest friend was being protective of me, and a wee bit sympathetic.

"We must make sure to compliment Carrie—this chicken is delicious," Sylvester said, drawing my attention toward his voice. I stared at his slender hands with their long fingers; I have drawn them millions of times over the years, and I longed to draw them now, but I am not allowed to have my sketchbook at the table during mealtime—I tend to spill stuff when I do. So, I traced their shape with my gaze, while lightly nodding in agreement with his remark about the dinner that I barely tasted.

Helena poked me with her toe again, so I shifted my eyes toward Preston and held his hands in my gaze to get to know them. They are large hands, well-manicured, soft, businessman hands; the palms appeared sweaty. I barely said two words to him that evening; I was too preoccupied with being *good*, and Helena's constant henpecking wasn't helping my state of mind. I wanted to get away—I wanted to go lie down.

The lying down idea infested my brain for about five minutes, and then I thought how nice it would feel to crawl underneath the massive structure of the dinner table. When I was little, I spent a lot of time under there; I would sit communing with knees and feet, using a pencil stump concealed in my pocket to scribble on the underside of the tabletop. If they were on display in a pair of khaki shorts, Sylvester's doorknob kneecaps, muscular calves, and bony, hairy shins would amuse me; I would tickle him as my finger stroked against the hair and with the hair, up and down that straight, narrow ridge of bone and flesh. Sometimes I would lay my head in his lap, and close my eyes. But I haven't done this in many years—I think I was twelve or thirteen on the last occurrence, and I haven't felt compelled to do it again, until now. Without a second thought, I did this impulsive thing. I certainly shook up the evening once I slid out of my chair; the last thing I saw as I dipped below the horizon was Preston's startled expression. *"Oh, my God is she all right?"* he cried as he leapt to his feet, scraping back the chair, nearly tipping it over. *"It's okay—she's right here,"* Sylvester assured everyone as his hand gently caressed my tired head resting between his startled thighs. *"She's just tired, right, dear heart?"* Sylvester inquired of me, and then I began purring deep in my throat to express my contentment; I wiggled the stubby pencil out of my pocket and began to work on a new design directly below his dinner plate.

❧

Honestly, I'm amazed the man kept coming around after my performance that night. Somehow, the dinner was the catalyst that allowed Preston into the family. At first, his visits were weekly, and then they became daily. After awhile, he'd take me out for rides in his red Camaro, and we'd go for long walks on the beach. Mostly he'd talk to me—always talking while tolerating my natural, absorbing silence; I liked listening to him, not necessarily to the content of his talk, but the sound of his voice was soft like his hands; his overall texture was *smooth*. That was how our courtship continued—*smooth*. With a seamless effort, he became part of my life. The first time we had sex occurred with the same smooth pace, but his realization that I wasn't a virgin irked him—apparently, Whitley had told him that I was—*well, of course, he didn't know because I never told him.* When Preston asked who I had been with before, I said it was none of his damn business; naturally, he became indignant. So much for *smooth*; after that, I thought for sure that our engagement was called off—but it wasn't; he came back the next day and said I had a right to my privacy—*"Everyone has a past."* I never asked about his.

❧

Our wedding day is here and now—I just exchanged vows with Preston Ackerman about two hours ago during a private ceremony in the front parlor—so now, I'm officially Mrs. Preston Ackerman—but I won't be *"Samantha Ackerman"*, I decided to legally keep my maiden name—*Samantha Ryder*—I like it better. Funny thing to think about now, but for the life of me, I don't know why he would want to marry me—*mememe*—me, autistic me—my weirdness and me. The flattering idea of his adoration slips from my brain's questioning fingertips all too easy when he's not standing here reassuring me. Sometimes it doesn't make sense, sometimes it does—there are more sometimes it doesn't than does, it's frustrating to think about it.

Averting my brain from distress, I think about other things—the things I am certain about. I lie here buried by the solace of memories, their weight crushing me into the mattress of the bed where I'm hiding. The bare mattress is musty, unused since Guthrie left us; his room untouched, except by me when I need to think alone—*no one knows that I come in here.* My being in his empty bedroom seems like a vain search for a scrap of his beloved essence; his old bed is a source of comfort. He would understand how I'm feeling right now, and I know he'd be hiding with me in his lonely room at the end of a hallway. We used to lie down together, making shadows on the walls, or reading comic books. I'd lie with my head pillowed on his broad chest, cuddling him like a large teddy bear, I'd listen to his heartbeat and his breathing; quite often it would be his growling stomach waking me up from a nap. He was such a good friend and I loved him then—I love him now. I remember telling him that I wanted to marry him.

He laughed. *"Aww, shucks, Buttons, I'm much too old for you!"*

I laugh to myself. *He'll be fifty-two this year—oh, Guthrie, I wish you were here!*

Age never mattered to me—age, what is age? It is only a demarcation of the progress of linear time in a life. Our age difference was the right excuse for him to make—after all, I was only five when I proposed to him, but I would have understood his reason to protest our marrying if he just simply told me the truth—he was already in love with someone else—Lenore.

❧

Preston Ackerman—my husband—did I really want this man for my husband? Why did I need a husband? I don't know if I love him—I don't know how I feel. He says that he loves me—in time, I will learn to love him too.

❧

Feeling inspired, I quickly rose from the hollow where Guthrie used to lie and left behind the seclusion. Stepping lightly down the hall, I tried not to make the taffeta rustle, but it whispered anyway. I ducked into my old bedroom and thundered up the stairs to the garret studio from the secret passageway inside the closet. The scent of linseed oil made me feel giddy—comforted. My hands picked up my sketchbook lying on the table, opening it, I turned the pages like a storybook; lines and washes, random marks manipulated into forms, scattered portraits and hands—my heart raced—*this is beautiful!* The voices of the twenty or so guests filtered through the wide floor planks; their festive noises invading my thoughts of the past—*how much longer does this have to go on?* The old gabled house seems overwhelmed by its guests; most of them are Preston's friends and family—he has two young boys from his first marriage that had failed. *"Why did it fail?"* Preston sucked in his breath when I asked him this question, then as he breathed out, he said, *"We were not happy together."* Well, that seemed simple enough—I understood that concept because I watched Lenore and Whitley struggle with their unhappiness—yet they knew happiness too.

After his proposal and my acceptance, I had to wonder if he expected me to be a mother to his boys. *How can I be a mother when people perceive me as a child who needs to be told what to do all the time?* On the day that we announced our engagement, I approached his young sons and said, *"I'm not your mommy, I'll never replace your mommy; I'll never pretend to be your mommy—I'll never be your mommy."* That clarification on my part made a sour beginning for the rest of that day—I certainly can ruin a good day by just opening my mouth. Oh, well, I always say what's on my mind.

So, here I am, still wearing my mother's wedding gown, dressed like a perfect china-doll—only I'm not so perfect; the decorative Victorian lace around my neck makes me itch and I hate the sound of the taffeta—it is such a loud fabric, I want to scream every time I move. The delicate veil of illusion netting that has annoyed me for the better part of the day is now crumpled from being underneath my body—*it's ruined. I can't go back downstairs like this*—

"Samantha?" A voice called, searching for me from the top of the stairs—*Preston.* The hall door to the garret opened, and his feet pressed on the creaking boards in the narrow stairway.

Shit! Trying not to panic, I spun around unsteadily three times, put my sketchbook back on the table where I keep it, and after another flustered spin, I met him at the studio door just as he opened it.

"What are you doing?" he asked; his eyes hooded with disappointment.

"I was tired; I came up to lie down—just for a minute." I told him with a smile that I hoped looked all right; I have tried practicing my smile for this day. I didn't want to make that weird crooked smirk in the wedding pictures—Helena says that I look like a psychopath when I do that. Feeling awkward, I lowered my eyes and studied his hands. In spite of the time we've spent together, I still feel unfamiliar with him, but I know the shape of his hands because I have drawn them many times in an effort to learn about him through drawing, but so far, only his hands have held my interest—*they're soft hands.*

"I was just wondering—just making sure everything was all right," he said with a hint of discontent. It's taken a lot of practice on my part to become aware of the emotions of others, learning to pay attention to the subtle nuances of mood. My obsessive interest in faces have filled numerous sketchbooks; this is a unique glitch in my autism, I look, I see, I draw, but I fail to react, to communicate, to acknowledge—*I've tried harder to understand just for him.*

With a distracted expression twisting his features, he looked around at my work laid out on the bench and the drying rail along the wall. He said nothing about them, he never does—he's not an artist—although he's the dean for the art school, he admits that he's a bean counter at heart, not a painter. He earned a master's degree in museum studies, so he has an understanding about the value of art to society and the monetary investment, but that is all.

My gaze left him, and wandered over to the rail where the commissions were lined up to dry, I barely saw them, I've already disconnected from them because they're done; Whitley will frame them after the paint dries. With a slight tilt to my head, I rolled my eyes toward the drafting table where my sketchbook sat waiting for me. It will be a relief when the reception is over; I really want to come up here to draw—*I want to draw hands today.*

༄

It is because of autism that I have a special talent—a gift. I can draw or paint anything—precisely copy anything in perfect detail; it gives me peace to do it. When I was four years old, I was playing in Whitley's studio with scraps of tempered hardboard that he had let me have; he even applied a layer of gesso on them and sanded them to a smooth finish. Using the tubes of paint he left out for me to practice mixing colors, I copied the *Mona Lisa* from a book I had found in one of Guthrie's dusty college boxes—it was my favorite book, and I imagined I could make the pictures I liked for my room. When Whitley came home from school, I held up my 10 x 8 inch duplication of the *Mona Lisa* for his inspection, it sent him into such ecstasies that it made me laugh—which was a rare sound for me to make aloud—though I do giggle inside my head a great deal. When the aging abstract expressionist painter showed the little painting to his young wife, he told her that he felt that this *talent* of mine could cause *"quite a stir"*—*"an attraction"*.

Lenore's eyes sparked with disapproval when she turned upon him, and he cringed, bracing for the words he knew she wasn't afraid to use.

"You oughta be ashamed of yourself to suggest exploiting her talent— you shouldn't encourage her to copy other people's work. Her own drawings are special—we should be nurturing those instead."

However, in spite of her protest, I was eager to please Whitley, and went on to copy everything out of the art history text precisely as I perceived it. If the pictures were in color, I matched the hues; if they were in black and white, I matched the tones, I copied everything exactly—precise-precise-precise and perfect—picture perfect. My defiance and Whitley's enthusiasm made Lenore very angry, so I stopped copying from the book and went back to my sketchbook scribbles that meant nothing to anyone but me— scribbles that would never cause *"quite a stir"* or become *"an attraction"*. I drew everything and anything—faces, hands, feet, or designs that my pencil's continuous flowing line created—random rhythms depicting the peace and quiet that the act of drawing generated for my overactive mind; serenity and focus rippled and swirled in the blackest blacks and the palest tints of graphite fading into white paper.

Once Lenore was dead, she no longer stood in the way of my father's craving for attention by living vicariously through my success. In his long life, he had two claims to fame that he felt quite proud of; he had been acquainted with Jackson Pollock, and he is a shirttail relation twice removed to Albert Pinkham Ryder. These two notable bits of background, along with his artwork and years of teaching, barely got him in the door of galleries—

so, he exploited my talent and we made lots of money—LOTS of money—more than he ever believed possible.

My talent became a quirky novelty for the world to enjoy. People came to talk to us—Whitley Ryder and his child prodigy. These visitors would bring me photographs, pictures cut out of magazines or books, they would hover over me, pleading—*"Can you paint this for me, Samantha?"* Of course, I could, I can paint anything I want, and I could do it quickly. I can do Hieronymus Bosch's, *The Garden of Earthly Delights* in two weeks. The entire ceiling of the Sistine Chapel takes about two months of eight-hour days because there's a lot of stuff in it; the last complete one I made was only 12 x 22 inches. I make each repeat copy smaller than the last, just so I'm not painting the same image exactly the same—I like to have some variety in my work—or at least a challenge. The *Mona Lisa* is the most popular, and my latest copy of her is 3 ¾ high by 2 ½ inches wide. Whitley says that I'm really splitting hairs by asking him to cut panels to such small denominations; it really pisses him off when I request something at a sixteenth of an inch.

As the word about my miracle talent spread, different people began to come to talk to me, to interview me for the newspaper, magazines, and then television. I would paint for them, my brush dancing across a canvas in deft strokes, my eyes clear, so focused, mixing paint, matching the flesh tone of the blush on a woman's cheek, or the hint of a man's five o'clock shadow on his chin. They'd talk to Whitley because I would be too shy to engage them in conversation—I couldn't even look at them; I feared them calling me names like *retard*; the worst one is *idiot savant*. *"I'm autistic, but not THAT autistic!"* I had shrieked at the offending visitor, who had also talked around me as if she thought I was deaf. I really just want to be left alone so I can work. *Why must these people see me? There is nothing to see.*

At the same time that museum curators pooh-poohed my talent, the world embraced it; I was the Gloucester, Massachusetts human-interest story that suddenly became a national treasure—or something like that. Will and Marie of the Kramer Gallery in Boston have handled my work for many years. They always say that no one walks away dissatisfied—although one woman did. She was an eminent pain in the ass; everyone knew that nothing anyone ever did could satisfy her, so I made Whitley give her back the money—that in itself made her happy. We later sold the miniature of Van Gogh's *Starry Night* to someone else who appreciated it.

Through the years, I have painted steadily every day; always busy fulfilling another commission that regimented my life from dawn to dusk. When it became clear to me that I could only paint what everyone else wanted, I felt sad. If I ever wanted to paint anything of my own, I don't remember what it was—it was so long ago. When I try to remember what I wanted to paint, I end up remembering people and the events surrounding those people—Whitley, Lenore, Guthrie, Helena, Sylvester, and now Preston—I have filled my sketchbooks with them, and doodles of nonsense marks, lines going nowhere, shadows cast by white light illuminating nothing. Today I want to draw hands, but I can't because it is my wedding day—the house is full of guests who want to toast the bride and groom—*which means I have to go back downstairs.*

❧

"Are you all right, Sam?" Preston asked.

His question reached into my foggy mind mired in memories and dragged me back to the present situation of us—he in a black tuxedo and I in a white wedding gown standing in my studio. I suddenly realized that I haven't heard a word he said; his voice has been droning along in the background of my drifting thoughts rehashing the past for an undetermined amount of time—*seconds, minutes?* It seems this milestone day with its celebratory distractions has caused me to slip through these tokens of my history with the slick ease of daydream escape—perhaps I'm seeking comfort in their familiarity.

"I'm all right, just looking at your hands—I want to draw them," I confessed weakly, suddenly feeling anxious about tonight in our wedding bed. It bugged me that I wasn't particularly enthusiastic about the pending event because I have yet to cultivate sensual feelings for him to make the anticipation of tonight enticing. I know he is looking forward to tonight; he's been like a child excited about Christmas.

"Come back downstairs to the reception." He gestured toward the stairway with a nod.

"But I don't feel comfortable—I want to be alone—" I sighed. My gaze once again sought the sketchbook, and I physically flinched toward where it lay on the drafting table awaiting my return, but I remained rooted to the spot in front of Preston, trying very hard not to whine, trying very hard to be good. "My dress is a mess because I laid down on it, and my veil is too—I can't go down there looking like this—"

"There now—you can change your dress," he coaxed, gripping my shoulders tight with his big soft hands. I held my breath when he began to caress my arms. "I know it's been a long day, but it is just for a little while longer—you can draw later, you can draw all day tomorrow."

"I know," I said through my expired held breath.

"Oh, Sammy, it's okay," he sighed, gathering me to his chest. His tuxedo jacket felt stiff and scratchy, the fabric held the chemical stink from the rental place. I didn't want to be near him like this, and struggled in his embrace. He held me tighter and I relented by going limp to placate his need to be close. "You will get used to me soon, I promise." He cooed into my ear, trying to be soft for me, but he said his words in a cajoling tone that I didn't like.

I narrowed my eyes, almost closing them, and then he kissed me. With a sudden twitch, I broke free, and he let me go with the slightest resistance. I could sense that he was worried that I might cry out, cause a scene, and perhaps embarrass him in front of his friends and family. Well, of course, he should be concerned since I've been known to do that sort of thing.

"Samantha is so unpredictable, she's always ruining a good time, pitching a fit when things don't go her way." Helena had crabbed about my absurd quirk a very long time ago—way, way, way back when Sylvester first came to us. We had spent the day Christmas shopping with him, and he seemed mad at her when she said it because he said, *"It's been a long day, you've dragged us from one end of this mall to the other—she's tired."* I think he was tired too—tired of her chronic nagging. If only she had just left us at the bookstore where we were quietly reading books, that way, she could' a shopped 'til she dropped without us two slow-pokey-toes driving her bat shit—it would've been a happy ending instead of a crappy ending.

"It's all right, Sammy, I know you need time; we don't know each other that well, but we will be fine." He stepped close to me again, his head lowered, and he looked at me with that intensity that always caught my attention in a curious way. I felt confused by the trill of my heart—*what sort of tantalizing excitement is this? It's sort of like fear.*

21

"Let's go back downstairs," I said, turning away from him, and lifting my skirt just like Helena had instructed me so that I don't *trip and rip*, I began to walk toward the top of the stairs.

"I wouldn't have gone through with this if I didn't feel something for you—I do love you, you know." His voice followed me; he said this with a meekness that I found unexpected from him. I looked back at him; he remained unmoved, standing by the bench, his large hands hanging at his sides; he looked defeated. "I really want you to believe that—I know I come off like a pompous ass sometimes—you know I don't mean any harm."

"We'll be all right," I assured him, holding out my hand.

"Do you love me?" he asked, taking my hand, he pondered it thoughtfully. "It just occurred to me today that I haven't heard you say so—even after exchanging our vows—I don't know where I stand with you."

"Oh, Preston, what is love?" I asked. "Is it a state of familiarity—a fondness for a body that one is intimate with? Or is there something more to it than that? I don't know—my concept of love is so different from yours—I understand the sensibility of it. I love Whitley, I love Helena; I loved Guthrie when he lived here with us, I loved Lenore while she was alive—and I still love them. Then there's Sylvester, I love him too because he's one of my oldest friends. I love them because I am familiar with them. In time, you will be familiar to me, and I will learn to love you too. You must be patient with me, Preston. I am different from you, so different I might as well be alien— don't ever forget that I suffer from autism, no matter how normal I may seem on the surface, I am not normal like you, no matter how hard I work at it, I'll never be normal. Don't expect me to change overnight; expect me to be different."

"I love you because you are different," he said, letting loose that short bark of a laugh. I've recently recognized that he uses this noise when I confront him with something he finds hard to hear.

"I'm sure you do, but I fear you don't really know what living with me will entail."

"Are you saying that our getting married today is a mistake?"

"No—but I know that you've made concessions to be with me—I know that you love me, but I'm afraid that you will have regrets someday."

"I promise—you will have no regrets, nor shall I. Do you know what I love about you? Your mind—I don't even think about your disability—I—" he tried to say, but I covered his mouth with my hand because his speech was well rehearsed; he had said this several times before, like on the night I let him slip his hand inside my panties that very first time.

"Don't say that, you're lying to yourself because you do think about it all the time."

I don't think he heard what I said, and wondered if I even spoke out loud—sometimes I forget to do that. Sylvester pointed it out to me once; he said that he could tell by a certain look in my eyes when I'm talking inside my head. *"Talk to me, dear heart, your eyes want to."*

"Don't worry, Sammy," he laughed and embraced me again, kissing me hard on the mouth, his hands crushing my wedding gown; at this point, I didn't care if he ruined it. When he lifted the voluminous skirt, I did nothing to stop him, then his groping hands tugged on my undergarments, causing the stockings to make soft, tearing whispers as the runs split open and traveled down my legs. I remained silent, focusing on his mouth and his face pressed tight against mine, trying not to flinch from the abrasiveness of his incoming facial hair while he kissed me. As he thrust into me, his face looked strange from exertion, and from something internal. He appeared dissatisfied, but I couldn't tell if it was with me or with the act of sex itself. Initially, he wanted to impress on me the importance of sex—how it was supposed to be *special*, but this isn't *special*. Although there was excitement in the urgency of the moment as we grappled together, I felt distressed that he didn't want to wait until tonight when we could be alone, to lie together for the first time as husband and wife. Suddenly, I wanted to cry, but I stayed quiet as he tensed and convulsed with a smothered moan into the puffy folds of my veil. The taffeta of my dress seemed extremely loud compared to his panting.

"Stop!" I cried, unable to bear it any longer.

He didn't stop until he finished, then with a grunt; he pulled away, and stepped over to the drafting table, plucking a handful of tissues from the box to wipe off his penis; he scowled at it with disgust. After he threw away the wad of tissues, he zipped his trousers and adjusted his jacket with wooden-like motions.

"I'll see you downstairs," he muttered without looking at me; walking away, he eased his broad-shouldered body down the narrow stairway.

Feeling apprehensive because of his sudden change toward me, I followed him, but detoured to spend an inordinate amount of time in the bathroom, whispering frantic curses while trying to make sense of my dress and veil. I stopped my monologue of foul language when I heard high-heeled shod footsteps clunking up the stairs like a deranged horse.

"Sammy, are you all right?" Helena called out from the hallway.

"No, come help!" I cried, allowing for the exasperation that I felt to enter my voice.

"What happened to you?" she exclaimed with exaggeration—*she's drunk*.

"What do you think? I came up here to just be quiet for a little while, then my husband came looking to get *some*—he got what he wanted after a sad puppy display and a bunch of pretty talk," I grumbled, mimicking impatient annoyance much like her own.

"Oh, Sam—I thought maybe that was what happened after the two of you *disappeared*," she laughed wickedly as she unpinned my veil and shook out the mangled material once she freed it from my hair. "What a fucking mess—gah! What did he do to you? Thank goodness, the photographer is done taking pictures! You know—if you come downstairs changed into something more comfortable maybe the drunkards will take a hint that you'd like to start your honeymoon."

"I think I will!" I expressed my relief with a growly sigh.

After she helped me shuck off the hideous gown, I tiptoed in my ruined stockings and sticky underwear into my new bedroom to find a proper dress to replace it.

"Wear something nice," she called, ruffling the noisy dress in my wake.

"No—I thought I'd pick through the hamper for the jeans with a hole in the seat and a dirty t-shirt with stinky pit stains—do you think they'd notice?" I sneered as I fetched fresh underwear from the dresser drawer.

"Sometimes your sense of humor is unbelievable," she smirked from the doorway. "Wear this one—it's pretty." She stepped into the closet and pulled out a red dress that I never really liked; she had picked it out for me one day and I agreed to like it just to appease her.

"No—this one." I picked out my favorite denim dress—I love it because it feels so soft, but I really selected it because I knew she hated it.

"Good lord, that thing! It's so ratty you've worn it to death—you're a wealthy woman, yet you wear the same out-dated rags."

"Lena, I'm tired, I just want to be comfortable," I whined at her to emphasize the fact that I am tired and uncomfortable; my crotch burned and felt abraded inside.

"Here, wear this one—it's similar, but not so beat," she sighed, pulling out an off-white linen dress of a similar style.

"All right," I muttered my compromise just to get her out of my hair, tugging the dress that vaguely reminded me of a sack over my head; it slid loosely over my body. "This is so much better," I sighed with relief to be free of the lace and taffeta confinement.

"It will take time for you to get used to him," she said with a sigh.

"Yes, it will—he's aware of that," I replied, brushing my hair.

"He didn't hurt you did he?" she asked, looking at me with concern as if finally realizing what had just occurred.

"No-no, I'm all right," I answered, turning my gaze to the floor, feeling an odd mix of shame and anger—the whole thing went wrong and somehow it felt like my fault. "It's not like I haven't done it before."

"Sam!" she cried. "I thought you said you haven't done it with him."

"Well, yeeaaa, nearly a month ago we started—and he ain't the only one I've been with!"

"You've been with someone else before?" she asked this with such surprise.

"April Fools!" I cried out and clamped my hand over my mouth, mocking her question.

"Who?" she asked, her curiosity was killing her. "Who did you screw around with and when—where—holy shit—Sammy, you never told me!"

"Jeez, Louise—none of your damn business," I grunted, crossing my arms in front of me—*why can't I keep my big mouth shut?*

"Holy shit, you've been holding out on me!"

A burst of laughter from downstairs interfered with our conversation.

"Happy Anniversary, I wish these people would go away! Maybe I'll stay up here."

"No, you're going downstairs to say goodbye," Helena said, narrowing her eyes at me, daring me to be defiant—but I'm going to be good. When I walked downstairs to rejoin the guests, Helena stalked behind me like a disgruntled shepherdess with a wayward lamb.

Upon entering the front parlor, I caught my husband's eye; he quickly looked away, turning red-faced, thus confirming that he had a major bug up his ass about everything he can think of that I did wrong since the second we met. Lucky for him, my temper didn't blow up in his calculating face because I felt someone familiar standing at my elbow, and turned to find Sylvester holding an empty glass in his hand. *Uh-oh, he's potted, the poor thing*—he never could handle liquor very well.

"Are you all right?" I asked my old friend, taking the glass away from him—*Whitley must've poured him a scotch—he can't drink that stuff—it does bad things to him.*

"Fine, fine. How are you, my friend?" He leaned in close to me—*oh, yes, it was scotch, damnit, Whitley!* I slipped my hand into the bend of his arm so I could steer him over to the alcove where he could get some fresh air at the open windows. The gentle ocean breeze through the screens caused the curtains to billow softly around us; outside of my studio, this is one of my favorite places in the house.

"Tired, dear—very tired," I replied, leaning my head on his shoulder, and nuzzling the seam of his sleeve; his suit smelled good, fresh in spite of the hint of cigar smoke—he must have been outside with Whitley smoking a few minutes ago.

"I'm sorry," he muttered.

"It's all right, it's just today—tomorrow I can go back to my routine," I said, putting a tune to it with a singsong in my voice.

"Right," he laughed. "You made such a pretty bride today," he said with an intimate whisper, his hand stroking my hair in a sweet gesture.

"Oh, Sylvester," I sighed. Grasping his slender hand, I made a bouquet out of his long fingers that I knew so well, and kissed the fingertips. "I've known you for such a long time—you are one of my best-est friends."

"That's so Dutch, dear heart," he laughed.

It always amuses him when I mangle the English language by making up my own words and using holiday wishes for curses—*he always understood me.* Feeling a sudden rush of affection for him, I kissed him on the mouth; he sighed against my lips as he pressed back with ardor equal to mine, and then he moaned as if suddenly afflicted by an impulsive agony. When we parted from our kiss, he swayed unsteadily.

"Oh, Samantha, I—" he mumbled with a sickly twist to his mouth that resembled regret.

"Oh, you poor thing, you don't feel so good, come along." Slipping my arm around his waist, he slumped against me as I led him from the alcove. Just as we emerged from behind the curtains, Helena was there, and thankfully, she caught him on his other side, and together, we steered him toward the small powder room down the hall; good thing it was unoccupied.

"I'm so sorry about this—I should have been watching him." Helena groaned as her man knelt between us and threw up into the toilet.

"It's all right—Sylvester can get drunk on my wedding day—there's no law against it." I leaned over him, gently rubbing his shoulders. "It's all right, dear heart," I soothed, mimicking his kind concern that he reserved for me. He laughed, his chuckle echoing inside the toilet bowl. A sudden premonition compelled me to relieve him of his glasses, fearing that they'd fall in. As I stepped back, Helena stepped in to hand him a dampened washcloth to wipe his mouth.

"Thanks," he moaned, flushing away the recently expelled contents of his stomach.

"Is everything all right in here?" Whitley asked, peering in at us through the doorway.

"We've got it under control, Daddy—Sy is just being himself," Helena winked.

"Well, we wouldn't want him any other way," Whitley shrugged. "But does the bride need to be preoccupied with this?"

"It's my wedding day—I can do what I want—I have so far," I remarked from my station against the wall just inside the doorway of the itty-bitty bathroom. Sylvester began heaving again; I reached down to pet the back of his head, my fingers traced the spot where his graying dirty blond hair is thinning at his cowlick.

"Yes, apparently you have—" my father said with a crooked smirk that he reserves for discovering mischief.

"You had no business telling Preston that I was a virgin," I snapped, suddenly angry that he had commented to Preston about my assumed inexperience.

"I thought you were," he shrugged, his face marked with a baffled expression. "I never knew that you had a boyfriend because you didn't tell me."

"It's none of anyone's business if she had a boyfriend or if she had a one night stand with someone she met on the beach." Helena said in my defense; the tone of sarcasm slapped at his indignant attitude, making him flinch.

"She's my daughter; that makes it my business—"

Just then, Sylvester heaved again with such gusto that he made us pause our conversation to examine his bent back. I petted him again, offering him reassurance.

"Daddy—why should it matter with who or when it took place—I didn't go off willy-nilly with my head up my ass—I thought about it, I did it of my own free will, and I used birth control—" I shot back. Helena yelped, quickly covering the reactionary grin behind her hand; Whitley sagged as if wounded by the past that reverberated between us; my words sang in a tone so much like Lenore—like mother, like daughter—the apple didn't fall far from that tree.

Sylvester gagged from a fit of the dry-heaves.

"He's clearing out the guests—your husband—not this one here puking his guts out." Whitley said, recovering with a good-humored laugh as he nodded toward Sylvester's crouched form wrapped around the toilet bowl. "He's telling them to scram because you're tired."

"Oh, goody," I giggled; I didn't care if anyone heard me.

Sylvester's roiling belch resonated within the toilet bowl. "Excuse me," he muttered.

"I guess I should go out there and say goodbye to them," I sighed.

"I think we should go too, Lena." Sylvester said, raising his upper body from the toilet and sagging against the wall next to me.

My poor friend looked so vulnerable down there; I stroked the top of his head.

"I'm sorry, Samantha—I didn't mean to get hammered like that—" he sighed.

"It's all right, Sylvester," I smiled; bending down, I replaced his wire-rimmed glasses on his face, carefully perching them on the bridge of his prominent nose, tucking the curved bows behind each ear. He smiled in return, but his expression held a note of self-reproach as he looked up at me. While I stroked his hair, he leaned his head against my leg; I wasn't sure, but it felt like he kissed my thigh through the folds of my dress—if he had done this unusual act, it was all right, I didn't mind; our long time affection for one another is sweet with familiarity.

Helena and I helped Sylvester to right himself, each taking a hand and tugging—the three of us laughing at the absurdity of our being jammed inside the tiny powder room.

Once on his feet, Sylvester, bent over the sink to rinse out his mouth, then he straightened his tie, and ran his fingers through his hair. I thought he looked much better now.

"You look fine—no one will know the difference," Helena teased.

Sylvester gave her a sidelong glance, his mouth turned down in the sour expression of someone still shaky from upchucking his innards.

As our small family group gathered at the front door, an outsider looking in would have wondered about our subdued manner in spite of the joyous occasion. Compared to the indifferent attitude of my bridegroom, I seemed much more animated as I waved my farewells with detached attention to our departing guests. Before they were all gone, Whitley complained about his aches and pains, and excused himself from the front stoop.

"Well, that's that," Helena said, her eyebrow flickered at me with carnal knowledge.

"Goodnight," Sylvester said, slipping a covert glance that tripped over my face with a hint of apprehensive embarrassment. I watched them walk toward the carriage house, together, yet separately; she with her arms crossed in front of her as if she felt a chill, and he with his hands in his pockets, his head down. I turned to my husband, but he didn't return my look while I studied his downcast face. He said nothing. I said nothing.

Only the caterer's truck remained; the clatter of the catering staff cleaning up the mess within echoed from the back of the house. And Preston's two sons—the clarion call of their upraised voices piped from the barn in the backyard.

"Well, you can go paint or draw to your little heart's content—I'm going to go change my clothes—I have to take the boys home to their mother—I'll be back in a about an hour," Preston finally said. I acknowledged this with a kiss on his cheek. He kissed me on the lips, but not with the passion he used in the garret; his disappointment in me was so blatantly obvious I should have taken the cue to ask, *"What's wrong?"* But I pretended to be oblivious to it—he'll blame my indifference on the autism, that's easy-peasy, right as rain.

In spite of the potential anger brewing inside of me, I relaxed once I was alone. After taking a shower and changing into studio clothes, I went upstairs to the garret where I sat down and began to draw hands in my sketchbook. First, I made long hands with thin fingers and knobby knuckles that I've known for years; these belong to Sylvester. Then I sketched feminine hands with almond-shaped fingernails that belong to Helena—she must have been to the manicurist just for this occasion—those nails are definitely not her own. Next, I rendered Whitley's paint-stained hands that will never come clean; they are ancient hands, sinewy with tendons, scars, age spots, and veins. After these familiar hands, I made a quick study of Preston's substantial hands with their neat fingernails and smooth skin—my pencil skipped away in reaction to the memory of the way his hands crumpled the skirt of my wedding dress; the flesh of my ass and thighs felt bruised by his grip, and my crotch felt raw. His love was rough—*maybe tonight will be different—I can only hope.*

Then I began to draw a pair of blocky hands with thick fingers, hands I haven't seen in a long time—these belong to Guthrie. They were manly hands, even as a young man, he had exceptionally strong hands—the hands of a sculptor. I have imagined that he has acquired many scars since I last saw his hands. I ask Whitley every now and then if he has heard from his stepson, but he still becomes angry whenever I mention Guthrie's name. *When will he forgive—will he ever forgive?* I had always hoped that Guthrie could come home again, but he won't until Whitley says he can—that's between them to work out.

Finally, my inspiration directed the pencil to draw another pair of hands, hands belonging to my mother, Lenore—they are small, delicate hands like mine, the fingernails uneven from carelessness or nerves. Her hands that used to bathe me at night, fold clothes fresh from the dryer; they are the hands that had mended a tear in the knee of my jeans with a nifty patch shaped like a flutter-by to cover the raw reminder of falling off my bike in the driveway.

Lenore and Guthrie, they have been gone for years, I miss them—*miss-them*—miss them both. *What would they think about my getting married today?* I know Guthrie would wish me well if he thought I was happy with my choice, but Lenore would hate it—she would hate the whole thing! Lenore thought she was going to be there for me long after Whitley died from old age—mother and daughter alone, we were going to have a wonderful life together.

I looked up at the bulletin board above my drafting table; my mother's portrait glanced at me over her shoulder. *"Are you happy, Sammy?"* her eyes questioned. I can almost hear her voice as if she was standing right beside me.

"Sammy wouldn't do anything she didn't want to do—right, Buttons?" Guthrie's portrait said, his deep-set eyes framed by heavy, dark eyebrows, and his thick frowning mustache seems to depict the serious consideration of the situation at hand. My finger touched the tip of the graphite nose, and then my gaze slipped over to Sylvester's sketched features; from him I looked at Whitley and Helena; all of them are watching over me with varying degrees of love and disquiet. They worry too much in their various ways. Guthrie's right, I've only done things that I wanted to do—but sometimes I was not happy about doing them.

The question is—am I happy?
The answer is—I don't know.

2 *Guthrie and Lenore*

Happiness comes and goes in various degrees—I try to keep track of when and where, and especially who I've been happy with. When I think of Guthrie, my happiness is painful—it makes my stomach hurt because the butterflies crash into each other. Before I knew Sylvester, Guthrie was the one who knew me best. Like Whitley, he was a giant, but in spite of his intimidating size, I would melt against his shape, holding his big blocky hands with my tiny ones, feeling safe. A long time ago, he had been my protector, but after Lenore died, he left. I miss him. I wish he would come home someday—*I wish he were here!*

My pencil doodled around a drawing of Guthrie's hands; the patterns of cross-hatching are the static keeping away the memories, until the dulling point eventually made smooth lines, drifting into the white away from the drawings of hands to make a circle—*circlecirclecircle*—circle. Slow—slower and slower, I made a black spiral, a tornado, a cyclone, the eye of a storm, a tunnel with a light at the end; it is into that spot of white light where I peer through and remember that day when Guthrie came home.

❧

Today—Guthrie is coming home again after being gone for so long. Summer always brought him home to us; the occurrence of his seasonal return caused me to associate the warm smell of sunshine-induced sweat on his skin with being happy—happy to have him home. Graduate school in Chicago had kept him away for extended periods of time in which semesters turned into years. School then turned into meager adjunct positions, but still far from home in the mid-west—Indiana, Ohio, Iowa, back to Ohio, and then Illinois; the competition for tenured teaching positions at art schools closer to home was saturated by artists who can't make ends meet making art. He called last night with good news that he will start a new job at an art school in New York City this fall, so now he'll be closer to home, and we'll see him more often. *He's coming home today!* I could hardly sit still in school because of the anticipation.

When I got off the school bus at the end of the driveway, I saw Guthrie's distinctive, black and chrome Delta 88, a.k.a. *Delta Dawn*, parked in front of the garage. With my heart singing, I ran inside, but I moved through the house doing sneaky-running because I wanted to surprise him. So, I crept on light toes up the stairs without making a board creak, and paused in the hallway, listening—their voices came from Mommy's room. I have found them in there before, Mommy folding laundry, Guthrie sitting on the bed, smoking—talking and laughing. The door was ajar, so I peered through the crack of daylight, and I saw Mommy standing with her back to the door. Her long black hair hung loose down her back, her arms crossed in front of her; she was wearing her black bikini, her skin already evenly bronzed by the June sun; she looked beautiful in a shocking sort of way—much like the enchanting splendor of an evil queen.

"Come down from there, you silly fiend," she scolded with a wicked laugh.

I pressed my face closer to the crack, careful not to disturb the door and saw Guthrie standing naked on the bed with his hands on his hips; his muscular body looked stunning in the sunlight blazing through the afternoon filled windows.

"I don't want to—come back to bed—I want to love you some more," he teased with a laugh, and started to jump up and down on the rumpled bed.

"Oh, you're being ridiculous—come down from there," she laughed, holding open her arms, beckoning to him. Then with a yell, he leapt from the bed to the floor, catching her in his arms just as she turned to escape from him.

"I got you!" he shouted.

She shrieked with laughter while struggling with him; their roughhousing caused one of her breasts to pop out of its bra cup, his hand quickly covered it with a greedy zeal that also seemed protective. Both of them laughed wildly as they grappled, and fell onto the foot of the bed, kissing. Unable to contain myself, I pushed open the door and jumped onto the bed with them. Naturally, they shouted with shared surprise because of my sudden interruption; Guthrie rolled away from Mommy, sat up, and modestly draped the bed sheet over his pee-pee that stood straight up in his lap, while Mommy scrambled from the bed in a panic, and stumbled into the bathroom. I laughed even more because I had scared them.

"Samantha, you know that you should knock first before entering someone's bedroom!" Mommy's voice called out with a frantic tone through the closed door.

"It's okay, Lenore, no big deal," Guthrie laughed. "Hey, Buttons, how was your last day of school?" he caught me in his arms, greeting me with a hug; his skin felt sweaty against my face and arms as I hugged his neck.

I latched my gaze onto his face, absorbing his being; his blue eyes came alight with amazement as I silently presented the drawing that I made in school. "Hey—let me see your picture—wow, it's a picture of the house, that's really beautiful—will ya look at that—hey, Lenore, you've got to see this!" he said, looping his arms around me as he took it in his hands to examine it. The picture was a perfect rendering of our house with its impressive gabled roofline, each tiny windowpane accounted for with a delicate shift of tone in the graphite. It could have been a better drawing had it been on the smooth plate-finished white paper that Whitley always gave to me for drawing on, but I had to settle for the linty vanilla colored paper that the kindergarten teacher gave us to use. It was great for making velvety blacks with my pencil, but I always hated how the eraser made holes in the flimsy surface whenever I tried to cut in highlights. Shifting into place on his lap, I leaned against his bare chest, rubbing my cheek on him; I loved how he was covered with fuzzy dark wisps and curls of hair.

"Jeez, Louise, this is something—she's a genius, Lenore—I can't get over how she draws like this—I've taught freshmen and sophomores in college who still draw like they're in Junior High, they can barely dream about becoming this good," Guthrie mused while his gaze lingered over my picture. "There's gotta be a special school for someone like her to attend—I bet there's one in Manhattan."

"We tried to get her into a private school for gifted children last winter out in Wellesley..." Mommy called out from the bathroom. "...but they wouldn't take her because her social skills are not on their level. You know how she is—she wouldn't mingle or *participate*—the teacher doesn't have time to focus on her. '*It's not the Samantha Ryder show here*'—that's what the school psychologist said—imagine that, as if Sammy's a big ego expecting the spotlight on her. I keep telling Whitley that we really should hire tutors to come in to teach her—that public school is going to fuck her up by treating her like a retard—and the kids are mean to her because she's different." She returned from the bathroom, barefoot, wearing jeans and a t-shirt; she began to drag a brush through her long hair, and she cursed sharply when she hit a snarl.

"Damn it, Sammy, get off his lap—Guthrie, get your clothes on," she roughly tugged me by the arm, and although Guthrie readily let me go, I dug in my heels, and sagged to the floor. "Sammy, come here—oh, you brat, well, fine, lay there!" Since I refused to cooperate, she let me go with a huff. Whitley has always claimed that I am definitely my mother's child—just as stubborn.

"Don't make a big deal out of it, Lenore—it was bound to happen someday, we were really pushing our luck today," Guthrie chuckled.

"Don't laugh, it's not funny—do you think it's funny?"

"Of course it's funny—don't get all wigged out because it only makes it worse for the kid when you make a big deal out of it—"

"Well, I don't think it's funny at all—get dressed, Guthrie!"

"Lenore—come on—she thought it was funny—she wasn't freaking out about witnessing the *primal scene* or anything like that—just go with it, all right?" He helped me off the floor and hugged me. "All right, Sammy? You're okay—you did nothing wrong—it's okay."

"Ugh, it's not okay, Guthrie—just get out of here!" Mommy shrieked as her face twisted into an angry grimace.

"Lenore—" he sighed; with his head sagging, he stared at his hands— hands roughened by his work, his fingers as misshapen as ancient ruins exposed to the elements. I wanted to comfort him, and I wanted Mommy to stop yelling at him, because *Guthrie is home*—I wanted them to laugh again, hearing them laugh made me happy—seeing them happy is so rare. "Cripe, Lenore, don't ruin it—I just got home."

She didn't say anything. I wanted to speak, but I stood still, quiet, my eyes tracing his outline, then focusing on his down-turned mouth framed by his thick, dark brown moustache, and his heavy eyebrows furrowed into an earthy depression.

"Lenore, I do love you, you know," he said, his face appearing like a wound. Just then, I became acutely aware that none of this was ever a game between them; it was something much more serious, and I started to feel afraid; I began to suck on my two favorite fingers for comfort.

"I never loved you, Guthrie. My mistake was fucking you in the first place," she muttered from a point beyond where we sat. Over the horizon of Guthrie's profile, I saw her light a cigarette and throw the spent match out the window.

"Yeah, right, I've been your sex toy all these years—come on, Lenore, be realistic! Do you think I come here just to fuck you? Damn it, I love you! Whitley can't keep his dick in his pants to be faithful to you, but he keeps you dangling around here just like he did Dulcie because you're the mother—the built in baby-sitter for his gifted daughter—Sammy is his daughter, right?" She said nothing in reply, her breathing behind us suddenly changed as it skipped in her throat, and she began to cry, now a victim of his words. "Don't cry, Lenore." Forgetting about his modesty in front of me, he strode across the space between them. "Listen, I'm sorry—"

"Get away from me," she shrieked, pushing him away as if disgusted by his nakedness.

"Fine, I'll go—I don't know why I bother coming back, we always end up fighting over the same shit—I should have stayed away—I tried, Lord knows, I've tried for years!" he growled, crossing the room with thumping feet that echoed his irritation on the plank floor. He began to thrust his furious limbs into the sluggish jeans that seemed resistant to his flesh, his big feet becoming entangled in the stiff fabric, and he cursed vividly when his big toe caught the hole in his knee and ripped it bigger.

Watching—listening—absorbing, I remained quiet with my fingers corked in my mouth. He squatted down in front of me, his hands gripping my shoulders tight; I stared into his eyes—those blue, blue, blue eyes—wanting to understand, wishing that he'd tell me—*tell me what? The truth about me.* At that moment, his eyes seemed to hold everything there is to know about me—and lots of love. Without saying anything, he softened his hard expression, his hands released my thin shoulders, and then he caressed my cheeks with his square-ish fingertips.

"I bet you don't even know who her father is—she looks like you—it's a good thing isn't it?" he said this with a tone of accusation meant to sting, but she didn't reply; she stared out the window with her back to us. "I love you, Sammy—always remember that," he said, then he kissed my forehead and he left the room.

Minutes later, his car revved to life and roared out of the yard. Mommy turned away from the window and began to sob, covering her face with trembling hands; her voice mourned with inarticulate words as if she spoke another language—the language of sorrow.

"Don't cry, Mommy—Guthrie will come back, I know he will." I plucked my fingers out of my mouth to tell her, but she didn't seem to hear me over her wailing. I began to doubt if I actually spoke. "Mommy—is Guthrie my father?" I asked loudly to make certain that I actually said the words.

When she dropped her hands from her face to look at me, I saw that her eyes were red and swollen from sadness; she suddenly looked as confused as a child would once she realized that she's lost and can't find her way home.

"No, sweetie, Whitley is your father, I got pregnant long after Guthrie left for school," she said, wiping her eyes and cheeks with the heel of her hand. "I wanted to have a baby for Whitley—you were my gift to him—I told him I was pregnant on Christmas morning—we went for a walk on the beach after Helena opened her presents. I remember how he was so happy! He told me that was the best present he ever got—he loves you so much."

"Does Guthrie love me?"

"Yes—he loves you—very much." She slumped against the wall next to the window and stared outside as if looking for Guthrie to come back. I hoped he would come back—come back soon. I hoped for her to say something more, but she remained absorbed in her thoughts.

"Why don't you love Guthrie?" I asked.

"I can't—" she gasped. "I want to and I do—he wants to be with us— you and me as his family. Oh, Sammy, I can't expect you to understand any of this—it's just so mixed up," she sighed, wiping her eyes roughly with the heel of her hand.

"Do you love Whitley?"

"No, I don't love him either—he's such an asshole," she huffed, her brow becoming a tangle of emotional upheaval. She was real mad at him yesterday—mad at him all week because of his drinking; then he got into a bit of trouble for driving home drunk. She keeps warning him—*"One of these days you're going to kill someone—or yourself—driving around like that! Do you think Sammy will understand why you're in jail or why you're dead? I don't want to try explaining that mess to her someday!"* She was livid, and he hung his head, meek with shame.

"I'm sorry," I said. When she looked at me, fear spread over her face after realizing she's talking to me—as if it mattered—sometimes they forget I'm there during their verbal assaults on each other—or to themselves.

"Sammy, I love you—you know that, right? You are so special to me. If I ever left Whitley, I would take you with me—I wouldn't be like Dulcie and leave you behind like she did Helena," she sputtered with a repressed sob. "But he's your father, he loves you so much and I can't do that to him. Although I say I don't love him—I do—in my way I do, I can't help it." She separated her body from the shadowy wall to come sit with me on the bed, and she gathered me into her lap; I sat limply against her body while she squeezed me tight.

"Do you think Guthrie will come back?" I asked, forcing her to sway with the rhythm of my fretful body rocking in her lap. My body has an independent attitude about people holding me, just like a cat. I prefer to choose when to get into someone's lap—I decide when to be hugged and when to be kissed; I go limp with tolerance, become stiff when I've had enough. My rocking is like a warning twitch of a cat's tail; after awhile, she'll be forced to let me go once she grows tired of keeping up with my persistent motion— she says I make her feel seasick.

"I believe he will be back, he won't stay away—he probably went for a walk on Good Harbor Beach to think for a little while."

"Yes, that's what he's doing," I agreed, feeling certain that she was right, and I envisioned his shape cutting into the horizon—water and sky—rather than slouched in the driver's seat of Delta Dawn going somewhere far away, like going back to Chicago or going to New York City. Maybe if it's low tide, he's walking out to Salt Island.

"Oh, Sammy, I'm sorry that I yelled at you like that—I just—" she hesitated over her words as if embarrassed. "I know you didn't mean anything—I overreacted."

"I should know better, I'm a big girl now," I said, hinting at my shame with expected words. I couldn't help it! Guthrie just fascinates me—his maleness and bigness—I fixated on him—*loved him!* I often found myself caught up in a frenzy of exhilaration because of his pending arrival and his being here. This high-charged emotive experience is most likely touched off by Lenore's impatient pacing as she waited, watching for the growling-gleam of Delta Dawn when he pulled into the driveway—her agitation sending invisible vibrations to nudge me over the edge. I rarely express such outright emotion, so it always surprises everyone when I fly out of control into his arms upon his arrival, covering his face with kisses; it's a pure outburst of affection so unlike me. It's not like I don't feel anything, I do, but most of the time I fail to smile, fail to cry, fail to be anything other than me, my face is usually a blank slate, but my insides are in turmoil.

Guthrie loves me—I love Guthrie—Lenore loves Guthrie—Guthrie loves Lenore.

The gleeful words sang inside my head; then I stopped rocking in my mother's lap because I suddenly made the connection between sex and love—at least a six-year-old girl's concept of the emotional actions of adults. I was always aware of the mutual thread linking Guthrie and Lenore together; they were natural companions—like boyfriend-girlfriend, husband-wife—only I never defined their relationship in those terms—only love defined them. They weren't playing a game at all—they are in love.

"Why do you have sex with Guthrie if you don't love him?" I asked for clarification. Her body tensed in reaction, startled by my question, and then after a tremulous sigh, she smiled; I didn't see her smile, but I could feel her smile.

"That's why it's so complicated—I do love Guthrie—but I'm trying hard not to; I shouldn't because I'm married to Whitley. Long time ago, when I first met Whitley—I was so young—I was crazy about him, and he—he was so wonderful to me! I never knew anyone like him before. After spending time with him—just talking—I had been dating a guy, you know him, my friend Noah out on Bearskin Neck, he had just opened the gallery out there, I worked for him—I was practically engaged to him—I dumped him for Whitley. I was so in love, I couldn't stand it—sometimes I thought I'd explode just thinking about him. When Dulcie left him, he was crushed. She thought we were fooling around, but we hadn't done anything, we were just friends. I had been posing for him in the studio at the university—she misinterpreted what was going on because he had done something before with another girl—she got me mixed up with her. But things changed after she left—I made them change, because I was so wild about him. Then after we got married and I came home with him to live, I fell in love with Guthrie practically the minute I laid eyes on him—before he had his mustache," she laughed. I laughed with her; I've only seen pictures of him without his mustache, and I thought he looked funny without it—he didn't look like Guthrie. "It's been this way for years—Whitley knows that I'm unhappy, but he doesn't know how I feel about Guthrie—you must promise me not to tell because he'll get mad at us. I want to be the one to tell him—that would only be fair—you know?" She looked to me for my promise, and I nodded, agreeing not to tell. Although she seemed relieved, there remained the unsettling sense of misery. She gazed out the window over the top of my head with the expectation of his return at any second.

"You know, if Guthrie never came back, maybe I'd be happier," she mused aloud.

After she said this, I felt mortified that she would ever say such a thing. But when I think back on those days in my early life, if he had never come home for all those summers, perhaps she would have been more content with her life—just Whitley and me. There wouldn't have been the pacing, the waiting, the watching—*but we'll never know.*

For supper, she fed me my favorite grilled cheese *sammiches*; the one big sandwich cut diagonally into four perfect little triangles, and served with potato chips and tomato soup—she even put the chips on top of the toasted bread to warm them up the way I like them. And for a special treat, she let me watch *The Flintstones* on the little black and white portable television in the kitchen while I ate the triangles oozing with orange American cheese, dunking the crisp crusts into the soup and crunching warm chips. She joined me at the table, eating a pasta salad she had made, which I found too icky because the sliminess of it made me want to throw up.

While we ate, Whitley called to say he was going to be late tonight, he said that he was going to Pinkerton's house to play poker with the guys. This news made Mommy sad again. So we sat together like a pair of bumps on a log while the news talked about things like trickle down *Reaganomics*, the never-ending problems in the Middle East, and the evil Soviet nuclear weapons threatening world peace, none of which impressed me as more important than the insignificant drama occurring in our house. Our domestic life went on peacefully without the influence of men for the rest of the evening. After my bath, Mommy tucked me into bed, drawing the shades in my bedroom so that the daylight remaining in the sky at eight o'clock didn't disturb my rest. But my antsy mind continued to crawl over Guthrie's absence, so I sat looking at picture books, copying my favorites into my sketchpad until I got sleepy.

Of course, Guthrie did come back. When he crept into my room long after dark, I could smell the salty surf on him; he sat on the edge of my bed and turned on my desk lamp; the night shadows and electric light carved gloom on his face. His blue eyes cradled tears within their lower lids; once he realized that I was awake, he roughly rubbed the tears away to hide them in his hands.

"Tomorrow, we will go to the beach—I want to go first thing in the morning—so come wake me up early; don't let me sleep all day," he said. I nodded my reply. He sat a little longer, just quiet, his dry eyes were red—I watched him—I loved looking at him, my eyes devouring his being there. It was on the tip of my tongue to say *I love you*, but I didn't say it.

"You know what? I've been looking forward to reading a story to you—and I know just the one I want to read!" he said, picking through my pile of books on the headboard shelf. To my delight, he held up the tattered copy of Dr. Seuss's *The Sneetches*. The book had been his—Whitley had given it to him on Christmas Day, 1961. He flipped to the back of the book to read *What Was I Scared Of?*. Only he did it the special way by inserting my name into the story so I was the one doing errands in the dark turquoise nights and running into the creepy pale green pants with nobody inside them; he made me laugh so hard about getting brickles in my britches that I had to go pee.

After my trip to the bathroom, he sensed that I was still restless, so he angled the lamp onto the wall, then he lay down with me, and together we made hand shadows into eagles, bunnies, wolves, serpents, and finally a moose. Then our shadows did mock battles—the fingers of my small hands nipping at his large ones, his big ones swallowing my little ones, and then they made peace with a fingertip kiss. They danced beautifully as our hands and arms twined around one another until they collapsed to our bodies for goodnight hugs that I had missed because of his long absence. He held me extra long, extra hard, and I likewise clung to his neck while wordless love passed between us; then he tucked me in and turned out the light.

Through the closed door, I heard him in the hallway talking to Mommy, but she wouldn't let him into her bedroom. He gave up after a bit, his footsteps traveled heavily down the long hallway to his bedroom; this room is above the sun porch, it's always freezing cold in there in the winter, and blazing hot in the summer.

A few minutes later, I heard Mommy leave her room to follow him, her knock on his door received by a low *"Come in."* Below the sullen drone of the window fan in his room, their talk in soft murmurs went on for quite some time, and then the familiar creaking of the mattress springs came after a brief silence. When laughter broke out between them, I laughed inside—I felt good about them being together because they seemed to be so happy—they are so unhappy otherwise. I knew that they must love each other—*how could she not love him?* She does because she said so. Some time passed by before I heard Mommy go back to her room, and the door clicked shut behind her like the final note to their love song.

Whitley came home after I had been sleeping for a long time, but I awoke as soon as I heard his familiar, careful tread creaking up the stairs; his steps were heavy from drinking whiskey at Pinkerton's house. He went straight into his studio without stopping to see Mommy or me because on nights like this he is too ashamed of his drunkenness to face either of us. I listened to his movements clattering across the planks in the garret above; after awhile he became quiet—probably working on his latest painting; his aching body is so full of arthritis that he is much too restless to sleep. I know he'll fall asleep from exhaustion sometime around dawn—passed out on the sofa under an old ratty blanket. It's been years since he slept through the night in the same bed with his young wife; he made many conjugal visits, and abandoned her side once they finished loving each other. It was rare for me to find him in a tangle of bed sheets with Mommy tucked in beside him, her long black hair draped over his bare chest; he would lie there with a pensive expression fixed upon the ceiling until he noticed me peeking at them, and then he'd wink and wave at me to come in. I'd sit on his side of the bed, and like co-conspirators, we'd whisper our schemes for the day, until our snickers woke up Mommy.

Whitley—Whitley is Whitley, and that's just the way he is, no amount of ranting and screaming will change him; he is such a child in spite of his advanced age—he was sixty when I was born. Whitley's self-absorbed behavior has often led him astray in peculiar directions that he cannot explain; but when he was on paternal duty, he was really *on duty*, which led him to spoil me rotten (like a doting father would). When I was five, he bought me a black and white pinto pony for my fourth birthday. I called her Pony, because I thought that was her name. I loved saying the happy sounding word; I would say it over and over and over and over again until I drove everybody up the wall, *"Pony. Pony. Pony-ony-ony-ony!"* We kept Pony in the barn out back and she grazed in the backyard. This lasted until the neighbors caught wind of her on the ocean breeze—literally—so they complained. But before we could find a proper stable for her, some naughty boys stole her to go for a joyride on the beach. Their fun ended when she escaped from them, and while they chased her, she ran out in front of a dump truck. Poor Pony. I was quiet in my sadness while everyone around me stormed with their outrage and grief. Sometimes I just don't react in the right way.

In the morning, I heard Mommy make her familiar wake up noises; she routinely goes jogging on the beach early in the morning. I could hear Guthrie's distinct snore coming from down the hall, but she didn't trouble with him; her quiet, solitary sounds moved down the stairs, traveling a daily path until she exited the house, the screen door lightly banging shut on her way outside. A little while later, I woke up Guthrie, early just like he had asked, otherwise, he would have slept the entire day away. He was quiet, not ornery like he can be when he first wakes up, just quiet in that typical sad manner. After we performed our bathroom rituals, we entered the kitchen and made French toast for breakfast in a joint effort.

When I finished eating, I took a tray of buttered wheat toast and tea upstairs to Whitley in the garret, where he was sleeping off his hangover. I laid a note on his chest to let him know where his family had gotten to just in case he wondered. WE'VE GONE TO THE BEACH—LOVE, SAMMY. I kissed him on the end of his nose. *"You and Guthrie have fun,"* he muttered with a chuckle as his hand plopped onto the note, holding it to his heart as if it was the dearest thing he ever received in his life. I left him to sleep.

Guthrie helped me into my bathing suit and let me wear one of his t-shirts like a dress over it. Then we took inventory of the items contained inside my beach bag: suntan lotion, flip-flops, hat, sunglasses, bucket, shovel, and a beach ball to blow up when we get there (and we'll let the air out of it before we go home, making fart noises with it.) After we added a clean beach towel, I was all set to go. He wore his swim trunks with no shirt, sandals, and those mirrored sunglasses that made him look cool. We went out to the garage to get the bicycle built for two, and we loaded the wire baskets with our stuff; he slung his beach towel around his neck like a long scarf, then we saluted each other—pilot to co-pilot—and mounted the bike. I'm still too little to reach the pedals, but he doesn't need me to pedal because he's very strong; I just hang on to the stationary handlebars, with my feet dangling free. He's the strongest man I know—stronger than Whitley—he's like Atlas; I could clearly imagine him carrying the world on his broad shoulders (I have drawn this image of him.) As I rode behind him, his churning efforts quickly built up speed, and we wheeled down the street like the wind. I watched the powerful muscles in his arms and back move under his flesh, his thighs and calves flexing as he peddled; my eyes eagerly memorized the dynamics of his anatomy to draw later.

Upon arrival at the beach, we parked the bike by the fence, and he held my hand as we walked out onto the soft, warm sand.

"Isn't that Mommy's umbrella over there?" I inquired, pointing at the bright yellow beach umbrella—the most obnoxious one she could buy so we could find her on crowded beach days, but today is quiet so far, because we're very early.

"Yup, but she's not under it—she can't be still running," he sighed, with a hint of a frown as he squinted left and right, hoping to catch sight of her heading back.

"Is she still mad at you?" I wanted to know.

"Yeah, maybe just a little bit—uhhh, we talked real late last night—I guess you can say we made up." With a queasy expression, he self-consciously staggered over his words as he remembered my awareness of their relationship. "It's going to be all right between us—it's just a misunderstanding—people have them all the time."

"I don't want to ever have a misunderstanding with you—that would suck." I tugged on his hand and held it to my cheek.

"You shouldn't talk that way, Sammy, it's not polite," he scolded me for swearing.

"Well, here's a newsflash, you taught me everything I know!" I accused with a giggle.

"Yeah, well, maybe I shouldn't have taught you some of it," he snorted, rubbing his head with a nervous hand; it seemed to me that he had less hair than I remember.

Sometimes I wonder if he preferred my silence to my constant chatter. There was a time when I didn't talk at all, and he practically tore his hair out trying to get me to string more than two words together—so he taught me the *bad* words—the bad words that made me laugh because they were *bad*; they made talking more fun.

After we made ourselves at home under the umbrella, I imagined Mommy coming back, she would be happy to see us, and then we'd play together like we always do. But Guthrie looked worried when he picked up the sunglasses lying in the sand a few feet away; it looked like she had carelessly cast them aside—or maybe dropped them.

"She doesn't swim," he muttered, squinting at the water and then both ways up and down the beach as if trying to spot her jogging along the tide line.

"She hates the water," I agreed. "Maybe she had to pee—I gotta pee, Guthrie."

"Didn't you go before we left?" he chuckled with a mock frown.

"I did, but I hafta go again because you made me drink that great big glass of juice!"

"Oh, yeah, the big glass of OJ that *you* insisted I should sieve out all the pulp—"

"Oh, Guthrie—I'm going to go pee with or without you!"

With our hands interlocked, we nagged back and forth in good humor, laughing all the way from the umbrella to the bathhouse. After I pushed on all the empty toilet stall doors looking for her, I became satisfied that she wasn't in the bathroom. So after I did my business, we returned to the brilliant yellow beach umbrella, where we watched and waited. Guthrie sat cross-legged in a stoic, stiff-backed, injun style on his towel, and I sat as an imitation of him. We didn't play, we did nothing, just sat—I was perfectly content doing so. But she didn't come back. The beach began to get busy and it quickly lost its peaceful appeal.

"Maybe she hooked up with someone, like Stefanie or Nita—she's done that before, Whitley and I have had that happen lots of times," I said with a deep sigh.

"Maybe you're right," Guthrie shrugged. After a little while longer, he folded the big yellow umbrella, packed her stuff, and he pedaled us home.

Without putting the bike away, he ran inside to check her room to see if she had come back, but it was empty, and then we asked Whitley who had just groggily shuffled downstairs if he had seen or heard her. He said that he hadn't.

What followed as the day progressed was a steadily growing male-oriented panic that became a search party as the three of us spilled out of the house into Whitley's Caddy, and he drove us all over Gloucester looking for her. Whitley stopped at each one of her friends' houses near the beach inquiring after her, but no one had seen her. By dinnertime, we gave up and went home, hoping that she had come along on her own, but the house was empty and that's when Whitley called the sheriff to report her missing.

She came back with the tide three days later, ironically making landfall on Good Harbor Beach within feet from where she had pitched the yellow beach umbrella—as if she came back looking for us.

Someone had kidnapped her—someone had murdered her. The medical examiner's report stated that she hadn't been dead for very long—less than twelve hours—the murderer dumped her body into the water shortly thereafter. According to the physical evidence, her captor kept her tied up, repeatedly raped her, and then choked her to death. I knew that being tied up was a bad thing—bad people do that to you so you don't get away. Being choked to death meant a great deal to me because last Christmas I nearly choked to death on a piece of hard candy; Guthrie had to tip me upside-down and whale on my back to get it out—I was terrified. Being only six at the time I had no concept what *repeatedly raped* meant, and imagined that it was like being stabbed with a knife several times—little did I know how close I came to the gist of that awful definition.

Kidnapped, tied up, repeatedly raped, and choked to death. What a horrible way to die.

Now that we know what happened to her, our house filled with tears. Guthrie cried. Whitley cried. Helena returned home from her internship at a museum in Boston, hid in her room and cried. But I didn't cry—my sorrow was beyond tears, I shut down—shut out—shut off; I was as if blind, mute, and deaf—lost, but they were too caught in their grieving to notice that I was so emotionally misplaced. I sat in my room filling my sketchbook with pictures of my mother who I missed—who I couldn't imagine being dead—murdered—never coming home again. I expected at any moment that she would come in and tell me it was all a lie—a terrible story—the *wrong* story. She would never allow it to happen—perish the thought! Kidnapped, tied up, repeatedly raped, choked to death—how silly of us to think that would ever happen to Lenore Ryder! *"I was sleeping, just like Sleeping Beauty— I'm okay now."* But no, she's dead all right; she's dead just like Pony was dead. Dead like Guthrie's mom, Margie. Dead is dead, you don't come back when you're dead. Dead isn't like sleeping.

The two men, the old and the young, got stinking drunk that night. Their low murmurs at the dinner table grew into grumbles and then growls as they became surly from their liquid comfort. Helena ushered me to my bedroom to get me away from them. *"Go to bed,"* she sternly instructed me as she closed the door behind her. But I didn't. Left alone, I listened with my fingers stuffed in my mouth, and I sucked on them with soothing focus. This old habit Lenore had tried to break to no avail, I was wily enough to wash off the various remedies she used to make them unappealing. Their noises coming through the floorboards grew louder, my body absorbed their wretched vibrations—I was scared of their potential male violence. I crept out and sat on the stairs, to watch; they circled each other with the postures of gunslingers at a showdown. I quietly slid down the steps on my butt for a better view, and I could see that Guthrie's face was red with anger, the veins in his forehead bulging. Whitley looked pale and shriveled, and he seemed frail, no longer the giant he once had been; Guthrie looked like a monster in comparison.

"Guthrie, I think you should just let it go—leave him alone," Helena said in soothing tones when she stepped in between them. Guthrie ignored her, stepping away and around her. Whitley followed him, slowly turning on unsteady feet.

"How do you think I feel? I've known all along about you two, sneaking around, flirting, and fucking," Whitley snarled.

"I loved her—Lord knows, I loved her better than you ever did—I should have made her leave you—I should have taken them both away—Lenore and Samantha—I love them both."

"I don't care how long you were fucking my wife—you can't breeze in here twice a year to *'play house'* with my family and claim that you would be the better husband—or the better father! She was my wife—you had my wife, but Sammy's my daughter, not yours—she's *my* daughter—I would never allow you to take her away from me!"

"Are you sure that she is your daughter?" Guthrie spat.

Whitley lurched at Guthrie, his fist swung, and bright red blood flew from Guthrie's face; the blow caused the younger man to drop onto his knees. Cursing, Whitley cuffed him again and again. Stunned, Guthrie toppled over onto his side and he lay still, covering his nose and mouth with his hands; his eyes were clinched shut so tight it didn't look like he had eyes at all.

When Whitley began to kick at the fallen body, Helena suddenly came to life and screamed, tugging on him to stop; he wheeled around, ready to slap her, but he stopped because I screamed—my scream split through the anger-filled room with the force of a lightning bolt cleaving the earth. Without their noticing, I had moved from my concealed spot, because I feared that Whitley wouldn't stop kicking him. I knew that Guthrie wouldn't hurt Whitley because he is old, because he is his stepfather, and because he knew that he would have killed him if he had hit him back. Whitley gaped down at me in silent disbelief upon seeing me shielding Guthrie from him in the stance of a crossing guard with my arms splayed out from my sides; I continued to scream like a banshee.

"Shit—what have I done!" he croaked, staggering out of the room with his hands over his ears, he thundered up the stairs to the garret. I stopped screaming with his departure.

"Jeez Christmas, Sam, I told you to go to bed!" Helena shrieked, dragging on my arm to make me move, but I dug in my heels, making a low growl in my throat.

"Leave her alone, Lena," Guthrie muttered into his cupped hands. He remained lying on the floor, battered and sad.

Corking my mouth with consoling fingers, I knelt down beside him, petting his shoulder, hoping that my touch would somehow ease his pain. Helena hovered over us, her agitation annoying me; I glared at her, and she glared back at me, daring me to tell her to go to Hell.

Finally, the fallen warrior raised himself from the floor; his hands covered in sticky blood, and his nose swollen out of shape. Helena asked him if his nose was broken. He said he thought it was, and then she said he should go to the hospital.

"I won't go there unless I'm dying—if even then," he scoffed. "You are up way past your bedtime, Buttons—let's go, upsy-daisy," he said, scooping me up in his arms. I hugged his neck and wrapped my legs around his waist as he carried me upstairs. In my room, he sat for a long time on the edge of my bed talking to me, but I trembled so hard because of tearless crying that he had to lie down with me. He stayed there holding me tight to his chest all night even after I finally became quiet, and I fell asleep with my head cradled in the hollow of his shoulder. When I woke up the next morning, I stared at his ruined face where it lay on the pillow close to mine. He looked awful because of the muddy purple and red bruises that seeped across his face in skin-deep contaminated puddles. I felt bad.

The detective came to ask more questions, and it seemed like he was suspicious of Guthrie or Whitley. I was the only alibi for the two of them. I wanted to help, but unfortunately, the detective couldn't understand my testimony without words—I haven't spoken in days because my sadness had smothered my voice. When the detective became frustrated with my inability to communicate, Whitley apologized for my silence on their way to the door. *"She's autistic—you've gotta understand, she's very upset—give her time, she'll tell you what she knows."* But as the detective left us, it became clear through my father's under-breath grumbles that my being a witness might not be any good because of my *handicap*.

Feeling bad, I went slinking out the kitchen door with my sketchbook clutched to my chest to find peace in the barn loft full of sunny flurries of dust motes. But as I trailed along by the leafy Rose of Sharon hedge with its buds close to bursting into pink and white blooms, I peeked through at our new tenant living in the carriage house; he stood on the back patio smoking a cigarette with a pensive expression etched on his youthful face.

Sylvester Hayden is a young man that Whitley knew from the university. He just moved into the carriage house a couple of days ago with his worldly possessions stuffed into his little car that Guthrie referred to as a *"Fix it again, Tony"*. The young man didn't notice me at first because he looked at the clouds in the sky, but it seemed like his disconcerted gaze remained focused on something troubling within him. I knew that the detective had just questioned him moments ago because I had watched from the upstairs window while the two men stood talking out on the patio before I came outside; it was a short conversation, just long enough for the two men to light-up and smoke cigarettes, put them out, and say goodbye.

When Sylvester Hayden finally noticed me by the maple tree watching him, we regarded each other with the perfect pitch of silence. But it seemed my presence unnerved him; his shoulders shuddered as if he felt chilled in the balmy June air. I stepped through a gap in the hedge made by the maple tree and stood in front of him, staring.

"Hello," he said, crouching to my level. "You must be Samantha—your father mentioned he had a little girl—I'm sorry to hear about what happened to your mother," he said with a solemn frown, his gray-blue eyes looked serious behind their wire-rimmed glasses. It was apparent by his reaction that my lack of emotion puzzled him, so I took my fingers out of my mouth and quietly thanked him for his kind sympathy; these were the first words I've said in days—he has no idea what he's done for me.

"I know—I do know how you feel—I just lost my mother too." He spoke with a discernible tightness in his throat that resonated with genuine emotion. "Last fall—it happened," he awkwardly added; his emphasis on the word *"it"* made it heavier than the two letters that this small word is comprised of. It fascinated me to see how his face expressed his feelings without saying *"I'm sad"* out loud; I wanted to draw his grief.

"I'm sorry," I whispered, wondering what had happened to his mother—had she been kidnapped, tied up, repeatedly raped, and then choked to death too—*is "it" that common?*

"That's okay, thank you," he replied.

"I want to draw your picture," I said as I plopped down onto the cradle of thick tree roots in the shade underneath the great maple tree, opened my sketchbook to a blank page. As he digested my request, his face made a spectrum of expressions, and then with a modest shrug and a smile, he agreed to allow me to do this.

"What do you want me to do for a pose?" he asked with polite curiosity.

"Just sit down and read your book," I instructed, pointing with the end of my pencil at the old Adirondack chair where I have spied on him enjoying the old maple tree's shade from my window; a thick, yellow hardcover book lay on the seat where he must've left it when he answered the door earlier. The tree's broad trunk and gnarled roots straddled our conjoined yards, breaking the thick hedge in two, and its low-slung leafy branches offered a shady place for reading without the sunshine's blinding reflection off the white pages. With a curious tip of his head and a quick nod, he did as I suggested, and settled into the weather beaten chair.

So, we sat in compatible silence—he reading and I drawing. From time to time, I could sense him watching me over the top of the book entitled *Wonderland,* but I never actually caught him looking; his face appeared relaxed behind his spectacles, his eyes as if intent on their task of visualizing the writer's word pictures. He was quiet; I liked it that he was so quiet (most adults always feel the need to talk)—even his motions while turning the pages were hushed. This is what I really needed—he asked nothing of me, and he didn't seem to mind my being there.

"I'm done," I announced, feeling sorry to end our peaceful communion. He shook himself as if waking from dozing off, and he leaned forward to see my drawing. "Oh-my-god, Samantha—look at what you can do!" he exclaimed with the typical adult disbelief that I've confronted before. I felt funny—I always feel funny when people notice me, and notice what I can do.

"It's just what I do," I said with a shrug as if to explain this thing I cannot explain—this talent that sets me apart from other children. "I'm not showing off," I added to reassure him that I was not committing the crime that annoyed the other children in school. *"You're such a show-off,"* they have sneered at me throughout my time spent in kindergarten. The meaner ones take away my pictures and ruin them if the teacher isn't watching. I want to cry, but I don't, and for some reason that seems to make them madder at me. Some kids will hit me because I won't cry, but when I hit back, I'm *bad*, and then I get into trouble. Whenever I got into trouble at school, Lenore always had to come get me because of my wretchedness—but she's dead—so, Whitley will have to come get me—*someone will have to*. I stared at Sylvester Hayden while waiting for further reaction from him; he stared back at me through his wire-rimmed glasses, and it seemed like his sensitive face perceived all that I felt without my saying a word.

"I don't think you're showing off—you have a rare talent—a gift—your father must be very proud," he said softly after some thought; the awe in his voice seemed to choke the breath out of his words. "Oh-my-god, what he must be going through right now—I wasn't thinking—does he know where you are?"

I shrugged in reply. "Was she pretty?" I asked.

"Who?" he asked, mystified by my question; I have changed subjects on him again—like I do to everyone—it's as if I had thumbed the radio dial to another station without letting him know—*Guthrie says it drives him bat shit when I do that.*

"Your mother."

"Yes, she was very pretty," he answered with a smile. I watched his face make this smile, his eyes crinkled in the corners as if the happy memory of his mother's beauty lit up something inside him—a happy memory—I'll remember this expression and will draw it later, and I'd make the drawing blue. Yes, I do remember thinking his emotions were made from a blue light.

"My mommy was very pretty too." I turned to a page in my sketchbook to my last memory of her alive, and I let him hold her image in his hands to view her.

"You look just like your mommy—tho' you do have a little bit of your father around the eyes," he said softly, returning my sketchbook to me. I stared at him—no one had ever said that to me before—nobody ever noticed seeing Whitley around my eyes before.

Just as he said this, and before I could reply, I heard Helena calling me. I used to think that my half-sister, hated me—but I guess not. I wouldn't exactly say that she loves me, but to say that she tolerates me is too harsh; her emotional attachment resides in a gray area where she considers my being when she feels guilty enough to think about me. It seemed like she felt irritated by the attention I received because of my disability. She annoys me most of the time, and we fight just like typical sisters do; but as far as sisters go, we get along all right. She sometimes tries too hard; she tends to be domineering, but she's too scattered and self-centered to focus on me for too long, so I wait her out; thus, her future attempts to replace Lenore as my surrogate mother were a failure. When she called my name again, I jumped onto my tingling feet and peeked out past the tree trunk to beckon her to come meet Sylvester Hayden. When Helena stepped through the gap, Sylvester wobbled to his feet from the comfortable depths of the chair. As they introduced themselves, his face turned bashful red. Her gaze ran over him, assessing him like she does everybody she meets; she didn't look particularly pleased to meet him—nor did she seem to bear any kind of an opinion about his existence beyond the hedge.

"Thank you for finding her for us, I hope she wasn't any trouble," she sighed as if relieved to see me safe in the company of this quiet young man with spectacles. I liked his face; I can tell by his looks that he is kind, and I wondered if Helena would think so too once she got to know him.

"Actually, she found me—she was no trouble at all." His words sputtered with nervous agitation; he was so much calmer while he was alone with me, but faced with Helena—pretty, pretty Helena—he seemed ready to go into convulsions. I wanted her to go away just so he could be quiet again—I liked his quiet and it seemed so did he.

"I didn't know where she had gotten to—with all that has happened, I feared the worst," she spoke with halting words, as if afflicted by his unease.

I furrowed my brow at her, but she ignored me, directing her attention toward him.

"She's quite talented for someone so young—how old is she?" he asked.

"Six—she's autistic—I suppose she's kind of like an idiot savant—she can copy anything, but I don't think she can produce something self-inspired," she quickly rattled the well practiced speech that she always used to explain me to strangers.

"Oh, that's—interesting," he paused as if uncertain about how he wanted to express his thoughts regarding my unusual circumstances; I was glad that he didn't want to take pity on me and say *"That's too bad."* "I think she is very inspired. She doesn't seem—I mean, she is quiet, but I wouldn't have guessed anything wrong with her—well, I took in consideration the circumstances—I'm sorry for your loss."

While they talked over me, I sketched him talking to her. They questioned each other like adults do—always asking questions, always wanting to know something. I tend to take people at face value, if they want to tell me anything about themselves, I won't stop them; if I want to tell them something I will when I'm ready—I don't like too many questions. So, I listened to him tell her about his dissertation on Edvard Munch and how he had gone to Norway to do research, she looked bored; however, I was fascinated, it seemed like he understood how I perceived the world as he described the emotional moods of color, line, and shapes that Munch used. I loved hearing him talk; his thick Down East accent had a musical quality to it that is earthy. His essence is as comfortable as the weather-beaten chair under the sprawling shade of the old tree with the soulful sigh of the ocean breeze expelled with a summer rattle through its leaves.

Helena perked up when he mentioned the art history seminar that he will be teaching in the fall semester about the psychology of aesthetics; she expressed an interest in taking his class. Then he asked about her studies as an undergraduate and she relayed to him her scattered interests comprised of the artwork of Élisabeth Louise Vigée-Lebrun, Artemisia Gentileschi, Georgia O'Keeffe, and of course, our distant relative Albert Pinkham Ryder.

He smiled and nodded rhythmically, his glasses glimmering in the waning sun; it seemed he was too dumbfounded by her enthusiasm to comment on anything she said, but he was perfectly content just to look at her and listen to her ramble on and on about herself in a flirtatious show and tell that said nothing of much consequence. My attention drifted to my pencil dancing from image to image, the point barely leaving the paper surface.

"Come along, Sammy, we should go, Whitley's waiting, and I'm sure Mr. Hayden has things to do." Helena said just as I started to sharpen my pencil to a fresh point.

When I looked at Sylvester, he twitched as if to protest our departure, but he said nothing; as much as I would have loved to stay there with him, I knew I should go home even if everything there was going wrong. So, in a meek gesture toward friendship, I tore a full sheet of pictures from my sketchbook and gave it to him; he made an incoherent noise that expressed his surprise to receive my gift as he took it into his fine hands. I thought perhaps the picture of Helena would please him the most; on this particular sheet, I had also drawn another small portrait of him and connected him to her with a thin pencil line that drifted between them as negligible as a spider web covered in dew on a cloudy morning—the thread linking them together while they talked.

"Good-bye, Sylvester, thank you for letting me draw your picture," I said with stiff formality that I knew Helena expected from me as she firmly gripped my shoulders.

"Mr. Hayden to you," Helena hissed.

"It's all right, she can call me Sylvester—you're welcome, Samantha—it was nice to meet you," Sylvester responded with politeness that equaled my inelegance. "Thank you for giving me this drawing, it is very kind of you." Our gazes met for a moment and we smiled in silent commiseration regarding the expectations of others as opposed to our personal lack of consideration for formalities, in that instant, we bonded and parted ways undeniably as friends.

The sun had begun to settle around us as Helena led me by the hand through the gap in the Rose of Sharon bushes, leaving the young man to his self-imposed solitude.

"You shouldn't wander off like that—Whitley is about ready to call the cops," she scowled at me; her angular, thin face was pale, and her dark eyes seemed enormous in the twilight. "That guy's a little weird, don't you think?

Like maybe he's queer or something—what's up with that long hair and scraggly beard, yuck—Whitley always picks some real winners to live over there," she babbled upon our arrival at the back door. I said nothing. I didn't feel like defending myself or arguing with her about Sylvester Hayden's peculiarities that made her uncomfortable. I was still absorbing his quiet and knew in my heart that he meant no harm to anyone—his underlying sadness is reminiscent of Guthrie's, only his is less volatile in nature, whereas Guthrie's growls like a bubbling cauldron of self-destruction.

A couple of days later, we were surprised to hear that the police arrested Noah Valentine. We've known Noah for years—he owned *Noah's Art Gallery* in Bearskin Neck, Lenore always said that he was her *old friend*. We later learned that a young couple—tourists from out of town—had identified him as the man they saw with Lenore when they had asked her for directions to Plum Island. After they had walked away, they over heard them arguing, and they said she had punched Noah in the eye during a struggle next to the yellow beach umbrella. When the detective questioned him for the second time, and asked again how he received that shiner, his guilty conscience blurted out his crime and he willingly confessed that he had kidnapped Lenore, tied her up, repeatedly raped her, and choked her to death.

The forty-year-old Noah Valentine told them how he was once engaged to Lenore, but she had jilted him to marry Whitley; although they had remained friends afterwards—he never got over that she had dumped him for *some old man*. He had obsessed about her and he felt she had treated him so poorly until he became obsessed with getting her back. After he captured her, he kept her tied to the bed in his apartment above his Bearskin Neck gallery so she wouldn't get away. He claimed that he didn't mean to kill her—he said it was self-defense because she attacked him after he had set her free so she could go take a shower because she had *gotten dirty*. He talked all kinds of crazy beyond that, saying stuff like, *"He made her dirty, I never wanted him to touch her ever again—I'm sorry—I told her I was sorry."*

The defense attorney naturally made a plea of insanity. The prosecutor called it a crime of passion; she had fought to escape, and he killed her in cold blood to stop her. Noah Valentine was tried, convicted, and sent to prison for the rest of his life—all because of passion; his passion for Lenore was a crime, his passion killed her, and his passion made a mess of our lives.

The woman who was my mother while she was alive is now a dead woman named Lenore—like Poe's lost *Lenore*—*Nameless here for evermore*—Whitley can barely bring himself to speak of her—even now.

The last time I saw Guthrie was at the funeral; he lingered against the back wall in the front parlor where we had the casket on display. I waved at him to come to me, but he looked away with his head down as if in prayer; his bruised face was flush with emotional trauma. When I asked Whitley if I could go stand with him, he told me *no*, and gently asked me to be quiet; he then took a hold of my hand to make sure I stayed put, and I remained good as gold so not to distress him any further. Guthrie didn't come home after the graveside ceremony at the cemetery. When I went looking for him, I found his bedroom barren of his life with us. While still in my funeral clothes, I sat on his empty bed with the hollow in the middle where his body had lain since he came to us when he was seventeen—long before I was born, and before he had a mustache. I tried to feel him there by lying down in the depression of his shape, and I tried to will him to come back. Although I lay there for hours, nothing came of my wanting, I had a funny feeling that he hadn't just gone for a walk on the beach to think.

Whitley came in and sat on the edge of the bare mattress, the springs creaked under his butt like one of his old man farts. "*Sammy—*" he said, and then stopped, because he was unable to speak beyond his grief. Then he cupped my face in his hands, his eyes so dark brown they were nearly black, like mine, like Lenore's—*I look like Lenore, Sylvester Hayden had said so, but he also said I looked like Whitley around the eyes.* But the catch in Whitley's voice warned that he only saw his dead wife in my face. When I asked him where Guthrie went, he said that he has moved away to New York City, and that it was for the best. That was the last time he willingly spoke of him, and to my disappointment, we never heard anything from him ever again.

After the funeral, it was as if Guthrie never existed in our family. So, it was just Helena, Whitley, and I living in our big old house with creaky floors, drafty windows, and the proud gabled roof; the constant, mournful sigh of the ocean from down the street often filled the silence. The ghosts of Lenore and Guthrie linger amongst us unspoken of, yet unforgotten by our hearts that had loved them.

A few days after the funeral, Whitley hired Carrie, a former math teacher from Ipswich to keep house, cook meals, and tutor me in math; her brother, Rick had been doing the odd jobs of a handyman and yard work twice a week for years, so she came highly recommended. Soon enough a new pattern of normal routine became established, Carrie came to the house by eight in the morning when Whitley had to catch the train to Boston to teach, and she stayed until I went to bed. It seemed she loved us like we were her own family, but she wouldn't cater to any of Whitley's flights of fancy regarding any hanky-panky; she was a no-nonsense, big-boned widow of about fifty-nine with Irish red hair and a temper to match. Carrie and I got along just fine—she loved me to pieces. I never gave her any reason to fret over my autistic tendencies. I'd sit at the kitchen table, making pictures in my sketchbook or playing with the creamer and sugar bowl while she baked soda bread, molasses cookies (and a decadent chocolate cheesecake served annually on my birthday!) I would be good as gold for her so I could lick the goodness left in the mixing bowl and on the beaters. I learned a lot about cooking by watching her prepare our dinner—if I'm ever given a chance to try, I could cook a Yankee pot roast to die for!

By the following autumn, Whitley took me out of the ineffective public school system because of my disastrous adventures in kindergarten the prior year, and Carrie helped him hire tutors in order to keep the state social worker off his back.

Sylvester Hayden became one of my tutors by default. The emotional attachment that I garnered for our tenant in the carriage house on the other side of the Rose of Sharon hedge quickly grew in intensity, and he managed to absorb my obsessive affection with an empathic amity. During the hours he spent teaching me how to read and write, I found peace and quiet.

Since Sylvester refused to be paid for the tutorial services, Whitley invited him to take his meals with us. Unfortunately, the first night was disastrous; Whitley encouraged him to indulge in an evening of drinking, but Sylvester wasn't that type of man—a drinking kind of man. He wound up passed out on the powder room floor after puking his guts out for the better part of the evening. I was small enough to sit on the floor beside him holding a cool cloth on his brow. I even fished his glasses out of the toilet, washed them off, and kept them safe until he felt better.

Helena acted so disgusted by the whole ordeal that she became scarce, only returning now and then to peer in at the unfortunate young man like a nosy buzzard. I really thought he was going to die—he looked so bad—but Whitley assured me that he would live. I fussed and petted him, whispering encouragement and comfort; when he finally rolled his eyes open to look at me, and he murmured his gratitude like a soft prayer.

Whitley laughed at him. *"I take it you didn't do much in the way of drinking up there on Deer Isle, didjya?"* he inquired of our guest as soon as he was lucid and sitting up. *"No, sir,"* Sylvester replied in a barely perceptible vocalization. *"Daddy, don't pick on him, that's mean,"* I pouted my warning in a mock imitation of Lenore. This parroting habit that I picked up during my years of knowing her has caused recent emotional outbursts to blurt out from my formerly expressionless visage. Whitley toned down his insults, and became more proactive in easing Sylvester's misery with his favorite remedies rather than prolonging it by making fun of him.

From that night on, Sylvester quietly sat amongst us at dinnertime in his place across from me—Helena kitty-corner from him, and I sat next to her. Whitley, at my elbow and seated at the head of the table, presided over the nightly conversation; it seemed Whitley felt relieved to have a sympathetic male in our midst, though it was likely Sylvester's retiring nature allowed Whitley to have a captive audience every night. When I set the table, I saved two empty places for Guthrie and Lenore, and they stayed that way for years unless Whitley's buddy, Pinkerton, came over to fill one of them and a special guest the other.

During the hours we spent over our meal, Sylvester would covertly admire Helena. Even though he tried to hide his thunderstruck expression, I could tell that he was in love with her. He'd remove his glasses whenever he could to impress her with his handsome features uncluttered by their presence, his self-conscious face naked to her casual glance in his direction. But she hardly looked at him; when she did, it was a tease—almost as if she just pretended to throw the stick for an expectant dog, forcing his eager gaze to chase her elusive eyes. Dejected, he'd finally look away to mind his plate and Whitley's pontifications.

Unfortunately, he never had a chance to attract her because she had already met Neil Shepherdson and fell in love with his broad-shouldered shape that stood tall and impressive, his boisterous and sociable manner making him seem larger than life. She once told me that she was the luckiest woman alive to possess such a man, because he was every woman's dream.

As the years went by, Helena muddled through what remained of undergraduate school, then she went into graduate school, and finally, she started to work on her doctorate degree in art history. She wrote her dissertation about Albert Pinkham Ryder and our father, comparing the intimate romantic inspirations and ideals of the early Ryder to the sprawling abstract expressionist meditations of the later Ryder. By this time, Sylvester had become Dr. Sylvester Aloysius Hayden, a tenured full professor at the university, and as her adviser, he pushed Helena to finish this rambling document. She hated him with a passion during this trial in her life, but he wouldn't let up on her. It would be easy to believe that he thrived on making her miserable since he couldn't get any other satisfaction from her, but I knew that he was never unfair to her. After she finished the chore of writing to *Dr. Hayden's* approval, Dr. Helena Tate-Ryder married Shep in a spur of the moment ceremony as soon as they both accepted teaching positions at Berkley. They departed from Gloucester in classic, happy-go-lucky fashion, driving off into the sunset with a *Just Married* sign on their rear bumper to go live happily ever after in California.

Once they left us, it was just Whitley and I in the big house with all of its distinctive historical features that everyone admired from the side of the road. But by then, the trees and bushes had grown too tall for prying eyes to see beyond them to catch a glimpse of the house where the murdered Lenore had once lived or in later years, the house where the famous autistic artist resides.

Sylvester continued to join us for dinner every night, and it seemed he intended to stay in the carriage house forever. So, the quiet man, preoccupied with Edvard Munch's romantic belief that humans are powerless before the great forces of death and love, remained alone on the other side of the Rose of Sharon hedge.

Night after night, I watched his hands unfold countless napkins, and manipulate silverware through his plate full of food. I loved the way his fingers held a tumbler of water or a glass of wine; he could balance a delicate teacup with elegant dexterity, and a coffee mug with firm control. On the rare occasions that he cautiously handled an offered shot-glass of scotch, he'd meet my eye with slight apprehension. With a glance, we'd silently recall his first dinner with us, and how the two of us had spent our time communing on the powder room floor. I'll never forget his blink of gratitude when I rescued his glasses from the acidic slime and chunks that had been the contents of his stomach—only a very good friend would attempt such a feat.

Meanwhile, I grew up sitting across the dinner table from him, and a time came when I was no longer a child; a budding adolescent suddenly became a young woman with coltish limbs and tiny breasts. Our interaction remained steadfast as he and I spent many hours sitting alone in complete silence; I always loved how he understood quiet. We were perfectly content not to talk to each other, sketching and reading, and at ease with our peaceful existence. When we did talk, it was about things that mattered—never small talk; however, there were things that we never talked about, that perhaps we should have taken care of long ago, but the opportunity to say what was left unsaid never came, or it did, but we neglected to rise to the occasion.

∾

Oh, poor Sylvester, puking in our powder room again! With a relaxed hand, my pencil drifted away from the spirals and made more crosshatching static from light to dark, then dark to light, fading to the edge, and then I turned the page to a fresh blank sheet of paper. The pencil point touched the white, and through my half-closed eyes, I began to draw long slender hands with knobby knuckles—the hands belonging to my first lover. *I'll never tell anyone.*

3

Sylvester Stargazing

"I miss you, goodnight—sleep well—I love you," I uttered the words into the telephone receiver with firm sincerity to maintain the sound of normal—*she doesn't have a clue that I suspect anything.*

"Oh, Sy, for godsakes—*you act like I'm going to be gone for a year! I'll see you Wednesday afternoon—goodbye, you silly-boo,*" Helena said in *the voice.* I recognized *the voice*, its particular crisp nuance always bothered me, but for the first time, I am able to comprehend the reason for its distracted timbre, the unnatural phrasing, and the concise, purposeful words. It's *the voice* she uses whenever she calls home from out of town; it's *the voice* she uses when she's on the telephone and I'm in the room—it's *the voice* she uses when she's not alone. As I stood with my cell phone crushed against my ear listening to her familiar voice, there was still a thread of hope clinging to my heart that all of my musing throughout this miserable day has been over nothing; but her admonishment directed at my sentimentality had the verbal resonance of guilt. When I had mentioned to her that Theodore Wilson had called, she laughed. "Oh, Theo—*that dumbass—he called to remind me that I'm going to New York—as if I'd forget!*" It was *the voice* that was incriminating, not the words. "*Is he with you?*" I wanted to know, but thankfully, I restrained my suspicions that begged to heckle her about her alleged infidelity. *This is stupid—I really have no reason to believe that she has been unfaithful.*

After she disconnected our contact, I stepped out the back door to escape the walls that are tormenting me with the echoes of lies—*her lies and my lies.* When I arrived at the outer edge of the patio flagstones, the soothing fragrance of lavender from the garden perked my sense of smell—I took several slow deep breaths of the herbal tonic hoping for relief, but found no comfort, only more anguish. *Damn it, Helena, why?* For years, I've garnered self-doubts because of my quirky personality and shortcomings, but I never doubted Helena until this morning when she left for a research trip to Manhattan. After all these years together, I had no reason to think anything was amiss—we both travel alone often enough, going wherever our research takes us. But today was different. No sooner had I returned from dropping her off at the train station, her graduate assistant, Theodore Wilson, called the land line at the carriage house looking for her—that in itself wasn't unusual, he's always telephoning to remind her where to go and when because she's chronically late for appointments. *But*—I didn't quite catch what he said when I first picked up the phone—it was something like *"Did you remember to pack your teddy?"* Whatever he said, the tone was unmistakably flirtatious, but upon realizing he had reached me instead of her, he began to blunder over his words with embarrassed muttering; the familiar background buzz of the North Station added to his frustration because he couldn't hear me very well. *"Oh, shit, I just pressed the wrong autodial to reach Helena—I mean—Dr. Ryder—I'm sorry to have disturbed you at home, Dr. Hayden—*(then he said something else that I barely understood)*—sorry—I'll try her cell phone."* I want to believe it was an honest mistake—or a joke gone wrong—whatever it was, he was clearly too tweaked-out for it to be just because he pressed the wrong autodial. *No, you're imagining things—she's not having an affair!* Unfortunately, the more I thought about her having an affair with a student right under my nose, the less absurd the idea became. *No, it is absurd, she's half his age—why would a young man of twenty-something want to fool around with a woman over forty? It's ridiculous. But is it ridiculous for her to want to fool around with a younger man? Well, yes, of course it is—because she'd look foolish.*

As I continued to mull over the evidence of the past few months and even digging into memories from years ago, there is a clear pattern—*there have been signs all along—why didn't I see them? Because I'm too trusting—I believed her.*

Well, now I have something in common with my father—he had no idea either.

Shaking out a cigarette from the crushed pack inside my shirt pocket—it's stale, but it'll do—the lighter, nearly out of fluid, flickered weakly, but the flame was just enough to catch the frayed tobacco—I inhaled, exhaled—inhaled, held it—exhaled long, slow billowing stream of smoke, my hand is shaking. *Maybe I'm imagining it.* Feeling dizzy, I cranked back my head to look up at the deepening night, getting my bearings by sorting out the stars.

Damn it, Helena, why?

❧

I fell in love with Helena when I spotted her on the commuter train—she didn't know I existed, but her father did—he was looking for a new tenant, and I told him that I was interested. When I signed the lease to rent the carriage house from Whitley Ryder, I had no idea what I was getting into—I hadn't anticipated the years of commitment. My initial plan was to work on my doctorate in the peace and quiet of Gloucester; it was the ideal location, close enough to Boston, but far enough away from the city's distractions. It was perfectly far enough away from my father's house in Deer Isle, Maine, but close enough if I needed to go home.

Whitley and I began our affable relationship during our morning commute on the 110 to the North Station. The initial icebreaker that bound us was an ongoing discussion about art because I noticed that he spent the entire train ride drawing in a small sketchbook. I always carried one too, but I never made a mark in it. I lost count of how many times I pulled it out of my backpack with the intention to do something, but once faced with the blank sheet, I couldn't think of a single thing I wanted to draw. When I mentioned this to him, he shook his pencil at me and spoke with a low chuckle.

"Anybody can draw, but it's up to you to begin drawing. Don't get hung up on fucking it up. Make a mark a day—don't dwell on making something that looks like something—that comes with practice. Listen, it doesn't have to be of anything more than getting to know how to use the pencil—but if something comes from it, you'll be pleasantly surprised." It was inspiring advice coming from an old sage, but I still had a blank sketchbook in spite of his encouragement.

My arrival next door to the Ryder family overlapped with the desperate three days that the community spent searching for Whitley's lost wife, Lenore. Of course, the transaction to rent the carriage house happened well before his wife went missing—I had no idea what was going on until the detective knocked on the door and grilled me for about ten minutes. Whitley had told me more than once during our conversations that his wife meant the world to him. He referred to the three women in his life as *my girls*, Lenore, Helena, and Samantha—they were his world. I had hoped that they'd find her alive, but when I awoke on that gray dawn to the sound of sirens on the ocean breeze, I knew they had found her. I couldn't imagine his grief—yet I could. Standing on the fringe of the Ryder family tragedy, my grief from losing my mother last fall was still too fresh—too bitter—I relived the crushing blow of losing her all over again.

It was several weeks after his wife's death before I saw Whitley again—I was glad to see him admiring my rusting '69 Fiat Spider in the driveway one morning—shaking his head and grinning—"*I always like black cars—this one is a real honey—*" he laughed. "*The salt water air is always tough on a car—we can work on that body, and make 'er shine again.*"

Our love for old cars soon occupied our free time, we tinkered with them for hours in the garage—his was a sleek, red '59 Cadillac Deville convertible. We'd work in compatible quiet, tuned in to the Boston Red Sox games as they played their ballpark drama on the radio, which became a topic of vehement frustration, especially in the midst of play-off season. It was amusing to watch Whitley destroy a hapless radio with the accessible variety of projectiles as if it were at fault for foiling the team's chances to win the pennant. His colorful verbal abuse and clever directions for sending the team to Hell would cause me to drop onto the oily concrete, rolling in a fit of hysterical laughter—I don't think I ever laughed so hard in my life, it was intoxicating.

Then, there was also our seasonal obsession with fly-fishing, which I never did before until Whitley persuaded me to join him on select mornings at his favorite trout stream. I spent several blissful hours of silence with water swirling around my legs encased in sloppy waders cinched up like old man pants with suspenders; the sound of the water filled my ears with hypnotic peace. I rarely caught anything, but that didn't matter—the peace mattered, and it seemed like Whitley felt the same way. Strange as it may sound, catching a fish destroyed that peace—the exhilaration of success completely spoiled the serene atmosphere of the day; we'd drive away from the stream, moody like a couple of grumpy bears awakened from hibernation.

For the duration of this exclusive time of centered musing, I told myself it was okay that Helena didn't give two shits about me—I knew that she would never give me a thought because I was just a spectacled, rangy, nerdy guy with a heavy Down East accent, and monk-like habits. Chances are she probably thought I was queer—*I can always concoct the worst-case scenario perception of me*—but there in the middle of the stream none of it mattered. Going home always dismantled the relaxing mediations— my state of misery was never far away, because by dinnertime she'd be there, and usually pouting about some slight or complaining about Samantha driving her nuts. The girl never seemed happy—I longed to make her happy. But in spite of my efforts to appease her, Helena tolerated me with the jealous attitude of a spoiled girl who felt ignored by her father; the forced pleasantries of her less than personable manner stung my faithful heart that loved her from afar.

Ever since the day my absurd crush on her took root, every moment that I spent around her was misery as I bumbled about in contortions of nervous jitters, stuttering, sweating, and breathing funny when I breathed at all. It took emotional feats of mental diversions to overcome my inhibitions whenever I found myself face-to-face with her, thinking she couldn't stand the sight of me, and when I was without her it took daring feats of bravery to recover my senses. *Ridiculous fool.* It became painfully clear early on that I never had a chance to win her over because of Neil Shepherdson, the built in boyfriend who seemed attached to her hip. *Shep* was a drawling, midwestern boy; yet in spite of the doggy/jock name, he was intelligent.

As I progressed from doctoral student to assistant professor to full professor, I missed several opportunities for positions in Europe where I could've continued my research, but I made excuses not to accept them because of my foolish obsession with her. Then as the department chairman, I found myself obligated to maintain a distant, professional relationship as her adviser. Herding Helena through her dissertation was perhaps the most maddening challenge in my life, which was mostly due to her lack of organization and flighty whims—it was a miracle that she ever finished writing the damn thing without my writing it for her.

By the time Helena married Shep and moved to Berkley, I was well established in my profession in Boston with a decent salary to live on, so it made perfect sense that I should give up renting the carriage house, buy my own home, and finally put the Ryder family behind me. But I didn't do it. Part of my reasoning was my personal comfort zone, the carriage house suited my needs just fine—*what would I want with a five bedroom Tudor in Cambridge? I love living in Gloucester.* I also convinced myself to stay because of Samantha.

From the day that I met the little girl, she became my *"dear heart"*; her quiet ways consoled my tormented mind—she became a source of peace in the emotional storm during that awful period after my mother's suicide and my heartsick obsession with Helena. Samantha always saved me from complete misery—surprisingly she offered a quirky comic relief. I think I survived many meal times at Whitley's table because of Samantha's timing. She would rescue me from her father's dinnertime pontifications, which usually included generous quantities of strong drink. As if she knew my *"limit"*, she'd rise from the table enticing me away with distractions, usually by pressing a book into my hands and requesting that I should read to her. We'd flee to a quiet place to read—the breezy screen porch in the summer, the front parlor by a warm fire in winter. Evening walks on the beach were always acceptable in any kind of weather—riding the short distance on the bicycle built for two—Samantha and me, whiling away the remains of an evening skimming stones—at least the ones she would allow me to throw. By the end of such evenings, she'd walk along beside me, every step producing the muffled rasp of stones shifting inside her loaded pockets. Then I'd read her a bedtime story and go home feeling good as long as I didn't see Helena on my way out—but I always longed to catch one more glimpse of her to end the day. If I did happen to see her—or worse, talk to her—the bubble of serenity that Samantha had instilled would burst, and I'd go home a muttering nervous wreck. *Stupid fool.*

When Whitley decided to pull Samantha out of the public school, I volunteered to tutor her because her disability fascinated me. It was the logical thing to do because of her receptiveness to my being there. A natural trust brought her to my patio door every morning throughout that first summer; she'd stand with her little hands cupped around her face as she peered through the glass for a glimpse of me as I groggily shuffled downstairs rubbing sleep from my eyes. I never knew how long she had been standing there waiting—five minutes or five hours, it seemed all the same to her. After a week, I expected her to be there, and so it became our routine to breakfast together. She loved my wheat bread and the way I buttered it in that *melty-way*. Then scrambled eggs with American cheese—it had to be the orange kind, or it wouldn't be right. She kept a small frying pan in my kitchen, and with a stool to stand on, she'd tend to the scrambling task without mishap. Then she'd divide the results even-steven between our plates. While I sucked on my first cup of coffee, I would sieve out the pulp from the orange juice for her. She'd watch this operation standing on tiptoe beside me with her chin resting on her hands clinging to the kitchen counter edge; dark eyes watching the glass fill—eyes so dark brown they were almost black. I could look into those eyes and see the intelligence churning there—still waters run deep.

There is so much going on inside her head she cannot possibly tell me everything, more often than not, she chooses to say nothing only because she cannot coordinate mind and mouth—this will come with time and practice. I longed to help her unlock her thoughts so that I could hear them—I always imagined that she would have the most beautiful things to say. During our sessions in reading, writing, and art history, it became my job to get her to sort it out—and I would wait for it to happen, which is very tricky because I must pay close attention. When her slow responses come, they rapidly gain momentum, and if I'm not on the ball, she can overrun me once her energetic mind cuts loose—then she tells me everything. She even told me that she knew I was in love with Helena—I don't know how she figured it out.

As if to express her gratitude for my efforts, she'd show me how to improve my limited drawing and painting skills. With the patience of an elder master, the little girl would tuck implements into my hand to teach me how to manipulate the various mediums and the mechanics of brushwork, pencil point, and pen nib—making marks. "No—*hold it like this—and then you do it like this—you will feel it when it's right—when you feel it, then you will see it,*" she'd say to me. It always astonished me when I achieved the results I aimed for in a drawing or painting.

Our daily one-on-one meetings were happy routines for us. As she got older and full of restless adolescent energy, we would go jogging on the beach together, and if low tide exposed the hard-packed sandbar, we'd race to Salt Island and back; she could run forever, and I'd chug along in her wake, watching her sassy ponytail swishing back and forth.

On weekends, we would indulge ourselves with a movie on Saturday nights, museums and galleries were always delightful excursions on Sundays, she also enjoyed the Symphony (especially performances of Beethoven), but lazy afternoons spent in the stacks of a bookstore were a sweet decadence in which we'd lose ourselves. At closing time, the store employees (who knew us well) would gently send us through the door with our shopping bags full, blinking our dazzled eyes in the daylight as if we had just awakened from a long nap.

Although I feared that our persistent efforts to overcome the debilitating effects of autism might not be enough, I had always held onto hope that she might achieve a level of independence to help her cope with daily living. I never imagined an outcome so rewarding—she is an exceptional young woman who bravely prevailed in spite of her disability; I'm proud of my part in helping her become who she is today.

Yes, it was easy to love Samantha for who she is.

༄

Damn it, Helena!

Trying to calm myself once again, I breathed in deeply, sucking the fragrant October night air deep into my lungs; as I exhaled, I tipped my head back to look at the dazzling night sky once again. The constellations glittered above the treetops; my gaze scanned north for Draco's tail curling between Ursa Major and Ursa Minor. I also found Cassiopeia's throne straight up above. Then I sought the triangle of Deneb, Vega, and Altair high in the southwest. Slowly turning, I looked for Pegasus in the southeast; the ocean breeze blew my attention toward the lights from the Ryder house peeking through the leafy fingers of the maple tree.

Samantha—she's still in the garret working later than normal. Lately, it has become a common occurrence to see the garret lights on well past midnight. I knew that things weren't going well with her marriage to Preston. Tonight, I noted a distressed tick in her fingers as they twitched beside her dinner plate, her head tilting away from Preston's presence beside me as if cringing from him because he was drunk. I noted how his verbal volume cranked another notch with every swallow from a glass filled with pure gin.

Whitley, Helena, and I have watched their five-month marital interaction in bemused silence. There is no telling what goes on between them privately, and neither of us wanted to interfere with the natural progression of the newlywed's relationship. Even though Whitley has mentioned a vague concern, he shrugs with a non-committal wait-and-see-what-happens attitude. Helena despises Preston in her typical black and white opinion. I instantly disliked the jerk when he started as the new dean at the School of Art; he is a swaggering, smooth talking, know-it-all bore with a big mouth. Each of us put up a front, hoping that they'll work it out between them, but really, we're hoping Preston will just go away—if not on his own, then with Samantha's persuasion as she kicks his ass out.

For the life of me, I couldn't figure out the attraction on her part; she barely looks at him, and when she does, she squints at him with her head cocked to the side like the RCA dog as if she didn't quite understand his voice. There is no sense of adoration visible in her eyes while the patronizing phony fawns over her with a great deal of fuss.

As I thought about this, my heart took on a distinctive ache. *Oh, Samantha!*

Although I was opposed to the idea of Samantha marrying Preston, I took comfort in knowing that Samantha wouldn't do anything she didn't want to do, but my silence irked me because as her friend I should have asked her—*"Is this what you want?"* I believe she would have told me the truth. I can't help but feel that I failed her when Preston first sidled up beside her at Whitley's retrospective, oozing his despicable charm all over her, his oppressive presence forcing her to focus on his being there, and sweet-talking her into his arms.

It's my best guess that he went after her for the money.

Since the wedding, I have covertly watched for changes, and have noticed signs of her regressing, she has developed a child-like manner these last few weeks, she makes involuntarily little whimpers like mock-sobs—I've heard these sounds before, back when she suffered from the distress of her mother's death and Guthrie's departure.

Recently, my over-active imagination has produced nightmares in which Preston has declared her incompetent and had her institutionalized. My mind embellished on this story line in a dream the other night; I came upon Samantha pleading for help through the tiny window of a cell, her little hand reaching for me through the bars, but no one would let me help her because I am *the outsider—I'm not family*. No one would listen to me, and a collective faceless *they* kept me from taking hold of her plaintive hand reaching out for comfort. I woke up crying because of my impotence. Thankfully, Helena didn't notice my emotional disarray because she's been taking sleeping pills—I don't know why or for how long this has been going on; apparently, my obliviousness has gone into the realm of *ass-up-head syndrome*. I laughed out loud at Samantha's personal favorite description for being stupid. When she first used this phrase, I thought she was being dyslexic and pointed out that it should be *head-up-ass*; she displayed her rare two-dimpled grin. "*Oh, that's an entirely different level of stupidity— it's 'not as'—which implies there is still hope that you can pry your head out of your ass, but when you're 'ass-up-head', there's no hope for you at all.*"

With a sigh, I smiled at the garret windows. Just then, the lights went out. *Sleep well, dear heart!* My heart quivered inside my chest with a familiar feeling. The light ocean breeze had cleared away the smoke from my spent cigarette some time ago, so that the lavender from the garden seductively tickled my nose; I took a deep breath. My mind flinched as it eagerly retrieved the blissful memory from a June night many years ago, and I looked up at the stars.

Oh, Samantha, please forgive me, I still love you very much.

❧

Recumbent Virgo lying low in the west, flirting with Hercules standing directly above—I still remember who they are. My mother taught me how to identify the constellations; she made the Deer Isle night sky come alive for me every night during hushed lessons in the dark, and ever since her death, I've made it a point to come outside to commune with the moon and stars—it was how I want to remember her. As I mentally checked the inventory of important figures in celestial mythology, I reluctantly ruminated about things that might have been had I been a different man—*if you were a different man, you wouldn't have let Helena slip through your fingers*—but I never had her—*You never tried—you were always daydreaming, never taking action.* Yes, it's ridiculous how I wasted so much of my time with chronic fantasies that caused a miserable tempest of unrequited love—*Maybe it's time you moved on*—but move where—Boston? *How about to the moon?* No, no, no—too far, I would miss the Earth—especially the ocean. With a long final gulp, I finished my glass of wine. When I set the glass on the table, I wobbled as my foot slid off an uneven flagstone and my hand knocked the glass over, it shattered on the patio. *Shit, it's too dark to see, I'll clean it up in the morning.*

I tried to laugh at myself, but only heaved a deep sigh, as if trying to flush out that spiny ball of depression caught in my throat with one deep breath, but it stayed there, a persistent ache. I often wondered if this is how my mother felt—chronically choking on nothing there. *Why?* I still wonder why my mother hung herself. Raising my chin, my fingers gently probed my throat, the cartilage of the larynx, and the lumpy Adam's apple—the fragile windpipe, easily crushed.

The soft slam of a screen door caused me to drop my attention from the sky to look at a phantom flitting in the darkness. The ghost was Samantha traversing the yard along the hedge, her white nightgown fluttered softly around her ankles as she trotted towards me. I knew that Whitley was not at home, he had departed shortly after dinner to go drinking with his cronies at their old haunt in town where they hassle any unsuspecting female in the vicinity; a bunch of old farts still horny enough to try to get laid. Whitley has been known to get lucky from time to time, often dangling a woman half his age from his nearly eighty-year-old fingertips. His friends lament how it is an outrage that he is still so damn good-looking that he turns the pretty heads of women of all ages. Feeling responsible for Samantha's well-being while he was away for the night, I became curious about her being out so late, so I stepped through the gap in the hedge dividing the property and called her name.

"Sylvester!" she replied to my hail with a wave. There was a particular clarity to her voice in the still air; normally she speaks in a low, soft tone that is earthy, but tonight there's a lilting timbre. It's not that singsong child's voice that often chirps from her lips during polite conversation when she feels uncomfortable, she doesn't use that voice with me unless she's being funny—she is very funny at times. No, this voice has a natural pitch—a musical connection with the night sky and the ocean, the words become stars and waves. I've heard this joyful ring when she's very happy and her emotions bloom to the surface, briefly accessible on rare occasions. I was struck by the way her face appeared luminous in the night shadows collected underneath the broad branches of the maple tree.

"I'm glad you're still outside," she whispered, stepping closer to me. I could smell the lavender bath soap on her skin.

"What are you doing up, are you all right?" I asked with a dim tone because I really felt too miserable for company, yet, I couldn't stand the loneliness tonight. Samantha's silence can be calming, and I often welcomed her quiet presence even when I felt miserable, she always reminded me that there are better things in life. *I'm being a fool for feeling shitty about Helena.*

"What are you doing out here?" Her inquiry jangled with laughter; it was unusual, girlish. As I looked at her, I thought she seemed different. There was something about the tilt of her head, the way she held it cast upward rather than its normal downward posture, it is rare to see her so animated—it was rarer for me to look into her eyes; that dark penetrating gaze latched onto my view of her and I couldn't let go—*she's so beautiful.*

"I'm wondering why you're outside at this time of night, is everything all right?" I rephrased my question hoping for an answer this time. I smiled to myself because of her tendency not to answer a question until the right kind of question is asked; it's almost like a game, one I believe she is smart enough to play.

"I want to see what you see in the sky," she said, staring into my face with her nearly black eyes wide open in the darkness, her mouth smiling with a secretive demeanor that made dimples appear in her cheeks; she turned her gaze toward the stars.

"I come out to look at the stars—and the moon," I told her, a smile tugged on my mouth. Her curiosity about what I see in the night sky is akin to her needing to know what I taste while eating gumbo at the restaurant that we went to last week—it was spicy, but she enjoyed it.

"I know—I've watched you from my bedroom window, many, many times," she said, gesturing toward the dark house behind her.

"Oh, really?" I laughed. *Why haven't I thought of teaching her the night sky before?*

"Can we look together? Please show me some constellations!" She grabbed my hands, pulling me toward her; we stepped out from underneath the tree into the open yard. "Is that the Big Dipper up there?" she looked up and pointed at the night sky sparkling above the trees.

"Yes, that's the Big Dipper," I answered, suddenly feeling taken aback as she turned around and pressed the full length of her back against my body, her hands possessively clasped my wrists against her torso. It isn't the first time I've hugged her like this, but as I slid my arms around her like I have hundreds of times, I felt self-conscious as my forearm brushed against the softness of her breasts. I could have easily broken free from her, but I didn't want to alarm her because my male urges don't know the difference between friend and lover. My friendship with Samantha has been a steady bond for years, I have always adored her, never once questioning the purity of my intentions, but tonight as my heart hammered inside my chest, I knew something had changed. It is not typical for me to respond recklessly—especially with my friend, Samantha Ryder. I don't take risks, even after drinking two glasses of wine. But the feelings stirring inside of me at this moment suggested something desperate and I loathed the implications as she leaned against me with such trusting innocence. I took a deep breath and hoped for the sensation to pass. As I cast my gaze toward the stars for a necessary distraction, I felt mortified that I may never think of her in the same way again. *This isn't right.*

"Okay—I'll show you the Little Dipper, look a little to the left of the Big Dipper's bowl—there's the long tail of Draco the Dragon, see?" I explained, pointing with a hand she had willingly set free; she nodded silently. "Then to the left of the tail is the cup of the Little Dipper, and the North Star, Polaris right there at the end of the handle—and in between Polaris and the tip of Draco's tail—there's a giraffe, that's his long neck, slanting right, and his legs zigzag up there—see?"

"Oh, I see—," she whispered; her fingertips stroked the hair on my forearm that remained crossed over her torso with the same curiosity that I've seen her touch the bark on the maple tree. "Sylvester?" she asked, leaning her head into the hollow of my shoulder, her pale throat exposed.

"What?" My response fluttered through the wisps of hair that tickled my lips as if they teased for a kiss; I drew back my head to avoid the temptation, yet I continued to hug her with both arms tightly closed around her.

"Why are you trembling?" It seemed as if she accused me of something with this question. Although I knew exactly why my body quaked with this nervous tremor, I held my breath, unable to answer her question because there is no way to explain that her sudden appearance tonight touched off a hormonal reaction inside of me much like a meltdown in a nuclear reactor. As her body turned within my arms, she brushed against me with a soft motion that drove me mad; I hugged her tighter, she clasped me around the waist, squeezing me in return. "Sylvester, what's wrong with you?" she pried with this question.

"Nothing's wrong," I said, feeling ashamed of the unsettling thoughts that my mind began to entertain as my groin felt heavy with its unexpected burden. I tried to extricate myself from her grasp, but her hands were reluctant to let me go. "Maybe you should go home now," I muttered as I gently shook free and backed away from the sweet attraction of her scent.

"I don't want to go home, Sylvester, I want to be with you," she whispered, stepping in close again, her hands gripped my shirtfront; she abruptly rose up onto her tiptoes and pressed her lips on the corner of my mouth. My reluctance melted as I turned into her kiss, and her arms clasped me around the neck, tugging my head down; her kiss might as well be the jaws of a lioness bringing down a weak wildebeest.

"Samantha, we shouldn't do this," I protested as I lovingly embraced her eager body as it slid against mine. When I tried to step away, I found myself even more hopelessly entangled when she kissed me again—I suddenly felt giddy with joy. "Oh, dear heart," I whispered as my willpower to resist her looked the other way. There was no question about how I felt—*I loved her*—and then I kissed her with an unstoppable passion that begged for satisfaction.

With a laugh, she suddenly pushed away from me, skipping a few steps backwards into the deep shadows of the maple tree—I held my breath, watching her, for a moment afraid that I had gone too far. Without a word, she lifted her nightgown with seductive slowness and then discarded it into the night air; stepping forward, I caught it before it fell to the ground. Looking at the girlish cotton in my hands, I knew that I had to stop this from going any further, but as I gaped at her pale beauty under the dark umbrella of the tree branches, I couldn't turn away my desire. As I stepped forward to cover her with the nightgown, she flung herself into my eager arms, and softly murmured my name with a low musical tone. Our lips met in a deep kiss; the nightgown fell to the ground.

Naked in the starlight, we wove our limbs together with passionate tenderness, kissing, kissing, kissing; now I've become the predator and she my prey succumbing to my hunger—I groaned feeling appalled by what I had just done to her. She clung to me with no intention of release while she nuzzled my bare shoulder with her face, her soft kisses danced across the bony ridge of my collarbone. I suddenly felt protective of her, petting her loose, silky hair; an uneasy delight ached inside me as intense pleasure trilled throughout my being. Feeling exhausted, I lay sprawled on the dewy grass, looking up at the stars; she rocked on top of me, the thin crescent moon nestled into the curve of her neck and shoulder. My heart ached with joy; I gripped her waist with my hands, and privately swore that I will be with her forever—*I love her.*

"Oh, Samantha—" I sighed, feeling so content—so complete—no longer so alone.

But these sincere thoughts only lasted until the headlights of Whitley's car entered the driveway. Fear crept in along with reality, shriveling any leftover enthusiasm and suddenly our bodies seemed very white in the darkness—I didn't want Whitley to see me lying naked in the backyard with his youngest daughter dangling her nude body over me while she performed experiments in sexual pleasure that left me breathless. *Shit!* I couldn't remember for the life of me how old she was or going to be—*sixteen, seventeen, eighteen? I can never remember these things. Her birthday is tomorrow—it's way past midnight, so it's today*—but it doesn't matter—to make the act even more despicable, she's mentally handicapped! Even with her consent or her seduction—it wouldn't matter. I will be the one held accountable for my actions because I'm the adult—I should know better—*I should have stopped her.* For years, I've acted as a guardian, a trusted friend of the family. I've spent hours upon hours alone with her without incident until tonight—*what the fuck is wrong with me?* Without a doubt, what I've done tonight would have an impact on my career. *I can't stay here anymore after this—I must go live somewhere else!*

Suddenly afraid that any hasty move on my part would alert Whitley of our presence, I lay as flat as I could on the grass, wishing I could sink into the ground and vanish.

"Oh crap, he's home early tonight, I have to go," she whispered, lying low over me, she reached into the darkness. "Here are your glasses so you don't step on them," she gently placed the wire rims on the bridge of my nose and over each ear. Cradling my face in her hands, she kissed my brow; the night air chilled the warm impression causing me to shiver. "You know how he is—he spends about fifteen minutes polishing the bug guts off the Caddy before he comes inside—don't let him see you or he'll guess what we've done." She crawled away, and began to heap my clothes over my stark nakedness.

"Samantha," I sighed, sitting up. I touched her cheek with my hand, and she placed her hand over mine. Looking into her eyes, I feared that this would be our only time like this; I longed to pull her back to me. "Dear heart—I—I don't know what to say," I fumbled with the truth of my desire as I rose to my grass-stained knees, completely disregarding the possibility that we might be seen as I clutched her to me and kissed her with staggering passion in spite of my angst. "Samantha—" I moaned soulfully when she parted from me.

With quick motions, she slipped into her nightgown. "It's all right, Sylvester, no one will know about it—I won't tell anyone," she sighed with the softness of a breeze. She then hastily kissed me, the tip of her tongue touching mine one last time, and she scampered away—a little girl again, when just a moment ago she had been a passionate woman. It was as if she passed through a barrier a yard away from where I knelt in the grass feeling abandoned and exposed.

My emotions were raw as I pulled on my clothes in the dark shelter of the maple tree, and as my head popped out of the neck hole of my t-shirt, I saw her slip through the back door without making a sound. I waited, keeping watch until Whitley finally staggered out of the garage—drunk again. He took a leak in the hydrangea bushes before he entered the house through the front door. A deep exhale escaped me just then, and I entered the carriage house in a zombie-like state. Shucking off my clothes to take a shower, I discovered that my cock, thighs, and stomach appeared ravaged by her stains. I felt sick. *What have I done?*

Through what remained of the night, I expected Whitley to come pounding on my door to kill me for what I have done to his daughter—he'd have every reason to—I should be drawn and quartered for my selfish irresponsibility. No matter what she had done to tempt me, I should have resisted—I should have made her understand why we shouldn't—*why it was wrong.* Then I further tormented myself, feeling angry and indignant, wondering how long she had designs on me without my being aware—or was it an impulsive act that sent her running across the backyard in the darkness to meet me—and like me, suddenly becoming aware of *a feeling.*

Whitley didn't come.

When I finally crawled into bed, my body shivered with inexplicable tremors until I finally fell asleep from fatigue.

The next day sent me on my way to work as usual—crisp white shirt, chinos, tie, tweed jacket, and polished shoes—I have an early morning lecture, so Samantha knows not to come for our routine breakfast. I moved through the day, it was no different from any other day—though I felt different. Throughout a full day of teaching, meetings, and advising, I found it difficult to concentrate because I was in a buzzing fog as if I had gotten stoned before coming into the office. The worst part of my affliction was how my cock felt painfully sensitive every time I moved; the focus of my thoughts on Samantha only inflamed the problem.

Anne, the department secretary, hovered maternally near my desk, and she even took it upon herself to feel of my forehead. *"You don't look right to me—no offense, Dr. Hayden, but you look sick,"* she said. It was all I could do not to say—*"Of course I look 'sick', I spent most of last night fucking my brains out with a teenager, I think my cock is going to fall off—if it does,*

I deserve it!" Thankfully, I maintained the decorum not to say such a crazy thing.

I was grateful when I finally got on the train to head for home, but my anxiety grew as my anticipation regarding the night ahead overwhelmed me with thoughts of endless possibilities. Tonight Whitley and I will celebrate Samantha's birthday, and then I will be escorting her to the movie theater to see the new Eugene Riley film. The spirit of the tortured romance *Dandelion Wine* seemed too fitting for us to see together.

"Well, look at you, so spic 'n span," Whitley commented upon my arrival for dinner; I had neglected to change out of my suit from work, though the knot on my tie was loose, I had taken the time to slick-back my hair with a wet comb, and cleaned the day's fingerprints off my glasses. Then he proceeded to remind me that Samantha is turning sixteen—if he said anything about her being sweet sixteen and never been kissed I would have self-combusted in an instant, but thankfully he didn't. Perhaps he thought that his mentally handicapped daughter couldn't possibly care about such things as kissing—only chocolate cheesecake and vanilla ice cream slathered in homemade hot fudge mattered. Little does he know, his *Little One* seduced me with what I suspected to be the premeditated candor of a teenager, and then made love to me with the astonishing passion of a woman driven by lust. Not to minimize my part in the night, I certainly wasn't chaste—like they always say, it takes two to tango—*oh, so true.*

When she entered the dining room and took her place at the table across from me, it became clear that I was at her mercy.

"Happy birthday, Samantha," I said softly, trying to disguise the unnerved tremor in my voice as I presented my carefully wrapped gift to her; a CD of a string quartet by Beethoven that she had asked for last week. After she opened it, a smile lit on her lips causing both dimples to bloom and she raised her downcast face, the gaze of her dark eyes skipped across my face like it normally does on any given day. "Oh, it has the *Cavatina*! Thank you, Sylvester," she said, expressing her gratitude with her usual soft tones.

I spent the entire meal on pins and needles waiting for her father to read my obvious guilt, and I would have allowed him the liberty to pound my stupid skull into a pulpy mess for my indiscretion. But nothing happened. The evening went on just like any other; the ceremonial decadent chocolate cheesecake and rich French vanilla ice cream with hot fudge drizzled on top only prolonged my agony. I felt sick to my stomach.

Whitley talked, I listened, and Samantha sat across from me, her demeanor never alluding to any clues concerning her feelings, which relieved and disturbed me at the same time—frankly, I felt disappointed by her silence. Throughout the day, I had nurtured a ridiculous notion that she would miraculously come out of the spell of autism, look me in the eye, and proclaim her love for me in front of her father because I had cured her.

After we cleared the table of dirty dishes, I shyly offered to accompany her to the movie, she reacted in her normal Sammy-way, clapping her hands, she cried, "Can we put the top down on the Fiat?" I assented that we could do that—it was going to be a beautiful night.

Whitley waved us on our way, never suspecting a thing; nevertheless, I felt like a wolf in sheep's clothing being there by her side inside the darkened theater. She sat through the film, completely absorbed. I barely watched it as my tempted gaze kept dragging toward and away from her sweet profile in the dim light; all the while, I suffered with my guilty conscience and distressed ethics. *What have I done—why did I do such a thing? I couldn't help myself—she made me do it—NO! I allowed it—I could have stopped her—I could have said, "We mustn't do this." I could have pushed her away, I could have walked away—I could have done a lot of things to prevent the events of last night. But I didn't—I let it happen because I love her.*

While these thoughts circled inside my mind with the persistence of vultures over a pathetic dying creature, there was not even a hint from her about how she felt, or what she thought. Although my mouth grappled with several attempts to utter words that I longed to say, I tormented myself into a silent misery, unable to speak to her, unable to bring myself to ask anything of her. I could only go through the motions dictated by the moment. On the way home, I began to wonder if I had dreamt the entire thing—the Samantha Ryder who I made love to last night was gone as if she never existed at all; the rare lucid light that I saw in her eye may have been a trick of shadows.

After the movie, I successfully delivered her home without succumbing to the temptation of taking a romantic sunset walk on the beach because I feared that someone would recognize us—everyone in town knew her—and me. It made me wonder what people saw when they viewed us together—to them, I am just one of her guardians. My being her lover is the furthest thing from their minds—*We all know that Doctorsylvesteraloysiushayden would never do such a thing, he's such a good man, the family is so lucky to have such a kind-hearted soul to help them look out for that poor child. Well, here's news for you, that child is not a child anymore, she's a young woman*—*no one has ever thought of that happening, have they? No one ever expected her to grow up. No one expected that she'd feel sexual desire. I certainly didn't*—*and I never imagined in a million years that she'd come to seduce me*—*why me? (Because she trusts you.) Trust. If she trusted me, I shouldn't have let it happen. If I truly do love her*—*I will not let it happen again.*

After I wished her goodnight, and left her within the safe walls of her father's house, I entered the dark carriage house doused by nauseous waves of relief and disillusionment. I cursed myself and wished to die; I even banged my head against the wall as my shame overwhelmed me. This self-inflicted torture went on until she arrived at my back door within the half hour, her little knuckles rapping on the sliding glass door. As soon as I let her inside, she kissed me with the same amorous mouth that I thought was only a dream, and I enveloped her body in my arms that had longed to hold her since she left me the night before, alone and naked, kneeling in the dew-soaked grass. Drawing her inside, I closed and locked the door behind her, and we cast aside our clothes, anxious to touch one another; this time, my bed absorbed the shocks of our passions as we writhed and shuddered, until we fell asleep skin to skin, cocooned in flannel.

Trust and love.

I awoke the next morning alone, she had gone home while I slept, yet the scent of lavender lingered on my skin, on the sheets, and the pillowcase. I breathed in this sweet essence and moaned, feeling wretched all over again because in spite of the love I felt, it was wrong to love her like this. *I shouldn't have done it*—*but she had come to me!*

෴

It was our secret—Whitley never found out. Every night at dinner, she would sit with her indirect face cast down, and greeted me with her normal mur-

mur, *"Hello Sylvester, how are you today?"* Occasionally, she'd meet my eye and smile, a private little smirk crested with a wink, and then she'd look away and return to being withdrawn and silent, her hands busy fiddling with the silverware or the surface of the tablecloth. As I watched from my place across from her, I wondered what was on her mind—*is she distressed, is she excited, is she bored? Oh, please, look at me!* I would plead in silence, feeling hopeless; it was as if she refused to look upon me with any form of tenderness—adoration—or love. Night after night, I struggled with guilt as I lay with her, wondering—*how long do I expect to continue with this secret?* At the age of thirty-three, I was nearly twenty years her senior, it was absurd for me to be with her, but I was so in love with her that I was convinced I couldn't live without her. *I wanted to marry her!*

By the time she turned eighteen, I plotted with myself to ask Whitley if I could court his youngest daughter. Even with all the best intentions, many evenings passed by while I sat smoking a cigar with him; the question lingered unspoken on my tongue. I even went as far as carrying my mother's engagement ring in my pocket; inserting my fingertips into it, twirling it around, visually measuring her slim fingers against mine, trying to determine if the ring would fit on the proper finger. I tried to imagine her reaction when I slipped the elegant oval-shaped diamond set in old gold onto her finger—but I never did it. I carried the ring for over a year; her nineteenth birthday came and went, and I did nothing beyond ponder the question.

I was a fool—an ass—I'm such an ass.

Samantha's declaration: *"No one will know about it"* carried the weight of our secret affair on broad shoulders that seemed content with the situation, and so we carried on in a mode of silence. In crystalline hindsight, I understand how this mute behavior created a deep hole of disservice to what our relationship meant to us; thus, we buried and eventually smothered ourselves with the clandestine passion that neither of us owned up to. Although in my heart I have always loved her, a part of me feared to confront her with the commitment I desired to share with her. So I have remained silent on my side of the dinner table, like nothing ever happened between us, and she went on with her life like none of it mattered. One thing that I am very grateful for, it didn't destroy our friendship—it didn't dismantle our original bond, the foundation of trust remained steadfast. If anything, the intimacy we had shared somehow gave us more leeway to forgive each other for our failure to communicate what we left unsaid.

◡

Helena returned home when her three-year marriage to Shep ended in a bitter divorce. I felt ashamed when my heart experienced a pang of chronic excitement the moment I heard the news that she had quit her job and was coming home—I couldn't believe that I felt anything at all since I hadn't given her much thought after she left. Then as if pre-determined, my relationship with Samantha ended. My heart hammered with agonizing confusion while I listened to her abrupt decision to stop seeing me. *"I know how you feel about Helena—you are not beholden to me—you are free."* She whispered the final words that released me from obligation as she kissed me goodbye that night. At the same moment that I felt rejected, I felt despicable because I was relieved that it was over, but I did not feel *set free*.

After the back door clicked shut, I rose from the bed to look out the window; I saw the familiar pale nightgown-shape traveling over the blue-black grass heading home in the pre-dawn darkness. Brutal anger suddenly infused the moment and I cursed myself for betraying her with my indecisiveness—overthrowing reality for a fantasy. *But was any of it real?* She set me free so willingly that I had to wonder if I really mattered to her—*did she ever love me?* In spite of my heart's contortions, I wasn't sure how I felt—if she hadn't seduced me that first night, none of this would have happened, I wouldn't have thought of having an affair with her because it was wrong. It was this sense of wrongness and my self-loathing that prevented me from slipping my mother's engagement ring on her finger every night for over a year.

Fumbling in the darkness, I plucked the ring out of my pants pocket, and returned it to the box where I kept it in the corner of my underwear drawer. Cursing and slamming the drawer shut, I glanced out the window just in time to see the phantom young woman vanish inside the house. *She's gone.* My brittle emotions wailed from my throat in a desperate cry as I dropped to my knees at the windowsill, giving myself a goose egg on my forehead to explain away at dinner with a lie about dropping my pen on the floor and bashing my head on the desk.

"Is the desk okay?" Whitley asked with a chuckle.

Samantha made no comment—not even a dimple of humor or a glance of pity, but she stared at me, her gaze locked with mine.

"The desk is fine," I laughed. After I said this, her gaze withdrew to attend to her fidgeting hand that played with a wrinkle in the tablecloth, and she made that whimpering noise inside her throat. *Was that an allergy tickle or a sob of anguish? I wasn't sure.*

Helena and I caught one another on the rebound. It was almost too easy once I confessed how I had felt about her in the past—I had expected her to laugh in my face, but she didn't. *"Oh my goodness, you're so sweet!"* she exclaimed, then began to cry. She moved into the carriage house within a month. Although our relationship intensified with the frenzy of newlyweds, she warned me that she didn't want to get married again. *"—at least not right away, you can't blame me for being a little bit gun shy,"* she said. I suppose she was entitled to feel that way after what she had been through; truthfully, marriage was the furthest thing from my mind. As much as I wanted to be with her, I felt on edge as her raw emotions ebbed and flowed through that first year we spent together. She verbally flailed painful stories about how Shep fooled around with students behind her back: *"He was bringing them home to fuck them in our bed—the pig."*

To make my internal contentment with her even more precarious, Shep frequently called to talk to her; she'd sit huddled on the sofa murmuring to him, and then sobbing after hanging up. When I asked, *"Why did he call this time?"* she'd say it was about a few things that she had left behind in Berkley, he wanted to know if she wanted him to ship them to her. *"He won't shove them up his ass, so I guess he'll ship them or throw them out,"* she sneered as she wiped her eyes with the back of her hand. So, along with some personal items that she had abandoned, he sent photos of their wedding and honeymoon as if to aggravate her. To my relief, this contact tapered off with time—or perhaps he ran out of photographs.

After reviewing the past, I realized there are two sides to every story—now I wonder what was his—*did she do something to cause him to stray?* It made me wonder if she had fooled around behind his back as well. It would explain why the returned photographs hit her like sniper shot reminders of what they once had—specifically aimed as if she had been the one who instigated the undoing. *Who walked in on who?* I wonder. It wouldn't be the first time I caught her in a little white lie.

As our years together accumulated, I continued living my life as I always did, only with Helena in it—I suppose that is how the rift began. It was evident from the start that my normal mode of behavior drove her up the wall. I wasn't social enough, I read too much, I worked too hard, I wouldn't let her redecorate the house her way, I made funny noises or I was too quiet, and my midlife male gaseousness grossed her out—the list goes on. Perhaps I bored her to tears.

Granted, she isn't the easiest woman in the world to deal with; she's moody, her demands on me are frustrating, and at times annoying. Her constant bitterness, negativity, and her persistent nagging about everything under the sun that she found fault with would often spoil our time spent together. She creates chaos in her life by being inattentive and disorganized, easily sidetracked. She passionately immerses herself in too many projects that she starts, but never finishes—the house and her office are full of them, hoops of neglected needlepoint, books half read, articles she started to write with enthusiasm, but the efforts are always discarded as *"works in progress."* Whenever I dared to remind her that she needed to work on anything for her tenure committee, she would have a meltdown and take to our bed with a mysterious malady that caused me to take her to the emergency room from time to time. Once it was for an ulcer, and other times it was for nothing at all other than stress-induced hypochondria, for which the doctor prescribed an anti-depressant. She's been like this for so long I can tune her out with the slightest roll of my eyes. Just keeping my mouth shut so not to arouse her irritation, and staying under her radar is a cherished skill. It seemed a toss-up: I have overlooked her shortcomings because I love her too much or maybe I don't love her enough for not pointing out that she needed to get her shit together. Either way, she tells me that I'm a good man for putting up with her, so it seems as if she is aware of her faults and appreciates my forgiving nature. In spite of the tribulations of our life together, I felt satisfied that this was how I had wanted it to be in my fond old fantasies that had dimmed to a vague partiality during the three years I spent with Samantha.

❧

Do you ever think of me? I inquired of the darkened garret windows staring at me with their blank expression. I always wondered if she remembered any of it—was our time together like dreams in her mind? As much as I wanted to believe that I understood Samantha and her disability, I never knew for sure how she felt about me. For three years, I maintained an intense and secretive sexual relationship with her at the risk of losing my mind, but they were three of the happiest years of my life. Nine years later, it is certain that my heart and mind are not in harmony—they have never been—especially when she's near me and the heady scent of lavender fills my heart with the addictive sensation of love all over again. Daydreams about Samantha trouble my peace of mind in a disturbingly pleasant way that I crave, often causing me to become mentally adrift during inappropriate times in which I shake myself free of their grasp with a spastic twitch that has caused Helena to exclaim: *"You really oughta get that checked out, Sy—that's just fucked-up."*

So, it seems I'm not content unless I'm obsessing about someone unattainable. As I sat through Samantha's wedding, I internally agonized over a scenario in which I would leap to my feet at the proper time to declare that there is reason for them not to be wed; but I missed the opportunity because I was too busy thinking about it. *So typical.*

Once the civil ceremony in the front parlor finished, I tried to pretend that I was happy—I went up to embrace the bride, I even wiped her happy tears for her, but I slowly became despondent that I had failed to follow through on anything that ever mattered to me. To ease my emotional pain, I began to drink myself numb—what made things worse, I found her newly married inaccessibility attractive. Once I became sufficiently drunk, I made my way to Samantha to confess my undying love for her. When she kissed me in the alcove I wanted to die; just feeling her soft kiss on my mouth and smelling the scent of lavender made my heart sing—*I still love her!* I emotionally seesawed between mortified and excited, I suddenly felt very ill. Moments later, while I puked my guts out into the powder room toilet, the two women that I loved tended to me. Helena with her impatience for my sloppiness hovered on the fringe, while the eternally patient Samantha stayed close by. When she relieved me of my glasses, so not to have a reoccurrence of the past, this final connection lead me to imagine in a watery toilet bowl hallucination that this moment meant something significant—that history is repeating itself in the cramped powder room for a reason. Whatever it is, it's beyond me to guess the meaning of this event. Consumed by a new misery, I briefly wept while embracing the porcelain altar, vomiting became a tearless heartbreak that longed for forgiveness.

I am a fool.

❧

Thankfully, the stars in the night sky remain unchanged, their patterns come and go with the seasons; I can rely on them to be in their places at certain times of the year. Tonight there is no solace to be found in the night sky as my thoughts returned to my mother, Elise. And without wanting to, I also recalled my godfather, Aloysius. The last time I saw him was when he visited me in Oslo. He said that he was in love, but he never said that he was dying from an inoperable brain tumor. He died two months later, and my mother died the very next day—because of *him.*

Two things appeared upon her death, a sealed box and a sealed letter. My father, Jacob, said that the box contained sketchbooks and a manuscript about a nineteenth century Welsh painter, Annachie Powys, who Aloysius exclusively collected; it was to go to a woman named Katharine Tierney. *The letter was to me*—in this letter, Elise explained that just before she and Jacob were married, she became pregnant during a careless one-night-stand with Aloysius. Damndest thing, I knew, but I didn't want to know. Looking at myself in the mirror, I recognized the features of that other man—*Aloysius Farnesworth. How could Jacob stand it? Raising me as his child—looking at me and seeing him. Why did they keep it a secret until now? Would I have been better off knowing that he was my father all along?*

After my mother's funeral, Jacob asked me to take the sealed box to Katharine—"*Aloysius asked me to hold this box the last time I saw him in London, he said that if something happened to him, he wanted you to deliver it to her.*" This request irritated me—*Why me?* I got around to it, but over a year later. When I found the box gathering a significant layer of dust on the floor of my closet, I felt guilty about neglecting the duty that Aloysius had asked Jacob to delegate to me. It wasn't until after I finished the semester that I finally got up the nerve to make the long drive to Syracuse, New York. I went there without calling ahead, foolishly thinking I'd ring the doorbell and leave it on the front stoop with a note, but when I stood on her front porch, I knew that I couldn't just ring the bell and run like some ridiculous prankster. I had to make sure she was still living there to receive the items that Aloysius wanted her to have. *If she wasn't still there, then what?* I had avoided talking to Jacob for several months, and dreaded having to admit to him that I hadn't delivered the package until now. So, I waited, and watched through the sheer curtain as a woman's slight figure descended the stairs from an upper flat. Ever since I learned about Katharine, I had expected someone older because Jacob said she had been Aloysius's lover, but when she answered the door, I was surprised to see that she was so young—*younger than me—an undergrad for godsakes!* The young woman greeted me through the partially open door with an astonished flutter of hands—she looked as if she saw a ghost, and I stepped back, equally startled by her slight resemblance to my mother. We stared at one another, dumbstruck until she finally found her voice, *"Who are you?"* she asked; a nervous tremor accented her disconcerted query. When I introduced myself and informed her of Aloysius's request that I bring her this box, I realized that she was the first person to hear me admit that he was my biological father. With an expression of guarded relief, she offered heart-felt sympathy for my losses, and she benignly invited me inside.

I followed her upstairs to the kitchen, and carefully set the box on the table. An awkward silence hung over us while she studied me thoughtfully, and then she said, *"I wasn't sure that he had anyone—his family was a touchy subject—apparently, painful."*

"He was always vague about his life—I hate to say, but I never really liked the eccentric old bird—" I laughed with regret, recalling how he desperately tried to connect with me whenever he came to visit. There were many times he appeared about to say something, but he'd say nothing at all—and I'd feel relieved. *"I guess it was hard for him to keep the secret from me."*

"Do you know what's in the box?" she asked after an uncomfortably long silence. Although her hand lay on the box lid, tracing the wax seal with her finger, she didn't seem anxious about opening it. Quiet and guardedly secretive, this young woman was clearly damaged by her involvement with Aloysius—it couldn't have been pleasant for her to witness his end.

"Sketchbooks and a manuscript—something he had been working on," I told her.

We talked about him—it was good to talk to someone else who knew him. We agreed that he wasn't a terrible man, though his manner could be puzzling, obsessive, very possessive—conflicted, I guess. *At least I come by it honestly.* When I asked her, *"Did you love him?"* I thought it was interesting how she verbally avoided the answer *"—we were worlds apart and on separate paths—no matter how we felt, it was impossible."* Enough said, I guess.

After our awkward, yet pleasant meeting, I drove home feeling angry with him. I had to wonder if he thought that maybe I'd replace him in her life. But perhaps he only wanted us to be aware of each other, because over twenty years later she wrote me a note: *"When I first received the box from you, I feared that you had left me with a burden—I did not open it for many years, but when I finally did, I felt overwhelmed and closed it again. When I recently opened it, I knew the time was right, and I know what I have to do, thank you for bringing it to me—Katharine."*

Aloysius is dead, Elise is dead, and Jacob lives on without them—and without me. Their patterns remain the same, but I have changed. There are so many unsettled, disjointed patterns in life, and now a new pattern has emerged in mine—I could go mad trying to make sense of it all.

❧

If Helena has done this—I have no idea where to go. My neck began to ache from looking at the sky for so long, but I kept looking at the cloudy vat of the Milky Way—*how beautiful.* Stepping through the Rose of Sharon hedge onto the adjacent open yard for a better view, a sharp bang startled me, causing my gaze to drop back to earth. It looked to me as if an old fantasy materialized in the darkness when I saw Samantha running toward me, but it was unlike the last time I saw this phenomenon; this time she appears to be running for her life while looking over her shoulder for a pursuer. She ran straight into my arms like a dream come true, but contrary to the tender fantasy of embraces and kisses, she crashed into me with such force that I staggered backwards until my back bumped against the gnarled trunk of the maple tree's reality.

"Holy shit, what's wrong, Samantha?" I exclaimed with bewilderment as I scrambled to maintain our balance with her firmly embedded in my arms.

"Preston is drunk—he won't leave me alone—he doesn't understand—I just don't want him touching me—I can't stand it," she said, her voice muffled by flannel, her hands clawed at my shirtfront.

"Did he hurt you?" I asked suddenly feeling outraged that he had done something so terrible to frighten her out of the house in the middle of the night.

"No, no—I wouldn't let him touch me, he kept wanting to do things to me, so I ran away—he fell down the stairs chasing me—he's so drunk—so stinking drunk." She started to laugh, but her giddiness quickly turned into tears. "I can't go back there—I'm too afraid!"

That drunken fool—a real class act. "Here now, come inside—it's all right." I pried her off my chest, and led her into the house, guiding her through the darkness to the sofa. The house felt chilly, so I wrapped a blanket around her shoulders as she huddled against the pillows.

"Are you sure he didn't hurt you?" I dared to ask, turning on the lights. When the room became illuminated, my apprehension flared into anger as my first impression thought she appeared beaten, but then I realized she was just normal Samantha, her inward gaze grappling with communicating; this is normal when she's upset, so I waited.

"I'm all right—just tired," she replied with half-closed eyes that were far from sleepy.

"I'm sorry, dear heart," I carelessly spoke the old endearment as my heart began to do a wild ricocheting dance against the wall of my chest, its enthusiasm inspired by my earlier reminisces of our former relationship and mixing with the pleasant dreams gathered in my brain.

"Why are you sorry?" she asked, turning toward me, and our eyes locked. With her attention leveled toward me, I felt self-conscious and shrank from her gaze.

"I wish there was something I can do—should I call the police? Has he been abusing you?" I asked, bending close to her. My racing pulse cranked up another notch as an overwhelming protectiveness surged through me; the idea of her husband mistreating her in any way disturbed me, reminding me of the dream that I had the other night.

"No, nothing like that—I wouldn't put up with that," she replied, shaking her head; then her body swayed in a steady rocking she does when she's upset. It seemed as if I struck a nerve, which led me to believe that she was lying about what he did to frighten her tonight.

"I'll call the house to tell Whitley you're here so he doesn't worry."

"All right—yes, he should know—he'll help."

My conversation with her father didn't last more than a minute, he was glad that she was safe, and he suggested that she should tuck in and spend the night with me. *"She doesn't need to see him like this—he's so polluted, he'll be throwing up half the night—or he'll just remain passed out here on the floor where he landed in the foyer—the bum, "* he laughed. My responding laughter hid my apprehension about her staying with me, but I agreed that she should try to get some rest. I handed her the cordless phone so they could say goodnight, and he reassured her that Preston wasn't dead, just passed out. After she hung up and returned the telephone to me, she sat on the couch, bunched up under the blanket, rocking.

"Are you hungry? I have cookies and milk," I said to draw her attention back to me.

"No."

"Thirsty?" I perceived a slight decrease in her motion.

"Do you have any wine—that will help calm me, please?" she shuddered.

"Yes, I have some leftover Shiraz from—last night." *Damn.* I had opened that bottle last night for Helena. When we toasted each other, she had smiled at me in what I thought was that *special way*, which led me to believe in her desire for me. I had made love to her last night, making her yelp with startled pleasure. I realized just now that I hadn't made love to her in a long time—our busy lives filled with the daily tremors of stress, the nervous tension is eating up the intimacy we once had during the stillness of our hours at home. *Damn.*

"What's wrong? You look so unhappy," Samantha asked.

"Nothing," I replied, surprised by her visual assessment of my frame of mind.

Thankfully, her mind is too busy chewing on in her problem to pursue my *nothing* and let it go. I fetched the bottle; there was enough for two glasses and I busied myself with building a fire in the fireplace. We drank in silence, sharing the sofa with Daisy, who lightly danced between us, mewling in her kitten voice, loving the attention, her fluffy paws batting at our fingers, making us laugh. After awhile she became annoyed with us and departed with a sassy hiss. Laughing at my silly cat, I met Samantha's gaze; she had that eerie direct stare that I haven't seen for years, and a hot flush traveled through me like an electrical surge of shame.

"Are you feeling better?" I cleared my throat as the inflamed debris of memories tried to choke me. She said nothing in reply as she leaned against my side, putting her arms around me. "Oh, there now—are you all right?" I inquired further; startled by her closeness, my hands clasped her thin shoulders, tightening the blanket around her.

"Hold me, Sylvester," she murmured into my neck as she burrowed her face under my chin. I hesitated at first, but the temptation to be near her and our years of companionship swayed me into relaxing. As soon as I wrapped my arms around her, we leaned back against the plump pillows that buoyed us in a comfortable nest. The smell of lavender filled my senses with its delicate perfume, and I sighed, feeling sated by her familiar scent; my heart began to race.

"There now, are you better?" I inquired; my voice shuddered with emotion.

"What's wrong, Sylvester? You're not right—" she pressed her hand upon my chest.

"Helena is having an affair." I gagged on my words and tears dropped from my eyes with unexpected forcefulness as I buried my face into the silken luxury of her dark brown hair, I gulped a long breath of her lavender essence and held it in so it would penetrate my senses.

"Shit," she hissed, agitated, she pulled away from me and stood up, emerging from underneath the blanket. "That bitch, she just doesn't know when she's got it good. What's the matter with her? Stupid, stupid—stoo-pid bitch!"

As she began to pace around the room, I watched her—*admired her*—and gulped down the remains of my wine, hoping to snuff out the feelings that I still have for her, but as a result, I felt sloppy, horny, and miserable. I set aside my empty wine glass before I accidentally broke it.

"Samantha—why don't you go upstairs to sleep on the bed—I'll stay here on the sofa—everything will be all right tomorrow." But she seemed not to hear me as she paused in front of my bookshelf and quietly internalized her distress while running her fingers along the colorful spines. Through heavy eyes, I continued to watch her. With a twitch, she suddenly turned to me, and sat on the edge of the sofa; her fingers caressed my brow and danced into my hair.

"Sylvester, Sylvester, Sylvester—I'm sorry, I shouldn't speak unkindly about Helena," she sighed, once again leaning against me; I let my arms fall back into place, and hugged her tightly. My lips lightly brushed the top of her head in an attempt to kiss her, but I couldn't do it.

"It's all right—" I assured her that I wasn't offended. We were quiet, but my head buzzed from my overwrought emotions; closing my eyes, I sighed, she shifted.

"I do remember," she said, her fingers lightly petting my forearms. "I remember your arms, I never forgot how it felt when you held me—I always felt safe."

"I never forgot either," I muttered; the strangling memories clawed at my throat making it difficult to speak. "Every time I smell lavender, I think of you—and our time together—"

"Please make love to me, Sylvester—" she whispered, sitting up, turning to look at me.

"Oh, no, Samantha—it wouldn't be right," I said as I separated myself from her. This stunning jolt to the raw emotions that I have been struggling with this evening forced me off the sofa. "Things are different now, dear heart—we can't—" But I returned to her as she followed me, and I gathered her into my arms, gently embracing her. "Especially not now because of how we feel—because of how we hurt inside."

"I know—everything has changed, but not you, you've always been so good to me—" she muttered as her fingers tugged on my shirt collar. Unable to deny my feelings for her, I lowered my head and I carelessly kissed her. It felt natural as we stood in the middle of the room quietly hugging and kissing one another, so when our impulsive desires sent us drifting upstairs, we went without hesitation. In spite of the emotional complexity of our situation, our physical passion was self-evident as we lay together entangled by love.

A very loud knocking on the front door startled us apart. I muffled a cry of exasperation because the interruption of the beautiful ecstasy from which I suffered caused my ejaculation to sputter without pleasure as I withdrew from her unsatisfied body.

"It's *him*," she whimpered, sitting up, and clasping her arms around her legs.

"It's okay, be calm—I'll take care of it," I assured her as I stumbled out of bed on wobbly legs. I quickly pulled on jeans and a t-shirt, and I fumbled my glasses to my face as I hurried down the stairs. The knocking quickly turned into violent pounding. "Who is it?" I called out through the closed door even though I knew perfectly well it could only be Samantha's husband.

"Is my wife with you, Hayden?" Preston growled.

"Yes, she's here—but I think it would be a good idea if you went home right now; she's very upset," I called through the door, trying to sound weary, but I feared that I sounded drunk instead. "I really don't know what you did to frighten her, but good lord, man—you need to pull yourself together—it's 2 AM, go home and sober up."

"You haven't called the cops, have you?" he shouted.

"No—she didn't want me to," I said specifically to imply that I would have done it in a heartbeat if she said so. "Please go home and sober up—she will talk to you tomorrow."

"Don't give me any of that fucking tomorrow crap, I want to talk to her right now!" He punched the door, causing the knocker to clatter with agitation on its brass plate.

"Preston—if you don't leave, I will call the cops," I shouted through the door. Then I heard the window upstairs rattle open, I looked up the stairway to see Samantha on the landing above the foyer, tightly wrapped in her robe, shivering against the chilly night air.

"Preston, please go home," her voice softly drifted into the night.

"I didn't mean to scare you away—" he bawled.

"Go home, Preston—I'll talk to you tomorrow," she soothed. But the man wouldn't hear of it; he continued to rage at her with inarticulate exclamations slurred up to the window like a fucked-up Romeo.

"Here, here, what's all the ruckus?" A new voice entered the fray on my front stoop. I couldn't see him because I didn't dare look out the window to see, but apparently, Whitley had come along to set things straight with his wayward son-in-law.

"Daddy, be careful!" Samantha warned. She stood with her hands clutching her robe shut as if being modest—I was sure that she wanted them to believe in her modesty in front of me.

"He isn't going to hurt me—right, Preston?" Whitley asked. I could hear the smirk in his tone; it is plain that his opinion regarding his son-in-law has bottomed-out on this night. "Are you all right, Sammy?" he called to her.

"I didn't hurt her!" Preston bellowed.

"I'm all right—I need to sleep now—please, just let me sleep—I need sleep."

"Come back, I said I was sorry!" The drunkard groaned with frustration.

"I know, but you frightened me—I just want you to leave me alone!" she shuddered.

"I'm sorry, Sammy—really I am!" her husband bellowed with a trailing whine.

"I know you're sorry, bud, but you are making things worse by coming out here and scaring the girl more than you already have; you should know better by now. Come along—you and I have had too much to drink for our own good. Leave your woman alone, come back home, and sleep it off—she's safe with Hayden for the night," Whitley coaxed him.

Safe with me? I stifled a noise in my throat that had the tenor of a laugh with the bass of a groan, a sarcastic sound of guilt.

"Okay, okay—" he moaned like a spoiled child who didn't get his way.

"Thank you, Daddy," Samantha called after them. I thought it was sweet whenever she called him that, and I figured it gave the old man's heartstrings a paternal tug to hear it spoken.

"Goodnight, Little One, get some sleep," Whitley chimed with pride. "Thanks, Hayden!"

With the crisis over, I collapsed onto the bottom step feeling wretched and I moaned into my hands because of what I've done on this night. I felt like completely losing it, opening the door and yelling at Preston—*"Hey, asshole, I just fucked your wife—I did it because I love her—I have always loved her because of who she is—you just love her money!"*

"It's all right, Sylvester, he's gone—" she spoke softly to me from above.

"I should sleep on the sofa—you need to get some rest," I sighed with open wretchedness. She carefully padded down the stairs, paused beside me; her hand stroked my hair. I leaned my head against her leg, kissing her warm thigh encased in the soft layers of flannel. "Oh, Samantha—you have no idea how difficult this is for me."

"You do love Helena," she said.

"Yes, still," I huffed with a bitter sound. "I do love her, I can't turn off the emotions because she has hurt me—I don't know how I'm going to get through this," I groaned, neglecting to confess my dilemma regarding my feelings for her.

"What has gone wrong?"

"I don't know—I—don't know—I don't understand." My voice faded. Actually, I did understand—*I am to blame.* My preoccupation with Samantha corrupted my life with Helena, she is much too needy to have someone only paying half attention to her—it's all or nothing, I knew that from the beginning, but didn't heed it. "I'm just stupid, I guess—"

"Hush—you're not stupid," she whispered, sitting next to me on the step.

"Oh, yes, I am—look at me—look at us—I let you in to protect you from your husband and whatever sex game he wanted to play with you tonight, only to fuck you myself—I'm ready to lose my mind—really, I think I'm cracking up," I choked on laughter and tears combined. She put her arms around me, and I accepted her quiet comfort. When she kissed me, I savored her soft caress and moaned with delight. Once again, my inner conflict failed to overlook temptation when it came to Samantha Ryder as I fell asleep holding her. When I woke up still holding her, I was surprised that she did not slip away like she used to in the past. It was delightful to lie there watching her sleep as my lover beside me. It was even sweeter to observe the awakening consciousness as it arrived upon her face just before she opened her eyes. Wishing each other good morning, skin softly brushing against skin, our lips kissed, and our limbs embraced.

"I should go home—" she said, turning her gaze to the clock. *She's late.*

"Not yet—stay just a little bit longer—I only have a lecture this afternoon—we'll have our coffee together before you go home." I didn't think she would, any slight step to the left or right of her routine disrupts the balance that she diligently maintains—but after last night's fiasco, there is no balance left.

"No, I won't go—not yet—he's still there—I'm not ready to see him."

"You should divorce him," I murmured, kissing one of her rosebud nipples as I pressed against her, hoping that she'd allow me to mount her again.

"You should have married Helena—maybe that's why she strayed from you, you wouldn't commit to her," she sighed. I nearly bit my tongue because of the mention of Helena. "You gave no definition to her life with you—other than being lovers."

What is Helena's definition? My lover—is that what she is? Not my significant other—not my wife. Truthfully, after Helena proclaimed her gun-shyness about marriage, I never gave the subject much thought. I had believed Helena and I were happily *"status quo"* and I had accepted this arrangement, perfectly content to be with her while I fantasized about Samantha. During my contemplation above Samantha's nipple, I wondered if I had emotionally alienated her while indulging in sex with her throughout the three years we spent together, which lead her to set me free when Helena returned from Berkley. Samantha was the only woman I ever considered marrying, but I felt too paralyzed by self-doubts and ethics to follow through. *Safe, sound, "status quo".*

"Forgive me," I moaned into her soft flesh; I wanted to cry—*I should have married her! If I had, Helena wouldn't have known the difference—but it would have been one of those "what if" scenarios nagging in my mind.* "Oh, please, forgive me," I groaned. I wanted to die. "I made a mistake—" I wanted to confess my jelly-kneed dithering nine years ago just to get it out in the air between us. "I—" I stammered. I wanted to say that I made the wrong choice—I wanted to tell her *"I love you—I loved you then, and I still love you now—please forgive me."*

"We all make mistakes, Sylvester—" she said, placing her fingertips on my mouth to stop my confession. "Just like before, no one has to know," she kissed my mouth, my brow, and then she revisited my lips with a soft lingering caress, the tip of her tongue touching mine. "You know we can't let this happen again—no matter how good it feels, we just can't—never again." We heard the distinct sound of Preston's Camaro roar to life and drive away.

"Now I can go home."

"Oh, Samantha—" I sighed, giving in to her logic. *Never again.* She's right—this must end here because we're not in a position to carry it further. Although stolen kisses during furtive meetings in secluded places *"to talk"* eagerly greeted my imagination—but I feared turning something beautiful into something ugly should our secret be discovered. For now, our feelings have nowhere to go, so, I reluctantly kissed my love goodbye. *Never again.*

With her robe firmly wrapped around her, she paused in the doorway to look back. Without my glasses on, her expression was softly blurred, but I didn't need to see clearly to feel the emotional brew afflicting her—*never again.* Then she was gone. I rose from the bed to watch her from the upstairs window. Her pale shape flitted through the gap in the hedge, and she walked quickly across the green lawn with her arms folded tight in front of her. I knew that it is for the best to let her go home to work out her problems—or not. And I need to do some thinking as well—it is time to put an end to the charade in which I live.

When I turned away from the window, I met the accusing gaze of Daisy; she lay on my pillow, her bushy tail twitching with annoyance like a regal lady with a fan. "Daisy, if you don't tell, I won't tell Helena that you peed on her brief case." The cat only narrowed her yellow eyes as if in contemplation of the deal that I offered; the fluffy rogue routinely pees on Helena's stuff to pick a catfight, and Helena screams at me because of something my *pissy cat* did to her stuff. After a while, Daisy looked away and yawned as if she had already forgotten my indiscretion. One thing for sure, my cat always liked Samantha. It's funny how animals seem to know things in that peculiar awareness they possess; through my cat's eyes, I'm finally seeing the errors of my ways.

How do I amend what I've done? I don't know.

⌒

Right up to an hour before Helena's return home on Wednesday afternoon, I had refused to change the bed sheets. I spent the last two nights relishing my infidelity through the fading lavender scent of my lover, alternately feeling sated and miserable. A part of me wanted Helena to come to bed tonight and know that I had been with someone else—my sweet revenge—but my guilt forced me to strip the bed to eliminate the stains of lovemaking.

"Why are you doing laundry?" she asked when she caught me carrying the tangle of clean sheets upstairs; my nervous hands were incapable of folding them neatly.

"I umm—I—" I sputtered with guilt, ready to confess what I had done.

"Eww, did you go off in your sleep again?" she asked, wrinkling her lips into a grimace reserved for amused disgust. Her intimate knowledge of my body's nocturnal habits sometimes makes me too human for her taste. I disgust her most of the time, awake or asleep, it doesn't matter; she's always had a hard time with the reality of me once the early novelty wore off.

"Ugh, last night—it woke me up." I matched her expression by crinkling my nose.

"Jeez, Luiz, you act like you had an affair," she snorted in an indelicate way that always makes me laugh, but my usual snicker got stuck in my throat because of the confession teetering on the tip of my tongue. Forcing a chuckle into the air, I climbed the stairs with the sheets.

While making the bed, I picked up a pillow from the floor and breathed in the scent of lavender; I had forgotten to wash the pillowcases in my panic to hide the evidence. After embracing what was left of that night, I exchanged the pillow with the one from my side of the bed; this one bit of proof of my infidelity I could not part with just yet, and if Helena smelled it, it would serve her right to have to wonder how the scent of her sister had gotten there. But this evidence was explained away later—"*Preston was drunk, he had scared the shit out of Sammy, so she spent the night here.*" She bought the story that I had slept on the sofa without batting an eyelash. It's the furthest thing from her mind that I would have an affair with anyone, and she'd think it especially ludicrous that I would have a fling with her autistic half-sister, Samantha Ryder.

4

Whitley

Poor, sad, Sylvester, I wish he could be happier! I hated to leave him like this, but I have no choice—*I must go home*. With one last glance over my shoulder, I witnessed the tormented image of him lying on his back staring at the ceiling with his head pillowed on one wiry arm stretched up behind his head. His skin lightly tanned by this past summer's sun, except for the hollow of his open armpit that remained pale from being unexposed. For a moment, my eyes remained transfixed with fascination on this spot with its raw thatch of brown hair fanned out like a natural cluster of marram grass growing in a protected contour of a sand dune—this is beautiful to me. This is just one small place on his body that I love to study, my mind breaking it down to its simplified shapes, then examining the way light and shadow drapes over his skin creating delicate shifts of color. It's my special way of seeing, I could look at him all day—and then draw all night the things that I have seen—precious flesh, fascinating bones—he's just a man, but so much more—structure and spirit—the things about him that I love.

With a slight twitch of my chin, I shifted my eyes to visit his profile. Upon sensing that I lingered, he turned his head to look at me; even with his glasses off, I knew that he could see well enough. Long ago, I always left without waking him with the purpose of avoiding the cast of his lonely gaze following me out the door—I always wanted to stay—to be with him all the time, but I always returned home, and filled pages of my sketchbooks with *him*. This time I stayed and this time I looked back to meet his eye—*this timethis time—this time will be the last time—never again—we can't let it happen ever again. It's our secret—no one needs to know.* Without uttering

101

a word, I looked away from his barren face, stepped through the bedroom threshold, and ran down the stairs to flee from my desire to remain with him.

Once outside in the cool morning air, I clasped my arms tight around me, the soft flannel of my nightgown now replaced the sensation of his warm skin against mine; I shivered. When I passed through the hedge and entered the green lawn beyond the maple tree, my thoughts paused over the memory of a girlish cotton nightgown that had once lain discarded on the grass alongside the bunched up pile of male blue jeans and flannel shirt that belonged to my anxious lover who had succumbed to my temptation. I remember how I had carefully removed his glasses and placed them on the white of my garment so they would not be lost in the darkness. It is funny how I remained aware of their location throughout our tryst so not to crush them while our writhing bodies struggled to achieve pleasure on the damp grass—in all of the concern for his glasses, I never took heed of the harm upon my heart that I inflicted by tempting him on that night. *And what of his?* My adolescent desires never took into consideration the pain that I had imposed upon him—his final kiss that long ago night, and his gaze this morning expressed the hardship—*his guilt. Poor Sylvester, I can't believe Helena has hurt him like this—he's so unhappy. Oh, Samantha, why have you done this to him again? Because he makes me happy. Because he makes me feel good—I wanted him to feel good—because I love him more than anyone in the whole wide world.*

When I decided to set him free to chase his dream of Helena, I cried tears of heartache that came from a bottomless well of sadness because I loved him. It was different from the tears that I have shed whenever a bemused glut of emotions arises due to an imbalance in my routine. It was akin to the distress that I felt during the loss of Lenore and Guthrie. While it was fresh, this emotion became as despicable as a thick, crackly scab over a festering wound that gives the appearance of healing, and it remained neglected with a furtive hope that it will eventually go away. Nine years later, the remaining scar is still raw and thin-skinned, the fluid collected underneath the protective tissue are the tears that I have left unshed. What is worse is how it aches because it is secret—I have told no one, and we have failed to address it together as if we don't know where to begin or where to end. I just don't know what to do about it. After last night, how can I—*how can we*—pretend that nothing happened? But we will, because we always have. *We can't let it happen again—never again.*

From the back-step, I confirmed that Preston has already left to make the drive to work; he never took the train like we do, and I am grateful that he goes off to battle Boston bound traffic early so I do not have to face him on this frail morning. I don't know what I'll say to him about anything. He had frightened me last night—*"Trust me,"* he had said. I flinched from the memory and clamped my hands over my ears. *"No—don't touch me!"* Fighting against my fear, I went upstairs, took a quick shower, and got dressed. My body ached from the lack of sleep—my body ached from Sylvester's love—ached for his gentle love. Preston's love is contrary; Preston's love does not arouse tenderness. His love is not love—his love is like greed—like a crime of passion.

The distant call of the cuckoo clock in the studio reminded me that I'm past my time. I ran down the kitchen stairs to make up a tray of toast and tea for Whitley. Long ago, Lenore had entrusted me with this task so I could spend time with him while she went out on her morning run. I would go up to the garret and sit for nearly an hour, trying to coax him awake; the armor of my ultimate patience reinforced by stubbornness never chinked by the arduous morning task. It is our game, our ritual. Once he is awake, we'd talk—father and daughter—about things—many things, anything—except he cannot talk about Lenore—or Guthrie. But this morning he is already awake, which is unusual.

"Good morning, Daddy, how are you feeling?" I inquired, curious about his wakeful face and watchful eyes; he looked rough—rougher than normal—his skin appeared gray even in the ruddy daylight of the garret, and his bloodshot eyes look as if he didn't sleep.

"Oh, dear, bread 'n beer—if I were whiskey, I wouldn't be here!" he greeted me with a laugh, stretching his arms above his head with a yawn; his joints made their tormented crunching sounds; although he is in dreadful pain, his smile continued to shine. I laughed at his silly rhyme that he always teased me with for as long as I have known him—I will never tire of hearing it.

"It will be a sad day if you were to drink yourself by mistake." I made my usual comeback to his joke as I bent down to kiss his wrinkled brow.

"It was him, wasn't it?" he smirked, his nearly black eyes sparkled with a hint of mischief—teasing. "It was him—*him!*" he repeated with a hoot, slapping his hands on his knees; it was funny how he looked so pleased about his discovery of *him*.

"By *him* do you mean Sylvester?" I asked, understanding who he meant, but not what he meant—though I feared what knowledge that he managed to ascertain from last night's events.

"Yes, him—Hayden—he was the one you slept with before you married Preston," he said, pointing his crooked finger at me and he laughed.

"We were lovers while Helena was in Berkley," I admitted to our history, feeling immediate relief upon unburdening my secret. My father's face paused as he changed gears from self-assured knowledge to unexpected surprise.

"You mean to tell me, you two had some secret affair going on? Well, Happy New Year, why didn't you tell me?" he exclaimed, wildly gesticulating with his hands.

"Well, Happy Birthday—do I have to tell you everything? What happened was so private—and I was so young, I didn't want him to get into trouble."

"Trouble! Yes, you were young, I would have kicked his ass from here to Timbuktu because his judgment was not the best—he was probably scared out of his mind or just feeling foolish—how much older is he? Well, let's do the math—let's see—he's nigh fifty."

"He just turned forty-five—I'm twenty-eight."

"Seventeen years older—that's all? I was in my fifties when I married your mother—she was only twenty-one—never mind that—I wish you had told me—he wanted to marry you."

"He never said such a thing!" I replied with mock disbelief and then scowled.

"No—he never said anything, not in words anyway—he was just as tight-lipped as you were—but a father knows these things—a young man coming around is coming for a reason, not just because an old man is offering a free meal, cigars, and booze! He spent those dinners with us because of you—he'd preen himself like a bird trying to attract a mate. The two of you made quite a pair, you know—I never suspected a thing, but that doesn't mean I didn't think a lot. You know—if you had told me, I wouldn't have been a bit surprised at all! Jeez, Louise—you two spent so much time together; it was natural for you to fall in love with each other."

"Ah, but it was Helena he loved—I broke off our relationship as soon as she came back—it was the right thing for me to do because I knew that he still loved her."

"If he loves her he's a fool—she treats him like shit! That little dick teaser never gave him the time of day all the while he pined for her—toying with him, driving him crazy, the wretched bitch, she's worse than her mother! If he hadn't gone chasing after Helena as soon as she got back, I thought about playing matchmaker with you two."

"If he had asked to marry me, I would have said 'no'—it wouldn't have been right because he does love Helena—even though he just found out that she's cheating on him."

"Don't tell me another soap opera! That Helena and her bullshit—I hope he kicks her out on her ass—she deserves it—it'd give me great pleasure to help him throw her shit out into the yard, but that would mean her bitchiness will move back in here—no-thank-you," he groaned with a laugh. "All right, enough about Sylvester—tell me, what did Preston do to you last night to upset you? I want a good reason to wring his fucking neck while I chew him a new asshole."

"Preston wanted to—I wouldn't do it—he just wouldn't leave me alone—I was afraid that he might hurt me—he was so angry with me because I wouldn't do what he wanted." I shuddered at the memory of him looming over me, intimidating. *"Come on, trust me,"* he said—*but I don't trust him.* I hid my face behind my hands, feeling ashamed that all has gone wrong.

"Come now, talk to me—tell me, Sammy, were you afraid of him because he wanted to do nasty stuff to you? He shouldn't be doing things that scare you—tell me, I want to help you, honey—tell me." He put his arm around my shoulders, tugging me toward him.

"No—I don't want to tell you—I can't," I wailed as I leaned on his shoulder, my hands still clamped over my face.

"Tell me, Sammy—it's all right—I won't let him hurt you." Whitley held me together so I didn't fall to pieces—I was so grateful for him—his love, his strength.

"He wanted to tie me up—he told me that it would be a sign of trust if I let him do it," I cried, and my body began to sway, rocking—*kidnapped, tied up, repeatedly raped, choked to death, and dumped into the ocean—just like Lenore.* "I was afraid he was going to do me like Noah did Mommy!" I sobbed feeling overwhelmed by the childhood fears; my palms quickly became flooded with tears.

"Bah, that sick bastard—has he ever tried that before?" he asked with a defined flinch at the mention of my mother. "Sammy!" Whitley held me tighter, to make me stop rocking. "Talk to me, Sammy, has he ever tried that shit with you before?"

"No—not really—no—he's not gentle at all, he hurts me inside—he isn't like Sylvester," I muttered, lowering my hands from my face at last. "Sylvester is so gentle and good to me—he would never hurt me—I picked him because I knew he'd be nice to me."

"Look at me—tell me—did you sleep with Hayden last night?" Whitley cut beyond my marital dilemma that had sent me running into the night.

"Yes, but it wasn't my intention—I only went there to hide from Preston. Sylvester and I—we were both sad—what we did was wrong—we won't do it ever again." I sagged heavily against my father, and he held me tight. I wanted to sleep—not much sleep, too much pleasure last night. *What is Sylvester doing now?*

"Do you love Hayden?" he asked so gently it was almost a whisper.

"I love him—I love him as well as I love you, as well as I love Helena. I had sex with him last night because I wanted to—I would never do anything I don't want to do. Oh, poor Sylvester, he is full of regrets because of everything—everything is a mess," I whimpered.

"Sam—what if it is you he really wants—what if, the reason why he never married Helena was because he wanted you?" Whitley put this question to me with an earnest tone.

"Don't overanalyze Sylvester's feelings—it's not worth the headache! Have your toast and tea—stop talking about it." I wanted to leave him; I wanted to run back to Sylvester to see him before he left for his afternoon lecture. I wanted to feel his arms around me again—to feel his kiss, to lie down with him—but I can't—*we shouldn't—no—no—no—never again.*

"If I had known that Preston was going to be like this I wouldn't have ever allowed him near you!" he exclaimed with frustration.

"Oh, Whitley—he fooled us all—don't start regretting things now."

"Listen to me, Sammy. Preston does not make you happy, and I feel responsible—I know things—" he hesitated. "Oh, Little One, I've heard about things he has done," he sighed, hanging his head. "He's been seeing other women—Pinkerton told me that he's seen him wining and dining some Spanish beauty in Chinatown just the other day, and there have been others before her—right up until your wedding—he's had something going on all the time."

"It means nothing what Pinkerton saw—Preston is often entertaining visiting artists or prospective students—did Pinkerton see him kiss her or fuck her—no—it was just lunch in Chinatown. I don't really care what he's doing—if he is having affairs, it is because I do not satisfy him—I'm not sexually attracted to him—I don't even like the way he smells."

"Well—there's nothin' worse than a stinky man to turn a woman's stomach," he chuckled; then he made his wrinkled face firm with serious thoughts. "What about Hayden?"

"We've always been friends—he didn't instigate it, I seduced him—"

"Oh, Hells Bells!" he exclaimed, clasping his hands over his ears in a mock imitation of me. "There are just some things a father does not want to know about his daughter—her sex life is foremost on the list," he laughed and I laughed at his foolishness.

"You brought it up, don't be so squeamish, Mr. Pot—Miss Kettle knows you are no angel," I chided him with blunt accuracy about his own sexual past.

"Not that it is any of my business, but was Hayden the only one—or were there others?"

"There was no one else, I trusted him—that was why I picked him to be my first." I crossed my arms self-consciously over my body, tucking my hands in between my thighs in a protective manner. Out of the corner of my eye, I could see my father staring at me with a mix of dismay and admiration. It's been hard for him raising me without Lenore. A lone man with daughters is like a beleaguered army trying to protect all fronts, but all it takes is one enemy combatant to sneak in under the paternal radar to raise havoc when his daughter falls in love. Even after she is married, he'll still try to protect her from harm.

"Oh, Daddy, I was so afraid that Preston was going to hurt Sylvester last night."

"Hurt him—what about you? I think Hayden could have held his own."

"I'm very concerned about Sylvester." I bit my lip as tears welled in my eyes. "He looked so—ruined this morning."

"He's all right," Whitley hugged me. "You're both all right—poor child, you were so frightened last night—when I heard you screaming I thought Preston was killing you. I gotta tell ya, I thought you had killed him when I found him on the floor in the foyer—well, you know, the bigger they are, the harder they fall when they tumble down the stairs. What a dumbass, passed-out, and so shit-faced drunk he was stupid—after he come to, I turned my back on him to make coffee and he was out the door after you—I'm telling you right now, Preston is not allowed to drink another drop in this house, that fool can't handle his liquor. I stayed up all night making sure he didn't go sneaking out again to mess with you—I even served his sorry ass breakfast!"

"What am I going to do? I don't love him—I tried—I thought I would get used to him; he really wanted me to love him before, but now he's become impatient with me," I muttered into his shirt collar; he smelled stale, and in need of fresh clothes and a hot shower.

"If you don't love him, don't stay with him; you should consider a divorce as soon as possible—it would be for the best if you do—I can only see this getting worse. I would feel better if you divorced Preston before I die. If something happens to me, Sam—after last night, I cannot trust him to take care of you. I've decided to change my Will with Jack as soon as possible—I called his ass out of bed at 4 AM to tell him. Preston's name will be removed so he won't have a claim to anything should something happen to me anytime soon. The house will be in your name only—no one can touch it or your money. I think I will appoint Sylvester to be co-executor along with Helena, just so he can have some say in things—I should have done that in the first place. He's a good man in spite of himself, although he's an odd duck, I like him—I wish I could see you and Sylvester together, but I don't expect I will," he chuckled.

"Oh, Daddy, don't talk like that!" I cried feeling distressed by his prediction. "If something happens to you, don't worry about me—I'll be fine." I looked out the window at the sky, feeling hopeful. "I should check on Sylvester—I'm worried about him."

"I knew he was in love with you," Whitley wheezed, and he shook his head.

"Sylvester?" I frowned, tracing the pattern on the blanket with my finger, feeling restless by this circular conversation—there's nothing we can do about who-loved-who right now.

"I want you to be happy, Sammy."

"You don't think I am?"

"No. I feel responsible—I never meant to do anything to hurt you."

"You haven't—"

"Haven't I? I went against all that Lenore begged me not to do with you—I exploited your talent—I was greedy, a greedy old bastard. I kept you under my thumb, forcing you to forsake any chance for independence by making you dependent on me all these years—I even handpicked your husband—the way I see it, I have made many wrong decisions—"

"Have I ever complained?" I asked, feeling impatient.

"No—but you should have," he sadly shook his head. "Your mother has nagged me from the grave for everything I've done—I should have listened to her."

"I had no reason to complain. I have done everything of my own free will; if I didn't want to marry Preston I wouldn't have done it—I had my doubts, but I failed to heed them." As I said this, I placed my hand on his shoulder. Looking at him up close, I noted that his once impressive frame seemed so fragile. *He's full of cancer, but he refused treatment—he's too proud, too stubborn, and too afraid—it's a matter of time.* "That isn't Mommy inside your head talking—that's just your conscience talking—you're just filling it in with her voice."

"Oh, Little One, it is a cold existence living with ghosts," he sighed bitterly, casting his gaze at the hazy canvas on the easel; its delicate surface appeared populated by spirits.

"Have your toast and tea, Daddy," I muttered feeling sad for him.

"I am proud of you, Sammy," he clasped my hand and kissed it. "Go work, I can tell you're itchy to start—or go see Hayden if you must." He caressed my cheek and stared at me with adoration. "You look just like Lenore," he smiled; but behind that smile, he struggled with grief. *He had loved her—what had happened to them? Why did they stray?*

"I do not—Lenore was beautiful," I said, covering my face with my hands, feeling ashamed, *I've heard this many times from others, but never my father.*

"You are beautiful, Sammy," he said, pulling my hands away. "I don't blame Sylvester for wanting you—call me partial, but I think you are much prettier than Helena."

"Sylvester is a sad and lonely man—I tempted him one night a long time ago, and I took advantage of him last night—I was selfish, just as selfish as I was at sixteen—I wanted to feel good—I knew that he would make me feel good—last night, I wanted him to feel good because Helena had hurt him."

"If you wanted him to feel good, then you didn't take advantage of him. You shared something beautiful with him—don't make it ugly by feeling guilty about it."

"Don't try to find the right in what I have done—it was inappropriate behavior, even your conscience must understand that." I forced myself to refrain from the childish phrase: *"I was bad."* Although he smiled, my father did not reply; to avoid arguing with me, he ceased the conversation by nibbling on his toast and sipping the cooled tea. And so I left him be.

Whitley may believe that he has herded me into exploiting my talent, but if I didn't want to do any of this, I wouldn't have done it just because my father told me to. Like him, I have regrets after the fact; mistakes, poor choices, wrong turns, and oversights—we're all in it together as a family— even Sylvester is not blameless. If he wanted to marry me, he should have said so. On that night when Helena announced her intent to return home, I had felt a change in him—unnamed anxieties plunged him into an internal melancholy, I saw the creases of stress etched into his flesh—I knew what I had to do then, just as I do now. His face that I have drawn so many times—his body—and his hands—*familiar-familiar-familiar—I trust-I trust-I trust—I love-love-love him—dearest heart—what are we to do? Nothing-nothing—there is nothing we can do. Never again.*

I didn't go see him after I left Whitley; instead, I went directly into my studio, skipping off the path of my set routine to visit with him over our morning coffee. *He didn't come looking for me either.* There was only satisfaction found with the point of my pencil; eventually, I made myself laugh as if tickled by making the rendering of my lover's nicely shaped buttocks, and then I pinned it up in a prominent space on the corkboard above my drafting table to display it along with the hands and faces of my family. After quiet contemplation, I wondered if Helena would recognize her manfriend's ass if she saw it. I secretly hoped she would, and it was my hope that she would inquire about it. *How would she form the question? Have you seen Sy's ass? When did you see Sy's ass? How did you come to see Sy's ass? Jeez, Louise, Sam, you saw Sy's ass?* There are so many ways to make such an inquiry, but I have only one answer. Here's another question—*if Sylvester came into the garret, would he recognize his own ass?* Maybe not; I wouldn't know my own, but then, that's just me—I don't even look at me in a mirror.

When I saw Sylvester at dinner, he was quiet as per his normal manner. His gaze tripped over my face as he nodded his acknowledgement to my greeting, and answered that he felt well. He then politely asked about how my day had been, and I told him about the progress I made on the commission of the *Ghent Altarpiece.* Longing to be alone with him, I wavered on indecisive feet, but I resisted the temptation to lead him upstairs to look at it. Then he announced that Helena had called, and she wanted him to pass on her *"Hello"* to us. With this said, our lingering gazes fluttered away, and therefore we left many things unspoken; I have released him once again.

Preston arrived late to join us at the dinner table; he was subdued compared to other evenings spent seated at his place beside me, usually competing with Whitley and Sylvester for my attention like the bluster of a storm. Earlier today, we had a brief talk on the telephone, he gently apologized for his drunken behavior last night, and although I remained wary of him, I accepted his plea. He even asked Sylvester to forgive him as well, and Sylvester was kind enough to scoff and shucks in order to make light of the awkward situation. I was pleased with my old friend's natural performance that only betrayed his kindness toward me without exposing the passion he had expressed during the previous night.

Throughout dinner, Preston continued to behave sheepishly as if too embarrassed by the spectacle he made of himself to be sociable. Although Whitley pontificated normally, he maintained an air of secretive amusement as his gaze roved from one to the other corner of the silent triangle that he now oversaw. At times, he appeared ready to launch on Preston should he so much as look at me cross-eyed, and then he watched Sylvester with something akin to a peg down from respect—it was as if he didn't know whether to shake his hand or take him by the shoulders to shake sense into him. Both men remained blissfully ignorant of my father's scrutiny, as their subdued gazes were too busy examining the food on the plates before them.

From my place amongst these three men, I felt completely turned inside out; each one of them knows something about me so intimate, so secret— yet, they know nothing about how I feel, only how they think I must feel. It seemed fitting that my period started on that morning—it is so symbolic of the way my emotions bleed and migrate, staining my being.

All day long, my thoughts have been churned with the internal combustion of rioting emotions, so that by evening, I set into motion a consideration for making a change in my life—I moved out of my marriage bed into my childhood bedroom. Although Preston gave off the impression of feeling distressed by my decision, he claimed that he understood my aversion to him because of what had happened as he fretfully cast promises from the threshold to be more patient, and then he begged for forgiveness. Right then, I told him that too much damage has already been done and I needed time to think. He then stormed and raged, and then I roared; he backed down, and backed out of my doorway because I was *being bad*. He didn't dare complain to Whitley about my obstinate attitude toward him—he feared his father-in-law might aptly tell him to go fuck himself in more ways than one until the Christmas after next, especially since Jack arrived after dinner to do his lawyerly duty for Whitley. Jack, his young paralegal, Bob, Sylvester, and Pinkerton settled into the parlor with Whitley for drinks, and all the while I was upstairs, I could hear their evocative male rumblings—their laughter was curious; the aptly dubbed *Nasty Jack* always had an endless supply of dirty jokes. After this bit of legal reaction to my husband's bad behavior, and Jack's severe parting warning, *"You're on my radar now, I'm watching you*" the disinherited Preston began to lurk around the house like a punished dog with his tail tucked between his legs for days.

As for Sylvester and I, a new version of *normal* began to cycle through our friendship. Helena returned home on Wednesday as scheduled, and it seemed like they remained at peace in the carriage house. At dinner on her first night home, I thought Sylvester looked a little smug, as if savoring his unspoken revenge—what's good for the goose is good for the gander, I suppose. But he also appeared uneasy—he's smoking again. It became clear that Sylvester began to drift away from me, and I from him because of our guilt—because of fear—because of shame—because of desire denied. There isn't much we can do about what we did, what's done is done—we shouldn't do it again, and so we look away from each other so not to incite further temptation. Yet we quietly continue our daily dedication to routines. Together, but separate.

∽

Many mornings of toast and tea came and went; my conversations with Whitley never returned to the subject of Sylvester, nor did he cast any comments in Sylvester's direction that he had figured out our secret. And I was also surprised that he didn't antagonize Helena about her discovered infidelity, especially since his eldest daughter made his ass itch—so she remained oblivious to everything as per normal Helena.

Another morning came, after many in which I applied a great deal of consideration about my future, and so today, I have decided to file for divorce. This time my routine expedition to the garret with the tray of toast and tea never felt so urgent before. I was terrified by the idea of divorcing Preston, yet happy to have finally made up my mind to do it. I wanted Whitley to come with me to see Jack about it because his solid presence would be a comfort—I needed his strength and the resolve that he always exhibited whenever I needed him—I needed his paternal love. Questions that had formed in my mind like thunderheads all night crashed into a storm when I found my father lying on the sofa, covered with a blanket—asleep, but he looked—not right; the storm calmed as I remembered how frail he has become—so gray—in so much pain.

"Good morning, Whitley," I called softly, beginning our game as I set the tray aside. My eyes strayed toward his latest canvas, and I noted that it remained unchanged from the previous day; perhaps he's still living with it while waiting for the right mood to inspire change. I thought it was beautiful, the wide horizontal motion of saturated color weaving in and out of a sweeping curve of translucent mist; its flat surface shimmered with a beautiful sense of dimension. I recognized that it was the beach—and what I thought may have been a lone weathered post, may actually be a solitary figure, feminine in stature—*Lenore*. At least, I wanted to believe that he still thought of her—maybe he expected her to be waiting for him to join her one day. Or would she be waiting for Guthrie instead? Would the three of them meet again in the after-life to forgive one another—husband forgiving wife, wife forgiving husband—father forgiving son—son forgiving father— the lovers forgiving each other; finally at rest.

"Daddy?" My hand touched his shoulder, then his arm, and finally his hand.

No, he's not asleep. He's not asleep-not asleep-not asleep. Dead.

5

Gloucester

Pinkerton called to tell me that Whitley had passed on, so I went home to Gloucester to attend the funeral for the only father I knew.

When Whitley Ryder married Margaret Collins in 1953, he understood that I came with the package, and along with this understanding, he loved me like I was his own flesh and blood. He never had a son—or any children for that matter, though he had been married twice already. When Margie took his name with their wedding vows, I became Guthrie Ryder. I was barely two years old at the time, so the details regarding the event of my adoption never had an impact, but when I first used the word *"Daddy"* as part of my daily vocabulary, Whitley Ryder was the guy who received that special designation because he was my dad.

My biological father's name, Luke McKeon, never meant much to me—I didn't know him—never met him—and he never met me. McKeon was just the man who had made a vague promise to *"make it right"* in a letter scribbled from boot camp when he learned that my mom was pregnant. He never came back from Korea to follow up on this proposal; he went AWOL while over there and eventually the military presumed him dead; for all we know, he might be living happily with a Korean woman with a pile of children—or maybe not—he might've run out on her too. I recognize him in the only picture of him my mom possessed, and it is obvious that I carry his looks; I grew tall and strong, with blocky hands and barges for feet, and I am vain just like him. At the age of fifty-two, I stand six foot five and three quarters inches in my socks, and I now display the potential he had for a small, yet just as despicable, paunchy beer belly on an otherwise fit frame, but I have

Margie to blame for my baldness. My granddaddy, Ike Collins, was bald as a cue ball by the time he keeled over from a heart attack at the age of sixty-five. I suppose, had he lived, Luke McKeon would have grown old and died with a full head of hair—*genetics, ya gotta love 'em.*

While I knew him during my formative years, Whitley Ryder had been my idol and I loved him. He was a playful, lovable man; he was the man with whom I bonded with, and learned basic guy stuff from until Margie kicked him out a week shy of my eighth birthday. After a whole lot of yelling and screaming, I gathered from snippets of her verbal assault that she had caught him *fooling around* with one of his models in the attic studio.

Being as young as I was and mostly oblivious of everything unless it had something to do with comic books or football, so I didn't quite understand the true meaning of this action requiring his sudden departure because young women came and went from the studio all the time. It wasn't like he was hiding them up there—many of them she knew by name, they'd hang out in the kitchen smoking cigarettes, drinking coffee, and talking girl-talk. I knew Margie posed for him up there from time to time—though I never peeked. It was how they first met—he was her teacher at the night school where she took drawing classes, and he asked her to sit for him once. *"One thing led to another,"* was the explanation for how they got together. I knew that these other women posed naked up there because I spied on them with rapt fascination. They'd lounge on the sofa with their pillowy breasts exposed—the more meek ones draped their furry crotches with a piece of silky white fabric that he kept hung on a nearby peg. He'd often stand over them with a sketchbook cradled in his elbow, his pencil dashing spare lines on the paper. He'd talk to them, and laugh in that low chuckle at their coy responses—they often appeared so helpless lying there in front of him like that, but it seemed natural enough to me that the woman would be in the vulnerable position—I learned differently many years later.

There was one time I came upon a curious sofa scene in which a naked woman straddled his lap and was slowly bouncing up and down on him while he sat holding her breasts in his hands; he had all of his clothes on, and a remarkable expression on his face that looked like he was in agony. They didn't see me, and I went away to ponder what I had witnessed; this curious event occurred just before I knew anything about sex—I figured it out once girls became a preoccupation, and I was thrilled with the convenience that a man doesn't have to be naked to have sex. Only it was inconvenient how a guy can be led around by his dick when a good-looking woman decided to latch onto him—hey, I'll admit that women ain't too far off when they claim men think with their dicks. Whitley pissed off Margie because of his, which is sort of what he said to me when I complained to him about their marital disagreement and told him I didn't want him to go away. Whitley had to help me connect the dots—*fooling around* equals sex with a woman other than Margie, and Margie is the only one he's supposed to be doing that with because he's married to her. He said he felt flattered that I thought he was the perfect dad—but he admitted that he wasn't the perfect husband.

"*Even though I've said 'I'm sorry', sometimes sorry isn't enough,*" he said with a shrug.

After their divorce was final, he left Cleveland as soon as he found employment teaching drawing and painting in New York City. Naturally, I felt crushed; his absence during the following years had a profound effect on me. I missed him, and at times, I longed for his influence to guide me because I wanted to be just like him. He kept in touch with yearly birthday cards full of money and a short encouraging note that spoke of *maybes: maybe* we'll get together this summer to take a trip to Wood's Hole to see Grandpa Ryder, or *maybe* we'll go fishing on Lake Erie, or *maybe* we can do just *something*. Until that *something* happened, he expected me to be good, and not give Margie a hard time. He knew that by stating this he had me by the balls; I loved my mom, I would move heaven and earth to make her happy, and I wouldn't dream of causing her grief, especially since he had fucked-up and made her sad—*the asshole*. Calling him an asshole felt good whenever I did allow my resentment toward him to break the surface, but I let it go most of the time because he was a good guy and I loved him; I don't really like crapping on him.

Margie told me that she had forgiven him, but she felt glad to be rid of him because she claimed he was a drunkard. Truthfully, I hadn't noticed because drinking was something he had always done; I suppose the signs of him being an alcoholic were there—had I known what to look for. I can't go into a bar and not think of him, because he did smell like one—it was part of his essence; unfortunately, I associated good feelings with that smell.

For years, the attic room Whitley had used for a studio with its skylights and openness still smelled of linseed oil, alcohol, and cigarettes as if the ancient wood floors had absorbed his presence; it was like he had never left. Naturally, I took over the room, first setting up the train set he had sent me one Christmas, and then my slot-car tracks that came as a birthday present. Later when I was twelve, it became a place to hang out with my friends; we'd drink beer, smoke cigarettes, and pass around the occasional precious joint we had managed to obtain from someone with a connection.

While growing up, I was a big kid, nearly head and shoulders taller than most—a bit of a roughneck—but in spite of my size, I was a *"sensitive child"*, and because of my size, I carried a responsibility that expected maturity. I was a hormonal mess as an early-blooming adolescent; by the age of thirteen, I had the appearance of a sixteen-year-old and with my abundant body hair, I could pass for older. All through adolescence, I tried out various facial hair trends before I settled on growing the mustache that I've had since forever. I only shaved it off once and that was a very long time ago during a vulnerable phase in my life; later, the mustache became a shield that covered my expression, especially any sensitivity that my mouth might betray.

At times, my early development had its advantages and I took advantage of this special *gift*—older girls were crazy about me because of my outer maturity, and they got off on my youthful sensitivity. After awhile, I shed the gang of guys and I brought girls into the attic to experiment with sex on the same sofa Whitley was doing the model on; it only seemed fitting that his stepson should follow the tradition, christening it with my own passionate stains.

It also seemed part of my natural progression to stretch canvases and slop gesso over the taut surfaces like I had seen Whitley do. The early efforts I made were naïve images from a boy's mind—cool cars, air-born football players, bloody battle scenes with body parts strewn about, and sprawling naked women copied out of porn magazines that I stole from the smoke shop. My work matured with the desire to emulate Whitley's familiar work, but I never did very well with the barren color-field sensibility, and then the spare gestures indicating a feminine form didn't do it for me either. I couldn't figure out how he meditated over where to splash that random blot of color to have it make such perfect sense. Whenever I tried the technique, the long-mused over blot never looked anchored; it didn't look like anything, whereas his marks always did. It became clear that I had to come up with my own style, so I decided to forgo painting and became a sculptor— the three dimensional reality and tangible textures made perfect sense to me. I loved using natural materials like clay, wood, stone, even marble when I could get it, then bronze when I could afford it. I made a lot of naked women; my big hands with stumpy squarish fingers could model a delicate female figure with the grace equal to a Harriet Frishmuth fountain nymph.

To perfect my eye, I sketched a lot—lots of girls would take their clothes off for me in Whitley's old studio; some would actually get annoyed that I really did want to draw them, so sometimes I'd have to fuck them first, then draw them after they had fallen asleep. It seemed as if I found my calling; Margie was pleased with my talent—in a sense—*"Just make sure you double wrap that thing of yours, I'm not ready to be a gramma yet!"* For her sake, I was careful, but on the occasions later in my life when I have been careless, I've had regrets. I can fully understand my mom's lingering misgivings, but I knew that she loved me anyway.

Margie never remarried. She was beautiful, a tall, curvy, brunette with shocking blue eyes and delicate porcelain skin. I noticed that plenty of men turned their heads to watch her walk by; some bolder ones asked to take her out, but she wouldn't tumble for a date. I guess she didn't trust another man after what Whitley had done, but I always thought it was interesting that she didn't drop his name following the divorce. He called her every so often and she'd laugh hysterically like he was in the room tickling her; her giggles reverberated as echoes from when he used to live with us and they were happy. They maintained contact mostly because of me, and partly because they still loved each other in some form. While I was still young, I always hoped that she'd ask him to come back, but it never happened. I've realized this hopeful shortcoming is why I never get anywhere—I bet on the long shot all the time. When I turned seventeen she did ask him to come back, but it was because she wanted to say goodbye and to ask him a big favor.

By the time the doctor diagnosed her with pancreatic cancer, Whitley had settled in Gloucester, Massachusetts after obtaining a tenured position in Boston. While he sat at her bedside in the hospital, she made him promise to take me in and put me through college using the money she saved up; holding her hand in his, he kissed her, and promised to do this favor—or anything else she wanted him to do. I pretended not to notice them weeping as they clung to one another in a long embrace that held up the weight of their regrets.

After her funeral about a week later, I packed my things, and Whitley drove me to Gloucester. Before Margie's sisters descended upon the house to haggle over its contents, I took what I wanted of her personal belongings for mementos. The gold wedding band and the diamond engagement ring from Whitley that I found in a hand-carved box he had made for her, and as an afterthought, I snagged the photo album with Luke McKeon's picture residing along with my baby pictures and photos of us with Whitley.

From out of the flat files full of archived artwork she made over the years, her fashion illustrations from the advertising agency where she worked since I was a baby didn't interest me at all, but her personal sketchbooks were the most valuable possessions that I laid my hands on. I learned a lot about myself when I opened the dusty spiral-bound books for the first time; like me, she loved figure drawing. She was a keen observer of people, and she loved recording them. She didn't just draw nudes posing on the model stand in the studio; her sketches were snapshots of life being lived, life in motion, life breathing in a body unaware of being observed. When I came along, she concentrated on me, documenting my growing up; it surprised me how un-aware I was of her presence, so self-absorbed in my playtime I didn't realize she was drawing me. She also drew Whitley—the love of her life. However, the portraits were idealistic as if she tried to believe a lie that she told herself about him by concealing his flaws with a desperate hope that he'd change so he would fit the picture she made of him.

In the final sketchbook, less than half of it had drawings, and the rest of it remained blank—*oh, look—it's a polar bear in a snowstorm*. It seemed as if after Whitley left, she stopped drawing altogether; not even the ghost of an erased shape appeared on the blank pages following their divorce. It made me sad that she not only had lost her trust in the man she loved, but her joy in making art left along with him.

Upon arriving in Gloucester, I was awestruck by the huge eighteenth century house that he bought for a song. It is located just up the road from

Good Harbor Beach; the expanse of ocean and sky appears as a blue horizon beyond the tangled bittersweet and lilac hedge that surrounded the entire property. The house stood back from the road on a park-like woodland of enormous oaks, maples, and twisted pine trees; they screened the place from the prying eyes of tourists cruising by, but the gabled roof profiled like the famous house in Salem, peeked out through the branches to tease them. There were early to mid nineteenth century additions spliced in like wings extending off the tightly clustered main section; the newer construction mimicked the original design with the same solid *"that looks about right"* sensibility so often practiced in that long time ago era when handtools were high-tech as long as they were well maintained. The property, run down from years of neglect when he first moved into it, became a labor of love that grounded him for the first time in his life; he has enjoyed puttering around fixing it up, making it his. *"I plan to die here—I love this house, I'll never leave—the undertaker will be carrying my dead ass out of here."*

There also was a nineteenth century carriage house converted into a cottage on the property that he rented out to help pay the bills. This quaint, one bedroom dwelling was tucked inside a small haven of its own, surrounded by a privacy hedge made up of pink and white flowering bushes; it had its own driveway that jogged off from the main artery leading to the garage. There is a barn out back where he made a carpenter's workshop, and it had an old blacksmith forge that Whitley said we could get it up and running with a little bit of elbow grease.

The whole set-up was awesome, and put on the front of wealth and well-being that I never expected to find because by this time in his life I thought that Whitley's career as a painter had piddled dry since the Pop Art crowd came along to redefine *what is art*. He told me during our drive that he paints for his own satisfaction now—*"Movements be damned—and that albino freak, Andy Warhol too!"* he cried, banging his hand on the steering wheel. Actually, I discovered that he revived his painting career through his association with the Cape Ann galleries where he promotes himself like a state of Massachusetts celebrity by taking advantage of his shirttail relation to Albert Pinkham Ryder.

He was never a big name; he just happened to know the big names, bumping elbows with the likes of DeKooning, Pollock, Rothko, Motherwell, and Frankenthaler from the Abstract Expressionist movement. Clement Greenberg briefly mentioned him once in an article about a group show, but beyond that, Whitley Ryder was just another lesser member of a huge art movement that had rocked the art world back in the forties when Jackson Pollock first started drizzling paint off his brush onto a canvas laid out on the floor.

They were a wild bunch, their divergent concepts shaking up the art world with their freewheeling action painting that expressed the chaos of the post-war world in which they lived, and the peaceful color-field swathes that represented the spiritual contemplation of the sublime. Jackson Pollock's violent death in a car wreck punctuated the one side, while Rothko's suicide accented the other. I remember the day when we heard the news that Rothko had killed himself; the old man became extremely depressed. *"That guy was the best out of all of us,"* he slobbered, sloppy drunk like he was prone to be at the time; then the next day while nursing his hang-over he changed his tune—*"Yeah, he was fucked-up, what a shame."*

Whitley's one of the survivors of a group that is now dying off from old age. Even though I haven't seen him in years, I can only guess what his musings are about the slow demise of his contemporaries: *"It sucks to be DeKooning—Alzheimer's, what the fuck? He's better off dead—he didn't deserve that shit—"*

The welcome that I received at Whitley's front door consisted of a young woman named Dulcie Tate, and alongside of her was their eight-year-old daughter, Helena. Whitley had explained to me on the ride from Cleveland that he's been with Dulcie almost nine years, but they're not married. When I asked him why not, he only shrugged—*"It hasn't been a priority,"* he replied lamely. It amazed me that Whitley could still get women; he wasn't exactly a spring chicken anymore, but apparently, the spring chicks thought he was hot. Dulcie couldn't have been a day over thirty, so he caught her young. He was what women referred to as a *silver fox*. He was a big dude with gray hair that he wore long and pulled it back into a ponytail long before it was back in style. He was rough around the edges and he wore black all the time, kinda like Johnny Cash. But whatever the deal was, I couldn't wrap my mind around why a young woman would want anything to do with an old guy like him, unless she's got a father-figure complex—which I think is weird.

Shortly after my arrival, Dulcie split—apparently for the same reason that Margie had kicked him out for because the crying and shouting seemed all too familiar. I started to grind my teeth at night because it was so spectacularly dramatic—and traumatic for the little girl too because Dulcie took off without her. I could never figure out why a woman would abandon her child, but I guess she did it because she feared that another man wouldn't take her if she lugged around the baggage of some other Joe Schmoe's illegitimate offspring. I guess Margie considered herself lucky when Whitley was so accepting of my presence in her life.

This man whom I had thought was some sort of god when I was a kid, now has his hands full being human. His toughest task was to make his eight-year-old daughter understand that her mother didn't hate her, and her reasons for leaving were because of him and his bullshit. So, he tried to pay extra attention to her, although it was painfully awkward because after all she was a girl. To him, girls were delicate, you can't wrestle with them, play catch or anything rough like he did with me when he arrived in my life. He seemed at a loss about what to do with her—she was always Dulcie's charge before; his part in raising her consisted of giving her presents and goodnight kisses. So, he gave her more presents, and practically turned himself inside out to make the dour child happy, but it was a losing battle to dote on her because she was a bottomless pit of discontent.

Helena, the poor thing—I figured Whitley's striking genetics was not responsible for her looks. She was a homely girl with bottle-bottom glasses, she was blind as a bat without them; she also had big buckteeth that needed braces in the world's worst way—those choppers were the fault of her mother. Although she was a head-turner, Dulcie, had a mouthful of teeth; she had one of those smiles that looked like someone held a turd under her nose. In spite of the grimace, she was sexy, nearly six feet tall, big tits, long legs, and she looked great in a miniskirt; it seemed likely that Helena was one of those knobby-kneed girls who would eventually grow into her looks by the time she reached her twenties.

I felt awkward around the girl, I tried to be a big brother for her, but as an only child, I was ill equipped for the task. To make things worse, the girl latched onto me with the desperation of a drowning victim because she had a major crush on me. Her clinging-vine-ness caused me to steer clear of her; I had no emotional attachment available since my own grief kept me preoccupied—grief that Whitley failed to address because of his immediate problems having to do with a woman who had left him with a child he didn't expect to raise alone.

Whitley was in his mid-fifties when he got married less than six months later to Lenore, she was a local girl who happened to be one of his students at the university. I figured she was probably the one Dulcie caught him screwing around with, but he had never brought her around to the house that I had ever seen—I'd remember this girl because she was drop-dead-gorgeous. Helena and I met her briefly on the night before the impromptu civil ceremony took place in the front parlor with a Justice of the Peace. The two of us were just hanging around watching television in the living room when Whitley came home with Lenore hanging off his hand like an adopted stray, wide-eyed and nervous—there was a stunning awkwardness to this peculiar meeting. She was a kid—no more than twenty-one, but still just as much a kid as I was at the time. After a brief chat, they vanished upstairs and it was hard to ignore the sounds of bliss coming through the bedroom door when the sleepy Helena went off to bed after her program was over; she was mortified, her glasses only magnified her feelings of betrayal.

Things got even weirder because I fell in love with Lenore—head over heels—out of my mind in love. I couldn't help being attracted to her because she was so dang beautiful. Her long, almost black hair flowed with the consistency of silk and her soft skin felt like a tender peach. Her exquisitely shaped body—slender and petite—was much like a nymph from a fantasy world with perky little tits that pushed out against her tight t-shirts, and the sweetest shaped ass ever seen in a pair of jeans. After their short honeymoon in Cape Cod, the groom carried his bride over the threshold of the old Gloucester house with its steep, crooked stairways, and wavy old glass windows. By the next day, a playful flirtation developed between us that I never dreamt in a million years would ever go anywhere since she hung off Whitley like an extra limb—not that I had any intention to follow through on my desire—ever.

Our affair began within a month after their honeymoon when I woke up one morning to find her standing in my bedroom doorway staring at me. It had been a hot night and I lay naked on my bed with the windows and door open, hoping to catch a cross-breeze from the hall window. When I heard her soft gasp at the threshold, I scrambled to cover myself, making startled expressions that went something like, *"Holy shit—I didn't hear you—what the fuck are you doing?"* She had very little to say about the matter as she dropped her robe in a seductive ceremony—I let her come to me, no questions asked. We were young and crazy—that's the only thing I could ever think of to explain what happened that morning. This affair went on for years undiscovered by Whitley—but I found out later on that it was just unacknowledged. We built our discretion upon an unspoken promise never to talk about us, or our future; I was too insecure to bring into being a verbal suggestion of a future—although I fantasized a lot. We talked, but only about the present; she didn't like to talk about the past either. During the first year, I became rail thin between heartsick appetite loss and the daily rigors of sex; I feared that if I stood sideways I'd disappear.

Another factor that caused this to happen was my being there for her more than Whitley; he maintained the same old habits that I remembered from when I was a boy—getting drunk with his buddies, coming home late, working in the studio all hours of the night, often not coming to bed—same old shit, different wife. Leopards don't change their spots even when their mate is a pretty little thing with a body that can go on all night. At least this time he didn't bring home any of the women he bedded on the side.

It was apparent that their age difference played its part in their discord; no matter how *cool* he was, there grew a disparaging rift between them in sensibilities regarding male/female dynamics. She was strong-willed and restless, but he had different expectations from her as his wife—he wanted her to stay home to look pretty for him and to come when called. When she kept her pre-marital job at Noah's Art Gallery in Bearskin Neck, he was pissed, and when he expressed his objection, I thought the roof was going to blow off like a launch to the moon—not him—*her*—her temper was so hot it could peel several layers of paint off the walls. He melted to her will rather than put his old-fashioned foot down. I figured he feared losing her like he did Margie and Dulcie—and the other two nameless wives he had before my time. So, their marriage was over when it began—they knew it, but they denied it—they continued being married.

The following year when I started college in Boston, I chose to live in Gloucester and commuted by train to school all because I couldn't bear to be away from her. Four years later, it was another matter when I left home to attend graduate school in Chicago. I thought I was going to go mad. I tried to talk her into leaving Whitley, but she wouldn't do it. Although she said that she loved me, she claimed that I had nothing to offer her; but with Whitley, she had the stability of money, the luxury of a house, and everything else a girl could want. Feeling betrayed, I stormed out of town on the first of August, but in spite of my wounded pride, I still loved her.

While in Chicago, I plunged into my work to forget, but I didn't forget. Everything I made had her in it, even when I turned my back on the realism of my figurative work to a minimal expressionist phase. The inspiration for the meditative shapes that I carved into wood, or modeled with clay came from the curve of her hip, the hollow of her armpit, the flatness of her belly, or the petals of her vagina opening in between her parted thighs. I became wretchedly depressed throughout the first semester, indulged in drugs and booze to ease my misery, and wound up on academic probation by midterm, but I managed to get my shit together once the semester was finished, barely hanging on to my scholarship. By Christmas, I defiantly stayed away from Gloucester just to let Lenore know that I didn't need her. Although I did call home on Christmas morning to wish them well, Helena was the only one home at the time. She said Whitley and Lenore had gone out to walk on the beach. *"They're acting funny,"* she giggled.

When I came home in May, I found out that Lenore was pregnant—very pregnant; I felt woozy—we were almost never careful, I rarely put on a condom and almost never pulled out when I came. Although we had the house to ourselves, we got into the car and drove out to Plum Island to be alone; we said nothing all the way there until we settled, tucked behind the sand dunes where no one was supposed to be. *"Why didn't you call me?"* I asked. *"Why should I call you? It's Whitley's baby, not yours,"* she shrugged. *"How can it not be my baby?"* I exclaimed with a laugh. *"Because I got pregnant in October—you were long gone."* I didn't believe her—I wanted to believe that the old man was shooting blanks, and that the child growing inside her belly was mine. I raged on the quiet beach while she sat Buddha-like on a blanket, her round body stripped down to a bikini; her full breasts sagged heftily in the bikini bra that was barely big enough to accommodate her maternity endowment. *"Did you expect me to deny my husband sex just because of you?"* she asked, once she determined my jealousy. That shut me up.

What I had perceived as infidelity only rekindled why I was originally pissed since last fall, but oddly enough, I fucked her on the beach that day. At first, it was awkward because of her belly, but I found sex with a pregnant woman is curiously erotic. To make things even more interesting, she was horny as hell, which I found hard to believe because she carried on grunting and groaning like an old man stiff with arthritis.

After our sexual reintroduction, she said that she loved me—she said that she felt unhappy without me. I don't know what I was thinking when I inquired if she'd come with me to Chicago in the fall—I should have known what her reaction would be, just because she missed me while I was away didn't make a damn bit of difference—she has an even bigger reason for not leaving Whitley now. *"You've got to be kidding—I'll have this baby to take care of—Whitley's child—there's no way can I leave, ever!"* She not only said it, she laughed too.

I quickly found out that getting pissed wasn't going to change anything—my anger is no match for the volatile hormones of a naturally hot-tempered pregnant woman, so I swallowed my pride, kept my head down, and tried to defuse the Lenore Bomb with my sense of humor. *"Oy vey, lady—ya can't blame me for askin', can ya? Forget I said anything!"* She giggled behind her hand and then sighed. *"I'm sorry—I hate it as much as you do,"* she said at last, thus easing the pachyderm weight of hopelessness that sat on my heart. So, we remained *status quo*—it's just the way it's got to be, I guess.

Near the end of the pregnancy, Lenore spent a day in the hospital for tests when she discovered that she was spotting. The doctor prescribed bed rest and sent her home, he assured us that she would be fine; the placenta was slightly detached, although it was a serious condition, the baby wasn't in distress, but we needed to be vigilant. *"It's a little early, but delivery can happen any day now."* I was a pins and needles nervous wreck right up until the stormy June day before Sammy's birth almost two weeks later when Lenore declared, *"It's time to go."*

Whitley, who had been at a gallery in Boston installing a show of his recent work that afternoon, called to say that he was stranded because of flooding over the tracks. *"Don't worry, Pinkerton is here, he sez he will give me a lift to the hospital as soon as the weather lets up."* But the weather didn't let up, thunderstorms rumbled and rain poured with Biblical force for hours. It was a long night. I paced the floor in labor and delivery, suffering like a first-time father. The nurses kept teasing me whenever they came in and out of the room. To make matters awkward, they kept talking to me like I was the father to be—which to look at us it would physically make sense—but it was priceless to say, *"No, I'm the father-to-be's stepson."*

"Lenore, how are you feeling?" I asked for the millionth time since she started timing her contractions yesterday when the whole nerve-wracking process began—it's now close to dawn.

"I feel like I'm going to crap out a watermelon," Lenore grunted as she peeled off her sweat-drenched nightgown; her breasts reigned supreme above her belly with the nipples dilated to the size of silver dollars. She plumped the pillows behind her as she obsessed over comfort, then she settled back with her knees up, her feet splayed apart to expose her vagina; it was gaping wide open as if in breathless anticipation. I couldn't stop staring at her; pregnant Lenore was awe-inspiring, although pregnancy had stretched out her petite shape beyond its original lines, her new manifestation made of roundness and curves took on a voluptuous stature of a Venus from pre-history. When she caught my eye, she smirked knowingly. "You'll have to excuse me, there is no dignity during childbirth, and modesty doesn't matter anymore when you feel like your crotch is about to split wide-open." I figured she had to say this for Helena's benefit; the girl sat in the chair beside the bed, a wide-eyed fourteen year old taking it all in, so, I feigned embarrassment. Since my choice of career is centered on drawing from the nude it would have been appropriate for me to say some smart-ass remark like, *"Ya seen one naked woman, ya seen 'em all"*, but I didn't have my shit together enough to be any kind of a smart ass.

As her labor progressed into the final stages, the obstetrician came in to see her through the worst part. Lenore pulled herself up into a crouched position, Helena and I, now draped in hospital gowns over our street clothes, stood on each side, holding her hands; she screamed and bucked, carrying on like she was going to split in half as the baby's head began to push through. I was sickened and fascinated at the same time as I watched her flesh stretch wide to accommodate the descending head. Childbirth always appeared so physically impossible to me, and as I witnessed the delivery, I came to understand the true meaning of the phrase *"the miracle of birth"*; my eyes grew wide as the female body spiked above and beyond acknowledged reverence, attaining a lofty pedestal so richly deserved—even with the accompaniment of bellowed curses—it is a miracle.

Helena coached Lenore's breathing, I was very impressed with the kid that night; they huffed and panted in concert while the emerging head and shoulders took their sweet time to come, finally the baby girl slid out onto the bed. The girls hugged each other, squealing their mutual relief that it was over; Lenore then let out a victorious cry, rocked back onto her fanny, and lay against the pillows with a sigh of satisfaction.

Feeling overwhelmed with relief, I cut loose a mournful wail because I was unable to hold back the tears that have ebbed and flowed with the motion of gentle waves in my eyes throughout the ordeal. When my knees suddenly gave out, I crashed to the floor, and bit my tongue hard upon landing; the pain was excruciating. As I sat on my ass crying like a baby, there was only one clear thought on my mind: *This could be my daughter*—in spite of her denials, I wanted to believe otherwise—*she is mine.*

After a bit of quiet commotion, hustle and bustle of the doctor and nurses, Helena gave me a kick. "Guthrie, stop fooling around."

As I struggled to my knees, I saw the bloody bed sheets bunched up between Lenore's legs at the same time that I tasted blood in my mouth; I cast a glance at Lenore; it looked as if she had fainted.

"Is she all right?" I asked, wiping my bloody mouth on my shirtsleeve.

"She's all right, she's just resting—we just delivered the placenta!" Helena giggled.

"The what?" I asked, clueless.

"Mr. Ryder would you like to do the honors and cut this?" asked the nurse giving me a pair of scissors. I stared at them as if I never seen them before—*cut what?* Fumbling my thick fingers into the sterile scissors, I cut into a tube that she held out to me. The sensation of the blades chopping through something stalk-like troubled me, and once I realized that what I mistook for a weird plastic that looked suspiciously fleshy and wet was the umbilical cord, I flipped out.

"Holy shit—the umbilical cord—are you sure we could do that—what if we hurt her—hurt them? Oh-my-god, oh-my-god—holy shit!"

"Jeez, Luiz, stop being such a baby, you're a grown man!" Helena cried out, frustrated with my squeamish losin'-it-bullshit; the nurse patted me on the arm and reassured me that everything was just fine.

"Don't yell at him, Helena," Lenore sighed from the pillows that bolstered her. "Where's my Little One?" she growled with laughter as she struggled to sit upright; she looked radiant and wild with her hair matted with sweat, and her eyes drenched with tears. "Oh, will ya look at her—oh-my-god, how beautiful!" she sobbed. One of the many nurses brought the infant girl to her, clean and swaddled in a pink receiving blanket; she informed us that the infant weighed in at a healthy 7 pounds and 1 ounce. Lenore accepted the baby girl with an awed expression on her face, the little bundle made bleating noises like a newborn lamb.

After a moment of stillness in which only the baby's soft sounds filled the room, thunder rattled through the hospital as we stood watching mother and daughter bonding in the florescent light of labor and delivery. She softly cooed as she examined every inch of the infant's wriggling body, counting the fingers and toes as if taking inventory. Then, she offered her breast to the fussy little thing; she became quiet once she began to suckle.

I stood by, feeling separate from them, watching their naked beauty that was primal and ancient; the scene made me think of Paula Moderson's earth-mother paintings. As this image inspired me, I longed to get a sketchpad to document this moment, but I stood as if frozen, not wanting to disturb them.

"Here, Guthrie, I want you to hold her," Lenore said, patting the bed beside her.

Fearing that I might jostle them, I timidly sat on the edge of their presence, and as she laid the child into my arms, she coached me in the proper way to hold her. While I pillowed the tiny head with silky black hair within the palm of my oversized hand, I thought I had died—or something like it. Upon taking this small life against my chest, I fell in love for the second time in my life, and I decided that this precious being could only be mine. As I studied her up-close, my eyes were drawn to her tiny mouth; there was something beautiful about the toothless mouth with its smooth, pink gums—so sweet, delicate, pitiful in its helplessness, but so perfectly exquisite. I started to cry again, blubbering nonsensical words of adoration. Lenore's hand gripped my shoulder as she leaned her cheek against my face.

"It's all right, Guthrie, I'm all right and the baby is fine—I'm going to name her Samantha—Samantha Mae Ryder—do you like that name?" she whispered, pressing her lips to my temple.

"I love it—it's perfect—Samantha Mae is perfect—" I said; then without thinking I kissed her on the mouth, she let me kiss her—her return kiss was equally zealous. "I love you, I love you both!" I cried, embracing the naked mother and child tight in my arms, loving them with all my heart.

When I peeled myself away from Lenore, I caught sight of Helena perched on a stool across the room; she stared at us, engrossed like a voyeur as she watched our unspoken connection as lovers. I gawped at her, stunned that I had dropped my guard; I just openly expressed my love for Lenore in front of someone for the first time—love so secret, no one knew. Only Lenore knew of the tenderness I can express behind a closed bedroom door— or when we're completely alone somewhere else—hotel rooms in Boston or the sand dunes of Plum Island—never a public expression, never a touch—I never walked beside her holding her hand; I felt ashamed—caught in the act like a deviant.

"Shit," I hissed. "I'm sorry, Lenore," I blundered over my words, prepared to confess, but she only laughed.

"It's all right—it's all right, we're all a bit emotional this morning," she said, kissing my cheek. "Lena," Lenore called to her. "Thank you—I couldn't have made it without you, honey—thanks so much—I love you, I love both of you." Somehow, Lenore's words denied our relationship to Helena at the same time that it confirmed her guilt to me. Helena only shrugged off the compliment as if she had no other choice but to act accordingly; my blubbering certainly wasn't helping anyone—I could have been—should have been better, but I wasn't anything more than who I am—pathetic—what a shithead.

Whitley arrived with Pinkerton in tow, making a lot of noise of relief and joy; I readily gave up Sammy to him as he held out his hands for her. To look at him, to watch his reaction to his daughter was an emotional scene that left me breathless—instant love. Feeling wobbly on my pins, I stepped away from the bedside, and collapsed into the chair by the bed. Whitley and Lenore kissed their expressions of love, naturally—as husband and wife, the parents of the newborn girl they should do this; over the years, I've gotten used to seeing them exchange affection, always pretending that none of it mattered to me even though it did. I leaned forward, tucked my head between my knees, and felt grateful to have the blood rush to my head.

Of course, after Samantha's birth, things between Lenore and me took on a different focus; everything we did revolved around the baby; so, our sex-life took a powder. That wasn't the only thing that changed, Whitley was home more, and although the potential of jealousy could have come into play, it didn't, we all drew in together with Sammy as a source of gravity.

When I went back to school in the fall, I used every excuse imaginable to go home so I wouldn't miss too much of Sammy's growing up; she grew fast while I was away, and I marveled over these changes. I loved that child—she'd cling to me when I held her, her chirping baby talk and musical giggles bubbled and sang. I'd stare into those black button eyes of hers and feel so much love I thought I could die from it or go mad because of it. Never in my life, have I ever loved anyone so unconditionally before. Of course, I loved Lenore, loved her completely, but the feeling's emotional impact was different, and of course, there's the physical aspect to our relationship that held a special sweetness I could not deny—thankfully, she never felt jealous of my love for Sammy.

By the age of two, we noticed that Sammy suddenly became quiet. She didn't talk much, although she made lots of noises, cat sounds mostly, but during her Silent Sam mode, she appeared preoccupied—almost obsessed, and her temper became stormy when she's *"interrupted"* from whatever activity occupied her. Otherwise, she was a happy little piker, so no one thought there was anything wrong with her—it was just Sammy being Sammy, a personality of her own. The pediatrician expressed concern about her language development, after he tested her hearing again, and did everything else he could think of to figure out what could be the problem, he sent her to see a specialist, which led to another specialist, and then another. The outcome after a year of running around from one doctor's office to another declared our little girl to be *autistic*. Until the day Lenore called me with the news, I had never heard of Autism, and I couldn't grasp the concept that Sammy was mentally handicapped because she was quiet and too preoccupied with playing. So, I made the decision to put my thesis work on hold and went home to help our family cope.

My being there provided relief for both Lenore and Whitley; Sammy climbed on me like a tree, cooing like a dove, her shiny button eyes intently peered into my face. *"Guthrie!"* she chirped. I was happy to hear her say my name, but sad that perhaps she only said it because they had prompted her. Occasional words would come out of her little rosebud mouth, but mostly parroting what she had heard someone else say—there was no sign of actual self-expression—her words spoon-fed, and then encouraged with repetitive prodding. The second and third opinion dragged on through the summer, then well into fall, and the next thing we knew it was Christmas. All the results came back the same: *Autism*.

Why her? No one could explain how this little girl came to be like this; the finger of blame seems unable to point to anything—or anyone. What was worse, her future seemed so bleak because there wasn't really a set treatment—no magic pill or a shot to fix this malady. We were told that it would be for the best to send her to a special school where she could be around children just like her, where professionals can help her learn basic skills, preparing her for life with a handicap. We felt outraged, and we were in denial—the common reactions to such a tragedy. I feared that a day would come when we'd all have to agree that we were kidding ourselves by trying to keep her home—but sending her away was so repulsive that it only made us more determined to make it work.

Once I settled in for the duration, I had to admire how Whitley stepped-up to take his paternal place as the head of the family, setting the pace for daily routines, and schedules—each of us taking turns watching Sammy, teaching Sammy, entertaining Sammy. Dangling the *Little One* on his hip, he carried her upstairs to the studio to give Lenore a break—it was during her time spent with him up there that she showed us what she could do with pencil and paper. It wasn't just the dexterity of her hand-eye coordination; it was the incredible sense of knowledge expressed in line. The latest specialist upgraded her condition to *"gifted"* when we presented the drawings Sammy made with the precision of a traditionally trained artist. To watch her draw, you would never know there was anything wrong with her, her keen sense of observation displayed on paper everything she saw—especially the expression of emotions on faces—for a child who rarely made eye contact, she knew every inch of our faces.

I didn't return to Chicago until the following spring to work on my thesis again. During the time I spent away from Gloucester, I agonized over what I left behind. From a distance, I mourned as if Sammy had died, but I reminded myself that she was alive, that she was the same child—and she needed me. Once I finished my degree, I tried to find work closer to home, but the closest teaching job I could get was in Cleveland.

Lucky for me, Margie's sisters never sold the old house, so I rented it after Aunt Stella went into a home—then I eventually inherited it after she died. Generally, I went to Gloucester for every holiday, sometimes for a weekend, driving all night on a Friday, to arrive home by Saturday morning—dawn on Good Harbor Beach, Lenore running on the sand, her long ponytail swishing as she launched herself into my arms. Then I'd leave by Sunday evening, arriving in Cleveland—or wherever—early Monday morning just in time to stroll into a classroom full of bleary-eyed freshman, kids with little or no interest in drawing from the frumpy nude model perched on the small platform before them. As soon as my class let out, I'd go to my home away from home, jittery from sleep deprivation hallucinations, and my heart racing from a nigh lethal combination of nicotine and caffeine. I'd call home to talk to my two girls, especially to listen to Sammy breathing into the receiver, whispering monosyllabic replies to my questions. Finally, I'd come to rest, after a snack, a few beers, and more cigarettes, then I'd crawl into bed, and sleep until the next day, almost evening—always plotting my next trip home in the back of my mind.

❧

Lenore was the love of my life—there has been no one else—ever. After Noah Valentine murdered her, I wanted to die right along with her. I can love no one else—no one except Sammy. I hated leaving her behind, but I had to go because Whitley offered me no other choice, during our last conversation, he made it perfectly clear that he did not want me around. And so, I was banished from my stepfather's house, and banished from the life of a little girl I believed in my heart to be my daughter. *Now he's gone.*

Today, I'm seeing Sammy for the first time since she was six years old— she turned twenty-eight last June. Upon arrival at the house, I kept my distance by first loitering out in the street chain-smoking until I was certain that everyone had settled in for the funeral so I could slip inside to stand at a discreet distance near the door. I didn't want them to see me—yet I hoped they would see me and recognize me so we could mourn together as a family—we are family—*Whitley's children*. As I inched my way into the front parlor, I watched Sammy and Helena from an angle that allowed me to remain unobserved by them; Sammy wore a wide-brimmed black hat draped in a black veil, which left her face indistinguishable, and she had on a sleek, high-necked black dress with a long skirt that swept the floor. Helena sat erect and prim beside her in black, but not as dramatic—no veil, no hat, she looked more severe in a tailored suit that contrasted the flowing costume of her younger sister. Her angular features took after Dulcie, and I noted that the bulky glasses were gone; I surmised she wore contacts or maybe she opted for the new corrective laser surgery.

A man that I guessed to be Helena's husband sat between the two women, his hand gripped within Helena's, which was my only evidence I had to make the connection. He is older than she is, perhaps close to my age, maybe younger by a year or two—he still had hair anyway, nearly shoulder-length dirty blond hair salted with some gray. He had an absent-minded-scholar appearance; he looked quite dapper in his black suit with a crisp collarless white shirt, and he wore trendy spectacles in a comfortable manner that looked appropriate for his bookish façade. He did not strike me as the kind of guy I would have envisioned her going for—but then her taste was a bit strange—she was hot for me once, so go figure.

Sammy leaned toward this man as if to say something, and he bent his head toward her, his hand lightly caressing her shoulder, a kindly gesture of comfort as he leaned closer to whisper something to her—an answer to a question. It struck me how often it had been my duty to sit in the middle, dividing the sisters, so Helena didn't have to deal with Sammy; this man sat between them like a natural bridge spanning a canyon, his hands connecting their distant rims. Sammy reached over to brush back a stray hair that had fallen out of place and dangled over his forehead; with this goodwill gesture bestowed upon him, he blushed scarlet and suddenly seemed unable to hold still. *What a curious trio!*

Feeling uneasy, I self-consciously tugged on the cuffs of my suit-coat sleeves; I had bought it off the rack five years ago without having it tailored so it never fit me right. Then I nervously rubbed the back of my head where I still had substantial hair; not only have I gone bald on top, but my vanity has yet to accept another issue as I removed my glasses and put them away in my pocket—I need what they now call progressive lenses—call them whatever you like, they're still bifocals. It is out of pure irritation with the aging process that keeps my reading glasses tucked in my suit coat pocket out of sight, and the prescription sunglasses that I use for driving usually lay on the dashboard of my car. *Use as needed.*

A few minutes into the eulogy by Whitley's old buddy, Pinkerton, a sharply dressed, blond man arrived late, ushering in two young boys toward the empty chairs next to Samantha. *She's married?* If this guy is her husband, it seemed to me that the children were too old to be offspring from their union—that is, if they are married—I just assumed their connection was marital as he bent as if to kiss her. Her shrouded head quickly shrugged away; her motions indicated that his sudden appearance had startled her. Upon perceiving this interaction, it reminded me of her disability, and I wondered if she had improved, stayed the same, or had gotten worse.

Once the service ended, I hovered at the end of the line to file past the casket to take one last look at the deceased before the trip to the cemetery, but it wasn't my intention to go view the body. Although I made casual motions toward the door, my hungry attention remained drawn to Sammy, watching her—I felt compelled to take a few steps forward after every step I made toward the door because I couldn't take my eyes off the petite figure standing alone in a crowd of people. She barely acknowledged the ones who approached her with their offers of sympathy; Helena kept verbally nudging her to pay attention, while the spectacled dude alongside her provided polite intervention. The self-important blond guy acted as if he had somewhere else to be, and stalked around the house like he was on a mission—which certainly had nothing to do with the two boys he showed up with, they needed supervision, and he wasn't making the effort to supervise.

As I found myself drifting closer to the front, my gaze visited Whitley. His body lay on display in the casket surrounded by a mountain of flowers; he didn't look eighty-eight, but he did look dead—not asleep like I heard whispered amongst a few of the mourners from the Cape Cod branch of Ryders bearing small children in their arms. I noticed Pinkerton hanging back behind Sammy and Helena like a protective presence, his eyes roaming over the crowd as if assessing the quality instead of the quantity of mourners; suddenly our eyes met and he recognized me with a strangled cry that I knew well.

"You made it! It's good to see you again, Guthrie! After I told her that I contacted you, the Little One said she hoped that you might come to see him off," he said, grasping my hand in a friendly handshake. *The Little One— Lenore and Whitley's pet name for Sammy.* He pulled me out of line and brought me to the front to stand where I belonged beside my family. "Psst, Helena," he hissed, giving her arm a poke with his finger. Helena and the gentleman beside her turned away from the casket to greet us.

"Hello, Helena," I greeted her, feeling strange; if Pinkerton wasn't hanging onto my arm like a guard escorting a prisoner, I would have bolted for the door and never looked back, because looking at that woman made my *she's-no-good* alarm sound-off.

"How nice of you to have come," Helena said upon recognizing me; the half-smile that crawled across her face exhibited her displeasure that her words denied. She bore the same turd-smelling smirk like her mom's, she acted very plastic with all the right polite things to say, but she's *oh-so-phony.* Then as if she remembered he was there, she introduced me to the gentleman shadowing her—"This is Dr. Sylvester Hayden—" I couldn't help noting the slight hiccup over his name as if she didn't know how to define him. While I shook hands with him, he reacted with a genuine *how do you do* that I recognized as if I've met him before, but couldn't remember where or when—his Down East accent reminded me of that scruffy hippie with a rusty Fiat who moved into the carriage house around the time Lenore died.

"Samantha, look who has come—" he said, reaching for her; she stood beside him, staring at the casket; it appeared she didn't hear him. "Come, come, dear heart," he coaxed, pressing her shoulders with his palms to encourage her to turn. As if reluctant to peel her gaze away from Whitley, she slowly turned to him. "Look, who's here to see you," he smiled.

"Who?" she whispered. When her dark eyes glittering behind the veil finally regarded me, her small hand, encased in a black lace glove, landed on my arm, grasping my flesh through the suit coat sleeve as if anchoring herself to me. With a soft sigh, she lifted the veil, which revealed a face that resembled Lenore's so much her name accidentally gasped from my lips. My hands came up as if to push her away, only they received her instead as I hugged her, feeling thankful—thankful to be home, thankful to see her again. Knocking off her hat, the perfume of lavender that wafted from her hair sent my memories reeling into a past that I have tried to forget—memories I have immersed myself into, drowning myself on purpose—*Lenore!*

"Oh, Guthrie, welcome home, I've missed you!" she exclaimed, clasping me around my middle, nearly squeezing the breath out of me with expressive ardor so typical of the child that I remember from long ago. Truthfully, I was surprised that she remembered me; she was so young when I last saw her. I always figured there would be the string of *"Who are you?"* questions to explain; but no, she remembered.

She stepped back to contemplate me, her hands petting my arms and chest as if frisking for my tangibility, and then she grasped my hands, studying them—like she always did when I came home; funny thing, she knows the back of my right hand better than I do. When she looked into my face again, her inward gaze sharpened with outer focus to perceive me beyond the image of her memory.

"Oh-my-god, you're bald—" Her clear voice rang out during one of those bizarre moments when a crowded room suddenly becomes still for no particular reason other than a random lull in the droning buzz of conversation. This is a typical Sammy observation—if there ever was a moment in my life when I could have died from embarrassment, now was the time, but I laughed at my stupid sense of vanity. Dying is not an option today, I just got here, and I've waited too long for this homecoming to let a little embar-rassment kill me. Though if I did keel over now, I'm sure the mortician is creative enough to come up with some kind of a two-for-one deal—they could cremate me and stick the box with my ashes in between Whitley's stiff hands in an eternal strangle hold. *Now, that would be a fitting end for me!*

"Some things change, but thankfully, you never change, Sammy," I chuckled, casting a second glance in the direction of Whitley. It took a heroic effort to return my gaze to the young woman standing before me; when I did, her resemblance to her mother startled me once again.

"It's so good to see you again, Button's." I wrapped my arms around her small frame; hugging her to my chest, and I heaved a great sigh of relief. Her reciprocating little arms clutched me around the ribs, and I felt the familiar pat of her tiny hands on my back. I couldn't escape now if I tried, and I didn't want to because it was good to be home again.

6

Little Pictures

Black eyes, black veil—her gaze penetrated through the smoky fabric with rapt adoration—and questions. I had so much I needed to ask too, and she knew it. *"Come see me tomorrow—we'll talk,"* she said. *"Yes, we need to talk,"* I agreed. Although I spent nearly the whole day with her, physically linked by the tight persistence of her tiny hand threaded through mine, we were in the midst of too much commotion to talk about anything significant. Within minutes of our reunion, we were herded into a limousine to go from the house to the burial at the cemetery, and then the reception at the gallery for the events choreographed around the celebration of Whitley's life. When Helena overheard Sammy's invitation, she smirked at me—*"Yes, please do, stop by tomorrow afternoon for lunch."* But late that night as I left the house to go catch some shut-eye at the hotel on the edge of town, Sammy clutched me in an embrace to bid me goodbye and whispered, *"Come in the morning by eight—we'll have coffee."* By this time, she had discarded the somber hat and veil, and applied a kiss on my cheek with a joyful pressure; the tip of her nose nuzzled my flesh just like the way she used to apply her little girl goodnight kisses; a chill shivered down my spine that was pleasurable and disquieting at the same time. Nothing pleases me more than to defy Helena's wishes, and so, here I am.

Before I could ring the doorbell, the heavy front door opened; Sammy peered at me with a shy smile, her eyes squinting as if the sunlight bothered her. I knew this expression well; she scrunches her face with the effort to focus her concentration to make sure that she is actually talking aloud as she greeted me with a low, concentrated voice, "Good morning, Guthrie."

We hugged each other tight—it seemed I couldn't hold her long enough, but I feared I would hurt her if I held her any tighter. When we parted from our embrace, I felt afflicted with shyness; her resemblance to Lenore has carried over into this morning, I had hoped that I had imagined it yesterday. I could hardly sleep last night thinking about her—and thinking about Lenore; the inner conflict flared up again, infecting the connection between my brain and my tongue, so I just gawked at her, speechless just like yesterday. Thankfully, Sammy didn't seem to notice as I followed her to the kitchen.

With a deep breath, I remembered every square inch of the room—I felt relieved that it hadn't changed more than a fresh coat of paint and a new refrigerator. My gaze focused on the table, it looked as if she had fussed obsessively about the placement of objects on the maple syrup-colored surface, the soft pine scarred by decades of meal preparation skirmishes, blunt trauma dings and water rings. The unmatched brown crockery sugar bowl and white porcelain cream pitcher, stood perfectly centered between our place settings. They hung out like two old friends conversing, the spoon sticking out from under the sugar bowl's lopsided lid like it smoked a cigar, and the tall creamer stood patiently listening to its squat friend pontificating about who tasted better in coffee. The coffee mugs postured as passive observers of the debate, and the spoons reclined as if napping on their narrow napkin cots.

While she poured the coffee, I helped myself to the old ceramic ashtray that Dulcie had made, and took my coffee black with a cigarette. Sammy interrupted the sugar bowl and creamer's affable discussion to take from them their sweet offerings. Her delicate hands restored the fluted wide-mouth spoon and lid back to their proper positions, so the two old acquaintances could resume their silent debate after her intrusion. I caught myself smiling because I remember how she used to play with these two objects—silent games—silent conversations—her intensity disturbing to watch as much as it was fascinating. My heart swelled with love, but it also wept with sorrow for her, wondering about her growing up. *Did she still get to play or did Whitley turn her into a painting automaton?* I would like to know what goes on behind those glittering button eyes as they tilt upward to peek at me with intermittent curiosity.

"I'm glad you're here now—before Helena comes. It's absurd how she has suddenly become over-protective of me—I can fend for myself all right—it's not like I'll set the house on fire—I'm autistic, not stupid—they all baby me like I'm a child," Sammy sighed, clattering her spoon inside the mug with musical *ting-tings* against its ceramic sides. The sound brought back memories of her sitting with me at this same table, sharing hot cocoa that Lenore had made after we spent the day building a snow-fort in the backyard that one Christmas when a nor'easter had dumped snow up to my waist on us—*how old was she then? Five, I think. Lenore and I always loved playing with her—we'd spend all day playing with her like a married couple with their child—Whitley hung back—Whitley wasn't home—Whitley was in the studio—Whitley was too drunk.* I wondered if he was only drunk when I came home because he knew about my relationship with Lenore and he made himself scarce on purpose.

"They care about you," I put in because she seemed so annoyed.

"Sylvester—Dr. Hayden—you know, Lena's man-friend; he's not like that at all—he has never treated me like a child—I love that about him. He's a quiet man, very accepting. He listens and actually hears what I have to say—I've known him since you left us—he's been such a good friend to me," she replied, with a curious smirk tipping the corner of her mouth like a private joke, a deep dimple in her right cheek appeared and disappeared with the smile. She then reached for a sketchpad and pencil lying off to the side; she began to make cross-hatching doodles that evolved into sketches of hands—for her, drawing is her version of a tick, if she isn't drawing, she rocks or her hands fidget.

"He was quite diplomatic yesterday," I nodded. The man certainly had a way with the chronically irritable Helena as he extended his hand to pull me within their circle. Then he selected gracious terms to soothe his woman to put an end to the tension that saturated our reunion as a family. I also noticed how he attended to Sammy with gentle concern, often taking hold of her hand whenever she became confused; the connection to him instantly grounded her—calmed her. I also noticed how she fussed over him; if a hair was out of place or his glasses crooked, she would tend to him—not as a favor to return a favor, but something more intimate than that—*love*—as if they have loved each other for a long time.

"Yes, he manages Helena very well—she's a handful," she snickered.

"I bet she is—" I chuckled. I instantly liked the guy once we started to talk and I had a feeling that his woman felt neglected and purposefully sent him on the errands to separate us. I felt a little sorry for Hayden having to cater to her every whim. Throughout the reception at the house, she had him fetching things, often sending him out to the carriage house to retrieve something or other, but he did all of it without complaint. There was only a trace of a smile when he caught my eye-rolling response to one of her requests that sent him running no sooner had he returned. He graciously put his hands together, bowed and said, *"Yes, Sahib, I hear and obey."* I nearly busted a gut laughing—Helena scowled at both of us. It must be love—no man in his right mind would tolerate that bullshit otherwise. The first words out of my mouth would have been, *"Are your legs broken? Get it yourself, bitch"*—but that's just me.

"How are you? There's so much I want to know about you—how your life has been—I have missed so much being away for all these years." I plunged in with what I came for rather than discussing Helena and her man-friend whom she treated like a retriever—*"Fetch, Sy, good boy!"* No, she didn't even praise him; some dogs are too loyal, and foolishly give their owners more than one second-chance. *If I were her dog, I would turn up on her leg.*

"I'm about the same; not much has changed—I'm withdrawn, I don't make eye contact, I'm obsessive/compulsive, indifferent, emotionally disturbed, unable to express love—you know, the usual," she said as her upper lip curled into an amused sneer while she rattled off the common symptoms of her disability.

"That's silly, I know you are capable of expressing love, you were very lovable as a child—and you expressed love as soon as you saw me yesterday," I muttered into my coffee mug. A passing wonder crossed my mind if Sammy and Hayden have something going on—or had at one time—or wanted to, but for some reason it never happened—because of Helena—whatever it is, there's something going on between them. I glanced at the sketchpad and saw that his face had just appeared; it seemed like the tip of her pencil was very familiar with his features.

"My husband will verify it as a fact—his latest dig is I'm *'friggin' insensitive'*," she said with a familiar childlike singsong voice, but there was a hint of bitter sarcasm within the melody.

"It isn't your fault—your husband is an asshole." I had made the assessment the minute I saw the self-important bastard sashaying around as if he owned everything—I know his type, the corporate man of action. His gaze upon me made a similar pigeonhole evaluation of me when we squared off with suspicious jealousy that instinctively emerged between us. *"Oh, so, you're Guthrie Ryder—I've heard about you."* I was so glad to hear that my reputation preceded me.

"Well, that goes without saying—he's made a career out of being an asshole so far," she snorted with indelicate amusement.

"I don't mean to criticize, but how did you wind up marrying *him*—no, don't answer that—I'm being unfair—it's none of my business." I immediately felt bad for articulating my impulsive judgment of her husband—even if she agreed with me—but I couldn't help noticing that Preston Ackerman is a first-class asshole. What Sammy needed for a husband is someone like Hayden—someone genuine who gives a damn about her. *Another thing I'd like to know is why is he with Helena? If she ever talked to me like that, she'd be the newest satellite orbiting the Earth.*

"I agreed to marry him because I felt it was the right thing to do after the man went to great lengths to court me—I mean—I'm not exactly able to go out and date like normal girls. Preston came along by invitation and tried to win me over."

"Tried? He must have *won you over* since you're married to him," I laughed, getting up to help myself to another cup of coffee, and warmed up hers. Her drawings of Sylvester Hayden changed to drawings of me. I noticed she didn't draw Preston.

"No—not in the sense of my falling in love with him; I became impatient with the ordeal—we would go around on drives, park, and make out—he said that he loved me, he was all right, not offensive or anything, so I figured I could learn to love him. Well, seven months later, I still don't love him—I no longer sleep in the same bed with him."

I said nothing, feeling shaken by her blunt reality bites that offered snapshots of her courtship and married life. I could understand Sam's hope to learn to love someone; I have done that same experiment in an effort to move on with my life after Lenore. My legendary conquests of young women are just what they are—conquests—nothing more—so few of them had any meaning beyond sex. My four marriages suffered because of my emotional detachment—how I came to be married to any of those women is still a mystery to me. I have children that I haven't kept in touch with outside of the financial support I maintained while they were little, but now they're grown; I never get a Christmas card from any of them—I don't blame them.

"Lenore loved you very much—you made her happy, Whitley always made her sad."

"Whitley had his faults—he made a lot of women sad—even you."

"Even me," she sighed. "You—I love you unconditionally. You impressed yourself on me from the moment of my birth. I haven't seen you since you left, but as soon as I saw you again, I knew you—I have trouble recognizing people I met yesterday, but you—I never forgot. When I first became sexually aware, I wanted to be with you."

"You what?" I spit out the coffee I had just sipped back into the mug, I couldn't believe what I just heard, and hoped that I had heard wrong.

"You were long gone by the time I sexually awakened—" She spoke with a soft even tone, not at all childlike—it had a seductive quality to it that made me uneasy. "I used to fantasize that you would come back to become my lover," she said with a smirk, her dimples dented her cheeks as the corners of her mouth lifted—*happy dents.*

"Oh." I felt too stunned to respond beyond that pathetic noise. Feeling slightly nauseous, I stared at the sketchbook surface as her pencil worked an image of my physical details; I looked up and met her eye once her pencil lifted from the paper. She stared at me, and those brown eyes of hers were like black holes that could consume me—*Lenore.*

"Guthrie, I love you very much," she said, trailing her fingers over the back of my hand like she used to when she was little, and she would say, *"I'm a little buggy-boo creepy-crawling on your hand, Guthrie!"* I flinched; somehow, the memory of the gesture didn't match-up with the meaning of the same gesture in the present—*she's flirting with me!*

"I see." I cleared my throat, and decided now was the time to say my piece because this conversation was a little too weird for comfort—the things she said are beyond any conception that I had for this moment. "Samantha, I am your father." *There, I said it*—but it didn't sound at all like the way I had rehearsed it in my mind, it came out like a confession from a cheesy melodrama. I watched as Sammy made a reactive motion as if she hiccupped, and then her gaze traded places in a strange withdrawing and advancing after a silent consideration.

"No you're not—Lenore said you weren't, although there were times when I thought maybe she lied because of Whitley, but she hadn't. When I count the months, you were not living at home when I was conceived—Lenore said you left in early August to drive to Chicago for school—I was conceived in late September or early October—we didn't need a DNA test to figure it out." As she said this, she scratched hash marks with her pencil onto the pad, naming off the months as she counted. "See, I was born on June 29th—as you know, because you were there, I came a little too early because of some trouble with the placenta, I was actually due on July 9th—but no matter, you were already gone." I felt taken aback by the same evidence that Lenore presented me with that day on the dunes of Plum Island. *I didn't believe her—didn't want to.*

"Whitley knew it—Helena was a shit putting doubt in the air, she was always jealous of me—Sylvester told me he can see a resemblance to Whitley around my eyes—plus, I'm a genius with a brush—I have no interest in sculpture. Lenore couldn't paint to save her life—how she ever got into art school is beyond me—she must have slept with someone—if he had a perky pecker she fucked it and Whitley certainly had one of those—" Sammy went on with rhythmic prattle; her pencil made random cross-hatching patterns on a fresh page.

"Sammy—" I moaned into my hands that now covered my tired eyes; it felt like my heart just fell out of my chest, rolled under the table, and she stepped on it.

"What?" she looked at me, cocking her head like a curious pup; she stopped drawing.

"Fucking perky pecker—don't talk like that—it's unbecoming." I spoke like a father, the way I always thought of myself concerning her.

"Bah—that! I overheard Lenore talking to her friend Nita that way—she said that before she met Whitley she was a total slut—they laughed hysterically when she said that about a perky pecker, when I started to giggle—delayed like I do—Nita said, *"Don't forget little pictures, Lenore"* —I was *'little pictures'*, you know," she laughed with a snort. She began to play with her spoon, pressing the tip of her finger on the lip and wobbling it on its rounded bottom then letting the tail-end clink on the table with a silvery clatter.

"It's still unbecoming." I gave up trying not to smile.

"Merry Christmas, Guthrie, you taught me all that I know."

"Yeah, back then it was cute to hear a four year old cussing like a sailor, and it pissed off Lenore—Whitley thought it was pretty funny—but I did get you talking." *("Say SHIT, Sammy." "SHIT!" "You like saying that word, dontchya?" "Sheeeeeyit! Weeeehee-hee-hee!")* I laughed against bitter disappointment mixed with a weird sweet relief. *Okay, so I'm not her father—I knew, but I couldn't stand it that Lenore had chosen Whitley to be the father of her child.* "It was the least I could do," I continued.

Sammy smiled that wide psycho grin she always made when she felt especially pleased—both dimples blooming with happiness, wordless and priceless.

"I have loved you—I always thought of you as my daughter," I said, rubbing my eyes because they prickled with unexpected tears formed by the prevalent letdown.

"And I have loved you, but I never thought of you as a father—because a father is there raising you—nor have I ever thought of you as a brother because that's a boy you grow up with—I loved you because you were my friend—you were there, but just to visit for a little while—you always went away. Then you left without saying goodbye—it was hard for me to lose both of you. I understood Lenore's death, but when you left and didn't come back that hurt more."

"I'm sorry, but I had no choice—Whitley wanted me gone—he loved your mother too, you know."

"I know—just a few weeks ago he started to talk about her for the first time since it happened—and finally, he talked about you too—he loved you—he wanted me to tell you that. When I asked him if you could come home, he said he couldn't bear facing you after all this time—he told me to find you because he said I will need you after he's gone—I am so happy Pinkerton knew where you were—happy to have you home again."

I stared at her—amazed by how far she's come—*I'm proud of her.* And I stared at her because she looked so much like Lenore at this age I had to *147* keep reminding myself that this young woman is Sammy. For all these years, I had thought of her as a dimple-cheeked little peep with black button eyes, but sitting here with her today, my heart kept tripping over old arousals associated with Lenore. I felt sick and confused—I felt like a predator—*I have been a predator.*

"What's wrong, Guthrie?"

"You look just like her," I murmured, keeping my eyes averted; the murky black coffee seemed a safe study. "I just can't get over how much you look like her."

"Lenore, yes-yes—I do—Whitley told me so—everyone who knew my mother says so—even Sylvester who never met her says so—he thought I was making portraits of myself one day—so I had to tell him, *'This is Lenore, but you never met her'*—I never draw myself, he of all people should know that!" she laughed. "I haven't forgotten her."

"You shouldn't forget your mother—don't ever forget her—she loved you so much!" I exclaimed. "It's so weird—so wrong—I am attracted to you." I accidentally confessed my unexpected emotional confusion; feeling stupid, I laughed.

"Yes, I know—I can tell by the way you're looking at me—you can't look at me at the same time you can't stop looking at me—it's kinda funny," she replied with a strange, private smile that reflected her pleasure to know this. She stopped drawing, and began to roll the pencil under her palm over the tabletop.

"Doesn't that bother you?" I inquired. I couldn't wrap my mind around what she could possibly be thinking; her attitude disturbed me, and the noise of the pencil clattering over the table surface set me on edge.

"It should—but it doesn't. I just don't feel that way—love is a very pure emotion. I guess what you expect me to feel is jealousy—but why should I feel that? Lenore is dead. I know I should feel it because you may make love to me someday and think of her—instead of me—"

"Sam—this isn't about us having that kind of relationship!" I felt stunned that she has taken a mental step light-years ahead of me into territory that I wouldn't have considered; my mind is still stuck with the long-standing notion that she is my daughter, while her mind has clamped onto her pattern of thinking. It became painfully obvious that we're on opposite ends of the spectrum regarding our feelings, and now we're trying to meet halfway, our individual perceptions of each other are clashing. "I just want to say— you're very pretty, just like your mother—and it's uncanny how much you look like her—I have to keep reminding myself that you are you—not her— it's just weird that's all."

"I'm not like her at all—don't ever compare me to her—that would be like me comparing you to other men I've been with." She ignored what I just said, her focus entirely on her own thoughts caught up with her mother, the past, and her adolescent fantasies about me. She started to draw again—*Hayden*.

"Men—I thought you said you didn't date?" I laughed even though I didn't mean to laugh; this odd twist to her thinking keeps knocking me off-balance. It is such a typical Sammy conversation—no point of reference, her stream of consciousness blurting out whatever scrolls through her gray matter and sometimes half of it leaps from her tongue. I'm more confused than amused. "Sammy, what are you talking about?"

"I didn't date—I had Sylvester—he was my first—before Preston. We had an affair for three years—it ended nine years ago when Helena divorced Shep, and I let Sylvester go because he's been in love with her ever since he first met her. You know—he's the guy who moved into the carriage house the weekend Lenore was murdered—he's been here ever since—I was fine until Preston came sniffing around like a dog marking his territory—I slept with Sylvester about a month ago when Preston scared me because he was drunk and he wanted to tie me to the bed, but I wouldn't let him—Sylvester had just found out that Helena cheated on him—it was rather nice—he's so good to me—Helena doesn't know—neither does Preston—Whitley knew— he figured it out—"

Gah! I was right, she and Hayden had a thing going on, and apparently, they still do in some form. "Sammy—honey, slow down, you're giving me way too much information!" I sputtered against the flow of her breath- less explanation; she babbled as if trying to get everything inside her head shoved out to make room for more. The bizarreness of the conversation has entered into another zone that I hadn't counted on—none of this morn- ing's conversation has gone the way I had foreseen it. I originally came here to make my paternal claim on the child I had abandoned, but I find she's a grown woman—and not my daughter—we're not blood relatives, we're related in name alone. My stomach churned with squeamish contractions. There is no reason for me to be here, and judging by the track of this conversation, my being here could complicate her already complex life.

"I don't know what to say—" I said, fumbling for another cigarette.

"You asked about how my life is and I'm telling you—this is my life. After seeing you yesterday I realized that I've been in love with you all these years," she said with a joyful song to her voice. Her hands reached across the table to grasp my hand, but then she let it go as if perceiving my unspoken apprehension, her fingers lightly caressing mine as they drew away, like a wave over the sand, smoothing, soothing—soft fingers.

"I see where you're going—I can't get into this right now," I sighed, rubbing my eyes. She's still the same, she says what's on her mind, she has no filters to apply to delicate subjects—yet she's different because her level of awareness is keener than people give her credit; however, it's distorted by her lack of social interaction and her internal fantasy.

"Listen, Button's, I'm leaving tomorrow, but not for good, I do want to come back to spend time with you. I feel responsible for you—please understand I wanted to be here while you were growing up—I hated leaving you behind like that, but because of Whitley, I had to go. I'm sorry I couldn't be here for you back then—please understand I had to stay away."

"Do you have to leave so soon? You can stay as long as you want—I want you to come back—I'd love it if you lived with us—the house is big enough—your old room is empty, Preston's boys have Helena's old room because I've been expecting you."

It was a letdown that she blew off my apology for abandoning her, not even saying something comforting like, *"Oh, that's okay, Guthrie, I got over it."* Nope, nothing, she zeroed in on what she cared about the most: *me staying here.*

"Shouldn't you check with your husband first? I mean—he and I didn't exactly get off on the right foot yesterday," I smiled nervously—*she's been expecting me.*

"I've told him already—he's not thrilled, but too fucking bad," she sighed, her gaze turned inward; she sat fiddling with the pencil on the pad, an endless scribble of symbols, designs, images of hands, portraits of Hayden,

Helena, Whitley, and myself filled the entire page, now a portrait of Lenore materialized. I held my breath; the dark eyes looked at me in that crazy way some portrait gazes will follow you around a room. Although the image is facing Sammy, Lenore seems to be looking up from where she lies on the table, discreetly trying to meet my eye.

"Oh, look at this mess—I need to go paint now—I'm working on a commission to make the *Ghent Altarpiece*. Maybe you can help me with the frame—I'm not a carpenter and you were always building stuff and fixing things—Whitley was going to do it, but he's gone now. Preston isn't talented, he wouldn't know what end of a tool to use—the only tool he knows how to use is the one between his legs, and he doesn't even use that very well—he hurts me," she sighed again. A tear formed and dropped into her lap; she seemed unaware of it. "I miss Whitley, even though he was a pain in the ass sometimes—I loved him as much as I could—I really did."

I sat frozen, unable to move to comfort her; I can't deal with women and their emotional shit, but there was only one tear, so I relaxed in spite of feeling on the edge of becoming royally pissed as I began to dislike her husband even more. "Does Preston abuse you?" My words felt sluggish in my throat.

"No—but he's not gentle—he hurts me because he's rough—he's not like Sylvester—I love him, really I do—he's so good that way—he's so quiet—I love his quiet—he feels good to me," she said, hugging herself, her hands rubbing her arms and shoulders as if in imitation of Hayden's gentle caresses. "But we mustn't, never again."

"I see," I nodded, feeling funny about the open assessment of her lover in comparison to her husband. It is sad seeing her face reacting to her emotions, as if their sharp existence puzzled her. How can anyone say she doesn't feel—she does, she just needs to learn how to use the tools to express them. "It's all right, Sammy," I assured her that if she wanted to cry it was fine with me, but she didn't. "Don't worry about the frame, let me take a look at what you're working on, and I'll see what I can do," I said to comfort her at least in one aspect of what troubled her—the one thing I could do something about.

Without indicating that she heard me or understood what I said, she stood up and walked out of the kitchen like a sleepwalker. I followed her upstairs to the garret. Along the way, I laid my hands on the narrow walls of the stairway, and immediately received a splinter from the same old beam that had bit my flesh when I first moved in a long time ago. I always loved it here because of the house's rustic character—twisting, narrow stairways, creaky plank floors, uneven horsehair plaster walls, and ancient beams with adze marks on them; many have the bark still clinging to the wood, exposed, and dusty with cobwebs. The drafty windows with tiny glass panes are original eighteenth century, wavy and full of bubbles, you can't see for shit out of half of them. Passing through the common area, I could see my old room down the narrow hallway by itself and the front room where Lenore had slept; both doors are closed, but my mind can easily open them with the verve of memories to fill their emptiness.

Upon entering the garret, I saw that it is the same as I remembered. Whitley's stuff is stored in a long line of vertical bins; his worktable is just as he had left it the last time he worked less than a week ago, and chances are the girls will let it remain that way like a shrine.

"Your things are still over there," she said, pointing at the window under the gable where I used to work; I barely glanced at the plastic covered table I had left behind all those years ago. I looked away from it not ready to think about the memories left there.

Sammy's studio is in the small room at the back end of the house that had been her playroom connected by a stairway leading into her old bedroom that gave her inexhaustible access. I can still hear the echo of her little kid feet stomping up and down the narrow stairs, which was an integral part of the home-life background noise.

The new studio that replaced the playroom is clean and warm; the walls constructed with crisp drywall, painted an earthy tint of white that might go by an exotic name like *Egyptian Linen*. The room feels well insulated to keep the temperature regulated so the girl isn't roasting in the summer, and to keep out the Cape Ann drafts of the winter. I never doubted that Whitley would go out of his way to do the best for Sammy. The windows facing the backyard, filled the room with natural light, I noted that the carpenter who updated the windows maintained the original design of their predecessors and reused the old glass. A futon against the wall to my right piled with

pillows and blankets made me wonder if she had slept up here recently—if she and Preston are having marital problems it is possible, or has she taken after the old man and can't peel herself away from her work in progress to come to bed? That in itself can cause marital problems. I couldn't help noticing the other comforts of home in the corner—a small refrigerator, a telephone, and a laptop on a small handcrafted desk. Around the drafting table to my left, a stereo system with a precarious stack of CD cases within reach of the artist's work place—almost all of them Beethoven. Storage bins, cabinets, and drawers loaded with art supplies and vertical bins on top of flat file drawers line the far left wall, and to the right, miniature copies of famous works of art stand like a police line-up of the usual suspects on the wall-mounted drying rail.

"That's a mighty tiny *Mona Lisa* there, Sammy," I laughed, when I saw the 3 x 2 inch painting mounted on a slightly larger, dark stained wood panel leaning on the rail. Along with the infamous portrait stood a Fragonard, *The Swing* measuring 12 x 10 inches; a Manet, *A Bar at the Foilies-Bergère*, measuring 8 x 12 inches, and then a petite 6 x 4 inch Vermeer, *Young Woman with a Water Jug*. I turned away from the rail because she didn't reply to my comment, and I found her tucked behind the open studio door, her concentration intently focused on the pre-cut panels for the *Ghent Altarpiece*. Stepping over to stand beside her, I plucked my reading glasses out of my pocket and sat down at the makeshift table made of a plywood sheet propped on cinderblocks to examine the photos of the original to check out the proposed construction—a bit complicated and fussy, but no big deal with the right tools and supplies.

"Yeah, I can do this—did Whitley order supplies for it?" I asked, self-consciously putting the glasses away.

"I don't know—he was always so last minute about everything. Take a look-see in the shop—maybe he did, he talked to me about it the day before he died."

"I have followed your career, you know—" I said in a meek confession; I have coveted a few magazine and newspaper articles about her over the years, but always felt robbed that Whitley never allowed her to be photographed. Considering what happened to Lenore, I imagined he was paranoid about someone kidnapping her—maybe for a ransom.

"I suppose being the art world's freak is okay," she shrugged.

"Do you see yourself that way?" I asked, curious about her awareness of the critics who have pooh-poohed her purpose though they appreciated her technical skill.

"I'd feel differently if I painted my own things; making these is just so—you know? *Miss Ryder, can you copy this for me?* I'm so tired of it," her sigh came out tempered with frustration. "Do you know why I make them so small?"

"I always thought you were translating how you saw them in books," I chose not to say *copy* since I noticed that term bothered her yesterday when people spoke to her about her work.

"At first, yes, but I make them small because they are insignificant to me, I make them small so that they're almost negligible. I make them small because they are not mine and I can do what I want with them. I make them small for the challenge—why don't I paint them actual size? I know some potential patrons have stuck their noses up because I only do miniatures— they think I should do whatever they want me to do because they're shelling out the money for it—well, fuck that. It would be too much like forgery for comfort. Plus, it would be boring if I painted *Mona Lisa* the same way over and over and over again. By making them small, I make them different. People like them, they're crazy about them, and they pay ridiculous sums of money for the fucking things. Someday, when I paint something of my own, I will paint it big," she said, holding her arms out wide with her fingers extended to exemplify the infinite size of the canvas that she dreamed of; then she smiled. Perhaps hers is the most genuine smile in the world, and my heart swelled again—this time with pride and awe.

She gave me a hug from behind, her arms crossing my chest, and her hand slipped through the gaps between the buttons on my shirt to feel for my heartbeat just like she used to when she was little. The rhythm of my pulse always fascinated her. When she was a baby, I would lie with her sleeping on my chest, her ear tuned in to my beating heart, our hearts beating together; I could feel hers hammering its baby tempo against my ribs. Right now, I can feel her heart pulsing in between my shoulder blades where her small breasts pressed against me, her hand inside my shirt felt cool on my skin.

"It's good to see you again," she murmured into the hollow of my neck and shoulder.

"It's good to see you too," I expressed with a long sigh as I squeezed her arms tight against my chest, my heart bursting with the love that I've always felt for her. Tears dampened my cheeks and gave me the sniffles, but she didn't seem to notice my overwrought emotions.

"I'll go out to the shop to see if Whitley got started and we'll go from there, all right?" I said, wiping my face with my palms.

"Thank you, Guthrie," she murmured as she stepped away, releasing me.

Leaving her to her work, I slowly went down the creaking stairways, thankful that my body memory had retained "the stoop" that I acquired years ago to avoid bumping my head on the low ceilings and doorways.

Once out in the barn, I found the plans and the intricate molding for the frame, but he hadn't cut anything down. Judging by his notes, it appeared that the hinging mechanisms had hung him up; small, lazy sketches only showed the beginning of his thought process—maybe he was too sick or too drugged, probably both, to think straight anymore. It looked as if I'll need to do a little research on this before proceeding. I doubted the local hardware store would have replicas of fifteenth-century hinges—I could go talk to the area blacksmiths to see what they might have, or maybe I'll just make my own. I knew it wouldn't take much to get the forge working again; the pile of coal remaining in the box appeared sufficient for the fire I'll need to maintain to complete the job. Putting my glasses on, I read over Whitley's notes, *"Helena says the panels themselves were taken out of the original frame and hidden in 1566 because the Protestant iconoclasts at the time of the Reformation were hell-bent to destroy religious images—the frame was either lost or destroyed at the time. Historically, it was a richly carved, two-storied, Gothic reliquary front that might've had clockwork mechanisms that moved the panels, and maybe played music (?) We're not going to go that far!"* My art historical memory recalls that the darn thing is enormous, close to twelve feet tall and fifteen feet wide when the panels were opened—Sammy's finished piece will be about three feet tall tops, maybe five and a half to six feet wide opened—big enough. I bet the person who commissioned it is paying a pretty penny for it.

Upon realizing the scope of the project, I knew that this will not take a day or two to finish, so I might as well move in for the duration—hopefully,

Preston won't have a problem with it because I can't afford a hotel room for a month. Thankfully, the house is huge, we can stay out of each other's hair for the most part—though dinnertime will be the sore spot, Preston and me—oh, yeah, and in another corner there will be Helena—*we're all gathered here for a glare-fest, may the best stink-eye win.* Hayden will be the referee, and Sammy will blithely ignore everything—Silent Sam. *This oughta be fun.*

There's no rush to head back to Cleveland, I lost my teaching job at a community college last spring because I fooled around with a student who I had hired to model for me. Not that I always do it, I had swore off fucking younger women for a bit of time—at least, I did while I was married to wife number four. Things went along mutually okey-dokey until the little chickadee didn't get an "A" in my figure drawing class—I never felt so used in all my life. The girl was a lousy student, but a good kid—she didn't know the difference between a turd and a squirt of burnt umber on a pallet, but she was a good lay with a great body, I loved drawing her—the sex was a bonus I didn't ask for, but didn't say *"no"* to when she offered herself. I gave her a B minus for her pathetic wannabe efforts in the classroom when she really deserved a C. Then she put on the tearful act to the dean that I had led her astray. I didn't fight it either—*"My fault, I should know better than to stick my dick into a twenty-year-old pussy—again! I don't know what I was thinkin'—I'm getting too old for this bullshit!"* I believe those were my exact words to the dean when he called me in for *a talk*. Frankly, I'm getting tired of teaching, the kids these days expect to get an 'A' just for showing up on time—no one cares about the quality of their work, especially since they can make it on a computer with very little effort on their part. There's only a special few who like to get their hands dirty, but they usually are arrogant little pricks who don't care what I have to say—*because when you're twenty you know everything, right? Whatever.*

Just to make life even more interesting, my ex-wife—the former wife number four—is still living with me in my mother's old house. We just overlook the fact that we've been divorced for the last nine months because I don't have the heart to make her move out. So, we mutually hate each other under the same roof. I guess I'll have to help haul her shit out of there just like I had to help haul her shit in when we started to live together over four years ago. I should just let her have the house, move to Boston, find a new job—or something.

After mucking out the forge and running the sweep through the chimney pipe, I went back to the house to clean up for lunch and I found Helena in the kitchen piecing together sandwiches with her long spidery fingers encrusted with rings. My entrance startled her, even though she knew I was here; she didn't know where I was and I could tell it disturbed her.

"I see you're here already," she said, her brow knotted with disapproval as she turned away from me to concentrate on the arrangement of the lettuce over the thin slivers of roast beef.

"She asked me to come early—we had a nice visit over coffee—she's been upstairs working for a couple of hours now—I've been in the shop checking out Whitley's plans for the *Ghent Altarpiece*—" I turned on the water and began to scrub my hands blackened by soot. "—and as you can see, I've been doing a little tidying up out there."

"I see," she said, puckering her mouth in that annoying way she had back when she was a kid; the urge to slap the shit out of her kicked in just like old times—*some things never change.*

"Sammy wants me to build the frame for it," I continued to explain. "I'm thinking about firing up the forge to make hinges if I can find a period design that would be acceptable."

"Ah!" she nodded, continuing to make the sandwiches tidy.

"What's up with you?" I asked, annoyed by her suspicious attitude.

"Why does something have to be up?" she inquired with a put-on act of innocence.

"Well, to put it bluntly, you have something wiggling up your ass, and if you have issues with me, I want them out in the open," I sparked; she twitched in reaction.

"Why did you come here?" she asked, folding her arms over her tiny breasts; I wondered if she might be leaning toward the anorexic side of dieting.

"I came here because Whitley was the only father I ever had, and I wanted to pay my respects in spite of what happened between us."

"That's funny—you could have come before he died," she glared at me as if ready to tear me a new asshole.

"I wanted to, but—" I stopped; there was no sense in starting the cycle of explanation—or blame. "Why should I stand here and explain any of this to you—you know damn well he didn't want me around."

"Well, then, I won't beat around the bush, why did you come here?"

"I came to pay my respects, and I came to see Sammy—I always believed that I was her father, and I felt that I should come back to be part of her life again."

"Well, here's news for you—you're not her father," she said in a haughty attitude that made my ass itch. She never used to be like this with me—I guess I'm paying for every little thing I ever did wrong—starting with not tumbling into bed with her when she batted her boogily-shit-brown eyes at me.

"Oh, you know this for a fact?" I asked with snide curiosity.

"Yes, I had the DNA tests done—for Sam's sake and for Whitley's peace of mind—it always bothered him not knowing if she was his or not. He loved Sammy so much—I'm glad he went to his grave knowing the truth."

"She doesn't seem to think it was necessary—she believed Lenore."

"I know—we had a time getting her to agree to the test—she's so difficult at times," she said sadly, her body wilting with the weight of her *"burden"*. *Way too much drama.*

"Well, if you didn't treat her like a child all the time, maybe she'd feel more cooperative," I said, making a dig on Sammy's behalf. Helena glared at me as if recognizing her sister's complaint in my voice.

"You have no idea—you haven't been around for over twenty years, so what the fuck do you know? She certainly isn't getting better," she snarled.

"You're right—I haven't been here, but I think she has come a long way considering what her prognosis was when they first diagnosed her and recommended that *'special school'*, which was just a small step above an insane asylum. They said she'd never talk enough to hold a conversation—seems to me she can not only talk, she can tie her shoes, make coffee, and balance her checkbook."

"You don't know anything, you've only been around her for a few hours—she's gotten worse since she married Preston," she hissed with a grimace. "Chances are—she doesn't remember talking to you five minutes after you left, she's so preoccupied—her clearest moments are in the morning just before she starts working—so you got to see her at her best."

"Was that the reason why you didn't want me here until the afternoon?" I asked, feeling I had finally achieved higher ground.

"No—I just wanted to be here when you came," she said, lifting her jaw and dropping her gaze; she always did that when she lied.

"Sure, whatever." *I can't trust her as far as I can throw her.* "Well, I should go up and tell her goodbye—I'm going to do a little research on fifteenth century hardware."

"I'll come up with you—it's really a little early for lunch, but close enough—you can join us if you like—I made plenty for all of us—and as I recall, you're a bottomless pit, there is more in the fridge."

We walked up together in uncomfortable silence and entered the garret studio; Sammy had Beethoven blasting so loud I thought that I was going to go deaf just like old Ludwig. Helena and I watched from this fringe vantage-point at the door as the young woman seated at her drafting table continued working, oblivious of our intrusion; her steady hand with the dancing brush accomplished feats of illusion under the lens of an illuminated magnifying glass. Lena flashed the overhead lights at the switch by the door to get Sam's attention; she looked up, smiled, and then turned down Beethoven.

"Oh, Guthrie! I'm so happy to see you again!" she chirped. Just as my heart began to sink, I watched her face go through a thought process that I recognized from when she was very young—like a swimmer struggling to the surface. "Duh, I mean, I'm happy you're still here—what do you think about the frame—did his plans make any sense to you?"

It was all I could do not to look at Helena; my childish impulse to stick out my tongue at her and say *"Neeeaahhh!"* begged to cut loose, but I behaved myself. I knew that she looked at me with a dumbfounded expression, and I didn't want to embarrass her with a glance; sometimes that's as bad as acknowledgement.

"The plans look great, Sammy; the lumber is there, it just needs to be cut—but I need to go to the library after lunch to do a little research on fifteenth century hardware design for the hinges so that they will look authentic."

"Can I come with?" She brightened as she made her typical abbreviated request.

"If it's all right, I wouldn't mind the company." Although I spoke to Sammy, I allowed my words to include Helena; Sammy's gaze narrowed as she glanced at her elder sister.

"Eat first, then go," Helena consented with a sigh.

I slid my gaze away from her, trying not to think about what Sammy had told me about Helena fooling around behind Hayden's back, or his knowledge of it, and of his history with Sam and their recent fling. What a huge kick in those perfectly straight teeth it would be for her to learn about it, but that is not for me to tell—however, I can privately gloat and wish to be a bug on the wall when she finds out. Seeing the various portraits of Hayden on the board above Sammy's drafting table made me think that their recent one-night-stand probably spoke more like an admission to their true feelings for one another than just a careless indiscretion.

"I want to walk on Good Harbor Beach before it gets dark, Guthrie, can we?" Sammy begged, tugging on my sleeve. "The tide will be out this afternoon, we can walk out to Salt Island if we want to—just like we used to!"

"We can do that," I agreed, my hand instantly caressed her soft hair, the gesture is ingrained in my being; dark brown silk threads, fell in a frame around her sweet face.

Helena gave me a dark look that I ignored. In spite of her and in spite of Preston, I intend to be part of Sammy's life from now on, and I'll tolerate both of them to be with her. I paused in my thoughts to adjust my original belief that she was my daughter; the demotion to friend or stepbrother threw a monkey wrench in my ideals about her. I have to admit that my preoccupation with the belief that I was her father never allowed me to cultivate any other mind-set, to me, she was my little girl and I love the shit out of her.

When Sammy sat across from me at the table, my stomach churned with nervousness as I considered our earlier conversation over coffee, her words spoken with the direct honesty typical of Samantha Ryder, almost brutal in that *tell-it-like-it-is* sensibility. It is perfectly clear that she perceives me in a way that I never expected—the notion that she fantasized about me in the capacity of a lover is too alarming to ignore. Friendship I can deal with—a friendship between us is feasible—being her lover—that's inconceivable. At this point, I feared her persistence regarding her feelings about me because

I knew her natural obsessive nature might not let it go; she'll gnaw on this idea like a dog worrying a bone. The girl is in a marriage with a man she doesn't love—or can't find the desire to love, and then the man who she had as a lover is preoccupied with the woman of his dreams. *Maybe my being here is not a good thing.*

After filling a glass with milk, I looked up to find Sammy watching me through half-closed eyes as if absorbing my presence; suddenly her gaze opened wide and I saw Lenore again. My heart lurched inside my chest and I suppressed a shudder because I had just seen a ghost, and suddenly, I wanted to leave and never come back to Gloucester again.

7

It's love
in some form.

"*I will die in November—it's as good a time to do it as any, I guess—why not, eh? Everything else is dying—I'll just be one more thing.*" Whitley blurted out while we watched the golden October sunset over the salt marshes—Sylvester was driving my father's Caddy; Whitley and I sat in the backseat, enjoying the view. The conversations with my father during the weeks before his death always had grim tidbits like this, punctuated with a wink to take the edge off. Often our talks were threaded with memories of Lenore and Guthrie; these reminisces grew like seeds sown in a freshly turned garden of composted grief. "*I loved them both, you know—I knew what was goin' on and it devastated me inside when I first figured it out. If Lenore wanted to leave me for Guthrie, I would have let her go—it would have been right. But they would have wanted you—I would have never let them take you away from me—you were mine—my daughter—I love you with all my heart and soul.*" After his tender words, he then shook his head. "*What kind of father am I? I have never forgiven myself for how I treated Guthrie—I kicked him out during a time when we needed to heal as a family—but I was too proud—too angry—too hurt. I loved that boy and I turned my back on him.*" He then leaned on me and cried; it felt so odd that I could ever be a source of comfort to him—for the first time in my life, I felt stronger than my father.

On the day before he died, Whitley charged me with the task to find Guthrie. "*I could never face him—I'm a coward—that's hard for me to admit, you know,*" he said with a gleam in his fading eyes. "*Once I'm gone—you're going to need him. He's still living at Margie's house in*

Cleveland—Pinkerton knows where to find him." I didn't know for sure if he'd come.

On that day after the funeral, Guthrie and I took the long chilly walk during low tide from the beach to Salt Island; we were silent most of the time, but it was our sunset return along the narrow sand bar that he reiterated his disappointment that he wasn't my father. *"When you were born, I wanted to believe that I was your father because it was the only way—in my mind—the only way that I could conceivably express my love for you."* I listened to him reason this out, and I felt sorry for him—the enormity of the letdown seemed to crush him. Then he went on to explain that my resemblance to Lenore is complicating his former paternal feelings; the weighty tokens of my being there, every gesture I made reminded him of *her* too much, and he said that he feels revolted by his thoughts. I persisted with a steady stream of *how come* questions, which he evaded by making dumb jokes or lighting a smoke. I poked at him until he finally growled his answer. *"Jeezus K. Ryst, girl, you don't give up do you? You're a pain-in-the-ass just like your mother—okay, I'll tell you how come—it's just wrong, that's how come!"*

His mustache failed to hide his angry mouth; I remained silent, waiting—*what next?*

"I'm sorry for barking at you, Buttons," he muttered after awhile. *"I should have come home a long time ago."* His entire face squinted against his emotions as he sent the words adrift into the November wind filled with ocean spray as the tide began to make its return to the beach. We laughed when our feet received a soaking during the last twenty feet of our trek on the sand bar. We've always cut it close—pushing our luck—Lenore always warned us *"One of these days, you'll be stranded out there until the tide goes out again—I'll kill you if she gets poison ivy because you sent her to pee in the weeds!"* It never happened, but once he had me climb up onto his shoulders as he waded back, falling down twice because the undertow tried to suck him out to sea. I never doubted for a second that he wouldn't get me home safe that day—I held on tight just like he told me to—we only lost one of my flip-flops, no big deal.

Once we reached higher ground, Guthrie turned back to look at where we had been, the waves now nearly covering what remained of our path to the island. *"But I suppose it was just as well that I stayed away,"* he said to finish his thought.

Although he said nothing more, I could tell by the cast of his brow that he thought a lot. To comfort him, I hugged him as hard as I could—he sagged as he clutched me to his chest, and it seemed as if he, like Whitley, had also lost his strength. My image of him as Atlas withered in the pale twilight beach—he is just a man, not a myth. He appeared far from perfect on that sullen afternoon with a gray sky, gray ocean, and his gray hair—but he was my Guthrie; he has come home to me at last and I will not part with him ever again.

More than anything, I wanted to believe that our reunion was going to be a good thing, but no, it hasn't. My emotions went supernova, it's been too much to process all at once—Preston's misbehavior, Whitley's death, my night spent with Sylvester, and Guthrie's return have rattled me to the core; so storms of tears, both happy and sad erupt with startling regularity. To make things worse—yet wonderful—I have fallen head-over-heels in love with Guthrie. The euphoria is addicting, impulsive, disquieting—there are times I can't stand being in my own skin. To combat this new stress, I go running on the beach—running helps me to refocus and fine-tune, and when I'm done running, I sit by the water listening to the waves—the water whispers *'peace'*. Unfortunately, the peace that I find after this effort doesn't last long because they're there when I return home—Preston, Guthrie, Sylvester, and even the echoes of Whitley. And of course, Helena could never be a soothing person if she tried. I feel like I have nowhere to go—except inside my head to be alone.

Whenever I have tried to express my feelings to Guthrie, he laughs. *"Look darlin', you're infatuated—you're just a little excited that I'm home again—your feelings are a little mixed up—it's okay—you'll get over it."*

But I didn't. My fascination with him brought me to the threshold of his bedroom door to watch him sleep. The first time that he became aware of my doing this, he woke up with a start and cried out *her* name. I laughed at him because he looked as if he had seen a ghost; perhaps he has—the ghost of Lenore has never left this house—it is her memory that has brought us back together. Then the next morning, I brought him toast and tea on a tray; he sat up with a grim expression on his face and he asked me not to do it anymore. His rejection caused me to crumble emotionally, and as my tears fell, he relented, unable to tolerate my sadness. His hands reached out for me and I cuddled close to him.

"There now, don't cry, Buttons. I don't mind having you come in to wake me—not every man has such a pretty alarm clock—but there is no need for doilies on a tray, no tea and toast either. Don't you remember—I could never eat anything before my feet hit the floor—but I will light up a cigarette, if you don't mind," he said, as his hand petted my head on his shoulder. I continued to sob weakly. *"I didn't mean to make you cry, sweetheart—but we need to set some ground rules here—I'm not Whitley and you're not Lenore, and as long as we can keep that straight, we should be all right,"* he had said with a cough after lighting a cigarette.

Heaving a deep sigh, I sat up, took the cigarette away from him and held it between my fingers in imitation. He relinquished it with a shrug and lit another one for himself.

"I don't know if I like it that you smoke," he grumbled with a paternal scowl. I laughed as we blew smoke into each other's faces in playful spite; I quickly forgot my tears.

In line with his curiosity about me, I hungered to learn about his life since he left us, but when I want to talk, he becomes uncomfortable and doesn't want to discuss any of his past. But he eventually made revelations while I held him captive in the garret for one hour every day, more like he was captivated, because he spent this hour sculpting a bust of me. I learned tidbits of information such as he's had four wives; he had two children with the first, and a child with the second; they—*his daughters* grew up without him being a meaningful presence in their lives.

"I didn't know you had girls—for some reason I always imagined they were boys."

"Girls—all three were girls—with every birth, it was like rubbing salt in a wound—none of them were you—it was you I wanted—I don't think a boy would have mattered."

"I was never your daughter," I reminded him.

"Yeah—but you don't understand—in my heart you were my daughter—biology didn't matter—I loved you with my entire being since the day

you were born—this is just so fucked-up," he muttered. *"I still love you—I do love you in some form—I just don't know what it is."*

His third wife was barely a wife, their marriage lasted a week, but the divorce took longer. The last wife continues to live with him as if she hasn't realized that their divorce is final.

"We've been together for four years, but only one year as a married couple—funny thing, it was her idea to get divorced, so go figure," he said, squinting at the bust as he rotated the turntable to look at the bust's profile; his gaze quickly flickered toward me, but caught me staring at him. It is unnerving to him that I stare, but I can't help it because I am so pleased to see him in the flesh; I adore him, I love him, and I obsess over his being. Every day, the tip of my pencil has rendered his large, scarred hands with thick fingers that look so incapable of doing anything delicate, but they maneuver over the surface of the clay face with the dexterity of a ballerina on a stage. His manly sensibility would hate that particular comparison, so I keep it to myself—there are certain truths that should never be mentioned aloud—I do have some discretion or *filters* as he refers to my *open-mouth-insert-foot* disease. Perhaps he would prefer that I thought he is molding me into a shape he desired. I watched as he caressed the curve of the muddy cheek with his thumb, and then he touched it with his fingers as a soft expression misted his eyes.

During this quiet interval, I also stood back to view him in the same manner of concentration as my brain squinted at his shape in the garret atmosphere. He isn't much different from me; by understanding him, I might learn something about myself. I want to know if my inability to connect with Preston is a personal deficiency that has nothing to do with my autism. Perhaps it's our creative minds; maybe we are too preoccupied with our work to allow us to engage our emotions in a way that is necessary to maintain a healthy relationship. Or is it possible that our love became disfigured by the long time ago day when the two of us sat on the beach waiting for Lenore, and when she came back with the tide we became disconnected from each other—disconnected by grief, disconnected from the love we once felt. He is right—I am capable of love, but love always becomes confused within the spectrum of human emotions.

"Why are you so unhappy, Guthrie?" I asked.

With a sigh, he glared at me—his deep-set blue eyes with dark brows knitted together, and his thick moustache placed a heavy emphasis on his frown.

"I am just unhappy—I often asked myself why am I so miserable? I have no idea why I am the way I am. I've never been happy," he grunted, passing his hand over his head and rubbing the back of his neck as if it hurt him.

"Even with Lenore? I always thought you were happy with Lenore." I slid off the stool where I perch like a bird while he worked the wet clay to his satisfaction, and sidled up beside him, briefly casting my gaze at the earthen face. It could be a golem for Lenore rather than a portrait of me, but no, it is of me after all—sweetly idealized by what his fingers could conjure.

"We were—but we weren't—our happiness was fleeting. I felt I could love her forever—then she'd do or say something to make me not want to see her ever again," he sighed, stepping away from the bust—stepping away from me. "I am having a difficult time being here—I never really dealt with what happened—that's mostly why I didn't come home—I just couldn't deal with any of it."

"I want you to be happy, Guthrie—I want you to stay here—I can make you happy," I whispered, clasping his clay encrusted hands, and kissing the patch of clean skin on the back of his left hand.

"Sammy—I would love to, but I have a life," he said with a laugh, retrieving his hands from my grasp, and then he withdrew to the sink to wash them.

"Such as it is!" I cried with a laugh, sticking my hands under the running water along with his to wash off the clay that had transferred to my fingers.

"Yes, such as it is," he said with a measure of shame. "But you have your life to consider too." He turned away, shaking his hands off, and drying them on the towel. When I picked up the dangling end to share it with him to dry mine, he quickly dropped his end, his hands still damp.

"I'm sorry. I do wish Preston was less of an asshole," I sighed, folding the towel and hanging it on the rack to dry. "I had hoped that he would make me happy, but it hasn't worked out that way."

"Trust me, your marriage isn't going to work out with me here—as soon as I'm done with this frame, I really should get on with my life—I have an ex-wife to move out of my house—"

"Just give her the damn house, move here, and work for me—I need a carpenter—you can sculpt—the shop can be renovated to accommodate your work, we can make a foundry in the barn," I said, tugging on his denim shirt sleeve. "Maybe you can teach at the university—"

"Sam—you can't make a foundry in a barn, it's a tinderbox—listen, you're being much too generous. Helena will really think that I did come here to sponge off you," he laughed sharply. "I'll come see you from time to time, but I can't stay—I need to get my shit together and find another job."

"Guthrie, I need you here—I want you here!" I said, hugging him. I could feel his body stiffen and then relax as he accepted my embrace, and he hugged me in return. "All that matters to me right now is having you home—I want you near me."

His silence spoke of the uncertainty he felt about this arrangement.

As expected, Preston was not thrilled about Guthrie's moving in with us, and since he has no say-so about the arrangement, he has chosen to complain about Guthrie's bad habits. I guess it's hard for him to control his bad habits if Guthrie is in his face night after night enjoying himself smoking and drinking beer. Although I have noticed that Guthrie does consume a significant amount of beer, I have never observed him drunk, nor have I ever seen him show any hint of being out of control. I never thought of Guthrie's smoking as a problem since Whitley smoked like a chimney all of his life in every corner of the house. But to appease my husband, I made Guthrie promise not to smoke at the dinner table in front of Preston's two sons who have come to live with us as per the agreement he has with his first wife to share custody part of the year.

Preston has also made it a hobby to nag about Guthrie's past. I will concede that the man does have a shameful pattern, much like Whitley's behavior with young women—but who is he to judge? Pinkerton has kept me apprised of my husband's flirtations, but so far, there is no evidence that his flirtations have gone to the next step—but as Pinkerton has pointed out, *"I can't be everywhere!"*

It has been over a month since these bumpy beginnings charged the atmosphere of home with out-of-the-blue sensations. Preston mostly avoids Guthrie until they meet at the dinner table, and Guthrie congenially holds his ground when confronted by my husband's presence. Sometimes it seems like the dining room is barely big enough for the two of them, so the escalating household tension becomes more concentrated during the dinner hour and Carrie eyes us warily as if waiting for Armageddon. Guthrie sits at the head of the dinner table, replacing Whitley; Sylvester sits at his left with Helena next to him, and I sit at Guthrie's right with Preston beside me; his pre-teen sons sit next to him and squirm with restless energy through every meal.

To make things even more interesting, Sylvester has made friends with Guthrie; he accepted him without doubts about his intentions. When we gather for dinner, they sit deep in their discussions while Helena and I look on, I am delighted, but she gapes at them, mortified by the instant camaraderie. Their appearances and manners are from opposite ends of the male spectrum as they discuss everything from physics to politics and their mutual passion for old cars, baseball, and fishing. While the weather remained nice, they made it a habit to disappear before the crack of dawn on Saturday mornings to go to Whitley's favorite stream to cast flies.

Every night since his return to us, I have observed Helena examining him while we gather around the dinner table. She used to be in love with him—now her gaze is digging around, trying to find the young man from her adolescent infatuation. I know that young man is here, only older—I can see him through his façade that has been weathered by the years away from home. How betrayed she must have felt after finding out that Lenore already coveted Guthrie for herself—she always claimed that she never knew about their ongoing affair.

She noticed my study of her and gave me the stink-eye, so I gave her the stink-eye right back. *How can she live with herself?* I think she hates everybody and everything—nothing satisfies her. Her dissatisfaction with life is reflected in the way that she treats Sylvester. Her recently discovered infidelity is just the tip of the iceberg breaking through her shallow surface. I hate what she's done to Sylvester.

Poor Sylvester—steadfast Sylvester, he overlooks her faults and re-mains beside her—so tolerant, so patient—accepting her infidelity as if it were his fault—his undeclared revenge became a guilty pleasure as his gaze dances in my direction and quickly looks away. My gaze dared to land on him for a little while longer, and my chest began to feel tight as I took in the familiar sight of his hands holding the silverware while he cut the tenderloin on the plate before him. *Why are you the way you are, Sylvester?* I wondered. As if he heard my question, he glanced up and we connected; he smiled. My foot that had slipped out of my moccasin some time ago poked him in the shin, and then my toes grasped and tugged on the cuff of his blue jeans. Without further visual acknowledgement of me, he vainly tried to make me stop as my chilly toes playfully probed inside his pant leg to stroke the warm flesh of his hairy shin. But Preston nudged me for attention, and to Sylvester's silent relief, I removed my naughty toes from his leg.

After I passed the butter to Preston, I turned my attention toward Guth-rie; he's eating—his appetite is huge. Carrie is impressed by how much he can pack away; she had to adjust meal proportions to accommodate his hunger. I studied his face in three-quarter profile as he slouched over his plate, elbows on the table, forking chunks of beef, mashed potatoes, and carrots into his mouth; his face is a stern mask of concentration that did not want to be interrupted while he devoured the food on his plate. I traced his outer lines with my eyes; starting at the base of his skull, my gaze glided up and over his head to climb down his forehead with its ladder of worry lines. Then I hung, dangling from the dark brows to peer at his deep-set eyes, bright blue and fringed with black lashes that softened their expression. When I was very young, I used to run my fingers down the scooped bridge of his nose like it was a ski-jump, and I'd drop off at the broad dead end to fall into the dark brown thicket of his mustache—it's now streaked with white. The mustache made his mouth a secret, his lower lip barely revealed above his sturdy chin that jutted out with a stubborn posture. I've noticed how his obstinate jaw-line has started to soften with potential jowls. *I am really seeing him!* My heart sang with joy as I let my hand touch his arm, the sleeve rolled up, exposing a muscular, hairy forearm.

I want him near me—always near me.

❧

With all that has happened since the morning Whitley died, I have been procrastinating about my decision to divorce Preston—I haven't mentioned it to anyone. Although I haven't slept with my husband since I decided to move into my childhood room, it hasn't prevented his demands for sex, and his visits to my bed continued in spite of my lack of interest. I have rebuffed him as often as I have given in and lain still while he grunted on top of me. I don't cry—it is futile to protest, but I have complained about his forcible manner that has left me feeling sore. *"I wouldn't hurt you if you would just relax and enjoy it, sometimes you're like fucking a knot-hole in a two by four,"* he said with a laugh. I cuffed him on the shoulder for being so rude, but then I softened the blow with my own bit of sarcasm, *"I feel like I got fucked by a two by four."* To this, he laughed—a nasty laugh as if proud that his manly member is stiff as a board. But in spite of my bluntness, nothing changed, and his sexual advances continued the same way. This morning, he woke me from a sound sleep, roughly pushing his way into my unprepared body. Once he left the house to go to work, and the school bus picked up the two boys, I rose from my bed, feeling bruised by his grinding on my body, and I walked down the hall to Guthrie's bedroom.

He lay dead to the world, snoring and exposed; lying there as if he had fallen over with his arms flung out like a plea for mercy; his broad, hairy chest bare, and his armpits full of dark hair left open to the temptation to be tickled, which I did millions of times when I was little. I padded lightly into the room and climbed into bed with him, sliding my hips in between his long hairy legs sticking out of the bunched up bed-sheet coil that reminded me of the swirling draperies from Baroque paintings that manage to become modestly snagged on the dangling male genitalia. He stirred with a grunt as his arms fell around me with sleepy decisiveness—perhaps dreaming of a past passion in the forgetfulness of sleep. I kissed his slack mouth, and he sighed, kissing me in return, his hips moved under the sheet with explicit awakening. I kissed him again while my hand cradled his warm arousal inside the soft cotton sheet; suddenly his mouth vibrated against my lips as a yell erupted from him, and he roughly shoved me aside as he bolted out of bed, dragging the bed-sheet with him to cover his nakedness.

"What are you doing, Sam?" he exclaimed hoarsely, his face pale and wild.

"I want you to love me—" I pled, desperate to resolve the knotted guts of my feelings.

"No, Sam, I can't—this is—it's just wrong—" he said through clenched teeth.

What do I feelwhatdoIwantwhat do I need? Lovelovelovelove. Love.

"I need to feel good," I whispered, withdrawing into myself, my aching body curled into isolation as I self-consciously folded my limbs tight against me and began to rock. Suddenly the feelings that sent me to his room made no sense—yet they do, it felt natural to go to him for comfort—to find love.

"Sammy—please, don't try tempting me—I won't be able to stay here if you start doing stuff like this," he gasped. He looked afraid—*yes, afraid*—I had not thought about the potential of fear—*his fear.*

"I'm sorry, Guthrie—I didn't mean to—" I said softly, burying my face into my knees, feeling afraid, just like him. I listened to his movements as he began to get dressed behind my back. *What have I done?*

"Sammy, I think it is for the best that I should leave, I'm going to leave today—as soon as possible." he said, kneeling down in front of me and draping one of his shirts around my shoulders; his wrinkled brow was full of concern as he peered into my face. "You know I can't stay here anymore—because I nearly let it happen—there's a part of me that wanted to let it happen—you have no idea how difficult it's been for me to be here."

"Yes, I know," I sighed; my mouth struggled to articulate how I felt, but in my confusion I uttered the only thing I understood. "I love you."

"I love you too—" he sputtered. "Honey, I really do love you—in some form, I do love you. I see you as Lenore—and I can't get past it—please understand—it's wrong," he muttered, looking away. "Jeez Christmas, Sammy, how did we let it get this way? I can't look at you and not react to how I feel—I don't know what to do, but I do know that we can't do this."

"I know," I said, squeezing my eyes tight; I couldn't look at him. His hands landed on my shoulders, his fingers gently kneading my flesh, forcing me to stop rocking.

"We need time apart—it's the only way to make it stop—we must until something changes, all right?" He stood back, keeping his distance, avoiding temptation. "I do want to keep in touch—I do want to see you again—I'll come back some day—once things settle down."

"All right."

"I'm sorry," he mumbled.

"Me too." I nodded.

We remained as we were—separate and silent; the fluttering wings inside my chest made me feel sick as I slipped my arms into the sleeves of his shirt and pulled it tight around me.

"Then you must go," I said and left his room so he could do what he needed to do to leave. I went on to do what I needed to do to move on without him. I got dressed and went to the garret to work, but I could not work; my distraction ate away at my concentration—*if only he would leave now. Go away, Guthrie—please go!*

When he came upstairs to say goodbye, I hugged him, and his arms crushed my small body against his chest. We stood locked in our embrace for a long time, swaying like in a slow dance. His hands with their thick fingers tangled in my hair as he gripped my skull between them, and at first, he allowed me to apply tender kisses over the surface of his face. He then crushed his mouth against my lips with gentle force; he hadn't shaved, so his thick, coarse mustache and unshaven chin abraded my skin. Suddenly, with a growl, he separated from me, and leaned against the doorway; he was breathing hard and I was hardly breathing as I dropped into my chair. His final goodbye rumbled in his throat—I said nothing.

After I heard Delta Dawn roar out of the driveway, I turned on Beethoven's soulful *Cavatina—he composed sorrow as if he knew it well.* I looked at the drawings on the board above my drafting table, and the pencil versions of Guthrie looked back at me, I turned away. *Why can't we be happy together? We were, we had been, until I spoiled everything by getting into his bed like Lenore used to—the way I had fantasized doing.* Then I slipped a peek at my latest sketch of Sylvester's sympathetic expression. While I absorbed his pale graphite gaze, I laid my head down on the drafting table and did nothing all day. I didn't sleep—I didn't move, the time passed at a meaningless crawl.

Hours later, Preston's boys came home from school, but they never paid any attention to my existence—*I'm not their mommy.* When Preston came home, he wanted to talk to me, but I did not acknowledge his being; his anger at my disregard for him echoed through the house. Apparently, his rage caused Carrie to call Helena out of the carriage house to come look at me. She came, and prodded me with impatient questions that I refused to answer. I just wanted quiet and stillness. Then after a flurry of shrill activity intermingled with trembling moments of hushed murmurings from downstairs, Sylvester arrived, still wearing his jacket and tie that he wears to lectures; I could smell the train on his sleeve as he knelt beside me. His kind words coaxed me to respond to his inquiries, his hands landed to caress my back, petting me with the familiarity we have maintained over the years. As I leaned against the sanctuary of his body and hugged him around the neck, I absorbed his comfort. His arms carefully slipped around me after he had left them hovering in the air with uncertainty, hesitating to hold me as if afraid of his old feelings—and the fear of being exposed.

"Samantha, dear heart, what happened—where is Guthrie?" he asked again.

"He has left," I replied after a while.

"Why did he leave?" Helena's hoarse voice drifted from the doorway.

"He finished the frame—he said it was time he went home," I muttered. I could hear Preston grumble something under his breath, but I ignored my husband's noises. "He is gone—I'm too sad," I made the simplest reply to help them understand my feelings.

"I'm so sorry, Samantha—I'm sure he'll come back to visit," Sylvester whispered into my hair. I remained limp, not asking anything more from him beyond the comfort he applied. I closed my eyes and listened to his breathing and the beat of his heart—I do love him—but not in the way that I love Guthrie. He loves me, but not like the way that he loves Helena. *How can I love him—how can I love Guthrie? How can he love Helena—how can he love me?* Feeling so hollow inside, I clung to him—oh, how I wished I could transplant a piece of him into the empty space Guthrie's departure carved into me, but I knew that would be too much to ask even if he wanted to give it to me. I knew Sylvester would give every bit of himself to me if I asked it of him, but I can't and I won't.

Sylvester spent the night propped on pillows against the headboard of my narrow childhood bed reading to me from *Our Mutual Friend* that he found on the nightstand; his steady voice calmed me with its gentle music. With my pillow lying on his lap, I lay cuddling his hand against my cheek. When I woke up in the morning, our fingers remained laced in a loose configuration—the book must have dropped onto the floor hours ago, but his hand still lay cupped on the pillow as if cradling its shape. I looked up at his face. He slept deeply, his breath expiring through his parted lips in soft puffs; his glasses hung askew on the narrow bridge of his nose as his chin drooped toward his chest. I smiled, because he's been drooling on himself; the telltale dampness on his shirtfront was unmistakable evidence that this has been going on for quite some time. I pretended to be asleep when he woke up, so he could adjust himself without observation, allowing him to believe that he maintained his dignity in front of me.

8

Helena

Oh-my-god, I gotta get out of here before I go crazy! Oh, shit, but I should take her with me. Damn. The time that I have been dreading ever since Lenore died has arrived—life without Whitley; with him gone, the responsibility to look after Sammy has fallen to me—and it's a good thing I'm here. Especially since I can't rely on that asshole Preston to do anything for her— he was completely worthless two weeks ago when she turned catatonic on us after Guthrie left.

On the day that he unexpectedly packed his bags and took off, Carrie called me to come over because she said she was afraid that Preston might become violent—*"He's wiggin' out cuz Sammy won't talk to him—you better get over here!"* Then I said something to the effect that I didn't want to get involved in their marital spat, but Carrie reiterated the gravity of Sam's condition. *"There hasn't been a spat, there's something not right—you have to come see her."*

When I confronted Preston in the narrow stairway leading to the garret, he appeared pleased to share his frustration with me as he growled, *"I didn't do anything—she was like this when I got here!"* But in spite of his *obvious* concern for Sam, he had no compassion for her condition. *"Make her snap out of it,"* he commanded. His attitude set my teeth on edge. I entered the studio determined to straighten her around, but once I saw her with her head down on the drafting table like that, my resolve immediately turned to fear. I had never seen her like that before; her blank, tearless stare gave me the creeps, and I was afraid that she was having some kind of a fit.

Where is Guthrie? Carrie didn't know, she said his car was gone when she arrived at three. *What the fuck? He's gone, and Sammy appears unable (or unwilling) to communicate.*

I called Sy on his cell phone, and by the time I finished describing her non-responsive behavior, I was in tears and begging him to come home as quickly as he could. When he assured me in his usual placid tone that he was already on the train just passing the stop for Beverly, he was still too far away to suit me, so I went straight into a panic attack. He patiently remained on the line with me while I breathed into a paper bag until I recovered my senses, by then he was off the train and getting into his car.

Once he started talking to her, she displayed signs of life. When he asked her what was wrong, she only said that she was sad. *Well, that's a helluva bad case of sad if you ask me.*

After Sy coaxed her into eating a little bit of soup, she went to lie down on her childhood bed, but he wouldn't leave her. When I last looked in at them at 11PM, he sat propped by pillows against the headboard reading to her while she lay with her head in his lap holding his hand in a white-knuckled death grip. He paused his reading and leveled his calm gaze at me. *"She's okay, go home, and get some rest,"* he said.

Feeling relieved that he had everything under control, I went home, took a sleeping pill, and fell asleep expecting him to come home at any minute, but when I woke up the next morning his side of the bed remained empty. I wasn't surprised; everything he did for her, he'd do it with that steadfast sense of duty with which he does everything—without a complaint. When he finally dragged in by 8AM, he told me that she was better, and explained that he couldn't leave her—*"She's very fragile right now,"* he said. The fool had to go to the chiropractor for his ruined back by the afternoon.

Over the years, I've always been so grateful for his ability to manage Sammy, but I don't know how much of this sort of thing he can take; he has enough on his mind right now. Two days ago, he took an unplanned leave of absence from the university; his father's health is on the downhill slide because of congestive heart failure. He left home early this morning to go to take care of the quickly unfolding ordeal on Deer Isle. So now, I'm alone to watch over Sammy until he resolves the situation—either his dad gets better or he dies. I'm glad Whitley went in his sleep rather than dragging out his last breath in the hospital with all the paraphernalia of modern medicine prolonging the inevitable. He didn't want to end that way—*no one does.* I'm sure Jacob Hayden would prefer to die with dignity in his pretty cottage on Deer Isle with the sound of the ocean in his ears.

Before all of this crap happened, I have noticed that Sy has become quiet—*quieter*—and more depressed than usual. I'm worried about him—*how much more can he take?* It seemed like his friendship with Guthrie helped alleviate the melancholy that always plagued him, but now that Guthrie's gone, he's making those noises again—soft sighs, mutterings, and grinding his teeth. But the worst are the inarticulate whispers and moans that I've overheard through the bathroom door—it's the only place where he can feel alone in the house. I can understand that feeling too; it's making me crazy—the smallness of the carriage house becomes so oppressive when he's like this. Over the years, there have been times when I've come so close to packing up my shit and leaving him, but I don't. I don't because I'm afraid that my abandoning him would destroy him. I can't lose him because I need him here. *He's a good man—such a good man.*

Thankfully, her *"sad"* went away after Guthrie called the next morning to let her know that he had arrived in Cleveland safely. Although they have maintained almost daily contact with each other ever since, her state of mind remains precarious. She's become prone to fits of crying and silent rocking, and when she isn't like that, she's in the studio painting all day and late into the night. I don't think she's eating very well— yesterday at dinner, I noticed how her jeans have started to hang on her hipbones, and so did Preston: *"I see Germany, I see France, I see Sammy's underpants!"* he teased. She laughed at his juvenile rhyme, but she also glared at him with that deadly *"don't fuck with me"* look—she really does look just like Lenore whenever she makes that face.

Since I'm on sabbatical this term to work on Whitley's catalogue raisonné, being on call for Sammy isn't really a big deal, but I'm not getting much work done. It isn't very inspiring for me to track down the surviving cronies and listen to the sordid details of my father's drinking, drug habits, and the countless young women, mostly students—*between his binges, highs, and fucking, when did he find time to make thousands of paintings and drawings?* His muses filled numerous sketchbooks and canvases with voyeuristic impressions of the intimacy between the artist and model; Dulcie was one of them, and then of course, Lenore. I studied his documentation of all of them with mild disgust. I do not relish the idea of sorting through this crap. It's just wacky how he drew on every available scrap of paper he could lay his hands on—there are some things that should not be saved, like that obscene drawing he made on a paper napkin from a pricey Manhattan hotel bar of a woman who must've rubbed him the wrong way—literally. *I could have used Guthrie's help with this! Damn, I would have paid him a thousand dollars to pour through sketch after sketch of nude after nude to pick out the ones worth keeping and what we should trash—why did he suddenly pick up and leave?* It bugs the shit out of me that Sammy never gave a clear explanation regarding why Guthrie decided to bail out—I thought she hired him to become *her carpenter*. Even though I didn't like him being around, I was relieved that he looked after Sammy during the day.

Today, I gotta get out of the house—and I'm taking Sammy with me. I took her out shopping at the mall last week, which made her perk up a little more—*I think we're both due for another perk.*

I let myself in through the back door and followed the sound of classical music to the garret—*Beethoven again*—I'm a little tired of *Ode to Joy*, so I tease her unmercifully when I rename her favorites as—*Old 'n Boring, the Pathetic, the Piss-on-it-a*, and *Snot-on-it-all*. She's obsessed with Beethoven's music because she connected with his genius and disability—I think she has a crush on him—who knows—it's hard to tell what goes on in that busy brain of hers.

I paused in the hallway when I noticed her old bedroom door was ajar, and I saw that the bed was a tumbled mess of slept-in blankets and pillows. *So—she's sleeping in her old bedroom—I didn't know about that, what the fuck, no one tells me anything!*

I climbed the stairs chewing on the evidence of a marriage gone sour. *It was a death-defying feat that Shep and I stayed in the same bed. Both of us seemed determined to deny everything until I finally couldn't stand it anymore and had a meltdown.*

From the studio doorway, I saw Sammy bent over her work, the brush daintily clutched in her fingers danced over the small board cradled in her lap under the lighted magnifying glass; her hair is a mess and she has paint from one end of her to the other. *Everything appears to be back to normal— well, Sammy's version of normal.*

"Come on, take a break, we're going out shopping," I called to her over the classical racket and flicked the light switch a few times to reach through her autistic fog. When she looked up to greet me, I saw that her eyes were bright in spite of the dark sleep deprivation circles under them and she made that handicapped poster-child jack o' lantern grin. If I didn't know her and love her, I'd be afraid of that psychotic grimace.

"Shopping, okay—books? I want more books," she said after switching off Beethoven.

"You bought fifteen books last week, did you read them already?" I laughed.

"I only bought three—and yes, I've read them all—I really loved *Belle-fleur*—you should read it, it's wonderful; I couldn't put it down last night and finished it. I want to thank Sylvester for recommending it—see—I made him this card!"

She gingerly handed me the card with the two fingers that didn't have paint on them and went over to the sink to clean her brushes. The image is composed with her typical stream-of-consciousness lines; they wend aimless-ly around until an image appears—*his hands, good grief, what's up with the hands?* I opened it to find no message inside, just more linear meditations— *oh, wait, there's his name*—written lightly like a whisper, she has carefully spelled out his name in a twisting *fleur de lis* penmanship that made it close to illegible. Then the message came through with the same lightness: *Thank you for your hands—Samantha.* Nothing about the book in that note, she's so weird, but ya gotta love her. Sy has carefully preserved all of the pictures she has given him since he first met her. It's cute when I find one hanging on the refrigerator door from a magnet, just like a father hanging on to his kid's drawings from school. *It's only natural that he should feel something paternal toward her*—just as I thought of this, an internal chill made me flinch—*she's the closest thing to a child he'll ever have with me.*

"Nice card, he'll love it, Sammy. We can mail it out to Deer Isle if you want—he'll be thrilled to get it—it'll cheer him up," I called to her over the sound of running water—she didn't hear me. I set the card on the drafting table and turned my attention to the latest miniature she's been working on and saw that it was one of the panels from the *Ghent Altarpiece. Eve and her fertility figure; she needs more than a tiny fig leaf to cover up with—no one needs to be seein' that unsightly flab.*

"Have you read it?" she asked, turning off the water.

I had to think a minute before I replied—*we're back to Bellefleur*—"No, I haven't, I'll have to borrow it," I muttered. My gaze wandered lackadaisically over the drawings pinned up above the drafting table—*more hands— oh, there's mine—faces, and there's mine—there and there—that one's really old, my hair hasn't been that long in years—Sy seems to be everywhere up here—he doesn't change much, just his glasses do.*

"Please promise not to take a year reading it, I want it back—I want to read it again soon," she said, tugging on my sleeve.

"I'll borrow it from Sy, if he recommended it, he must have it around," I groaned. She always gets mad whenever she loans me things and I don't return them promptly—and sometimes not in the condition in which I received them. Books especially fall victim to coffee stains, nail polish, chocolate fingerprints, the dog-eared corners, and creased covers—I've ruined several books reading in the bathtub; only one book was completely destroyed after being dunked because I fell asleep while reading during a long, hot bath.

"He does have it; it's in his study on the shelf over his desk, second from the top, fourth book in from the left—I'm ready to go," she chirped, slapping her hands together.

Her visual memory always astounds me. "You are not ready—go take a shower—you look like you rolled out of bed and came up here," I laughed after taking a good look at her; she's in a ratty old t-shirt and sweat pants that she's been using to sleep in since she was twelve. She looks absurd with the *Teenage Mutant Ninja Turtles* stretched across her boobs—*it's just wrong I tell ya.*

"Oh, yeah, I did—wait—I'll just be a minute."

"Take your time—you have Eve all over you," I called after her. Sam giggled as she skipped down the stairs to her bedroom, childlike in spite of her twenty-eight years, and her laughter continued to echo all the way to the bathroom.

She's in a great mood today; Preston left with his brats yesterday to see their grandparents for a few days—so, she is free for now, but he's due back today. If only she could be truly free—she is always going to need someone watching over her—*what will happen after I'm gone?* Preston doesn't do shit; if she doesn't divorce the asshole, they'll be prying his neck out of my cold dead hands just so he isn't left to be her guardian. Then there's Guthrie; he's older than I am, and he looks like he's seen better days—we're not going to live forever—*and neither is Sy.*

I still would like to know what the fuck happened that day Guthrie left. It happened so quick—there was nothing leading up to it, and the suddenness of his departure seemed guilty—*I bet that lecherous scumbag went after her—if that's the case, I hope she popped him in the nose!*

My gaze refocused on the drawings again and paused over a sketch of a man's butt—*That's a nice ass—it's new—whose ass is that? Can't be Preston's, you can park Bruce Springsteen's tour entourage in the shade of his butt. That certainly ain't Guthrie's ass; although he's a big guy, he has no ass—he always sat on a crack; the seat of his pants hang loose as if void of gluteus padding—it's just weird. Men are just weird. It kinda reminds me of Sy's ass, he has a pair of sweet cheeks for a skinny guy—clothed or naked— it's a visual treat to watch him walk away—it's all that running he does that keeps it nice and firm.* My mind drew a blank when I thought of Theo—*I don't want to think about Theo or his ass.* I decided that the idealized buns in the drawing cannot be someone's actual ass—it must be some kind of a fucked-up Sammy joke. Like father, like daughter—they both shared a strange sense of humor.

I wandered out of Sam's studio and explored the rest of the garret; I saw the clay bust that Guthrie had been working on was still sitting on the turntable pedestal. Turning it slowly, I admired how he had captured her features, but I found the stillness unsettling. Sammy's face is probably the most animated visage I've ever known, she's always making faces to reflect her inner thoughts—but sometimes her poker face is as impeccable as stone. For a moment, I softened toward Guthrie, he spent hours with her working on this bust, his blocky hands modeling the clay into this perfect portrait; her head slightly turned to the left, her gaze cast down in thought; I could see her sitting for this, her hands busy to compensate for her quiet head. *What happened, Guthrie, why did you leave?* If only I knew. *Sammy knows, but she ain't talkin'.*

I stepped out of the small gabled studio and confronted Whitley's sprawling studio space at the front of the house. I pulled back the plastic draped over his last painting on the easel; it's a composition of pure November gray, the ocean and sky; an echo of his past as an abstract expressionist. I stared at its grayness and became angry with him. *Whitley, that manipulating bastard!* He took advantage of Sammy's talent as soon as Lenore was cold. He kept her at home under his control. Sammy would have benefited from interaction with other children—even college would have been good for her, learning about biology and calculus. She should have had the chance to take piano lessons so she could learn to play her favorite Beethoven sonatas instead of her fingers wiggling in the air in coordination with the notes trilling from the stereo. Maybe she would have met someone else other than Preston, fallen in love and married—she probably would have been happier. But he wouldn't allow it; he was afraid of losing her. He needed her to produce—he needed her income. Suddenly feeling disgusted with my father, I trudged downstairs to get away from his residual influence. I suppose he could have done worse, he could have sent her away to an institution where she would be locked up for life, her talent left unexplored while she sat rocking and rotting. *He loved her*—he looked at her and saw Lenore—he also saw himself in those dark eyes. I was jealous of her and how he spent hours with her; they'd paint together—they were compatible that way. I could never be close to him like that—I know he tried. He was afraid of me, yet he respected me because I was smart like Dulcie; she kept him in check, calling him on the carpet and cranking on him for every little crime he committed. I could look at him in *that way* that I had inherited from her and it would please me to see him cringe. I always wondered if he was mildly autistic, and managed to muddle through life without it crippling him.

"I need new jeans!" Sam cried out as she stomped down the stairs like a herd of elephants, nearly scaring me witless. "There are holes in the pockets."

"Sew the pockets, you know how," I gently reminded her after taking a deep breath; I think we have the same conversation every week.

"Yeah, but I hate doing it," she pouted. Yet another Lenore characteristic—like mother, like daughter—filling her pockets with treasures from the beach, causing gaping holes to form so that important things like house keys, cell phones, and loose change trickle down her pant legs, lost forever.

"Okay, new jeans and fifteen books, let's go." I gave her the once over to make sure she looked presentable. These jeans didn't hang on her too badly, but that's because she has a man's white shirt tucked in at the waist, before I could say *"Well, that's new"*, I recognized it as one of Guthrie's shirts because of the scorched mark of a cigarette burn on the sleeve cuff that Sammy just hid away as she rolled it up. I chose to say nothing because I felt too disturbed to inquire about its significance.

"Here, let's take a look," I said, inspecting her hands and face for traces of *Eve*. I was glad to see the paint on her face is gone; I didn't feel like washing her face for her. Her bobbed brown hair is still wet and she wore it slicked back in a boyish look; thankfully, she won't need a haircut again for a while. I had taken her in just before the funeral and asked the hairdresser to bob it short. As much as Sammy wants to grow her hair long, she can't manage long hair, it just becomes a frustrating rat's nest of tangles that I always end up having to monkey around with. The hairdresser had told me that dreadlocks would look cute on her— *cute—as if the girl isn't freaky enough—why not stick a KICK ME sign to her back.*

Sy had to take over the last time Sammy's hair was a mess and pried apart the snarls after he doused her hair with conditioner. I remember standing in the hallway outside the bathroom (it was over a year ago, well before Preston came into her life) Sammy sat on a stool wearing only a bath towel, Sy stood behind her, picking apart the tangles from her shoulder length hair with the greatest care using a stiff comb. Their reflected twins in the mirror showed me another view of the picture of his patience and her stillness. The tears that I caused dried, her reflected gaze in the mirror clasped onto his studious face bent over her head. *"Looks like you know what you're doing,"* I commented to his reflection. He glanced up into the mirror to meet my eye, and curiously, his face turned red. *"I had some practice while you were away,"* he replied. Sammy uttered a giggle and covered her mouth with her hands, nearly losing her towel. After a shriek and scramble, she affixed the towel snuggly around her body again, and Sy went back to work, his face redder for getting a free show of Sammy's rosy nipples blooming on her pale breasts. I laughed to myself at this memory; it seemed they couldn't look each other in the eye for a few days afterwards.

"I really like your hair short, it's nice—let's go," I said, after finishing the assessment of my little sister. She smiled without commenting, choosing to ignore my praise because she hates her hair short.

Later, when we arrived at the café in our favorite mall bookstore, I let Samantha go get the coffees; it's good to let her do stuff like that, especially when she is willing. I found a table and began to thumb through one of my perspective purchases while keeping an eye on her. It appeared as if she was holding her own, the person behind the counter knows her and that is always a plus when someone familiar is dealing with her.

I glanced around the café to study the people; people-watching is an old favorite pastime of mine. My gaze first found a forty-ish man seated alone by the window—possibly waiting for his significant-other to finish browsing; his wedding band looked so shiny against the skin of his third finger. There's something sexy about a man wearing a wedding ring—*he looks content with being married.* He reminded me of Sy a little bit because of the way he sat reading, with a tilt to his head to accommodate his reading glasses. I remember years ago when Sy used to wear bifocals, the line across the center of the lenses always bugged me—*they made him look like such an old fart!* I have tried to get him to go for the laser surgery, but he refuses to do it. *"With my kind of luck I'll end up blind!"* he exclaimed with indignation. *"You're nearly blind now,"* I laughed at him. *"I'm not taking any chances with what I've got left."* We dropped the subject because he turned snitty with me; it was so rare that he snapped. *What the fuck, Sy!*

When the Window Man's gaze tripped up my way as he turned the page of his paper, my gaze skittered away guiltily, skipped over two old women passing photographs of children and grandchildren between them, before coming to rest upon a young couple putting their baby in a stroller. They both cooed while snapping the pink bundle into place, and then they stood back, looking as happy as can be. When he helped her into her denim jacket, I sighed—*did Shep ever do that? I don't remember. Sy does, he's always the perfect gentleman. If he's so good—such a good man, such a gentleman— why have I strayed from him? Why are there times when I can't stand be-*

ing around him—almost hating him as much as I love him—why? I don't know that's why. I did the same thing with Shep—except I hated him more because we were married—I felt trapped.

My sigh came out louder than intended, catching the attention of the man seated by the window. I smiled at him; he smiled back as if he wanted to reassure me that life couldn't be so bad to heave such a sigh. He went back to reading; his gold wedding band is a gleaming advertisement of his vowed chastity. I suddenly felt mean. I wanted to disturb him, I wanted to make him question his fidelity—I wanted to rattle him deep into the bones of his faith. I wanted to make him want me—to make him mine—even for just five minutes.

"So, how much for that guy in the window?" Samantha said with a laugh when she arrived with our coffees.

Oh, she's sharp today.

"Window shopping costs nothing—and it's mostly harmless," I laughed a little too loud, as I crossed my legs with a slow, elegant movement, putting them on display for Window Man to see; he looked up over his reading glasses with a bewildered expression, I winked at him, and he blushed and looked away. "So, what's going on with you and Guthrie?" I asked, feeling bold enough to get pay back for her teasing me about the poor unsuspecting man by the window. The fact that she's wearing Guthrie's shirt indicated a certain intimacy. A woman smitten with a man always absconds with a garment belonging to the object of her affections; autism doesn't exempt her from being a woman—smitten or otherwise.

"What? Nothing, he's gone back to Cleveland to stay." Samantha said, taking off her coat and draping it over the back of the chair. "He called this morning to tell me he got a new job."

"Is he in love with you?" I asked, ignoring the smoke screen that she threw in front of the issue motivating my curiosity.

"Yes," she replied without a flinch.

"Damn, I knew it!" I exclaimed, banging my palm on the table; Window Man looked at us again, startled by my noisy victory for having guessed correctly about Sammy's dilemma.

"I feel weird talking about him like this," she sighed; worry lines wiggled over her forehead as she frowned into her coffee, not sipping it yet—a hard lesson learned, especially the unforgettable time with the hot cocoa and a straw. *She's always a disaster waiting to happen.*

"Are you in love with him?" I asked just to cover all the bases.

"Helena!" she exclaimed, whining.

"Come on, you can tell me."

"He says that I'm just infatuated—maybe I am—he can't believe that I'm really in love with him because he's so old and bald," she shrugged, but her eyes didn't meet mine. "I know it's more than infatuation—in here—I feel it," she said, placing her hand over her heart. She looked like she was in pain, and I suddenly felt sorry for her; expressing emotions is like an afterthought for her; they are so black and white, there's little room for ambiguous gray or transitory feelings. Her love/hate sensations are so overwhelming in their passion that she becomes confused like a left-handed person thinking their left hand as their right hand—*your other right.*

"I'm not judging you—cripe, look at what you're living with now—Preston makes Guthrie look like a prize."

"I don't want to talk about this," she muttered to her coffee cup.

"Don't shut down on me—tell me what happened," I prodded her hand with my finger.

Samantha flushed. "I can't talk about this right now," she said through gritted teeth.

"Commme-onnnn!" I coaxed with a persistent whine.

"Well, there's an attraction—it's different." She slowly dragged out the words at that reluctant pace she uses when she feels under duress.

"Merry Christmas, that's for sure!" I laughed.

Window Man got up to leave, and as he passed by our table, I smiled my best smile, and he smiled in return. I blew him a kiss, "Bye, cutie," I said sweetly.

"Bye," he acknowledged my boldness and his face flushed bright red. The man was clearly flummoxed as he departed, he looked over his shoulder a couple of times, nearly running down the folks browsing in the stacks.

"Ohhhhh, you are so cruel," Sam hissed.

"What the fuck, I gave him a thrill; he'll go home and screw his wife's lights out tonight," I laughed.

"Yeah, if she lets him," she snickered.

"Yeah, poor thing, I sure do hope he gets some—he's too fine to leave unattended," I mused. It struck me as odd that it's been awhile since Sy and I have done it; I don't think he even came on to me when I returned from my trip to New York—in fact we haven't done it since the night before I left for New York. *Do you think he knows about Theo?* A low-grade fear muttered inside my head. *Nah, he doesn't know a thing, he's too oblivious.*

"He is in love with me and I'm in love with him. We had to separate before anything happened—but he wants to see me again—soon!" Sammy whispered each word in careful staccato to assure that I didn't miss anything. "And I want to see him too," she added, her hands caressing the sleeves of his shirt.

The shirt! "Merry fucking Christmas!" I cried; my exclamation caught the disapproving attention of the two biddies with the photographs. Sammy blushed deeply and squirmed, her face crumpling with visible discomfort. "Well?" I prodded.

"I don't know what to say—I'm married—" she murmured.

"Oh, yeah, so blissfully," I snorted.

"Still—"

"Has he talked about coming back?"

"Yes, but we need a better reason beyond fucking each other's lights out."

"It was suggested?" I asked, intrigued—however, the visual was repulsive—Guthrie rutting on my little sister was just—*sick.*

"In a fantasy," she asserted with a nod.

"Well, trick or treat—is it Halloween?" I grumbled, not liking any of this at all.

"It was so good seeing him after all these years—I have missed him ever since Lenore died," she sighed with a lovesick tone that made me want to slap some sense into her.

"What happened between you two to make him leave?" I snagged her back from drifting.

"I got into bed with him while he was sleeping and he totally flipped out, so we decided it was best we parted ways before things got—you know— too far."

"That's it, I've heard enough, jeez, Louise, let's get out of here—I need a cigarette!" I cried, bolting out of my chair.

"I thought you quit!" she shrieked after me.

"Fuck that, I started up again weeks ago—as if you would notice, li'l-Miss-I-have-my-head-up-Guthrie's-ass-so-far-I-can't-see-where-I'm-going—" I groaned, walking away from the table without the books I had picked out to buy, leaving Sammy behind to scoop them up. *I can't believe what I just heard; I can't believe that she was the straw to break the camel's back. All right—so he's not as bad as I thought—cripe, Sammy!*

I left the store while Sammy got in line with the stack of books; my hands shook so badly I could barely light the cigarette crimped between my fingers. *What fucking next?* A throat cleared, a cough, and a quiet *"Hello, my name is Martin"* made me look up to see Window Man leaning against the post across from the café window also smoking and looking just as shook up as I felt; we stared at each other like a pair of deer caught in the headlights, and then we smiled.

∾

Cutting through the backyard from the carriage house, I saw Preston's car parked in the driveway. Feeling unnerved because he came home earlier than expected; I walked through the house, tromping extra hard to make sure he knew that I was downstairs rather than upstairs.

"What are you doing home? I wasn't expecting you until tonight," I asked when I found him standing in the bedroom in his underwear, buttoning his shirt.

"Hi, honey, I thought you were in the studio working—I didn't want to disturb you," he smiled and came up to greet me with a quick kiss; he felt sweaty and smelt funny—perfumy.

"Are you happy to see me or is that a one-eyed monster inside yer boxers?" I giggled when I noticed the head of his penis poking through the fly of his shorts.

"Sure, Sammy—I'm always happy to see you," he laughed. "I spilled coffee on my suit—I had to change before going into the office; I have a meeting this afternoon that came up—I didn't mean to disturb you," he said, scowling at his suit that he had left cast aside on the chair. "I didn't even know you were out of the house—where were you?" he asked.

"I just got back from the bookstore with Lena—let me try to clean it— you shouldn't let it sit, especially since you drink coffee with cream—"

"No, no, it's all right—I cleaned it, its fine."

I picked up the jacket and looked at it. "Where's the stain?"

"It's on the pants—look, Sammy—it's fine," he said, plucking the jacket from my hands.

"I don't see anything wrong—" I said, while examining the trousers. When I stepped in close to the slightly rumpled bed to look for the stain in the daylight coming through the window, my foot caught on something that moved and a soft noise emitted from under the bed; I jumped. "What the— there's something down there!" I shrieked.

"It's just the blanket," Preston muttered as he tried to interfere, but not before I found a woman under the bed in nothing but her panties, her large breasts pillowed on top of her clothes clutched in a mangled mess in her hands. I stared at her for a moment—no longer than a heartbeat— but my heart had stopped and started again during that moment—or so it seemed.

"Honey, I can explain." Preston sputtered, tugging on my arm.

"Don't you touch me," I growled at him, jerking my arm out of his grasp, I bent down for a closer look. "I can see you—you're not invisible, tho' I imagine that you wish you were right about now—just get your ass out from under the bed, take your clothes, and get the fuck out of my house," I said with an eerie calm that surprised me. She said nothing, she didn't move; her wide blue eyes didn't dare reflect acknowledgement that I found her. I stepped back to give her some room. "Get out of my house you piece of shit whore!"

"Sam, let me explain," Preston persisted.

"You shut up!" I whipped around, jabbing my finger toward his face— he stopped cold. Behind me, I heard the scrambling chaos of the naked woman extricating herself from under the bed, her bare feet quickly padding down the worn boards of the stairs as she scurried away.

"You've really done it now," he grunted.

"Me? What did I do? You're the one with a woman hiding under the bed. Did you think that you could do this shit in my house and get away with it? I am not stupid, I am not deaf, and I am not blind," I screamed at him, my face burned with mixed emotions, twisted with confusion as shame caused tears to erupt from my eyes.

"What about you and Guthrie, huh? You can't tell me that there wasn't some monkey business going on between you two with all that kissy-face shit going on—I'm not stupid, I'm not deaf, and I'm not blind either. That man is hot for you and it was just about killing him every time you touched him."

"You're doing this bitch in my house because you thought I was screwing around with Guthrie?" I snarled through clenched teeth.

"I've been doing her and many others just like her all along, sweetheart—you are just figuring it out," he sneered.

"I already knew about *them*, dick-stain—get out of my house with your stinking blue-eyed whore—did you think I'm just some retard that you could fool? Did you think you could bang sluts behind my back in MY HOUSE— don't forget this is MY HOUSE—not yours—it's MINE—Whitley left it to me—not to YOU—he didn't trust you—he said my marrying you was a mistake—a BIG MISTAKE—getoutgetoutget OUT!"

"Shut up, you stupid bitch!" He slapped me, and I slapped him back in reaction. He caught my wrist, hauled me around, smacked me in the face again, and threw me onto the bed. When he tried to get on me, I kicked at him, but my feet missed their mark and he slapped me for the third time. "Stop it!" he shouted into my face as he tried to pin my hands down, but this time I shoved him in the chest with my knees, he flew back, landing on his ass. I started to laugh at him because he looked so funny, as if his hard landing must have scrambled his brains a bit. During my amused assessment of him, I realized that he didn't even take his socks off to fuck her—*I hate when he does that with me.*

"Get out of here or I'll call the police," I gasped; picking up the cordless phone, my trembling fingers began to dial the first two numbers—9-1— "I wouldn't want you to miss your meeting this afternoon," I said, narrowing my eyes at him.

Glaring at me, he picked up his clothes and shoes, and left the room without saying another word. I sat on the edge of the bed, waiting until I heard him leave the house, the front door slamming in a wake of curses; the car engine revved as he left the yard. Exhaling deeply, I clicked off the receiver, and then clicked it on again to call Helena.

"Jeez-us, what's up, Sammy, I just saw Preston tearing out of the driveway like he had the Devil in the backseat needing a ride to Hell—"

"Lena—come quick," I said and then clicked off the phone. I sat still; the left side of my face felt hot where he had hit me. When the back door slammed a minute later, I covered my ears.

"Sammy, where are you?" Helena's muffled voice filtered through my hands.

"I'm upstairs!" I screamed so she would hear me.

"What the fuck, Sammy?" she asked, arriving at the bedroom door, out of breath. I looked up at her and dropped my hands away. She stood in the doorway, staring at me in disbelief. "Oh, my god, he hit you, holy shit—that fucking asshole—you've got to divorce him—that bastard has gone too far this time."

9

Boston

Boston. I wouldn't go into the city alone without a good reason. For the last eight years, I've been riding the train on my own to Boston once a week to meet with Will and Marie at the Kramer Gallery, but not today. I already met the Kramer duo on Monday to discuss my new commission to paint Correggio's *Jupiter and Io.*

There is no one to meet for lunch at the university; Helena has been in New York City doing research for Whitley's biography for a couple of days; she promised that she'll be back tonight in time for dinner and maybe we'll go see a movie. *"I'm sorry that I haven't been around lately—I've been busy,"* she said on the phone last night in that funny voice—the *phony voice.* It is phony for its falseness and phony because she only uses it when she talks to me on the phone; the phoniness of the *phony voice* suggests the cover-up of guilt. I think she's fucking someone—the guy from the bookstore perhaps; I saw her exchange phone numbers with him while I stood in line buying her books; both of them were grinning and blushing like foolish teenagers plotting their first date—*he's married!* It's obvious that she doesn't care about Sylvester—*whywhywhy why does she stay with him? He's security that's why—she's not ready to hop to the next available lily pad until she's sure she's got a good one to land on—what a bitch—I hate what she's done to Sylvester, he might not be perfect, but he doesn't deserve that.*

Sylvester is still in Maine tending to Jacob. He replied to my card with a long letter written during the wee hours of the morning after an exhausting day at the hospital. It was apparent that he originally started it as just a note on some stationary he found in his father's desk to express his gratitude that I had thought of him, and to suggest another book for me to read—*My Antonia*. Then he included a second sheet of lined paper that went on to describe memories of his father. He composed the third sheet with memories of his mother; a fourth sheet eventually spoke of his regrets about blaming Jacob for his mother's suicide, which continued onto a fifth sheet where he described the stars and the sound of the surf striking the rocky beach. On the final, sixth sheet he told me about the delicate colors in the sunrise, after that he began to excuse himself with a long goodbye... *"I am tired, dear heart—I must try to sleep before this day begins, but writing to you felt so good to me—I just couldn't stop. I apologize for rambling, but it was as if we've been together having a conversation all through the night—I could clearly see your lovely face in my mind's eye. I miss you, my friend—I will be home soon. All my best, Sylvester. P.S. Please go play with Daisy for me, she loves you!"*

It pleased me that he had poured his heart out on those six sheets of paper—so much said in his spidery longhand—I felt honored and stunned. His letter inspired me to make another card in reply; while composing it, my pencil lines longed to express what I have left unspoken all these years, but only the words *take heart* fumbled from my pencil. When I put it in the mail this morning, I hoped that he would understand. My hands have unfolded and refolded the precious sheets from him several times already this morning, trying to absorb the words, fearing that my card in return fell short. The letter now rides in my coat pocket, and I kept touching it from time to time to make sure it's still there.

My reason for going to Boston today is to meet Guthrie. When we talked on the telephone yesterday morning, he persisted with his need to see me, and I agreed that we should find a way to see each other—*"I'll be there, tell me when,"* he said, his tone fervent, gasping. *"Just come,"* I told him. He called back ten minutes later and said that he'd meet me at the North Station between 11:30 and noon tomorrow—today! *"We'll go to lunch, just to talk—nothing more."* That is what he said. *Lunch and talk* is all we can afford—*nothing more* implies the wistful things that caused our separation—in spite of our feelings, anything more would be too much trouble.

Why did I agree to meet Guthrie in Boston in the middle of February?

When the taxi came to take me to the train station, it occurred to me that there was no one at home to tell where I was going—for the first time ever, no one was watching me. Carrie will be in at about 3PM to start dinner, and I figured I would get home well before Preston put in an appearance should he chose to stop in to pickup more of his things.

Thankfully, the weather is good. I rode all the way to Boston filled with nervous anticipation. I couldn't be quiet even though I consciously made an effort not to make noises or rock, but I can't help it. I know that people stare at me with pity or disgust because they can plainly see there is something wrong with me. The conductor knows me, he is kind and patient, and he feels it is his duty to look out for me, he has asked passengers to yield the seat near where he stands when he spies me waiting to come on board; his fuss often embarrasses me. *"What's this—no sister, no professor—you're all by yourself today? Well, it is too pretty a day to stay inside—it's cold, but it's nice with the sun shinin'—what lousy weather we've been havin' this winter—"* he chortled with his amiable humor that I always liked about him. I agreed that it has been a harsh winter.

Once I stepped off the train at the North Station, the platform was crowded with people; I couldn't see Guthrie anywhere. I half expected that he'd be there waiting at the edge of the platform for the train to stop. I had also hoped to observe him from a distance while he searched the multitude of faces for mine; I wanted to surprise him. However, because of the cold everyone is bundled up and indistinguishable from male or female—at least, the sensible females who knew enough to wear warm clothes on a day like today. The nitwits who skittered around in fashionable shoes and skirts deserve the discomfort they suffer. I dressed sensibly for the weather—a heavy sweater, jeans, SK's laced up past my ankles and my bulky parka with the hood drawn up over my head. I also didn't want to send the wrong message—in spite of the fantasies that I have had for this moment, I didn't want to come here as a prepackaged enticement to tempt him into fulfilling his desires that he has alluded to during our recent telephone conversations that instigated this meeting. The bitter wind that whipped off the steel gray ocean welcomed me with its chilly breath, making my eyes tear and my nose runny. *Oh, how attractive—a snotty nose and watery eyes.* I giggled at my vanity as I wiped my nose on my coat sleeve and my eyes with my mittens. Suddenly, I felt so small in the crowd, and became afraid that he would have trouble finding me. While I wavered with uncertainty, panic started to take hold, so I stood still, my eyes scanning over the people shapes around me—*I can't do this, he'll have to find me—someone will find me.* Then a tall man wearing a navy blue pea-coat standing alone caught my eye; he stood with the *looking for someone* posture, and although he wore a knit cap pulled down over his ears, and dark glasses—I knew his profile and the turned-up collar of his coat failed to hide his familiar moustache. *It's him!*

"Guthrie!" I called out, waving.

He turned to focus on me, smiled, and jogged toward me. "Hey, Button's, is that you? Sorry, honey, you're so swaddled in stuff I didn't recognize you." We twitched forward as if motioning toward an embrace, but we kept our hands riveted inside our pockets—afraid to touch one another—we remained separated by cold air—for now.

"It is you; it always amazes me that you're so tall," I laughed; my body began to quiver, I longed to hug him.

"Yep—it's me." He ducked his head and smiled bashfully. "Let's get out of this shit and get something to eat—do you like chili?"

"Love it." I chattered my teeth, being funny with the pun; he laughed.

"Follow me; we can walk—it's not far from here," he nodded, lowering his gaze. "So, how's it going at home?"

"Okay," I shrugged, not really wanting to talk about the situation at home.

"I'm glad you filed for a divorce—you need to get away from him after that woman under the bed business," he grimaced. "So what does Nasty Jack have to say?"

"He says it will be easy-peasy and there is nothing to worry about, it's an open and shut case, the new judge is a bit conservative, but a fair judge, we just have to give him a chance—but we're in limbo until the judge returns from his vacation in Florida."

"How nice for him," he grunted. "Whitley always said Jack could get anything done."

"I can't wait until this bullshit is over—I guess Preston has given up on playing pin-the-scarlet-letter on me because he has no evidence that I've been unfaithful, but Jack called early this morning to tell me that Preston claims I'm incompetent and can't make decisions for myself—so now everything is on hold until after a competency hearing." It is absurd how something so simple can become so complicated when others from the outside get involved in the decision process—Jack and Jill, then judges, doctors, and social workers. For years, people considered my widely publicized autism a medical novelty because of my talent, and no one ever questioned my successful (and miraculous) autonomy outside of the specialized realm of state-sanctioned education. Now my independence is on trial because I'm trying to divorce a man who never loved me beyond my financial worth to help dig him out of debt.

"Are you afraid, Sam?"

"Yes." When my teeth chattered this time, it seemed to emphasize my fear.

"You have every right to be, I guess," Guthrie nodded, keeping his head down against the wind. "Maybe you shouldn't have come—I would have understood, ya know? I would have figured it out that you weren't on the train and called you at home."

"I needed to see you," I muttered, leaning in close to him, but we still refrained from touching.

We walked with the bitter wind at our backs; it pushed us along, and its persistent whine as it rushed by us made it difficult to talk without screaming "What?" every other sentence, so we gave up trying. With our feet sliding in the slushy snow, I caught hold of his coat sleeve so not to fall; his strong, bare hands grabbed me and kept me upright; we laughed, and he looped his arm around my shoulders, clamping me to his side as we hurried along. Twenty feet later, he pulled me into a doorway where we instantly became engulfed by the warm air filled with the musical mutter of voices and the clatter of plates and silverware. We took off our coats and hung them on the available hooks in the coatroom.

"Hungry?" he asked.

"A little." I wasn't sure if I could eat anything, I was so scared I thought I'd puke.

"Nervous?" he whispered.

"Yeah." I nodded and smiled at him.

"Me too—you're not alone," he said, placing a reassuring hand timidly on my arm, but he let it drop away, his posture sagged as if he were embarrassed.

My nerves jangled just because I'm near him and seeing him for the first time since our passionate kisses in the studio, I didn't know how to act around him—*everything has changed since then*. I looked up at his face, his brooding brow, his stern eyes hooded by shadow and his grimly set mouth framed by his mustache—my heart hammered with apprehensive delight. He wore faded blue jeans, a baggy black turtleneck under a blazer that disguised the little paunch around his middle; I thought he looked thinner. I felt tempted to reach out and pinch his love handles just to check, but I didn't dare. During my study of him, he looked me over with the same hungry assessment; our eyes met, and he ducked his head in response to my gaze; he looked guilty, and I knew that I looked guilty because I still felt bad about what I had done to cause him to leave. The feelings that drove me to climb into bed with him are still there, ready and waiting for me to act on them again. Just as my fascinated hand began to drift toward him, the waitress came and asked us to follow her to a table. Once we sat down, we listened while she began to rattle off the list of specials as she gave us menus and laid down the silverware wrapped in a napkin bundle—I didn't hear a word she said because I was too busy watching Guthrie; he caught my gaze that examined him.

"Okay?" he asked after the waitress left us.

"Yeah, this is fine, it's warm," I smiled, rubbing my arms.

"Yeah, warm—ah-h, Sammy, you are so pretty," he smiled and shook his head. I laughed, feeling too excited to speak. "It's so good to see you—are you growing your hair long?" he asked as his gaze darted from my eyes to look at my hair and then toured over every inch he could see of me.

"Yeah—Helena keeps trying to get me to cut it, but I keep telling her 'no'—Sylvester told her to leave me alone—that really got her panties in a twist—she really has a thing about hair—his especially drives her nuts," I giggled. Thinking about Sylvester's shaggy, dirty-blond hair with its streaks of gray suddenly made me so happy I felt myself blushing, and shyly glanced at Guthrie. I loved the sculpted contours of his skull, I mentally noted that if he kept his remaining hair trimmed it would put more emphasis on the shape of his head rather than the lack of hair on top, he would look so much better, but I refrained from saying anything.

"I'm not so pretty." He noted my study of him with a smirk, as if reading my mind he self-consciously ran his hand over his baldhead to the fringe of hair in the back.

"Men aren't supposed to be pretty—that's just wrong," I laughed, feeling giddy. Helena didn't think he had aged too gracefully, but I don't care—it is the heart of the man I want—the part that makes him *Guthrie*—to me, he is perfect. "It's so good to see you." I reached across the table and grasped his hands that were still cold from being outside; he eagerly enclosed my small hands within them—captured. He stared at our joined hands as if marveling over the miracle of them in spite of their ravaged, chapped appearance due to the harsh elements of the weather and labors in our respective studios.

"Do you need a little time yet?" The waitress asked; both of us twitched, startled by her being there, and our hands slithered away from each other like sneaky creatures trying not to be noticed, though we knew by her smirk that she noticed, but apparently wasn't surprised.

"Yeah, just a few, thanks, ummm—let's order our food so we can—you know—talk," he said, prodding me to look at my menu by taking up his. I only nodded in reply as I picked up the menu in front of me. I saw that he was playing trombone with his until he plucked his reading glasses out of his blazer pocket and put them on; I sneaked a quick peek and thought he looked nice wearing them. As if he sensed my peeking, he then made a noise in his throat as if to encourage a comment. When I pretended to drag my eyes away from the menu, and found him looking at me over the tops of his glasses, he wore a stern *I dare you to laugh* expression on his face. I smiled, and without making a peep, I let my gaze fall back to the menu page as if there was a big choice to make between the chili and a sandwich.

Guthrie's insecure vanity made me think of Sylvester and the way he wore his glasses with dignity; taking them off was like stripping him naked—vulnerable. I would kiss his exposed eyelids as he lay beside me in the bed. As my kisses loitered over his face, he'd remain quiet; a phantom smile would curve his lips to express his silent pleasure, and then I would kiss that smile, first at the center and then each corner because there is a sweet curve to his upper lip that I loved—*loved, adored, and treasured.* I have drawn that beautiful element, often the simple line left alone on a blank sheet. *Take heart—dear heart.* I bit my lower lip against the sick feeling that lingered within my stomach. Suddenly, it was all I could do to remain in my seat, and focus on the menu. I wished that I had the letter in my purse instead of my coat pocket and feared that it would become lost in the coatroom.

The waitress returned to take our order; Guthrie asked for chili, and I decided on the gumbo just to be different—to assert my independence from him, because when I was little I would always order the same food that he would order just to taste what he tasted—somehow my mimicking him brought him closer to me. *Gumbo is something Sylvester would order.* I asked for tea and he decided to get a pitcher of beer. After the waitress left, we sat for a moment in silence; the surrounding noise felt oppressive. I looked around, taking in the restaurant, the walls, pictures, waitresses flitting around balancing heavy trays, and the other people seated nearby. No one seemed to notice us, the May-December couple sitting on the edges of our booth seats, trying not to be seen.

"Did you come all this way to stare at the walls?" he asked, putting away his glasses.

"Sorry—I don't mean to disappoint you—I had hoped you would be disappointed because I think you forget how I am—my reality isn't your fantasy." I purposefully spoke about our reality to ground the euphoria revving our pulses to inhuman speeds.

"Now why are you talking like that?" he asked, his brow rising, and his eyes became bright with curious surprise.

"I've just been anticipating disasters—this is so weird."

"Yeah, weird, ummm—damn," he sighed, shaking his head. "It is good to see you—" he said with an eager smile.

"I'm afraid that I can't stay too long—I want to be home just in case Preston shows up at the house," I said, chewing on my lower lip. The fact that Preston hasn't completely moved out since I filed for divorce is a touchy subject that caused tension during our last telephone conversation, and I hoped he wouldn't start in on it again.

"Didn't you tell him you were going to Boston?" Guthrie asked with a low tone, leaning forward onto his elbows. "Not that it's any of his business what you do anymore," he scowled.

"I doubt you told your former significant other anything," I shot at him feeling harassed.

"I told her I was driving to Boston. When she asked me what for, I told her none of her damn business," he grumbled.

"Oh, that's nice—no wonder you're divorced," I laughed, feeling disappointed that we're going to bicker over this sort of crap.

"Hey, you don't live with her," he lowered his voice and ducked his head.

"And you don't live with Preston," I reminded him.

"Don't forget, I lived under the same roof for a little over a month and that was long enough," he said with a chuckle.

With his mouth tucked underneath his mustache, it's hard to see what his lips are doing—smiling or frowning. I stared at his mouth; it seemed as if his normal frown had deepened into a grimace of despair. I dared myself to look into his eyes, and the conflict raging within their blue made me sad for him. Seeing him like this reminded me of the old pictures of him without his mustache, how his exposed mouth appeared sensitive, and his pensive brow seemed to overwhelm his young face; the mustache created harmony, hiding his mouth's true emotional response—*but no, I can see*. Just like Sylvester's mouth, I have examined Guthrie's with pencil on paper; I have studied its subtle nuances that are lost behind the thick curtain of hair.

"I haven't forgotten, but I thought perhaps you have," I sighed. My gaze became downcast with disappointment in his selfishness.

"No—I haven't forgotten—I'm sorry, Button's." He held his hands out to me, but I refused to fill them with my hands. "Look—Sammy, I don't want us to get defensive and start building walls around us. It doesn't have to be this way." He sat back with a sigh and rubbed his face with a pass of his hands. "There's nowhere for my emotions to go in this because I know there's no way this will work—you understand that don't you?" he asked as if admitting defeat.

"I know. So why are we here?" I asked, feeling the confusion that has been sloshing around in my brain for several weeks beginning to solidify inside my guts.

"I don't know. I hoped we could see each other—" he stammered with the sound of misgivings. "I just needed to see you, I have missed you," he sighed with frustration.

His gaze shifted with internal discomfort, and suddenly my heart leapt with realization.

"You know what is wrong with us? It's the being in the same space that has us freaked out." My finger stroked the back of his hand where he left it lying on the table limp with hopelessness. I love this familiar patch of Guthrie; I have drawn his hands to memorize them—I have become intimate with his hands. "I'm a little buggy-boo creepy-crawling on you..."

❧

Being in the same space—yeah, that hits the nail square on the head. After her fingers danced over the back of my hand, she quickly withdrew and tucked her hand away when the pitcher of beer and the cup of tea arrived. I examined her closely while I filled my glass; the poor girl is shaking like a leaf because she's scared out of her mind, other than that, so far, she seems pretty normal—well, normal for Sammy. Hell, she's better than I ever imagined she'd turn out. Much of her success is due to Hayden's patient influence.

Hayden.

The stream where we spent hours fishing was an ideal conduit for finding out his story—but in spite of his openness with me, he maintained a cloak of Puritan privacy. We mostly shared stories about Whitley and his paternal influence on us, which lead to a conversation about the maternal absence from our lives because of the sudden passing of our mother's, and the saint-like reverence in which we covet memories of them. After I inquired about how his mother had died, he hesitated at first and then cleared his throat. *"Suicide,"* he muttered. I offered my sympathy, but he waved it off with a vague gesture as he cast his line into the water. *"For years I blamed my father—and I blamed myself for not being home when it happened. We should have been more vigilant because of her chronic depression—she was always so frail in spite of her inner strength—we never thought in a million years that she'd take her life.*" Those were his last words on the subject, and I let the conversation flow away with the stream. I got the sense that the soft-spoken New England gentleman took after his mother and that fact disturbed him.

Every now and then, he'd tell me a story about Sammy; he always spoke of her with such reverence. It made me uncomfortable to see the way his face would redden because of something that he left unsaid in a story, he'd fumble over the memory as if he couldn't recall the details, then he'd grow quiet and drop into a melancholy hole; I figured *that something* had to do with his sexual relations with her. He never told me about his affair with Sammy—and I never asked. I imagine he feels weird about it—possibly ashamed, for good reason he should be. When I asked her about how things started between them, she supplied the gory details with unblinking candor that made me regret asking. I don't blame him for not wanting to tell me about it. It was all I could do not to lambaste him when I found out that he fucked her when she was only sixteen, but I let it go—for Sammy. I sat down at the dinner table that night and pretended I knew nothing. I should have won an Academy Award for my performance. Although I understood the situation better after listening to her hypnotic rationalization for seducing him, my overall respect for him dropped to its knees. Yet, I respected his painfully obvious feelings for her, which in turn made me want to knock some sense into him—*good grief, if he's in love with Sammy, he should just tell Helena to get lost, and take care of business. But I guess it isn't that simple, nothing ever is.*

When she reached over to caress my hand resting on the table, I understood his feelings perfectly—she isn't making it easy for me to look the other way; the wayward accumulation of lust is testing my resolve. I leaned forward in my chair, and studied her hand on mine. I still can't get over how much like Lenore she is—she used to do the same thing, subtle little touches, teases, and temptations, but I would always withhold my response for the right moment. Sammy's dark brown hair with a fringe of bangs that covered her forehead just above her eyebrows framed a pale face that had the essence of her mother in every feature. Now looking at her up-close, I can see the wear and tear of stress on her face—horizontal worry lines on her brow and dark circles under her eyes; she's thin, perhaps a little too thin. She looks like someone who has been hiding out in a studio for years—unlike Lenore who jogged every morning and sunbathed; her skin held a golden brown tint almost year round.

Lenore would come to meet me for lunch dressed to the nines, and she'd turn heads everywhere we went. I never touched her in public; I'd walk beside her, but always a half step behind. Everyone notices Sammy's natural beauty first; then they thoughtfully narrow their eyes as if trying to pinpoint what's wrong with the picture before them. She looks normal enough, but if you put a level on the picture frame the evidence becomes clear that she ain't hung straight—or maybe the canvas itself is crooked—whatever it is, something's not right, and from a distance it is troubling enough to spoil the image of a pretty girl.

We sat in silence, struggling to find something to talk about other than the weather; I wanted to tell her that I had a room, but I didn't dare. Although I feel emotionally drawn to her, I began to chastise myself for thinking about her coming back to the hotel with me. I had to remind myself that this young woman was the child I had once believed to be my daughter—but she's not a child anymore—nor is she my daughter.

Who is she to me now? Dunno.

Since I left Gloucester, we've exchanged tender words laden with desire over the telephone, and we've playfully suggested sexual encounters to fulfill fantasies—*or was it just me making the suggestions and she just giggling?* Sitting here with her, I feel like a scumbag in comparison; I've become obsessed with her in a way that has become unwholesome. She innocently came here to meet me, and all I can think about is taking her back to the hotel and fucking her eyeballs out. *This is wrong.*

For some unknown reason, Sammy burst out laughing and started to cough. I pushed her water glass closer to her and watched quietly as she gulped it down to soothe her troubled throat.

"Jeez, Luiz, I hate when I inhale spit, I thought I was gonna bust a lung," she gasped.

Actually, I was more afraid she was going to toss her cookies, but I didn't say so. She is very nervous and I felt sorry for her. *Where the fuck is our food?* As soon as I turned to look for the waitress, our food arrived and without ceremony, we started to eat.

"How is it?" I asked.

"Very good. Have you been here before?"

"Yeah—I used to come here a lot with a friend while I was in school." I spilled the words out of my mouth and then shoved a spoonful of chili in to stick the rest left unsaid in between my teeth, and then I proceeded to endure the searing fresh-from-the-pot temperature in silence.

"Oh," she said, staring into the bowl before her, poking around the thick broth with her spoon. The way she said that left me wondering if she didn't believe me. "How is work?"

"It's a job at a retail frame shop—the money stinks more than the hours. How's your work coming along?" I said after I swallowed the mouthful of molten spice.

"All right, it's quiet now that Valentine's Day is past—do you know how many images of Venus and Cupid I've had to do over the years? It's absurd. Easter is coming up—I expect that will inspire someone to ask me to do some famous dying, dead, resurrected Jesus pictures."

"Ohhhh—so, there is a holiday pattern, I always wondered about that," I chuckled.

"Yeah—like greeting cards, last fall I painted *The Last Supper* for Thanksgiving—it's just wrong I tell ya! I'm getting tired of it."

"If you're tired of doing commissions why don't you just start painting something that's yours—you must have things that you want to paint," I said this out of curiosity; wondering if she ever followed through on the scribbles in her sketchbooks. It was easy for me to visualize the intricate organic patterns that are reminiscent of art nouveau forms becoming something more. The hands and features of people growing or rather metamorphosing from a chrysalis of lines—it is easy for me to envision watercolor bleeding over a saturated paper surface, curling like mist in the sky around the moon and stars—if I can see it, she must.

Years ago, I had a student when I was teaching at Syracuse—Katharine—she painted scrolls several feet long, they were breathtaking—I would give anything to have Sammy see one of those; she'd love them more because they were inspired by Beethoven's music. *Good grief, Syracuse—that's forever ago—that's where I met Millie.* Millie, the weird, big-hearted girl with whom I had a steady affair during the short time I spent in Upstate New York. She had been good for me—weird, but good—being with Millie was the closest I had come to falling in love with someone after Lenore died. When I got the job at Pratt, I wanted to ask her to come with me, but chickened out—she was too young. Millie came looking for me three years later, but I was already hooked-up with my first wife—a model who I carelessly knocked-up because I thought she was on 'the pill'. *"I never said I was on 'the pill'—I don't believe in messing with my body's chemistry like that,"* were her famous last words that sent us to the altar. The temptation to fuck Millie dragged me to the edge of a hotel bed, but before things became hot n' sticky between us, she told me that she was pregnant with Eugene Riley's baby, and was scared out of her wits about it. I immediately backed away from the edge of that bed and told her to go home and sort it out; although I felt sorry for her, I didn't want any part of that shit.

Disturbed by my wandering thoughts, I focused on Sammy again.

"...I never get a break from the commissions; there's always about five waiting for me while I'm working on one," she said, sounding a bit disgruntled with the production process into which Whitley had pigeon-holed her since she was a little girl.

"Tell the Kramer's you need to do something for yourself—can't you take time off from it? Take a year off—take two years off even—you can afford it, right?"

"I have tried, Guthrie, but I can't—there isn't anything I want to paint," she said sadly.

"I do not believe that—and neither should you—you have more to offer as an artist than the miniatures." I stumbled over the word *miniatures*—I almost said *copies*—that would have sent her off into a tirade, she hates it when someone refers to her work as copies (only she can do that). I was even pushing my luck saying *miniatures*—that was too close to saying *mini-forgeries*, which some snobby curator had said about her work once. Cringing, I dared to look at her, but she seemed unruffled.

"A man from Chatham has commissioned Correggio's *Jupiter and Io*—that's a new one for me, so I'm making it bigger than normal—it feels good to paint something and have room to move around," she said with a hopeful tone as if painting something else from the art historical greatest hits list is a treat.

"That Jupiter, I don't know what he thought he was getting away with; Juno was no dummy—that goddess could smell another woman on him before he walked through the temple door," I laughed from experience— my wives always knew—Lenore always knew when Whitley had been with someone. I took a hearty spoonful of my chili. "This chili is hot," I mumbled with a slurp, while wondering if I would know if she's been sleeping with Hayden again—*has she gone visiting him through the Rose of Sharon hedge lately?* Jealousy seized me by the throat and I had a hard time swallowing my pride along with my chili. She told me that he had stayed with her that night after I left—*would she tell me if he did more than "sit" with her?*

"How are Hayden and Helena?" I inquired to satisfy my nagging curiosity.

"Sylvester is in Maine—Jacob is dying; Helena is in New York today— or so she says," she rolled her eyes. "She's been screwing some guy she picked up in the bookstore a couple of weeks ago—she must think I'm stupid to not see it—I think the only guy in Gloucester she hasn't fucked is Preston."

"She didn't fuck me!" I feigned shock.

"Lucky you," she laughed. "So—what are your plans after lunch?" she asked as she scraped the last drops from her bowl.

"Ummm—nothing," I muttered, feeling angry with myself for thinking that I had any right to be jealous. *So what if she is screwing Hayden—I should be happy about it; they should be together—I'd offer to give her away at the wedding because it would be the right thing to do.*

"Are you driving back to Cleveland tonight?"

I swallowed hard. "No—I ummm—I got tomorrow off from work, I'm staying over in a hotel; it's been a long drive—I started to drive here after I got out of work last night, I got in at about six in the morning—I haven't gotten much sleep—" I couldn't look at her. She sat there staring me down, her eyes prying into my soul as if trying to root out what I don't want to tell her. Suddenly, I felt angry with myself for my indecent thoughts aiming to get her into bed. *Am I that transparent?* Is she looking into my guilty conscience and seeing my strategic plan so blatantly spelled out that I might as well have been wearing a sign around my neck reading, *"PLEASE FUCK ME, I'M HORNY!"*

"You got a room?" she asked, scraping the last molecule of gumbo from the bottom of the bowl—*any minute now she'll start using her finger to get what the spoon missed.*

"Yeah." My heart skipped a beat; I stared into my chili unable to eat it, waiting for what she was getting at—I suddenly felt very tired.

"Did you plan to invite me over?" she asked, licking her finger.

I dropped my spoon and it clattered against the side of the bowl loudly. "No," I lied.

"Whew—I thought you wanted me to sleep with you!" she laughed, licking another finger that swabbed out more leftover broth. Now it's my turn to choke, a fragment of skin from a kidney bean became stuck to the sensitive tissue at the back of my throat; I hacked fiercely, and then drank some beer to wash it down. Looking at her through watery vision, I saw immediately that she was kidding and we both burst out laughing.

"Startled you didn't I?" she snorted.

"Sure did," I chuckled, and then coughed into my fist. "You don't have to," I mumbled, feeling embarrassed; the people seated around us were checking us out, this sort of attention I didn't want.

"We're just going there to talk, right?" she asked, tilting her head.

"If that's all you want to do, that's all we're going to do; I won't lay a finger on you."

"I see, you want me to make the first move."

"Sammy—" I sighed, feeling uneasy; I looked around to make sure no one was paying attention to us; it seemed as if the interested parties have returned to their meals.

"Guthrie—I didn't fall off the turnip truck yesterday," she laughed, parroting my famous last words from a long time ago—goes to show that she was really listening to Lenore and me when we had our lover's spats. "Don't try to tell me that you drove all the way from Cleveland just to have a bowl of chili and say *howdy.* This is the restaurant where you used to bring Lenore after meeting her at the North Station; you were looking for me in the place where she used to wait for you to pick her up—and the hotel is probably the same one where you two spent many afternoons together screwing until your dick nearly fell off, right?"

"Oh-god," I moaned, rubbing my eyes, now I really felt like a scumbag.

"What oh-god? Happy Valentine's Day, Guthrie, I only do what I want to do—you're not going to force me to have sex with you if I don't want to," she said softly while her fingers caressed the contours of my knuckles with seductive slowness.

"Do you want to?" I asked around the lump that conflicted with my breathing.

"Yes and no—there's a part of me that is intrigued by this whole thing. While coming out here to meet you, I racked my brains trying to figure out what I would do if you set it up for us to have sex in a cheesy motel. I might go in there and throw myself at you because I'm dying for affection from someone who really loves me—or at least says he does in some form."

"It's the Wyndham," I said, feeling offended that she'd think I'd put up in a cheap dive.

"Okay, so it's not a motor-lodge in East Boston," she smirked, rolling her eyes.

"I do love you, but I would never force you into anything you don't want to do. I gotta tell ya, I don't trust my emotions right now. It might be for the best that we part here. I'll walk you to the North Station to see you off, okay?" I gulped down the last of my beer, wadded my napkin, and picked up the check, squinting at the typical waitress scrawl with a smiley face following the total that I was vainly struggling to see. I felt wretched. *I don't think I can continue with this relationship without—without what? Her—without having her. I'm a fool, I should walk out of here and never see her again, somehow that would be all right—it would have to be.*

"Hey." She grabbed my hand and took the check away from me. "I know you love me, as much as I know I love you. Know what? I am terrified and happy. My instinct is to go with you to your room and see what happens—do you know what I mean?" she whispered.

I knew exactly what she meant. Our kisses in the garret laid the foundation weeks ago; I have mentally groped this woman since our separation, so now I have high hopes that we might get in there—*alone at last*—and pick up where we left off. Just like I did with Lenore.

"What do you want to do?"

"Let's go to your room and see what happens," she shrugged.

❧

In spite of my collection of fears, I went willingly; it was the only way to find out for sure what would happen between us. I watched him fumble with the key in the lock and knew that he suffered from similar doubts. I knew that Sylvester always suffered with nervous expectation that was overeager to satisfy his pent-up urges, but I knew that he also enjoyed the anticipation—I saw it when he smiled, and those little crinkles would form around his eyes. I imagined that Guthrie would be different from Sylvester, different from Preston—with different expectations—different desires—*differentdifferent-different*. This difference scares me a little.

Guthrie opened the door and stepped aside so I could go first. With a runway model spin, I looked around the room, sat down on the nearest bed, and bounced lightly on the mattress when my bottom hit it—*this feels so unnatural—so unprepared.*

"This is nice!" My exclamation seemed too loud—too unreal, insincere.

"It's okay," he said quietly, leaning against the dresser with his arms folded across his chest. He's been quiet since we left the restaurant; neither of us could speak until now. The air around us is charged with our nervous energy; I felt like jumping on the beds, making a lot of noise and then becoming so still, so quiet, silent, silent, silent—just to lie beside him in silence, our heartbeats filling our ears with their mortal rhythm. Whether we have sex or not is irrelevant.

Feeling warm, I realized that I was still wearing my coat, as was he. Taking my coat off, I laid it on the bed. He picked it up and put it on a hanger, and then he removed his coat and hung it up. After what seemed like an excessive struggle to hang the two coats, and then a brief delay while he fussed with light switches, he finally returned to stand in front of me with his hands on his hips and his head down; he couldn't look at me. I went to him and placed my cold hands on his cheeks—he felt feverish.

"You are so tall," I said, looking up into his face—the face that I have loved all my life. There is no question in my mind that I do love him.

He smiled and laughed a little. "Yeah, I am tall—you're a peanut."

"Kiss me, Guthrie," I begged, rising up on my tiptoes, straining to reach him.

"Sammy, you don't have to," he sighed, resisting by turning his face away.

"Please, kiss me—I want you to." I slipped my arms around his neck, tugging on him to my level. We kissed timidly on the lips, and then his hands slid around my shoulders and down my back as he pulled me close. We kissed again a little more bravely this time, yet still uncertain, as if we were out of practice. Then we eagerly lingered in a heartfelt kiss that was no longer self-conscious. Sighing, we embraced one another and laughed.

"There, that wasn't so bad," I said, cuddling against his chest, my arms looped around his waist as he held me tighter. I could feel his heart beating against my cheek.

"That was pretty nice," he agreed with a chuckle.

Kissing again, we lay down together; his hands shyly slipped inside my sweater as he began to caress my skin, I prickled all over with goose bumps. Then he leaned over me, and with a gasp, he pressed his hips against mine and I could feel the hard warmth inside his denim crotch against my inner thigh. When the thin sliver of flesh between my legs responded with a pleasant twinge, I spread my legs to allow him to rub against me in the right spot, and so we moved together, our blue jeans offering resistance that was maddening; our kisses deepened as we moaned in our passionate communion—pressing, touching.

"Oh-my-god, Sammy," he grunted. Then with deep exhales, we abruptly sat up and fell apart—moved aside in a mutual denial—unable to follow through with our desires.

❧

"Are you all right?" I asked; I thought my heart had stopped, but no, it's still going lickety-split in my chest as per normal.

"I'm okay, and you?" she whispered, her pale face is now glowing with a flush as if I had breathed new life into her.

"I'm fine—ummm," I started to say something, but I didn't know what.

"Where are we going, Guthrie?" her hand touched my shoulder.

"I don't know—as much as I want you, I can't do this with a clear conscience. I respect you too much to just bang you for an afternoon, put you on a train, and send you on your way home—I think I'd go completely mad if I did that." I said this with a strong conviction; at least my relationship with Lenore taught me that I could never play second fiddle to another man in a woman's heart—this time it will be all or nothing—before I can become physically involved with her, I need to be sure there is nothing happening between her and Hayden.

"Having sex would be making a physical commitment we can't keep—we have to go home when we're done, and end up feeling more miserable than we did when we left home. Maybe after my divorce is final, we'll be okay," she said.

I kept my mouth shut; although she's pretty much in concurrence with my feelings about this, it's obvious to me that her perception of our situation is different—*she's denying Hayden's importance. Am I a substitute for him because he won't leave Helena? What if Helena leaves him someday, will that change everything?* We lay on the bed side-by-side and stared up at the whiteness of the ceiling; it stared down at us unconcerned with our trivial dilemma.

"We're doing this for all the wrong reasons," I said finally, just to break the silence.

"Yes, we are," she replied, nodding.

"Yup," I echoed for the lack of anything else to say.

"We are so pathetic!" she laughed, rising up on her elbow to look down at me.

"Oh, yeah, that just about says it," I chuckled, hugging her.

"I should go now," she said, sitting up; my arms that had just gathered her close dropped away, setting her free.

"All right." I agreed. "I'll drive you home—it's silly that you should take the train."

❧

He parked the car and we took a walk on Good Harbor Beach. I insisted that I didn't mind walking home from the beach, so he agreed after some persuasion. We stood down by the empty shore on the hard packed sand, just facing each other with our hands clasped tightly together. My fingers were spread so wide apart to accommodate his large fingers interlaced between mine that the fragile dry skin in between them began to crack from the stress.

"It was great to see you again," he said.

"Yeah, it was a good day—I really had a good day," I nodded.

"We should do it again sometime."

"Sure, I'd like that," I agreed. "I miss you already."

"If you miss me too much call—we can always talk—I know you hate the telephone, but it's better than nothing, right?"

"Yes, but I need to see you—to touch you." I cradled his cold hand to my cheek and my heart took a sickening roll and dive.

"I won't get a room next time—that was such a bad idea," he said, shaking his head.

"No—actually, it was a good thing; we learned from it—if we didn't, we'd go crazy wondering *what if* all the time—we needed it."

"Yeah, whatever—I'd still like to fuck your lights out someday, but only when the timing is right," he said with a naughty laugh.

"Yeah, well, someday," I snickered at his cheap-ass-ghetto comment as I flung myself into his arms. We kissed hard, our front teeth banged together in our haste.

"I love you," he sighed, backing away from me.

"I love you too," I murmured, taking a step backward of my own.

With this last admission, we said goodbye with the same awkward grace with which we greeted one another earlier today. Wiping tears from my eyes, I walked away, feeling his gaze on my back as I headed for home. I knew that if I looked back I would have begged him to come home with me, so I pulled my hood around my face and tried to resist the painful tears. Upon approaching the driveway, I decided to go to the carriage house to play with Daisy, my hand wiggled out of its wooly mitten and my fingers caressed the folded letter in my pocket.

Why is it when I do the right thing I always feel like I did the wrong thing? I didn't move until I saw her crossover to go down the street toward the house; relief and anxiety tormented me when I lost sight of her, so I walked up to the corner to watch her turn into the driveway. She never looked back, which was just as well. My gaze continued to follow her green winter coat shape through the denuded bushes as she skipped along, then her path jagged to the left, going toward the carriage house. I remember in the mix of her chatter that she had mentioned going there to play with Hayden's cat because he asked her to.

Getting behind the wheel a few minutes later, I wiped my eyes with the heels of my palms, turned the key, and pointed Delta Dawn onto the first road heading out of town—back to Cleveland—I'll sleep somewhere along the way if I need to, but I doubt that I will.

10

The Fractured Hues of White Light

It is a beautiful day. From the place where I am lying, I can see through the studio window to the outside. Even with fractured awareness, I observed the morning light as it changed from twilight blue to pearl dawn, and now I'm watching the crystallized air shimmer with the movement of an ocean breath. I sighed, rubbing my thin arms inside the bathrobe; my body ached and I needed to pee, but I didn't want to go downstairs until I knew Preston was gone. Last night, he arrived from work with his two sullen sons in tow, which caused Carrie to scramble in the kitchen to adjust her menu because she wasn't expecting them. *He said he was here to pack more of his things—he'll be gone in the morning.* I closed my eyes to wait for the right noises. Although he has recently moved into an apartment in Boston, Preston has not moved out all of his things yet. *Because he still has hope.* Lately, he's been begging me to forgive him; his *turning the corner* rhetoric also repeated by his lawyer, Jill, to Jack. Jack brought this plea to my attention, he said, according to Jill, Preston is on medication for depression and undergoing therapy—"*She says he's having a hard time adjusting.*" I made it clear that Preston's *turning the corner or having a hard time adjusting* is not going to change anything—especially because of the way I feel about him. I simply want him out of my life, and I have asked Jack to do everything he can to make it so.

Ah! There's the sound I've been waiting for. I opened my eyes again after I heard Preston's car leave, but I couldn't move because I feel broken; lying on the floor felt safe for the time being, not moving at all feels like bliss. My face prickled like a reminder—*what happened?* I laughed out loud upon realizing how my life is mirroring Guthrie's—his ex-wife is still living with him. They co-exist by staying out of each other's way, which is easy enough to do when they work different hours. *"I work late afternoons and evenings, so I leave the house before she gets home from work, and I come home long after she's gone to bed. I often stop for a few beers at the bar with my friends just to be sure that I avoid her—"* he chuckled into my ear over the telephone when we last spoke the other night. *Guthrie!*

"Samantha?" A distant voice called out; I opened my bleary eyes in reaction to the voice—*have I been sleeping?*

"Leave me alone," I muttered, my gaze began to rove around the studio—*what a mess—what has happened?* The tiny panel mimicking Correggio's *Jupiter and Io* lay on the floor—of course, it had landed face down like the peanut-butter side of the bread. My brushes are scattered like a game of pick-up sticks, and there are puddles drying on the floorboards that smell like turpentine—*it is turpentine.* I am thankful that the *Ghent Altarpiece* is long gone and avoided the early morning disaster that had befallen me. I have missed it; its absence has left an empty hole in the area it had occupied for so many weeks, and the associations with it that remind me of a time in my life that has passed: *Whitley dying, Guthrie coming home, and Guthrie leaving.*

Guthrie. My gaze landed on a crumpled card depicting a sentimental sunset with a couple walking on a beach holding hands, it stood out like a stark accusation; its surface scarred by abuse. I reached for it, but my fingertips only nudged it, causing it to lightly rock on its edge, then it fell over so that I could no longer see the picture, but I caught a glimpse of Guthrie's block-print penmanship inside. *Guthrie!*

The garret door opened. "Sammy, are you up here?" A voice asked as timid footsteps creaked on the stairs.

"Go away!" I pressed myself against the floor, wanting to seep through the gaps between the planks to hide. The sound of my heartbeat became arrhythmic with fear. *Oh, Guthrie!*

"Jesus, Samantha, what's this about—Boston—he met you in Boston, when did you go to Boston?" Preston crumpled the card and threw it across the room, it bounced off the wall and came back at him, and then he stomped on it with disgust as if trying to kill a cockroach. *"That man is a scheming*

piece of shit—he's after your money! He came sniffing around here as soon as your old man died to see if he had anything coming to him—when he got nothing, he went after you. It's because of him that we're in this fix isn't it? We were fine until he came along."

"*You know nothing—Whitley left Guthrie plenty of money—and no, we weren't fine before or after Guthrie got here! I do not love you, Preston—I don't even like you, we're not even friends—we never were—if anyone came sniffing around looking for money, it was you—*" I had kept my voice level—a notch past monotone. They were practiced words, he's heard them before—Jack has heard them, Jill has heard them, but the new judge deciding our case has yet to hear them because he's in Florida while I lie here freezing to death waiting for him to get his ass back to Gloucester.

Preston leaned against the doorway, insisting that I am not able to make the independent decision to divorce him because I'm *mentally handicapped.*

"*Your father had arranged our marriage.*"

"*Whitley only arranged that we should meet, but I was allowed to make the independent decision to get married—if I am incapable of making such a decision wouldn't that make our vows null and void?*" I laid this fact down like a trump card between us; he frowned.

"*No—he consented on your behalf when I asked him for your hand,*" he argued.

"*You make it sound so gallant—I'm glad you don't feel Whitley held a gun to your head and told you to marry me because he caught you with your hand in my panties. That sort of consent you're suggesting would have been put in writing—but you can't show me that, because there isn't such a document—it was just between you and me. I was taken in by your charm—you put on such a good show, you had me convinced that you were sincere. There was a time when I wanted to love you—I wanted to believe in you, but it was all a lie—you don't love me at all.*" When I said this, he shut up—for a little while. Then he began to make wild accusations about Whitley's manipulation; he accused Helena of being a conniving, money-grubbing bitch, who had nothing better to do than to meddle in our life, and Dr. Sylvester Hayden is in league with her—he may as well be the Devil, sitting beside me whispering lies in my ear.

"*Pursuing this ridiculous claim that I am incompetent will only make you look like a predator—and that is what you are.*" I spoke with moderate gentleness, hoping to make him see that his quest is going to go nowhere.

"*You never gave me a chance,*" he sighed with a pathetic quiver in his throat—I've heard this before, quiver and all. I'm not the only one practicing a speech. "*Guthrie Ryder comes back like the prodigal son and is welcomed here in spite of what he did to this family—while I get nothing—not even a chance to prove myself.*"

"*I've given you plenty of chances. I find it amazing that you think you're so above him with your morals—I catch you with a naked woman hiding under the bed and you think I'm a whore for meeting Guthrie in Boston for lunch—*"

"*I never accused you of having an affair—you jumped to that conclusion all by yourself—must be you're guilty of something,*" he snarled.

"*You did accuse me—it was the first thing out of your mouth that day I caught Ms-Blue-Eyes-with-Big-Knockers under the bed!*" Funny thing, I was less disturbed about him accusing me of doing something with Guthrie, than I was afraid of him thinking of Sylvester. All through this conversation, I kept my eyes averted away from the board above my drafting table where I have images of Sylvester posted—his lean face with sensitive lips, his hands with long fingers, and his firm ass. Preston began to yell at me, I guess he sensed that I wasn't listening.

"*Oh, shut up—you're being over-dramatic.*" I gave him a shove.

"*What did you just say?*" He looked at me with such a stunned expression I laughed.

"Sammy, are you all right—what happened?" The voice asked just as hands touched me.

"Nooooo—noooooo, go away, don't touch me!" I grappled with the hands.

I slapped his face. His hand clapped against my cheek so hard, my head snapped to the side. I staggered away, reeling, but he caught my wrists, his hands practically crushing the bones; my feet struck out at his shins. Growling, he hauled me by the arms, shoving me face first onto the drafting table, causing my work to scatter across the floor; then grabbing me by the hair, he pounded my head against the tabletop; stars erupted in my darkened vision.

My consciousness wavered like a thin veil between him and me until he forcibly ripped into me, thrusting through my body's resistance, a brutal grinding, pushing, raw, burning; the side of my face and breasts smashed against the unforgiving hardwood, the rigid table edge rubbed an excruciating indentation into my belly and hipbones. When he finished with a satisfied moan, his hand slapped my buttocks in rhythm with his pelvis as he made a few more thrusts against me, and then he gave my flesh a tender caress as he pulled out and stepped away. Set free, I screamed into my hands unable to articulate my agony; his leavings dribbled from my sputtering vagina as if it too felt shocked by his attack. Dizzy and weak, I gripped the table, my entire body convulsing with tremors, my vision fading into a gray fog.

"There now—that was good, wasn't it? We haven't had a good fuck like that in a long time—it reminds me of our wedding day, only better," he said, leaning over me, his lips brushing my ear with a tender kiss; I whimpered, afraid that he was going to plunge into me again. *"You know—you never told me who fucked you before me—who did it?"* He breathed his words into my ear, and I began to shriek. *"I bet it was Hayden—who else could it be? You don't go anywhere, see anyone—he's convenient, right over there in the carriage house—you're pretty accessible to him too—you've got his picture plastered all over the place on that board—and not a single one of me! I bet he fucked you that night—didn't he? You went running over there— when I knocked on the door both of you were upstairs together because I heard him come down the stairs—there is only one bedroom in that house. I swear to God, I'll kill him—"*

Feverish with fear, I slithered away. When he tried to catch me, my hand snaked out quick, and my palm stung when the impact struck his face. *"Fuck you!"* I growled.

"Sammy, what happened—tell me what happened—what did he do to you?" the voice screamed.

"Fuck you!" I cried, flinging my fists out at the voice.

"Sammy, don't—it's me, Helena—calm down—he's gone, I'm going to call for help—okay, calm down." The hands grabbed my wrists and began to struggle with me.

With a flick of his fist, Preston punched me; the impact against my temple caused me to stagger. After aimless falling against obstacles, I crumpled onto the floor, and then he stomped on my chest, crushing the remaining breath out of my lungs.

"*Don't talk to me like that ever again, you got that, bitch? And if you make it a practice to slap me, I'll make it a point to slap you back,*" he scolded, shaking an angry finger at me; the cheek where my hand bit him appeared inflamed, much redder than the rest of his infuriated face.

"*Coward,*" I wheezed. He said nothing in reply, I didn't know if he heard me; he left the studio, and I heard his feet thump down the stairs.

With an effort, I opened my eyes and looked up at the drawings on the board; seeing the drawing of Sylvester's ass didn't make me feel like laughing, and that made me sad. I heard something downstairs and wondered if it was the boys. *Did they hear their father rutting on me? Did they hear my screams? Don't they care that he hurts me? Did he do the same shit to their mother, making this the norm? Or did he tell them that I'm a crazy bitch and to ignore me?*

"Sammy?"

I opened my eyes to see Helena crouched beside me.

"Lena—hey, what's the matter?" I asked, so thankful to see her.

"What did he do?" she asked, her entire face knotted as if with pain.

"I don't know why," I said, cringing, the memory of his violence suddenly flashed through my mind. I closed my eyes as tears welled up into my eyes, but I started to see him again. "Make it stop!" I cried, opening my eyes to turn off the nightmare still vivid in my mind.

"Look what he's done to you, that bastard hurt you—" she cursed. "Oh, baby—poor baby—" she whimpered, petting my hands.

"I don't know why he did it," I sniffled and wiped my eyes; she helped me sit up. "I slept up here last night—he came up to talk to me this morning—we talked about the divorce—and then he got mad, I guess; I can't remember—he read something—the card Guthrie sent me made him mad. It happened so fast, Lena—I don't know why—" I stared through the sunny window, the tears in my eyes refracted the bright light blurring my vision, fracturing white light into the pure hues of my emotions—my private colors for all that I feel. I jammed the heels of my palms into my eyes and wished that I could stop crying. My face hurt and I couldn't remember why.

I looked around my studio and saw the disarray, and then I remembered everything all over again.

My gaze met the pencil rendered eyes of Sylvester, and I remembered that I had hit Preston. I left a dandy red mark on his cheek, and I hoped it turned black and blue so everyone could see that I stood up for myself—*Samantha's last stand*. "I got him, I got him good this time—I slapped his face red," I laughed and burst into fresh tears. Helena began to wail.

Sirens came as if in reply to our grief. First the police, and then the ambulance crew fetched me from where I lay on the garret floor; I began to fuss about leaving until Helena explained that I had to go to the hospital; although I had no broken bones, he had knocked me unconscious and a concussion was their main concern. I also have a rainbow of bruises on my face, arms, and chest; the inflamed abrasions inside my vagina were an intimate detail of the violence my husband is capable of doing—to add insult to injury it hurts to pee.

Later on, Helena told me that the state troopers plucked Preston out of a meeting with all the university hotshots, and led him away in handcuffs. She also told me that his ex-wife picked up their brats—"*What a mouse that woman is—I just can't see them together at all,*" Helena exclaimed with a roll of her eyes. She's always critical of *the other woman* as if she's some great judge of marital compatibility. But in spite of everything, Preston got out of jail after his arraignment the next day—Jack's protests on my behalf weren't enough because Jill plead something ridiculous like it was his first offense, plus the extenuating circumstances that have had a profound effect on his state of mind. Apparently, the first time isn't enough to prove anything amiss in our dissolving marriage—I guess the third time will be the charm.

Sylvester returned from Maine special to see me. While he stood over my hospital bed, the late afternoon light dimmed toward night; the window behind him framed his somber shape draped in his black greatcoat. While I told him about what happened, he kept my hand cradled to his chest, and raised it to his lips to kiss it several times; he looked pale and shaken.

"He guessed it was you," I murmured.

Without further explanation, he understood my meaning with a nod. There was so much to say, and I knew by the set of his mouth that he ruminated over words of his own, but he didn't speak. Our silence resonated with all that we left unsaid between us for years; my hand remained in his, and I pressed my palm flat against his chest to feel his heartbeat. There is so much power within his pulse; little does he know there isn't a truer heart in the world.

"I got your letter—I sent another card, did you get it?" I asked, feeling anxious that it hadn't arrived.

"Yes, I got it—it was lovely—thank you, dear heart," he smiled while lightly caressing my cheek with his fingertips, but his expression wavered and faded to sadness. "Samantha—" he murmured, but stopped because Helena entered the room talking; she had stepped outside to smoke a cigarette when he first arrived—she seemed upset with the world, and his arrival didn't ease her.

She took control of the conversation, sending our sad thoughts to the matter at hand; she paced back and forth, her trek at the end of my bed much like a wild animal in a cage, dramatically gesticulating with her hands and ranting about what we needed to do—*"to keep that asshole out of the house."*

Sylvester slipped out of his coat, laying it across my lap; my eager hands began to knead its familiar woolen texture. Picking it up, I rubbed my cheek on the collar, and nuzzled it where I could smell his male muskiness from that magnificent spot at the back of his neck under his hair; this special scent mixed with cigarette smoke, winter snow, and salt from the ocean mist reminded me of winter nights spent with him. The two of us swaddled in our coats, lying flat on our backs on the freshly fallen snow, looking up at the stars in the deep sky, holding hands. We also made love in the snow. I didn't dare look at him just now—but I knew he watched me, I knew his expression—curious, probably wondering what I'm thinking, then suddenly, his face became flushed as if he might have made the same recollections.

As Helena continued to rage in her revision of this morning's Preston-diatribe, he slumped onto the edge of the bed, his hands caressing my feet through the blankets; I wiggled my toes, curling them around his fingers, holding his hands so he wouldn't take them away. Without looking at me, he calmly agreed with her about changing the locks on the house. *"Will it be easy-peasy?"* I asked of him; he smiled. *"Easy-peasy,"* he nodded. Then he went on to suggest that he could put deadbolts on the garret doors, and perhaps a couple of sturdy brackets in which a two by four could be placed as an extra brace, just in case Preston did get in the house, he wouldn't be able to get into the studio to attack me again. He also suggested that he should permanently install the collapsible fire escape ladder so if I needed an escape route from the attic, I could climb out the window like I had during childhood fire drills that Whitley insisted upon while I was growing up. Helena listened to his suggestions with wide-eyed appreciation, and then became calm for the first time today, her eyes glazing over with exhaustion, and a *"Thank god he's here"* expression. Sylvester promised that he could finish these tasks before noon tomorrow.

After a brief silence passed through our little group, Helena ducked into the bathroom to pee, and then he bent down to kiss my forehead goodnight. *"Take care, dear heart—try to get some sleep,"* he whispered into the part in my hair as he kissed me there. I kissed his sandpapery cheek with its evening beard that had grown since he last shaved this morning. Just as he stepped back, Helena emerged. He helped her into the heavy duster that's just like the one I bought—the woman has five coats to every one of mine and she always has to buy one just like the one I picked out for myself (always in the same color) it pisses me off when she does that. Sometimes we go shopping together looking like absurd twins. One time I gave her a ration of shit by refusing to wear mine, and left it in the car while we shopped—she wouldn't speak to me for days afterwards because I embarrassed her when Sylvester came upon us and draped his greatcoat over my shoulders, and he scolded her for not being considerate of my feelings.

Sylvester then retrieved his greatcoat from my hands in preparation to leave my bedside, he moved with stiff reluctance as if sitting still for so long pained him, and he looked back at me with expectation. I knew that if I asked him to do it, he would have stayed with me, and it seemed like the hesitation in his step at the door held onto a glimmer of hope that I would make the request, but I let him go with Helena—*it is where he belongs tonight.* I turned off the light above my bed and settled in to sleep, but something caused me to wake up in the middle of the night, a cough or a groan, a familiar male sleep-sound that reminded me of a time long ago, and there he was, sleeping in the chair next to the bed. Although a book lay open in his lap, his glasses were off and were set aside on the bed tray beside him, his chin propped in the palm of his hand in the *resting his eyes* posture that I've seen hundreds of times. I watched him sleep until I drifted off again. When I awoke in the morning, he was still there, awake and reading; he looked up at me and smiled, putting his finger in the book to hold his place. We said quiet good mornings, and after I ate my breakfast, Helena called to say she was coming over, so he left to go home to tend to the locks.

Helena stayed for several awkward hours being a nuisance to the staff. I quietly drew in my sketchbook while she sat glaring at the television. To my relief, she left at eleven-thirty to check on Sylvester's progress with the locks. He had told me earlier this morning that he had to return to Maine this afternoon because his father is not expected to live for much longer, so I didn't expect him to come back. Helena wasn't gone for more than a half an hour when he walked into my room bearing a huge bouquet of brilliant yellow flowers; my eyes already weary of the sterile room became filled with their wondrous reflective light—*he knows that I love yellow.*

Dressed in his greatcoat, he sat beside me on the edge of the bed with a quivering tension as if he was coiled to spring away, ready for departure. I lay staring up at him, and he stared back; his expression was soft, but his pale eyes blazed with a strange fire. With slow movements, he leaned down, and cradled my head within his trembling hands, he kissed my lips with the tenderness that only his mouth understood, and then his arms enveloped me in a gentle embrace that allowed me to absorb his tenderness into my raging bruises. I clutched him by the shoulders with my arms, my fingers combed through his hair that he has let grow shaggy again, and then burrowed my face into his neck just below his ear, nuzzling the soft flesh of his earlobe. He shuddered with a soft gasp in response, gripping me tighter. We held on to our silence.

When we finally separated to say goodbye, he kissed my hand, stood up, and left after promising that he would come home again soon. He didn't say it, but I guessed that he expected Jacob to be dead before he got back to Maine.

Before I went home the following day, Jack insisted on Preston's immediate banishment from my house, but he didn't show up at the appointed time to move out the last of his belongings. Jack had already anticipated this contingency, and had arranged for a moving company to come take his things out and he forwarded the bill to Jill so she could pass it on to him at their next meeting. According to Jack, Jill is becoming fed up with her client. Jack also convinced the just-returned-from-Florida judge to institute a restraining order warning Preston to stay away from me. Although the language of this court order is impressive, its papery treatise on my behalf offers me little comfort. I am afraid for my life. It seems as if no one will do anything about it—unless he does something to me again—even then, he might get away with it because of the *extenuating circumstances* that are causing him to do things that he cannot help.

11

Locked Doors and No Worries

"Why is the door locked, Samantha?" Preston's voice boomed from the hallway door at the bottom of the stairs. I decided not to offer an answer to that question, and quietly lay on the futon smoking a cigarette in thoughtful reverie. Between the ceiling and me, we're trying to remember a time in my life when I didn't have a worry in the world—*well, that would be before I met Preston, that's when.*

Once I had found myself in the thick of courtship, I found it appealing to feel the heady sensation of anticipation that I associated with time spent with him. But in reality, it was nothing more than nervous anxiety that I am prone to feel when my eagerness to please someone comes into play. I am now aware that this feeling came from the realization that I was at a deficit; compared to any woman that he could have chosen—a handsome and virile man like him could have any woman. *So, why did he choose me—why would he choose someone handicapped? He thought I was an easy target. He was right.* From the beginning, I felt as if I had to prove myself worthy of the attention that he generously bestowed on me. Honestly, I was flattered that he wanted me—just because I'm autistic doesn't mean I don't have an ego that likes to be stroked—I enjoyed the attention—attention that I wasn't getting from anyone since I gave up Sylvester. But being flattered didn't equal being in love. I had tried to convince myself that I could *learn* to love him in the same way that I love Sylvester or Guthrie—although I had the best intentions to try my darnedest to love him, my heart wasn't up to the task. Ever since the wedding, I have learned that I've had it all wrong—love doesn't work that way. Long before that night when I slept with Sylvester, and long before Guthrie came home, I felt that I had failed Preston—but it isn't just about him—I failed myself too. Hindsight is a wonderful tool to use to club oneself over the head—so, the ceiling and I have reached the mutual agreement that it's not worth beating myself up over past mistakes. I need to deal with the situation behind the locked doors at the bottom of the stairs—I just don't know how. Staring at the pristine white ceiling above me isn't going to accomplish anything—*I must get up—I must make him go away.*

"Why is the door locked, Samantha?" Preston repeated this question now from the door in my bedroom that he had just finished abusing with his fists. He has been alternately banging on the garret doors, going back and forth from my bedroom to the hallway for the last ten minutes, grunting, slamming, and cursing. The sturdy old doors didn't creak, nor offer any give when he hurled his body against their density; the cross bars that Sylvester installed three days ago remained steadfast; after this treatment, I have acquired a new appreciation for how well-built this house is—*oh, there he goes, jiggling the knob again. I just wish he'd go away.*

I knew that Preston has been stalking me since I was released from the hospital because I've seen his tracks in the melting snow circling—*circlecir-clecircle*—circling all around the house like an impatient predator hungry and wanting to make a kill to fill his empty belly. I have reported this evidence to the police, and I have complained to Jack. So, he went to Jill and told her to tell *"that jackass to knock it off—or else"*, but apparently, Preston doesn't care to heed the big trouble of *"orelse."*

"Sammy, I know you're in there—and I know you can hear me—why is the door locked!" he cried out in frustration, banging his fists against the door again.

"I locked the doors to keep you out," I shouted, unable to stand being quiet as a mouse any longer, he's really starting to get on my nerves now.

This morning had started out nicely—the day after a snowstorm kind of day, crystal clear blue skies, and the sunshine was so intense because of the whiteness. It was the first day that I felt like going for a walk on the beach; the latest nor'easter that blew through yesterday had blanketed snow all around; the image of a snow-covered beach intrigued me, so, I decided to venture outside to indulge in the view. Shuffling down the driveway through the snow that had drifted overnight, I came upon the startling presence of a black Volvo parked in the driveway to the carriage house (the car belonged to Helena's latest paramour, *Bookstore Man*). While I stood hypnotized by the way the snow had swirled itself around the Volvo's body like frozen waves, Preston pulled into the end of the driveway and slid his Camaro into the snow-bank next to the mailboxes; he hit so hard that their doors rattled open as they shook on their posts. Upon seeing him, I darted back toward the house; he bellowed at me to stop as he plodded through the drifts in the driveway.

My wet boots with snow-clogged treads sent me sliding across the polished plank floors after I locked the front door behind me. I tripped and clomped upstairs, where I locked myself inside the garret to wait—waiting, waiting, waiting for him to go away.

He must have broken a window to get inside. The jerk—all the years we have lived in this house, no one has ever broken any of the windows—I love the old glass and the way its unevenness distorts the outside world. Asshole—assholeassholeasshole—ass-hole!

"Let me in, I need to see you," he moaned now from the door in the hallway.

"No fuckin' way, dick-stain," I stifled a laugh; it's hard for me not to giggle at Guthrie's pet name for Preston. Then I let loose my laughter because the absurdity of this moment struck me as funny—*this bickering through the door can go on all day.*

"I swear I'll break it down!" he groused, banging on the door with his fist.

Without offering a response, I walked to the top of the stairway leading to my bedroom; I glanced back at the windows overlooking the backyard—the fire-escape route is there if I need it to get out. I dragged on the cigarette with satisfaction. I really should call the police to report this incident, so they can catch him in the act, but I can't because I lost my cell phone last week, and the cordless phone from the studio is downstairs on my nightstand where I left it last night after I talked to Guthrie. *"Say the word, I'll come home and cave in his head."* I smiled. Guthrie's been in a rage about what Preston did to me, but I told him not to come home because Jack says his being here would only complicate everything because of Preston's accusations.

"Fine, don't come out; stay in there and rot for all I care!" Preston shouted; there was a distinctive whine of frustration by the time he said the word *care*. I stayed silent knowing it'll make him nuts. "Are you listening to me?" he shrieked with panic.

"Fuck you," I sneered at the door.

"Aaarrrgh, you little bitch!" he growled, banging on the door with intense irritation, the flat of his palms making distinct stinging slaps upon making contact with the wood—*Oak*—*I think Whitley once told me that the doors are made of oak—that's a good strong wood, right? A hardwood. They're twice as thick as normal doors—modern doors—they don't make doors like these anymore. Oak is better than pine—Guthrie once told me pine is a soft wood.*

"Look, I'm sorry, okay? Please don't be like this, come out so we can talk," he pled with a plaintive noise wheedling in his voice—*too familiar.*

"We're done with talking—Jack and Jill will do all the talking from now on—the restraining order says that you are not to drive near my house—you are not supposed to come on my property—what part of *you are supposed to stay away from me* don't you understand? You're in big trouble now, mister—I'm going to call the cops if you don't leave right now," I shrieked at the door, my entire body began to shake. Vocalizing my anger felt good, but I started to lose control—*I must keep control*—I'm trying hard not to cry—trying hard not to let him know I am weak—*I am afraid.* I wrapped my arms around my body to try to stop the shaking as my tense muscles kept pressing for motion; I began to sway.

"That's it then—you are just going to write me off?" his voice crackled with dismay.

"Yeah, that's it—nothing you can say to me now will change what happened—don't you remember what you did to me? I do—how can I forget—I have bruises to remind me every day. Here's a tidbit of information for you—this morning was the first time that it didn't hurt to pee."

"I'm sorry, I didn't mean to hurt you," he moaned pathetically. *Thud-thud-thud-thud.*

I swear it sounds like he's banging his head against the door, slow, steady thuds—flesh of a different consistency from that of hands—*fists*—the flesh stretched over something hard—bony—like his forehead. *Thud-thud-*

thud-thud. Forehead—flesh and bone, the skull of a man—an angry man, emotions all mixed up because he's sick in the head. Jack says Preston has some serious problems. Jack also told me that Preston used to knock around his ex-wife. He has a history—*a history*—of abuse. Banged up college girl-friends who never pressed charges—one cute little sorority girl got her front teeth bashed out, but she never pressed charges—*"It was an accident"* or so she said at the time—Jack says that she tells a different story now. *"Sammy, that guy you married is a real piece of work—a manipulative sack of shit and a total nut job, if Judge Davis has any common sense, he'll dismiss the whole competency hearing thing and you'll be home free."*

"You wouldn't know what sorry was if it bit you in the ass," I said to lighten my mood away from my persistent apprehension—sometimes it works, it sort of did, just saying the word *ass* was humorous enough for me to smirk behind my hand with secret humor. *Homefree!*

"Samantha—I love you, I will not give up on you—I still love you—please listen to me, I'm sorry for hurting you, believe me, I've learned my lesson—I want you back, please take me back, give me another chance—I want us to be happy together!" The pounding stopped and started in-termittently as he changed doors, his anguished pleas becoming more desperate.

Even though I knew that he couldn't touch me, his manipulative words were doing their job on my head; I became illogically terrified, second-guessing my own mind, feeling that I have been unfair to him—*that I have wronged him.* My knees grew weak and I collapsed onto the stairs, my body rocking as I tried to block out his voice. Struggling with my senses, my fin-gers clutched my hair as a wordless cry built up inside my throat. *Hang in there, Sammy.* The voice of encouragement popped into my head—*Guthrie's voice*—he had said the words in my ear last night, hundreds of miles away, through the telephone line. *"Hang in there, Sammy—everything is going to be all right."* I internally listened harder, wanting to hear something other than Preston's rage. *"I love you, dear heart."* I had felt the words breathed into the part of my hair, it wasn't even a whisper—words I wasn't meant to hear because Sylvester had suppressed them with a kiss. My eyes flew open and I stopped all motion—only my heart fluttered with anxious wings inside my chest. *HomefreehangintbereIloveyoudearheart.*

"I'm calling the cops, right now!" I shrieked at the impassive door after overcoming my wavering resolve.

"You fucking stupid bitch! I swear to God, Sam, I will get you back—I will make you see what a big mistake you're making." Preston slammed the bedroom door with his fist and stomped away, grumbling. He tried the hall door again just in case he might have been turning the doorknob wrong the last gazillion times. After a proper measure of belligerent thumping and growling, the front door slammed. Thrilled that he fell for my bluff, I ran to look out the window to watch him trudging through the snow to his car; he got in, and after some ingenious maneuvering that made our mailboxes lean over, he plowed out of the heavy snow.

"So long, fucker, don't come back now, ya hear."

Within minutes of his departure, the black Volvo parked in the frozen wave, slid through the drifts, and after a brief struggle through the chunks left by the snowplow at the end of the driveway where Preston got stuck, it fish-tailed on its way in the opposite direction.

Preston and Helena's paramour weren't gone for more than a minute when I heard Helena racing through the house screaming my name at the top of her lungs. I met her at the garret door just as she reached the top of the stairs. She was hastily dressed with a combination of jammies, jeans, boots, and a coat that looked just like one of mine. "I called the cops as soon as I noticed his car in the driveway just two minutes ago—are you all right?" she asked, out of breath and wide-eyed.

"I'm all right, he didn't get upstairs—he couldn't get me because of the locks Sylvester installed on the doors," I exhaled relief, it felt as if I have been holding my breath forever. *I'm thankful—thankful—so thankful for Sylvester and his care for me.*

"Oh-my-god—I'm so relieved that you're all right!" She gasped, leaning against the wall. "I wish Sy was here—this is too much—it's going to kill me if I have to deal with what I had to deal with the last time Preston got a hold of you."

"Have you heard any news from Sylvester?" I asked, trailing downstairs behind her.

"He called late last night—he's nearly dead himself! There's no change—Jacob is still miserable—what's worse is he's aware, but I guess it's giving them time to talk—which is good; it's been hard for him—hard for both of them," she said with a deep sigh as she poured coffee into her favorite teacup. "There's gotta be euthanasia for people suffering at the end of their life—I mean, we do it for our beloved pets when they're suffering because it is the kindest thing to do—why not do it for people—what makes us so special that we have to lie around suffering in some stinky hospital wasting time and money? You'd think the insurance companies would be on that so they're not pissing away any of their precious profits to prolong some poor slob's life—really—you'd think they'd be all over Congress about it! Fucking asshole politicians are hand-in-hand with the banks, the pharmaceutical and insurance companies, then the conservative rich-bitch religious right and their high-'n-mighty attitudes, if it weren't for them fucks we would've had nationalized healthcare back when Clinton was in office—the bastards, they're all in bed together—you know they've got their bean-counters figuring out how to fuck the American public up the ass for the almighty dollar. Bend over, Jacob Hayden—nope, we're not taking your temperature—we're taking advantage of your slow, painful death—CHA-ching—there now—here's a dose of the best drugs money can buy and all kinds of profit for us, we'll just keep you comfortable until you expire."

"That's sad—the poor things," I shuddered. My head readily tuned out Helena's tirade regarding Jacob's right to die with dignity—a man she never met. I had met him once when Sylvester and I went to Deer Isle for a weekend to cat sit. We had stayed longer than intended, lingering in Sylvester's boyhood bed, enjoying every minute of our unrestricted love. Jacob came home just as we had decided to emerge from our bliss; the elder Hayden's eyes watched me with curiosity as I stood beside Sylvester on the front porch with our hands clasped. Father and son spoke in quiet embarrassed fragments, shook hands, and regarded one another with strained smiles. *"I hope to see you again soon,"* Jacob said with a hopeful tone as I transferred the persnickety Petunia to his arms when we finally bid him goodbye. He was such a nice man—too bad I didn't get the chance to see him again. *I wished that I could be there for Sylvester.*

Sylvester has told me many things about his life with his parents—things I knew he could never talk to Helena about because she never shuts up; she blabs on and on pronouncing her opinion like she's the expert on everything under the sun, never hearing a word that he said—or what I said, or what anyone said. She had gone on and on ad-nauseam at Whitley about how he should die—that pissed him off, but he wasn't in any shape to tell her to shut up, so he let her blah-blah-blah at him just so he could spend quality time with her during his final days. After I complained to him about how I thought she was being selfish to carry on so much like that, he just laughed, and his dark eyes twinkled in that naughty Whitley-way that said a thousand words. *"She makes noise just to make noise—it's how she deals with things that upset her—it's like blowing off steam—her mother was the same way."*

Although Whitley's last days were rough, he never said a word about the pain. The hospice people from St. Theresa's came and went as per their schedule to administer his medications and monitor his vitals; he really didn't want them around—he said they depressed him with their offer of comfort and preparation. *"I know they mean well, but I don't want to be reminded that I'm dying; I know that already—I'm just trying to live for as long as I can and not waste a minute thinking about the inevitable!"* He took his medication to ease his pain, and he moved slower through life as if dragging out every last second he had left. Against the advice of the experts (Helena included), he maintained his daily routines. He slept in the studio on the ratty old sofa wrapped in the comforter, so he could see his latest painting first thing in the morning, greeting it with fresh eyes. When the stairs became too difficult for him to navigate for potty-breaks, I never complained about disposing his leavings in the chamber pot. Although I always offered to help him, he refused with a valid complaint about there being no dignity left at the end of one's life. *"The last thing I want is to have my daughter wiping my ass for me."* I was thankful that he died at home—thankful that I had been the one to find him in his final sleep.

What would Whitley think of this nonsense with Preston—what would he tell me to do? Whitley would have dropped everything to take me out of harm's way—no questions asked.

"I have to get out of here—can you take me somewhere?" I asked Helena after making a quick decision to get the hell out of here while I still could.

"Where do you want to go—the bookstore? How can you think about shopping at a time like this?" she cried, her face crimped with impatient curiosity.

"No—no, not the bookstore—I need to get away from here."

"Sammy, do you want me to take you to a hotel or something?"

"I want to go somewhere far away; I'm not safe here anymore—my safety is not guaranteed with him running around free—I doubt that after this they'll do anything to him because he didn't touch me; they'll just warn him again—nothing sticks to him. Guthrie says he's as bad as a Teflon Republican."

"Oh, Sam—I don't know what to do—" Helena groaned.

I had expected her resistance—I shouldn't be disappointed, but I am—especially if she's concerned with having to deal with the results of Preston getting a hold of me again.

"Please, just get me out of here—can we go somewhere together for a few days? At least until they catch him."

"Well—I guess we could take the train to New York—ummm—when do you want to go?" she considered with uncertainty.

"Today—right now."

"Now?" she exclaimed, her coffee cup rattled in its saucer. The sound grated on me; I prefer drinking from a mug for that reason. The cup and saucer thing is her ideal, she wants to look sophisticated or some image bullshit that she has concocted—like she's playing house or having a tea party—Lenore used to rag on her about it. *"Girl you are going to be disappointed all your life if you don't begin to deal with reality! Life is about broken glasses, chipped cups, cracked plates, and tarnished silverware—life is fragile at the same time that it is hard—it can all be taken away by one false move—if everything is picture perfect, then you're not living life, you're glossing it over to hide something shitty."* In my opinion, Helena is like an obsessive cat scratching in a litter box, but never covers the shit.

"Yes, today, the sooner the better—I want to go right now—I can throw some stuff in a suitcase and be ready to go in five minutes."

"We can't just take off now, we need a plan, Sam—" she sputtered nervously as she brandished the cigarette between her fingers in an elaborate gesture that expressed an affectation of dominance—or expertise.

"This isn't fifty ways to leave your husband, Lena," I laughed, but my funny went over her head as she scowled over my proposal to leave today.

Before she could parry my response with a witty reply, sirens arrived in the driveway; she glared at me. "We'll talk about this later—right now we have to deal with what just happened—your stupid almost-ex-husband broke into the house and tried to get at you again—that restraining order has got to have something to say about that bullshit."

12 Whitley's Cadillac

"Helena, you can't go on milking the 'victim card' for sympathy—it gets old fast, no one wants to hear that 'I'm a victim' shit—it's no excuse for any-thing. They're going to say, 'Well, that sucks your mom abandoned you, but that was years ago, move on—get over it.' What will impress people more is how you rose above it."

Well, that's out of the blue—Lenore had the knack for saying the right things that I didn't want to hear. She has been dead all these years, but ev-ery now and then, her voice comes from the past and lays it on thick. *That bitch.*

"Listen here, you—I'm taking care of Sammy, so get off my back about my mother."

After two hours on the road, we're now driving in the blinding gray of winter twilight, I glanced over at Sammy sitting—no, more like leaning against the passenger side door. *She's too quiet—is she crying?* I have asked her fifty times if she was all right, and she answered fifty times, *"I'm fine"*, but each time she replied, she sounded less fine—more like terrible.

She's safe now—I'm glad to get her out of there, I'm taking her far away from Preston.

When I saw the red sports car blocking the end of the driveway this morning, I nearly had a heart attack. It also didn't help that Martin was shitting bricks because *he* was running late—the gravity of the situation was completely lost on him—but I cannot fault him for being on the outside looking in at my family's asinine soap opera. After I saw Preston staggering down the driveway right after I called the cops, I quickly shooed Martin out the door. *"What's wrong—is there anything I can do?"* he asked. *"No, just go, it isn't anything that you need to be concerned with!"* I bravely told him in spite of the horrors that my imagination had begun to conjure, but I didn't want him involved. As it turned out, Sammy's safe, and now, I'm going to make sure she stays out of harm's way—*at least that's what I am trying to tell myself. Why did I open my big mouth and say—"We can go to New Mexico and look for Dulcie—is that far enough away?" I was really just kidding. She's crazy for suggesting that we do it. ("Let's go, I've always wanted to see the Grand Canyon and Yellowstone"), and I'm crazy for go-ing along with it. ("But, Sam, the Grand Canyon and Yellowstone are not in New Mexico!") She didn't care, once the bee got in her bonnet, we were as good as gone. This trip is fucking crazy!*

When I complained about the cost of such a trip, she disappeared into Whitley's bedroom, and came back with a wad of cash. While I looked through the twenty or more fat, banded bundles, I saw that they mostly consisted of small bills, nothing larger than a fifty, but there were a few Ben Franklin's peeking out here and there for some variety. I've never seen so much money in my life. When I asked her where she got it from, she laughed. *"Didn't you know? Whitley always kept money in a safe—he called it 'just in case cash'—I think there's about $10,000 here, is that enough? There is more if we need it—a lot more."* Sammy said with wide-eyed innocence. *Holy shit—there's a lot more?*

When we left Gloucester, Preston was still *at large.* I can't believe they couldn't find him—*he's too big to disappear.* It was the official consensus that he didn't hurt her—*Well duuuhhh, he couldn't because she barricaded herself in the attic.* I guess it doesn't mean anything that he busted a window to break into the house, it isn't enough to show his intent to get her that he left muddy boot prints on the floors outside each of the doors leading to the garret where she was hiding. Is she supposed to let him get her before they do anything about it? *What bullshit! Is that bastard paying off you assholes to say that shit?*

Even though Jack appeared on the scene to voice our concerns to the Boyz-in-Blue about the escalating situation, he admitted to us later on that until they caught up with Preston, we were supposed to sit tight and let the law enforcement people do their jobs. *"They'll catch him—if he's re-*

ally beginning to lose it, he's going to do something stupid soon," Jack said with that self-confident grin that ignited my historical aggravation with him. Back in the day when I tangled with him, he wore that grin like a badge after every time I let him fuck me. Today he had the nerve to ask me how things were going with Sylvester. *Asshole—bastard—fuck-face—jerk, it's a good thing he's a good lawyer or I'd fire his ass.*

Sammy sat like a lump through most of the day—not even rocking, not even crying—I caught her taking a couple of shots of Whitley's scotch to calm down from the hysteria-attack that came on after the police showed up, so now she's numb.

This whole day has been over-the-top weird.

We're driving because she wouldn't fly—she never has, never will—she's too terrified to try now. Good grief, I know spending an hour in the car with Sam can be a trial, but four—possibly more days driving to New Mexico! *Oh, my god, what was I thinking? I wasn't, I was infested by the idea of going to find Dulcie. I'll need to be committed after tonight.* As soon as I suggested it, I regretted it—I only suggested it because she asked me to take her to Cleveland to see Guthrie. Initially, I thought about taking her to Deer Isle to drop her off with Sylvester—but I didn't want to go up that road—*I can't deal with him right now.*

When he called last night he sounded beat, but underlying his apparent exhaustion was another tone—*I think he knew that I wasn't alone.* There was a suspicious tone in his voice when he said, "Get some rest"—it seemed almost accusing. *If he knows, then why doesn't he say anything? Because he's afraid—just like you are afraid. What do you expect—after all these years, do you think it's going to be easy to confront what is wrong in your relationship and walk away? We've been living status quo for nine years— we've been living a lie all along.*

Making the suggestion to go to New Mexico only encouraged her— almost as if I played her just like I have done in the past to get her to agree with something I wanted to do—*but I didn't mean to!* Then I tried to defuse the idea because that stupid old T-bird Whitley gave to me is a piece of shit.

"*I've got a car we can use,*" Sammy's childlike voice piped in. "*Whitley's Caddy.*"

Stupid cars! I always hated how Whitley's passion for old cars spilled over into my life—it drove Dulcie nuts too; we could never rely on those clunkers to get us across the street in a hurry. When Guthrie came along, Whitley sucked him into his fetish; first, they took apart and put back together the '59 Caddy, and then the Super 88—a.k.a. *Delta Dawn.* They drove down to Louisiana and picked up the hulking monstrosity that was in pieces with a trailer; they came home cocky and strutting as if they had conquered the world. I would sit in their periphery watching them work—wanting to be a part of their world, but this was the *boyz club*—NO GIRLS ALLOWED.

When Sy moved into the carriage house, he filled in the vacancy Guthrie had left; Whitley took him under his wing, and the two of them spent hours bent over that shitty Fiat, fuss-farting around with the engine and then the body. During that first summer, Sy turned into a grease monkey just like Guthrie; his refined hands coated with black crap most of the time, and he reeked like exhaust and the greasy dust of the garage floor. Seeing him bare-chested, sweaty, and filthy turned me off. The fool could make moony eyes at me all he wanted, but I wasn't about to let those grimy hands touch me—even though once in awhile I wanted him to, but he was too polite to perform my version of a dirty, sweaty rogue. There was an unusual appeal about Sylvester Hayden that was a curiosity to me—even after all these years, I still haven't figured him out, and I don't really want to.

When they dragged home the 1966 T-bird via tow-truck, it was heralded like the arrival of a new baby; the two men puzzled and fiddled under the hood for hours that led to weeks, fucking around with some engine bullshit; tinkering and tweaking. Whitley let me drive it after I came back from Berkley—I hated it—the friggin' thing was like driving a boat, but I drove it because it pleased him. Of course, I could have gone out and bought myself a new car after he died, but I haven't had time—*and Sy hasn't had the time to pop the hood to take a look at what was wrong with it either.*

At three o'clock this afternoon, we retrieved the Caddy from the winter storage at Jimmy's—a climate controlled storage lock up, leaving the T-bird in its place.

I can't believe I'm on my way to find my mother! As much as I would like to find her, I don't want to find the disappointment that could be waiting for me out there.

Ever since I started the research into Whitley's life, I kept finding clues about my mother in his desk, even in his checkbook; it seemed like he kept in touch with her after she left us—why he never told me, I'll never know, but her letters in reply to his were not encouraging.

Apparently, while I was still young, Whitley had offered Dulcie money to help her to support me if he sent me to visit her for the summers, but she refused. *"I know you believe that Helena needs her mother, but I am in no position to take her even if it is part time—she's better off with you. As you can see by the green shreds enclosed, I ripped up the check because I don't want anything from you—please keep your money for Helena."* It pleased me that Whitley made the effort to connect us, but it also struck me that he tried to dump me with her to wash his hands—especially after the arrival of Sammy—he really tried to get rid of me then. There was nothing more from her after 1977, nothing even to acknowledge the event of my turning eighteen and going to college; it made me wonder if he kept writing to her and she ignored his letters, or if he had given up.

Crushing out the remains of my cigarette, I exhaled a stream of smoke like a pensive dragon. I can't believe that I've become caught up in this hare-brained idea of hers—*leaving town*—but the more she brought it up throughout this wretched day, the less it sounded like a bad idea. She's right to suggest it; her safety is not guaranteed, if Preston is determined to get her again—who knows what he might do the next time—*he might bring an axe to break down the doors or worse, set the house on fire.*

I punched the cigarette lighter to charge it up—*if I hadn't already started to smoke again a few months ago, I would've started today.*

I do need to get away from here just as badly as she does. I need time away to think about what to do; the pressure between Sy, Theo, Martin, Whitley's book, and Sammy's divorce are going to make me implode if I don't get some distance—physical distance would be ideal. *This is crazy— I spent the afternoon gleefully plotting with my little sister to run away from home like a disgruntled fourteen year old—this is such a bad idea, it's* ridiculous!

"You know—when I was little, I used to watch Dulcie serve Whitley hand and foot—it used to make me so mad. I thought he was such a jerk back then," I said while fumbling for a cigarette from the pack that I kept partway stuffed in the seat where we could both pick from it. "I hated seeing her work like that—I always told myself that I would never become some man's servant." I lit the cigarette, exhaled, and lowered the window a little more. "So right up until I was around twelve, maybe younger—yeah, I guess I was younger—I had wished that I was born a man, so I could grow up with the expectation that there would be someone who'd look after my every need, pick up after me, and see that I'm fed and watered. Sometimes I still wish I were born a man. I wonder—since I am a woman and I love men, but I wish I were a man, and if I were to be granted that wish would that make me gay?" I mused over this absurd concept—I'm talking just to hear myself talk. Sammy certainly isn't talking—at least she isn't freaking out—*yet*. I should count my blessings, I guess.

"Nonsense! You just need a cleaning lady—you can ask Carrie to come in a couple of times a week," Samantha giggled through her nervous tears that have sprouted on and off since she confidently got into the car beside me to leave her problems with Preston behind.

"I'll ask her when we get back," I smiled. Carrie, the faithful housekeeper—she will be the first to sound the alarm that Sammy is missing. She will come tomorrow afternoon at her regular time to find the garret uncannily quiet, empty, and unused all day. I shuddered. *We should have left a note, but we were in such a hurry to go—I was anxious to go—to get the fuck out of Dodge as soon as the cops cleared out, and Jack took his smirk out the front door—leaving notes wasn't a priority. If we left a note, Preston might find it and then we'd be screwed.*

I heaved a deep sigh. "I used to think Sy was queer—don't ever tell him I said so—but I thought so because, well, you know, because he's so—peculiar—so damn *nice*—I figured he had to be gay." I rambled on just trying to keep her with me; I can sense the tension across the bench seat—*she's going to break down anytime soon and start to demand that I take her home.*

"I never thought he was a homosexual—I always thought of him as being sad," she remarked in between nose blowing into a tissue.

Yes, he is sad—sad like Eeyore—he can be downright "I'm going to go eat worms" pathetic, it drives me bat shit. I wasn't able to reach him before I left town, so I left a message on the answering machine at Jacob's cottage telling him that I was going out of town and would be in touch with him soon. It dawned on me that I forgot to mention Sammy was with me—*oh fuck.* I'll have to call him tonight because he'll automatically assume that he's going to look in on her while I'm gone.

"Sammy, don't let me forget to call Sy tonight—I need to tell him you're with me."

"You forgot to tell him?" she exclaimed.

"It's all right, he probably won't get the message until later—we'll be settled in by then."

"Can I call him on your cell?"

"Duh, that's right, I'm an idiot—fish it out of my purse," I said, poking my purse out from under the seat and tossing it to her.

"I can't find it," she mumbled as she groped in the dark.

"Cripe, dump out all of that shit—it's gotta be in there—that purse is such a fucking black-hole!"

"It's not here—maybe it fell out—are you sure you brought it?" she asked over the clatter of various plastic cosmetic implements that I had pitched in there at the last minute.

"Hey, easy with that stuff, don't lose any of it," I scolded. An image of the cell phone lying on the dining room table at Sammy's house right where I left it made my stomach turn. *I plugged it in to charge it—I can't believe I forgot it!* I frisked my coat pockets—no phone. "I'll have to look in my suitcase," I sighed, although knowing that it isn't there, but saying it is just to declare that it *might* be there made me feel better. "Where's your cell?"

"I told you, I lost it," she muttered.

"Crap, fuck—fuck-crap—the next one I get you is going to have a dummy string."

"Oh, I hope he's all right, I'm worried about him," she fussed.

"Sy's fine," I assured her. She really cares a lot about him, and I always thought it was sweet how he was so kind to her, looking out for her, and talking to her about books. It was cute how they'd sit at the dining room table drawing like a couple of kids with coloring books on a rainy day;

their roles reversed, she'd teach him how to use his pencil to create the right marks. His quiet mannerisms always soothed her. Her odd behavior never ruffled him, like the night Preston first came for dinner, and she had slid under the dinner table—*now why didn't Preston get up and say, "Well, it's been real—see ya!" I have no idea.* Sy's expression at the time was comical, but he took it in stride as he smiled down at her—*that rare smile*—his smile is so fleeting, it surprises me to see it; his melancholy is so pervasive it drapes him like a shroud.

It was wonderful that he took a break from the deathbed vigil to come down from Maine to see her in the hospital, his being there cheered her up. It was especially nice of him to spend the night at the hospital—though he had every reason in the world to not want to be at home. In spite of a night with little or no sleep, he was out early in the morning to buy and install those locks and fix the collapsible fire-escape ladder for her. I thought it was so thoughtful of him to bring her those yellow flowers before he left town—chrysanthemums I think they were; mums are nice, but they remind me of funerals too much—it was nice of him to make the gesture anyway, and it pleased her because she loves yellow—always the gentleman—*he's a good man.*

"I hope Daisy will be all right—do you think she's going to be all right?" Sammy asked; her voice raised an octave due to her apprehension.

"Daisy will be fine; I filled her kibble and water dispensers, and I even fixed up a second litter box with extra litter just in case he doesn't come home right away—she'll be all right for a few days," I assured her. The darn cat is so fussy, she couldn't care less if anyone was around; the bitchy thing always glares at me with the tip of her tail twitching—*that cat knows too much.* I'm still fooling around with Theo when he makes himself available—in spite of my promises to myself to stop—*they* always make me change my mind. Martin has been coming over nearly every night since Sy's been out of town. I sighed. *I didn't even call to tell him that I was leaving—I really need to get out of that relationship, he's worse than Theo—he is much too needy for my taste.*

After Martin made love to me the other night, I stared at his sleeping man-shape thinking about Sy; he hasn't instigated sex in weeks. He comes to bed, reads a book from the stack by the bed, and shuts off the light when

243

he gets sleepy. I have stared at his white t-shirt back on nights when my guilt is eating me alive while he sleeps untroubled—unconcerned. I have waited for him to turn over onto his side and slip his arms around me, his mouth and hands intimately probing to see if he can encourage me to accept him—it never takes much—he knows what to do and when he does, it's like falling—*I won't deny, the man is good in bed.* After his nightly silent rejection, I take a sleeping pill and zonk out until morning.

There is comfort in our familiarity—we have existed in status quo for years. His quiet, bookworm habits, and scholarly endurance nearly drives me insane, but his steady manner of always being there when I needed him for anything keeps me with him—because he is a good man. Sometimes the guilt just about strikes me dead. There have been so many times that I've come close to confessing, so many times I've wanted to leave him, but so many times I've held my tongue, promising myself that I'd be faithful to him—I'd change—I'd learn to be happy. No. I'm not happy. *If he's so good, then why have I gone around fucking anything in pants? The "grass is greener" syndrome, I guess—I'm too much like Whitley—he had a good thing going with Lenore and fucked it up, just like he fucked-up with Dulcie, and before her Guthrie's mom, Margie. What a fucking asshole—no wonder I'm so fucking fucked-up—it's goddamn genetic.*

"Daisy's such an independent kitty—if she had thumbs, we'd have problems," Sammy snickered. I was relieved for the interruption of my unproductive thoughts and laughed. Sammy had been rubbing the cat's fur the wrong way this afternoon to drive her crazy; the silly thing loves it, hissing fit to spit, and cuffing with those cotton-ball paws like she means business, but she comes back for more ruffling of her feathers. Sy is fiercely allergic to her, but he loves the cat anyway and tolerates itchy, watery eyes while he rubs his face into her silky fur until his eyes swell up and he can hardly see his way to the bathroom to flush them out—*what an idiot.*

The glimmering green of billboard-sized highway signs loomed ahead announcing the next exits, and *wherethefuckarewe.* I am eternally thankful that the weather is good, and the roads are dry; their surface is white from salt—today was a good day for clean up from the storm—such a perfect day, now turning into a perfect night for driving. *Preston.* How long will it be before he realizes Sam isn't at home? *What if he followed us out of town?* It crossed my mind more than once to watch for his stupid red Camaro, and then it crossed my mind that he might have been crafty enough to ditch it, rent a car, and start chasing us in some piece of shit we'd never think to look out for. *I am really glad that the roads are dry*—I figured I would drive for as long as I can tonight to put distance between him and us; I might feel better once we're in New York State—*maybe*.

"We're making good time, the roads are great." I sounded out the quiet woman beside me a few minutes later. "See, that's the exit for Sturbridge Village, do you remember when we went there?" There was a vague acknowledgement from the passenger side. I remember bringing Sammy here when she was little—Guthrie, Lenore, and I. Sammy quiet, Sammy making weird noises, Sammy quiet again, but her hands flew about her face in a private sign language while making sounds only she could understand. Once we got there, Sammy started to scream that she wanted to go home because she didn't like unfamiliar places, and then Lenore began to freak out because she was exhausted with frustration, and regretting the long ride already. Just when the situation seemed like it reached the point of no return, Guthrie showed up; he had been out on his reconnaissance of the place while we were in the bathroom trying to get the fretful brat to pee. It was as if he rode in to rescue the day as he knelt down in front of the little girl who was no more than three or four at the time and he grabbed her undivided attention. *"Sammy—hey look, there's a blacksmith—he bends metal by heating it in a fire and then he bangs it into a new shape with a hammer on an anvil—come watch with me, he's making shoes for a horse—maybe he'll let you pet its soft nose, but you've got to be very good—and quiet—shh, okay? You don't want to scare the horse—he's a nice one, look at his face with the white star, ain't he pretty? He must be special to be getting shoes put on, don't ya think?"* That man had a way with her; she'd follow him into a burning building if he said, *"Hey, that's cool, let's go check it out."* At least she'd shut up for him; she'd stuff her fingers in her mouth, sucking on them until they were wrinkled pink raisins at the tips, and her eyes stood wide open as if she needed them that exposed to take in everything—to pay attention to his every move. Apparently, he still has the *magic touch*.

All the while this scene played out, I looked on feeling helpless, unable to move—being the older sister, I should have taken charge of my father's youngest child—*but I didn't.* To protect myself, my random thoughts then fell back to Whitley—*where was my father—where was Whitley during this time?* He stayed behind—he always stayed behind—probably screwing any pretty little thing in paint-spattered blue jeans that he fancied, although the only evidence of his sins amounted to a few sketches of his nude paramours left lying about on his drafting table. Lenore looked the other way; apparently, she didn't care since she had Guthrie doing mattress gymnastics with her down the hall where no one could hear them. Truthfully, I was surprised that Sammy turned out to be Whitley's biological child—it just didn't seem likely, but I guess if I can juggle Sy and a string of lovers over the years, then Lenore can certainly have her cake and eat it too. I always wondered if she ever did both of them on the same night. There were times when Sy would try to fuck me after I had been with someone earlier in the day, but I would put him off—usually by picking a fight with him about something trivial, like his breath if he had been drinking or smoking. I'd crank on him, and he'd get bent out of shape, and go sleep on the couch. *That poor guy, I really put him through the wringer over the years.*

The sun dipped below the horizon and the darkness that had been creeping up from the east behind us, passed overhead, and zoomed westbound to snuff out the last sliver of red, turning the atmosphere above the rim of the world ahead into brilliant indigo.

"What the fuck are we doing?" Samantha suddenly wailed, thumping her forehead against the passenger side window.

"What I'm doing is getting you as far away from Preston as possible—he's never going lay a finger on you again—I'm doing this for you because you asked me to, remember, sweetie? Come on, don't cry, it's all right." I wiped my eyes as tears tumbled down my cheeks with swift release. "Damn, don't bang your head anymore—you're freaking me out, all right?" I cried, ready to lose it if she didn't stop.

"Don't get angry with me, Lena," she whimpered, cowering in the passenger seat. I reached over and patted her arm to offer comfort.

"It's okay—I'm just as upset as you are—this is big—we're running away from home."

"Why are you running away from home?" Sammy asked; her pale face seemed to glow in the darkness.

"I guess I'm running away from Sy. I love him, I do love him—he wants to marry me, he asked me the other night when he came home to see you at the hospital," I blurted out. I hadn't planned to say anything about it—*I can barely think about it!* He had come to the carriage house first before we went to the hospital to see Sammy, and he asked, *"Lena, will you marry me?"* I was dumbfounded; he stood in the living room, his face deeply furrowed with grave creases while he spoke—he looked awful—tortured and old.

"He did?" she asked with a squeak of surprise. "So, what was your answer?"

"I told him *no*," I sighed. "It wasn't the easiest thing for me to do—to make things worse, he became despondent after that—he barely said goodbye when he left town the next day. I don't know what to do—I can't stay in that kind of atmosphere," I moaned. I feel like such a bitch for saying *"no"*—*he looked so crushed*—the expression on his face, and then his reaction only drove home how terrible he must have felt. *"Why not? Can you at least tell me why not?"* he asked. I just couldn't—it wasn't that I didn't want to—it was because—I didn't know why—just like I don't know why I fuck every Tom, Dick and hairy bastard I meet.

"Arrgghhh, he had to pick now to pull this shit on me—all these years we've been together and he's never said a peep, and *now* he's obsessed with the idea of us being married, I'm ready to lose my mind!"

The whole scene just looked wrong to me, so—*false*. When I mentioned our marital conversation on the phone last night, he heaved a deep sigh. *"Listen, I respect your answer and I've accepted it—we'll have to move on from this point."* He spoke firmly, not at all angry, just—sad. *What the fuck does he mean by saying that? "Move on"—does he mean to leave me? Is he going to kick me out of the carriage house? It is his—Whitley gave it to him in his Will, he owns it free and clear. Maybe I can buy it from him—why should I move? Most of the stuff in it is mine anyway; he only has a bunch of books, the shelves that they're in, his desk, and that ugly leather chair that he loves so stinkin' much.*

"Did you tell him?" she asked.

"Tell him what?" I asked, uncertain about what she wanted to know.

"That we're going to Taos."

"Fuck no, have you forgotten Cape Cod? I can't tell him where we're going to be because he'll follow—and he should just stay out of it anyway—I don't want him involved with any of this shit."

"That was so sweet when he showed up—it was nice having him there," she cooed. "We had such a nice time in Provincetown—you should have come with us!"

"You want him?" I laughed. "He's in the market to get married, and you're getting divorced—" I teased her.

"Ohhh, no-no-no, he's yours!" she exclaimed. "I know for a fact that he does love you immensely. If it were me, I would feel flattered if someone loved me that much," she murmured.

"I feel smothered," I lit another cigarette and rummaged for the CD case. "Here, pick something out for us to listen to—I can't drive and search for music or I'll get us killed—anything but Beethoven, okay?"

After Sam flipped through the full CD wallet, she put *Dust in the Water, Dust in the Sky* into the portable CD player. After a joint effort fussing over the cigarette lighter and the adapter gadget, Dusty Waters began to pound lively notes on her guitar as her gravelly voice wailed and moaned about men being oppressive assholes and a woman's daily sacrifice to survive or something depressing like that. *What the fuck are we listening to?*

"I need to tell Guthrie," she said while lighting a cigarette with a green lighter she had bought at the gas station—we had laughed earlier about the message printed on its side: *Marriage is not a word, it's a sentence.* I can see a truck driver picking that up and having a chuckle or two with the cute little cashier as he laments his *sentence* left behind in Shit-hole Alabama US of A. *"I just picked it because it was green and white,"* Sammy had snickered. I always thought it was funny how she'd see something with writing on it and see it as a design rather than as words, her eyes detecting shapes and negative space rather than the message.

"You don't need to tell him anything," I grunted.

"Helena—I want him to know—he'll be frantic if he doesn't hear from me!"

"The fewer people who know where we are the better off we'll be—I don't want Preston finding out and chasing us down—"

"I feel so bad," she moaned.

"Why?"

"For Guthrie, it's going to kill him wondering."

"Are you really in love with him?" I asked. Even though she had admitted as much to me before, I got a sick pleasure out of hearing her say it—it's like watching people eat bugs on one of those stupid reality TV shows; I can't look away from the gratuitous, off the wall-ness of the idea—*Sammy and Guthrie in love! Whitley is spinning in his grave—no doubt about it—he's going to dig himself out of the grave as a pissed-off zombie and kick some ass—Guthrie's.*

"Oh, I don't know—there's something going on between us—that day in Boston, we wanted to, but we stopped—we couldn't start something with a clear conscience," she mumbled like she was ashamed of her behavior that day.

How far did they get? Did they actually get naked and come to the conclusion or what? Maybe he couldn't get it up—"I still can't believe you did that." I shook my head, struggling not to laugh. I cannot envision it, the two of them together doing it. *Nope, I don't want to go there—it's not a pretty picture. It's just gross how hairy he's gotten—hair in his ears, his back, his shoulders—UGH, he even had a hair sprouting on the end of his nose—what is up with that shit!*

Sam sighed with a loud exhale.

"Are you okay?" I asked.

"I'm okay." Sam lit another cigarette immediately after putting out the last one. "I have a confession to make."

"What's that?" I laughed. *Oh, boy, here it comes—this oughta be good!*

"I slept with Sylvester," she said with a bland tonality that didn't register as highly important in my ears, but I whipped my head around to look at her because I couldn't believe what I just heard.

"You did what?" I cried. My distraction caused the car to swerve wide and the people in a minivan in the passing lane had a panic attack on their horn. "Holy shit!" I corrected course; my heart went on a stampede through my chest. "When did you sleep with Sy? You're kidding me, right? Please tell me that you are kidding!"

"It happened before Whitley died—that night while you were away in New York *doing research*," Sammy said with a snide attitude that caused my head to do the herky-jerky again.

"Why do you say it like that—'*doing research*'?" I asked, mortified by the implication of certain knowledge.

"Whose dick did you *research* in New York, Helena?" she asked with an inquisition manner that pissed me off. Then she giggled.

"Shut up!" I took a swipe at her, but she ducked; I detected a smile when the headlights reflecting off the side mirror outside the passenger window lit up her face. "You bitch, what possessed you to do it?" I panted as the tears crowding in my eyes dribbled down my cheeks—*what possessed HIM to do it?*

"That night—I had a bad night with Preston, he got polluted with Whitley, and he scared me—he—he—I was sleeping and he woke me up—he tried to tie me to the bed—he always talked about wanting to do that, but I would never let him. He said it's all about trust and he tried to convince me it would be so sexy—he talked dirty, and then got a bit crazy when I fought back—I told him no. I got scared, so I ran away—I ran to the carriage house and found Sylvester outside stargazing—you know, he did tell you that I spent the night there. While we talked, he told me that he had put two-and-two together about you fooling around, because that kid you've been fucking mistakenly called the carriage house phone looking for you— he might've said something dirty before he realized who he was talking to. So, we comforted each other—and one thing led to another," she said, her voice tightening with strained emotions.

"Oh, that just explains everything—I can't believe you would do that to me!" I shrieked. My aggravation caused the car to swerve toward the passing lane again. "Holy fuck, I can't believe you're telling me this!" I began to gulp deep breaths of air, trying to get a grip on myself; my hands clenched the steering wheel as I promised myself not to get us both killed even if it did seem like a good idea at the time.

"Oh, yeah, I should tell you, that night isn't the first time I slept with him. It all started after you married Shep. I saw him from my window one night when I was home alone—Whitley was out doing Whitley things—you had just left town for Berkeley with Shep—so I went outside to see what he was doing—he looked so lonely, the moonlight reflecting off his glasses like that—beacons beckoning to me to come to him. So I seduced him and we fucked in the backyard," she proclaimed in a more confident tone—she almost sounded a bit self-righteous.

"You were only sixteen!" I cried, appalled that Sy fucked her when she was just a kid. "You were under-age—that pervert—that fucking old pervert!" I sobbed. *This cannot be happening, I'm dreaming all of this—this bullshit—it's all a bullshit dream.*

"It was beautiful—there was nothing perverted about it—I never regretted it, ever. I'm glad I chose him to be my first—I had decided it would be him long before that night."

"What are you talking about?" I gasped. As angry and distraught as I was, I felt intrigued at the same time in that same sick, twisted way that goaded me to watch people eat bugs on television—I needed to know even though I don't really want to.

"I was nine, I think—it was dinner time—he removed his glasses to impress you, but you ignored him. I always loved looking at his naked face, he's so handsome—he always looked so resolute because he knew what he wanted. I decided that I wanted him for myself, but I didn't know for what until I saw his glasses reflecting the moonlight that night years later," she said, singing her words with a joyous tone that caused me to waver in my anger and hurt—*she loves him.* Suddenly everything started to make sense—I became pissed all over again—pissed at Sy for taking advantage of a young girl, and I was pissed at Sam for taking advantage of him when he was vulnerable—I knew that he was vulnerable. It was my favorite sport to torture him—I knew that I had hurt him—I wanted to teach him a lesson, and make a fool of him. *He screwed her because I had made him miserable.*

"You are sick—both of you are sick. Oh-my-god-oh-my-god! I can't believe you did that! Eeeuuuuuuuuoooooo—" I wanted to vomit. Clenching the leather-covered steering wheel between my two hands, they began wringing—wringing whose neck, I couldn't decide, one neck for each hand I guess. I wanted to pull over, leave her on the side of the road, and then call Sy to tell him about where he could find her. But I couldn't—it would be like abandoning a child in a wolf-infested forest if I left her on the side of the highway. I wanted to get off the Mass Turnpike just to get out of the traffic full of Mass-holes who drive like they own the fucking road—I needed to look for a place to land so we can hassle this out without causing an accident.

"We had been sleeping together until you came home after your divorce from Shep," she said with a meekness that seemed meant to calm me down, only it didn't.

"You—you never said anything about it before! He never told me that was going on between you!" I cried as a torrent of fresh tears made it hard see where I was going. I was thankful to see the green signs indicating an exit coming up within the next mile.

"Yeah-well, we didn't want to tell you—it was our secret—Whitley only figured it out after he had to come over to scrape Preston off the front stoop of the carriage house that night—" she shrugged with a nonchalant care that I found disturbing. "Whitley told me before he died that he thought for sure Sylvester was going to ask to marry me once."

"Do you want him?" I asked this question for the second time tonight and quickly cast a glance at her. *Whitley condoned this relationship?* He knew, but didn't realize what he sensed about them—so typical of him to be oblivious of the world around him—he had his dick up some bitch's twat and wasn't paying attention to Sammy. How many times did I call home from Berkeley at night to find no one answering the phone, not even Sammy chirping her timid home-alone *"Hello?"* I had to call during the dinner hour to catch any of them around—sometimes Sy would answer the phone—he always sounded so—so—*happy. That bastard!*

"No," she replied in her typical flat fashion.

"Why, Sam—why?" I heaved a sob-laden moan.

"Does it matter? He loves you," she said, touching my arm with her hand. I shook her hand off and cringed from her as I started to slow down for the tollbooth.

"I can't believe that you're telling me this shit!" I cried.

"You need to know. That man is so in love with you—it's real sweet. When you came back, I let him go—I knew how he felt—I didn't want to keep him from fulfilling his dream to be with you."

I didn't reply as I fished for the ticket and money for the toll, then shot through to the off ramp that quickly dumped us onto a main drag of a town—*wherethefuckarewe?*

"He never said a word to me."

"I told him not to—no one needed to know about it."

"So you decided to do the honors? Fuck you very much!" I was so close to screaming at her I thought I was going to burst the blood vessels in my eyes—I was so glad we were at a stoplight. *I want to puke, just spew my guts everywhere.*

"Yes, because you need to hear it; he loves you and the guilt has been killing him ever since that night," she sighed. "Oh, for cryin' out loud, there are some days when being the passenger is great because you get to see stuff, and then there are times you see stuff you don't want to see," Sammy sang.

"What are you going on about?" I asked, wiping away tears with my coat sleeve.

"Here we are trapped at a traffic light in some godforsaken town and the view I have is a guy rummaging inside his nose for boogers!" Sam shrieked with laughter.

I cranked around to have a look and saw the guy with his finger jammed up his nose—not even being subtle about it, he was really digging deep, concentrating on mining out that crusty crumb of dried snot stuck wayyyyyy up his nose.

"Thanks for sharing!" I shouted, leaning on the car horn, startling booger-man. Sam giggled behind her hands as she slithered down into her seat so not to look at him anymore. "I think I'm more embarrassed for him being caught in the act than I am for seeing him," I chuckled and poked her in the arm. "Wave at him—hi, honey, woo-woo—hey, gold digger!" I shouted, sticking my finger up my nose at him, he cringed and yelled at us—I didn't need to hear what he said, I could lip-read *"you fucking bitches"* with no problem. We laughed hysterically; the light turned green and the booger-man squealed his tires on the salt-scoured pavement in his hurry to get away from us, and the cars behind us started to honk with annoyance. Gathering my senses, I flipped off the guy directly behind us via the rearview mirror and let the Caddy float smoothly through the intersection like we were the lead car in a parade.

"He still loves you," Sam whispered, the giggles all gone away.

"He loves me—he fucks you in our bed, and you are telling me that he loves me?"

"Yes, he loves you—he asked you to marry him."

"Whatever!" I moaned.

"I told him that I thought you were a stupid bitch for cheating on him—"

"Jeez, Louise, don't mince words—I'll have to come up with something just as despicable to label the two of you," I grumbled, pulling out another cigarette. "Give me your death sentence lighter," I asked, holding out my hand for it, she tucked it into my fingers.

"He didn't deserve that, Lena! He's been so good to you, but you nag him, tear him down, and treat him like he's a friggin' golden retriever fetching your slippers and cigarettes—he's so unhappy—I don't know how he has stayed with you for all these years," she said with an edge of resentment in her voice that I felt was uncalled for.

"What about what you guys did—does what I've done wrong make your little one-night-stand right?" I lamely shot back, feeling like a shitty whore, I threw the lighter on the seat between us, and it tumbled onto the floor. "Oh, fuckin' A!"

"Yes, it was a one-night-stand—we didn't do it to have a steamy sexual fling, we just did it because we were sad. We comforted one another, I know it isn't the best excuse in the world, but it's not like we're ever going to do it again—it just felt good, we needed to feel good, even if it was just for one night," she sighed with resignation, leaning her cheek against the window. I glanced at her, she stared out the window with her gaze turned upwards—I've seen Sy do that, looking for stars—reading the constellations. *She can't be seeing much, we're in a friggin' city full of light pollution.*

"How can he do that to me? Here I've felt guilty all this time for the things I've done and he turned to you the minute he found out—for revenge, that's what it was, he used you for revenge," I agonized. *Yet maybe not—he couldn't have slept with her for three years and not cultivate some emotional attachment—love.*

"Hello, Pot, this is Kettle, you are soooo black. You had a good thing with him, he stopped servicing your ass 24/7 to do what he has to do to live life—no different from anybody else—but no, you had to go off to screw some guy just because you've got the seven-year-crotch-itch, I'm-over-forty-and-it would-be-nice-to-fuck-someone-else-for-a-change. I could wring your stupid neck you're such a moron."

"You wanna talk pot and kettle—look in the mirror!" I screamed at her.

"I didn't go over to the carriage house to screw him just because he was there, I was running for my life, scared out of my wits because my husband wanted to do nasty things to me, and possibly beat the crap out of me if I put up a fight. Sylvester was so sweet, he took care of me like he always does—he is a good friend. Even though you're here with me now, you're not really here for me—you're here because it suits you to do it—I'm your excuse to go do whatever you want to do—and that's to go find Dulcie—you wouldn't be driving me anywhere if you didn't want to do that. I'm surprised you didn't just drive me to Deer Isle to dump me off with Sylvester and wash your hands of the whole mess. You know what? Sylvester wouldn't have made love to me if you hadn't been fucking Theo and Bookstore Man—he was faithful to you right up until that night."

The last shot jolted me—*she knows about Martin—how did she know about him?* It disturbed me that I had thought about taking her to Deer Isle to leave her with Sy so I could go on my merry way to do whatever. I'd probably go home and call Theo, the boy wonder, to come over to fuck me until I forgot about why he annoyed me—*to help me forget about Martin—to help me forget about Sy.* Without a doubt, I would have just left them together trusting that their friendship was chaste. I would have happily left her with him to do as they pleased together like I do every other time I've watched them walk off into bookstores or to a different museum wing, arm in arm, his head bent toward hers as they conversed in soft tones. *It never crossed my mind that he'd be tempted by her—that steadfast Sylvester Hayden would fuck a girl whose brains are scrambled by a freakish abnormality—what the fuck was he thinking?*

I made a right turn and continued to cruise around, getting significantly lost in a strange town. "Listen, there's more to why I've done what I've done, don't get all judgmental on me," I muttered. "Let me tell you, missy, it hasn't been easy-peasy—your precious Saint Sylvester isn't the easiest person to live with!"

"Happy Easter, I'm Peter Cottontail and Jesus has risen—stop thinking about yourself and think about him for a change—how do you think he felt once he realized what you were doing? I saw him—he was miserable because he never suspected a thing, he had trusted you. Then he was miserable after what we did. I'm sure a part of him secretly felt justified fucking me to spite you—and even if he did it with that purpose in mind, I don't think he truly meant any harm to me. I know Sylvester would never hurt anyone intentionally—especially me," she said with tenderness. I looked at her in the dim light of the residential neighborhood; porch lights and old-fashioned street lamps illuminated the interior of the car, and I saw that her expression was calm, distant, yet accessible—*she is "on"—there is no sign of her autism.*

"Are you in love with him, Sam?" I asked of this lucid young woman beside me whom I rarely see and talk to—*is this how she is with Sy? What about Guthrie—she said that she loved him? Who does she really love?*

"I love him in my way and he loves me in his, but he's not in love with me like he is with you—that man is nutty about you. You just had to fuck it up, didn't you?" she said sharply. "You had to hurt him—he would do anything for you, he was good to you, he would stand on his head for you— why did you have to hurt him?"

"I didn't mean to—" I began to defend myself, but stopped—there is no excuse for hurting him. "Well, I'm good at fucking up my life—I never learned to say '*no*' to a man. There were plenty of others before I went to New York—this has been going on for years, Sammy—practically since the beginning—once I started I couldn't say 'no'," I confessed with a deep sigh.

"Well, learn the word *no*—it's spelled N – O and it means the opposite of Y – E – S, that spells *yes*; it is a negative answer, a refusal, a denial, or a disagreement. Here I will use it in a sentence: *No*, I won't spread my legs for you—"

"I think I get the gist of it," I groaned. I caught sight of a green pilgrim's hat sign and turned left to follow the trail back to the Mass Turnpike.

"No-no-no!" she taunted, leaning toward me.

"Shut up already," I laughed and she giggled. I couldn't help it—I have to laugh at myself, because the alternative isn't available as an option. I pointed the Caddy at the on-ramp for the westbound Mass

Turnpike because I'm too pissed to stop for the night; I'll drive all night if I have to. As I drove, I puzzled over what I've been told and examined what I've known about him and her—them together—her obsessive attentiveness toward him, fussing, picking fuzz off his suit coat, smoothing his hair, straightening his glasses—grooming him like they're a pair of primates in the jungle. *Him— him sitting with her all night after Guthrie left; him sitting with her all night at the hospital.* Then I recalled the image of him standing by her bedside at the hospital the other day, her open hand flat on his chest, and his hands holding her hand in place—he looked as if he was in pain and she wanted to comfort him by putting pressure on a wound—his heart broken by me. Then the giant yellow bouquet of flowers the next day—the day after my rejection—and her gaze trained on their radiance, smiling even though tears drenched her cheeks. *"I miss Sylvester"*, she whispered when I asked her what was wrong.

I looked over at Sammy—she's asleep. I let her sleep and kept driving. *She doesn't understand why I have done what I've done—neither do I, so we're even. What the fuck is the matter with me—I have royally fucked-up everything again. I shouldn't have come back to Gloucester—but I had nowhere else to go. I had a break down. I had to pick between being fired or to quit my job because of my indiscretion with an undergraduate student. I got caught, but Shep didn't—or if he did, the old double standard—"I say, good show, old boy, but as for her, for shame, fire her ass!"*

It was ten o'clock when we crossed over into New York State; Albany didn't seem far enough away, so I kept going. It was well past midnight when I finally stopped in Syracuse and found a hotel. Once inside our room, Sammy collapsed onto the bed by the window, and I tried calling Sy. What I thought was his cell number turned out to be a wrong number. There was no answer at the house on Deer Isle. When the machine picked up, I left a message. *"You must be exhausted or you're still at the hospital—I hope everything is all right—we're fine, oh, yeah—I forgot to mention earlier that Sammy is with me, so don't worry about her. I also forgot my cell phone—I think it's on the dining room table over at Sammy's—anyway, I'll talk to you tomorrow night, love you, bye."* The words just rolled off my tongue like they always do, without a hitch.

On a whim, I called home, but there was no answer, the answering machine didn't even pick up, which I thought was weird, I wondered if Daisy did something to it out of spite—*fucking bitchy cat.* Returning the phone to its cradle, I sat staring at the wall, my body humming from the road vibration. After awhile, I lay down with the intention to sleep, but when I closed my eyes, the road showed itself to me as a dark pavement serpent with white hash marks sliding under the tires, a series of demonic taillights drifting ahead, and headlights like cosmic alien eyes coming at me. I opened my eyes and stared at the ceiling. *Does he love me—do I love him? Does he really love Sammy and does she love him?* With a sigh, I got out of bed to take a sleeping pill—*I need to forget about this shit.*

13

Vigilant. Adrift.

I departed from Deer Isle for Gloucester in the pale glow of a February afternoon. Jacob had passed away an hour ago, there is so much to do, but there is nothing more I can do; the arrangements were made months ago, his body is being cremated, and the memorial service will be performed this spring. *I'm done here.* I need to go home, but my emotions trickled into the lower gutter of grief upon hearing Helena's false tone hurrying through the practiced monolog left on my father's answering machine. It's so typical of her to be physically gone or emotionally unavailable at a time like this. In spite of the problems in our faulty relationship, I still needed to hear her sympathy, and at the very least, I needed her presence making Helena-noises in the carriage house when I returned home tonight. The place always feels so large and empty without her there filling the extra spaces. If she wanted to hurt me, she achieved her goal.

Her sudden departure today stirred my heightened suspicions, which automatically concluded that she's gone to meet her lover. Once my mind articulated the thought, it leapt to the next thing that distressed me even more—*if she's gone, who is watching out for Samantha?* I couldn't believe Helena left her alone with Preston walking around free—*can she be that selfish? Yes.* Anger ignited my grief into something ugly and bitter. I had tried calling Helena back, but her voice mail came on, I didn't bother leaving a message. Then I tried to call Samantha, but there was no answer at the house. My mind concocted several logical reasons why she didn't pick up the phone based on my knowledge of her routines—*she might've gone to the beach*—*I know she wouldn't go on a trip with Helena.* Some of my more worrisome notions revealed their grim possibilities because of my fear that Preston has done something to her again. *Samantha.*

My mind began beating its guilty drum. *"He guessed it was you,"* she had said, pressing her palm on my chest—not to push me away, but to draw me in—just her touch, a small gesture of concern—concern for the core of my feelings. While I held her delicate hand in place, I wished she could reach in to grasp my heart within her gentle palm, to cradle it until it calmed—until I felt peace. I never felt more wretched in my life; Helena had rejected my marriage proposal less than an hour before, which confirmed my fear that it was over between us. Before I arrived at Samantha's hospital bedside—before I saw the bruises—I was prepared to say goodbye forever. I meant to tell her that I planned to tender my resignation to the university and leave Gloucester—*I was finally going home to Deer Isle.* But I never declared my intentions; it was her hand resting on my breastbone that caused me to reconsider my plans. *She needs me now more than ever—I could not abandon her. I love her.* When I kissed her hair, I almost said it out loud—*I love you*—but I only mouthed the words within an exhaled breath, sampling their impact, and feeling besieged by their potential consequence.

"It's simple, Sylvester, you love her—don't overanalyze your feelings," Jacob had said.

The weeks that I have spent in Maine have helped me deal with the loss of my father before I actually lost him—I am thankful for this exclusive time with him. Our quarrel after my mother's death had become an embedded wedge between us; sometimes words are hard to take back even after you say you're sorry, but forgiveness has to start somewhere. The time that we spent together helped us conquer our grief and discard the blame.

"Let it go—don't ruin what time we have left with feeling sorry—" he told me.

"How could you stand it—knowing that I wasn't your son?" I asked him. I wanted to understand him—the position he must've been in when he first realized what had happened between Elise and Aloysius. Jacob had always treated Aloysius like a brother whenever they were together—shaking hands, hugging (even *him* hugging *her*), the three of them laughing, and *knowing*—how could they pretend that it was all right? *"We did it for her,"* he said. *"I forgave her because I loved her—but I don't think she ever for-*

gave herself." It seems men do strange things to please a woman they love—I know, because I've done my share—*I'm such a complete fool.* When I expressed this to him, he laughed. *"Don't be so hard on yourself."*

"After I learned about Mother's affair with Aloysius, you can't imagine the shock I felt—the anger. I want you to know that he didn't matter to me—you are my father—and I always loved you as my father." I said this while watching his stoic face remain impassive.

"I knew that—he knew that—he said that was how it should be," he replied with a nod.

"Remember that sealed box?" I asked.

"The one I asked you to deliver to Katharine?" he asked. I nodded. *"Yes, I remember it—and the contents—those beautiful watercolors by Annachie Powys, and the journals. He spent his life searching for them, only to receive them when his time was running out. I remember he was so frustrated at the time. When he said that she would write the book, I thought he was daft to suggest it. But she did a fine job—it's such a lovely book—he would've loved it."*

"It is a beautiful book—I'm glad she did it," I said. I remembered the day I delivered the sealed box to her; she seemed besieged by his intrusion into her life a year after his death. *"She was very young, much too young for him—"* I stopped and started to laugh—the parallel of my long ago dilemma with Samantha seemed too ironic. Jacob looked at me and smiled.

"I met her once—she was a very lovely, intelligent, young woman—yes, very young—but an old soul," he said thoughtfully, and then he smirked at me. *"How is Samantha?"* he asked. I started laughing out loud then, and he laughed with me. Thankfully, it wasn't the last time that I heard him laugh.

"I was a fool." My father's voice resonated in my head as I crossed into New Hampshire. *"It was Aloysius who brought us back together—what had happened between us was due to my negligence. We lived under the same roof, but we were light years apart in our emotions. After she had a breakdown, we moved here to start over—we wanted to be artists. I always believed that she was happy here—I never thought her melancholy was a bad thing—but she felt too keenly. After I found her dead, I felt so betrayed—I knew it was because of Aloysius—after we learned of his death, I should have been more vigilant—but I realized later on that it wouldn't have*

mattered, once she made up her mind to do it, there was no way I could've stopped her. She disappeared into the woods, just like a dying cat. I loved her—I believed she knew that—but after she died, I couldn't remember the last time I told her 'I love you.' You'd think after the years spent together that words don't matter—but they do—even the simplest words matter." His tear-drenched words were a revelation that I needed to hear.

Elise had been our bridge. Without her bright incessant chatter guiding us, we couldn't talk, but we've done nothing but talk these last few weeks. It's so odd, yet natural how we found things to talk about. He died peacefully while we were idly talking about the weather, and I promised that I would see to the cottage after the winter finished battering the cedar shingles.

"*Paint it yellow—she loved yellow,*" he sighed. "*I always wanted you to be happy, Sylvester,*" was the last thing he said to me.

It's time for me to move on with my life, I said in return after a comfortable silence, but I don't believe he heard what I said—he was already gone.

The simplest words.

What is wrong with me? This dysfunction—my inability to say the things that need to be said aloud has handicapped my relationships with the two women I have professed to love. My lack of vigilance allowed Helena to slip away, and I set Samantha emotionally adrift. Vigilant. Adrift. I've been a fool.

It was just past ten o'clock when I arrived home. As I drove up, I was glad to see the lights on in Samantha's house. The timer that turned the downstairs lamps on at dusk will shut them off after eleven—her bedtime. It made me feel good knowing she was still awake, probably reading in bed or maybe she's in the garret—*no*—from where I stood in the driveway, I could see the dark windows in the gabled peak of the studio.

Upon entering the carriage house, I flicked on the lights. Daisy ran to me with her sassy tail straight up and fanned out like a big feather, and she danced around my feet on her fuzzy slippers, mewing at me. I picked her up to squeeze her for a minute, and she immediately began to struggle— "*Unhand me, human, who do you think you are?*" I let her drop onto the sofa; she bounced and bounded away, leaving two wads of fluff behind. I really need to brush her later. I sneezed—*it's good to be home.* I took note of the extra food and water Helena left for the cat and my heart sank—*she's not planning on coming back.*

I stepped out the back door into the moonlit backyard and passed through the Rose of Sharon hedge, now made spindly by winter, and followed a path beaten down in the heavy snow by the tracks of both Helena and Samantha. I smiled at the companionable nature of the side-by-side tracks they made walking together—it appeared as if they were getting along all right. I let myself into the house from the back with the new key that felt a bit sticky in the lock. While kicking off the snow from my shoes, I found the house uncannily still; even if she's in bed reading a book, I should still feel evidence of her *being there*, at least I should hear music playing or her voice calling in response to my initial greeting through the upstairs floorboards that are the ceiling above my head. When I passed through the dining room, Helena's cell phone lying on the polished table surface caught my eye—plugged in, fully charged. *She left town without it—that's odd.* I took off my heavy great coat and left it draped over the table. When I entered the foyer, the plywood over the broken window by the front door made my heart gag on its pulse. *Shit—he broke in. Now that I'm home, I'll install an alarm system.*

"Samantha?" I called. It's entirely possible that she barricaded herself in the studio out of fear that Preston might come after her in the middle of the night—*I would feel better if she had.* It's never been in my nature to cause harm—*but I want to tear Preston limb from limb for what he did to Samantha.* My heart aches when I think about it—*I should have married her—if only I hadn't let her go—but you didn't let her go—she released you.*

My brain's playful devil's advocate has made a career out of being a pain in my ass. With almost ritualistic practice, I have gone over that final night with Samantha a million times—agonizing over my stupid inability to protest against her suggestion that I should go fulfill my fantasies. What was worse, she was right; I had to do it just to be sure—if Helena had rejected me—if she had laughed in my face, I would have gone back to Samantha with a clear conscience no longer teased by nagging dreams. I was relieved to be set free to figure out what to do—relieved that Helena was receptive. Then one night after supposed bliss with Helena, I looked up at the star-lit sky with her right there beside me like a dream come true, but my mind strayed back to Samantha. An uncanny, yet pleasant, melancholy took hold of me that night; this state of mind only intensified with the passing of time, it caused an unhealthy distraction that left my mind wandering in daydreams of someone unattainable.

When I recently divulged my conflicted feelings to Jacob, he considered me with a thoughtful cast. *"It's never too late for a second chance,"* he had said. I remember feeling so embarrassed when he caught me at the cottage with my young lover, both of us still damp from the shower we took to wash away our passions; his expression had been more curious than surprised when he met her, small and shy, clinging to my hand. I saw that particular expression after I told him about Helena's rejection of my proposal. *"It's just as well, she isn't the one you love—I know who you love—you just have to tell her."*

Can I call it love? Yes—it isn't anything else—when it comes to Samantha, there is only love. I climbed the stairs with a heavy heart; I longed to hold her tight, longed to tell her that I love her more than anything in the world—*most of all, I want to ask her to forgive me.*

"Hello?" I peered into her bedroom, turned on the light, and as I suspected the bed was empty. Stepping inside the room, I saw that the garret door stood wide open, and then I noticed the muddy boot prints on the floor outside the door. My gut clenched with growing concern; *Preston's been here.*

"Samantha?" I called, feeling sick from apprehension. I went to the garret door and looked up the dark, narrow stairs, the silence greeted me with a roar that caused a parasitic fear to grow deep in my bowels, and its chilly sensation went swarming up my spine to prickle my scalp like thousands of insectile feet.

What if Preston got in and—

"Samantha, it's just me, ummm—Sylvester." There was no reply. I had hoped to hear her bare feet running down the stairs; I had expected to have her tumble into my arms, and then I would breathe in deep the delicate smell of lavender—*lavender.* Her room smelled of it, but the scent was faint— she hasn't passed through here for several hours, probably not since this morning—or earlier in the afternoon. *How funny is that? I know her scent so well that I can tell such things!* My hand caressed the wall in the darkness to switch on the studio lights, and my heart lurched inside my chest as I entered the steep narrow stairway—my entire body cringed as I prepared for a gruesome sight—*what has he done to her?*

What I saw appeared ordinary in comparison to the dread that had provided my mind with imaginings of horrible conclusions. I sighed deeply, the studio is empty and tidy, everything is in its place, except discarded empty Beethoven CD cases, and the ashtray with cigarette butts in it. Helena had spouted paranoid concern about Samantha smoking. *"The idea that she might burn down the house is a possibility we must consider."* Helena's frantic remark echoed in my head with shrill intensity. *Damn it, Helena.*

It was an act of desperation when I asked Helena to marry me; I did it because I didn't want to believe that it was over between us—I did it because I believed in the delusion that I could say the magic words and everything would be all better. I had hoped that if she had said *"yes"*, everything would be all right, but I knew as soon as I put the question into the air that the old feelings were no longer there—whether she said *yes* or *no*, it was over. Her negative response only confirmed my fears—now we're just together because we're afraid to move on. Asking her to marry me was the stupidest thing I've ever done in my life. *I'm a fool.*

My gaze turned to the drafting table and the drawings pinned above it. I studied our portraits, bodiless heads floating in open white fields, Helena, Whitley, Lenore, Guthrie, me, and then sketches of our hands—portraits in and of themselves, and an ass. *Good lord, is that my ass? Why on earth would she draw a picture of my ass and have it there in plain view?* Feeling flush with a mix of embarrassment and thrill, my body memory recalled the last time that I made love to her. At the same time that I have savored the memory, I have punished myself for the pleasure. I shook myself away from this reflection and became disturbed all over again by her absence from the house.

Is she with Helena?

A loud noise downstairs startled me; the tread of footsteps coming up the stairs were much too heavy to belong to Samantha. I stepped out of the studio, closing the door behind me. Just as I crossed through into Whitley's side of the garret, I met Preston at the top of the stairs.

"Oh, it's you," he said with a smirk.

"Oh, it's you," I returned the mocking salutation.

"I want to see her, please step aside," he sneered.

"She's not here," I snapped at him, pissed at myself for leaving the back door unlocked which allowed him access—*stupid—stupid idiot!*

"Yeah, right," he laughed.

"Suit yourself, she's not in there." As I stepped aside to allow him to pass, he brushed by me with a classic *bully-bump*—our shoulders and gazes making contact—he smirked while I remained passively expressionless. Then he bellowed her name as he stomped across the floor planks, his voice rising in pitch as he continued to receive no reply to his inquiries. When I heard him thump down the stairway that led to her bedroom, I echoed him by coming down the stairs that emptied into the hallway, and we met in the common area where the hallways branched-off to the bedrooms.

"Where is she?" he asked.

"I was about to ask you the same thing," I returned.

"Don't be funny, Doc-tor Hayden—you know where she is—what did she send you back here for? One of her sketchbooks or a pencil? There must be something she wants."

"She didn't send me, I've been out of town for several days—I have no idea where she is, God forbid if you had anything to do with her disappearance."

"Disappearance—" he snorted. "She has not disappeared, I bet she's hiding somewhere in this house—probably in a closet—never mind, I'll find her myself."

"I must ask you to leave the premises," I politely extended the invitation for him to leave.

"Excuse me?" he asked, cocking his head with menacing curiosity.

"I want you to leave this house—you're trespassing."

"Fuck-off—I'm going to have a look around—"

Without giving much thought about it, I swung at him just as he turned away, luckily his guard was down when my right fist cuffed him square on the jaw; the pain in my hand was terrific—much worse than I ever expected. Then my left fist clipped him on the cheekbone below his right eye when he turned on me; he growled ferociously, pissed that I had struck him.

As we grappled in the hallway, I knew that I was in for it. I'm strong, but he's a lot bigger than me, and I'm certainly not a fighter; though fight I did with all that my instincts focused during the brief moments that I remained upright. There was no doubt that Preston intended to kill me; oddly enough, I didn't really care, I acquiesced to the notion of being a goner once my glasses exploded from my face. I longed for oblivion after he hurled me into a wall by my right arm, creating a sickening crack; gravity pulled me to the floor in a cloud of shattered plaster. My playing opossum didn't faze him because he was having too much fun making goulash out of my guts with his booted foot. When I thought it couldn't get worse, he dragged me to my feet and threw me headfirst down the stairs. As my body tumbled down the hard wooden planks, my right arm flopped at my side with painful uselessness, and I tried to keep my good arm over my head in a vain effort to protect my skull. At the landing, my momentum carried me to the foyer floor where I came to rest in an agonizing heap. At this point, I felt so much pain I stopped feeling the specific source of pain—*I am pain.*

Preston thundered down the stairs, and prodded me with his foot. He kept shouting at me, but I couldn't focus on his extensive diatribe, though I did grasp onto the gist of his anger. *"You were fucking her, weren't you? You were fucking her!"*

Just when I didn't think it could get any worse, he hoisted me by the scruff, and heaved me out the front door face-first into the snow. The initial cold was so shocking it snuffed out my burning lungs, and as I lay gasping for air, the cold soothed my pain.

After a rumbling quiet, things began to crash and shatter inside the house; I felt glass from an upstairs window fall on me.

"Where is she?" he bellowed to the night sky.

If I knew, I wouldn't tell him—I would rather die than betray her. I hoped that she was with Helena, not hiding in a closet where that monster will eventually find her—but their tracks through the snow showed them together—*they must be together!*

From where I lay, I could see the figure of Orion above the house, his arm raised in a threatening gesture, but he is frozen in the sky just like I am frozen to the ground, neither of us is able to do anything to stop the unfolding events, so we patiently waited.

Preston pounded down the front stoop and aimed one more kick into my prone body as if checking to see if I was still alive. Unfortunately, my writhing in the snow in response to his abuse alerted him to the fact that I was still among the living, so he punched me in the head just in case he had missed a spot. Stifling a moan, I gratefully listened to the sound of his footsteps crunching down the driveway. For a long time—or maybe it wasn't very long, I can't be sure—I lay enveloped in the bosom of heavy wet snow feeling it soak through my clothes. It hurt to breathe—*broken ribs for sure, probably a punctured lung.* I tried to move, but the pain was excruciating; I had no way to gauge how much damage he had done to me until I realized that I was bleeding from my mouth—*that isn't a good sign.*

While lying there, drifting inside my mind, thoughts of Samantha shook me—my legs and arms twitched as if I just awakened from a deep sleep. Bracing against the pain, I began to gulp air, forcing life into my broken body, and with every ounce of strength, I dragged myself out of my bloody snow angel and crawled up the neatly swept front stairs. The door stood wide open, for which I was eternally grateful to Preston for his carelessness because it would have been a chore for me to try to reach the doorknob let alone fiddle with keys if he thought to take the time to lock me out. All I have to do is get to a phone to call for help—easier thought than done—it felt like hours passed while I lay halfway through the front door trying not to pass out. Whenever I moved, I wanted to puke, but I used the reflex to let loose a sound inspired by anger; though I meant for it to be more like a growl, the resulting sound was the primal noise of a wounded beast waiting to die from a slow, painful death.

Oh, Samantha, dear heart—I hope you know that I love you—it would be a pity if I die tonight without ever looking you in the eye and actually telling you how I feel. Then with dogged effort, I commenced crawling on my belly.

14

Cleveland

Well, it's another fine night at the frame shop. Not only am I cutting mats and putting together frames for artwork I wouldn't give my last nickel for, I'm now covering for the recently fired night manager. I caught that nerdy little ass-wipe making special deals for himself on so-called limited edition prints (more things I wouldn't buy or go out of my way to steal).

Other than his lack of taste, his first mistake was having me do the framing and matting; he's perfectly capable of doing it himself—but he's the kind of management sort of guy who wouldn't lower himself to do such labor when he can delegate it to the peons below him. If he had made the effort to do it himself, then I wouldn't have noticed anything amiss until he used up something I'd miss, or if he left a dull blade on the cutter. The girl who cuts mats during the day shift appreciates it when I put a fresh blade on before I leave at night; she wasn't shy about nagging me the next day if her first cuts of the day didn't glide true. The tattletale *something's-not-right* at *Picture Perfect Gallery* was a certain batch of *special orders* that he filled out with no prices tallied as if money had been no object. Whenever I questioned the ass-wipe about the paperwork, he always claimed the orders came in after everyone else had left, and the register was already spitting out the daily report. Apparently, the women named *Michelle Belle* or *Tori Tuttle* ducked under the half-closed front gate, and begged to make a purchase for Aunt So 'n So's birthday present. *"You know I can't say 'no' to a customer, especially a pretty one,"* he told me with a wink as if I was supposed to understand his meaning—which I did, because plenty of pretty ones with money to burn do come in wanting to buy something pretty to decorate their boudoirs—

or shop for a favorite aunt. This bunch of crap comes from the guy who regurgitates the store policy whenever someone else bends the rules. What gets my goat is he's got a pregnant wife, so the wink and nudge didn't sit well with me. Although I wasn't the most faithful husband in the world, I never looked at greener pastures during my wives pregnancies. Granted the temptations were always there, but it just seems worse to go behind the back of a lady who's body is being stretched beyond recognizable shape and cries over greeting card ads; they were just so helpless that I felt obliged to cater to their every whim since I got them that way.

As I walked away from the conversation, I said to myself that it's none of my business if the sleaze-ball is sticking his dipstick where it don't belong, but I was suspicious because his insinuation of after-hours nookie clunked like a phony. The guy isn't an Adonis; no pretty girl in her right mind would go for it with him even if they got a great deal on cheap-ass-ghetto art. I mentioned the fishy *special orders* to the general manager, and after spending a morning with him going over the receipts, he then thanked me for my observations, and asked if I'd be willing to keep an eye on the situation.

Three nights ago, while I stood outside smoking a butt around the ashtray by the mall entrance, I caught the ass-wipe carrying out one of these *special orders* that I had just framed for the woman named *Tori Tuttle*. She's become quite a regular—according to him, things have become hot 'n heavy, and this particular piece was going to hang in her bedroom (wink-wink, nudge-nudge); I guess I was supposed to be impressed by the little nerd's intimate knowledge. After he dropped the gate in front of the store behind me, I waited outside the mall entrance to keep an eye on his parked car, and as he stepped out the mall's front door, I hailed him. With a flustered giggle, he claimed to be carrying the package out to her car. When I offered to help him with it because it was large and the Lake Erie wind seemed primed to turn it into a sail, he then melted into a guilty puddle of thief, crying and confessing all over the snow bank. The two guys from mall security whom I happened to be chatting with by the ashtray became very interested in the spectacle he made of himself; I didn't have to lift a finger to accuse him of anything.

With him out of the picture at *Picture Perfect Gallery*, I'm currently thinking up the 200th way to choke the living shit out of that little ass-wipe because I'm wasting time sitting at my recently inherited desk tallying a register drawer that got fucked-up by the new cashier he had hired. Just moments ago, she sat across from me, sobbing her apologies for being a dim-bulb; I couldn't stand watching her heaving bosom nearly popping out of her skin-tight shirt anymore, so I sent her home to scrape together a few brain cells for tomorrow afternoon. Computerized cash registers are only as smart as the humans who push the buttons, although I only have a rudimentary knowledge of their workings, there's one thing for sure, if the damn thing was on the blink, I'd be the only one in the entire mall that could make change without the stupid machine spoon-feeding the math for me! Nothing like technology to turn the brains of an entire population into malleable mush.

When the telephone rang with irritating shrillness, I stopped short of smashing the fucking thing onto the floor with one swipe of my hand. This is *not* how I had envisioned my life!

"Guthrie Ryder," I barked without declaring the store name.

"Hi Guthrie," a small voice murmured softly into my ear.

"Hi, uh—can I help you, ma'am?" I didn't know too many people who would call me by my first name, and I have yet to become intimate with any of the staff or customers to let them use my first name—*nor do I intend to*—I have to keep reminding myself that this is only temporary.

"It's Samantha," the voice sighed.

Suddenly her voice became recognizable to me; she sounded exhausted—and relieved. A rush of emotion caused sparks to go off in my vision. "Sammy—honey, I've been worried about you—are you all right?"

"I'm in Cleveland," she garbled; it sounded like she choked on a giggle.

"You're—did you just say you're in Cleveland?" I laughed, feeling that weird giddy euphoria of butterflies in my stomach like an idiot schoolboy with a crush; I get like this whenever she calls, and the idea that she's come to see me has sent me on a heavenly rocket-ride showered with fireworks.

"I'm at a payphone near the mall's main entrance—I don't know where you are in here—please, come find me!" Her voice quivered as if breathless with excitement or almost in tears from fright.

"Shit," I sighed. "Are you all right?" *Out there all alone, she must be terrified.*

"I'm fine—I just want to see you for a little while—I can't stay long."

"You're here—you're really here—how did you get here?" I lowered my voice and took a quick look around. I wondered if anyone heard me; the other employees were busy out front and thankfully, there was no one in the break room sucking coffee with their ears flapping.

"Yeah, I know I'm here; I thought I'd come to say *hello*—can I do that or are you busy?"

"Uh, sure," I sighed, leaning back in the chair; I looked around again to make certain that I was alone. My head began to spin with confusion—*she's here—what the fuck is this all about?* "Shit," I sighed, I felt sick to my stomach, and my head pounded a beat that felt a half step behind my heart in rhythm.

"Guthrie?" her bodiless voice inquired of me.

"Listen, Sammy, just look directly ahead of you—the elevators are right there across from the payphones—all you got to do is ride up to the third level, I'll meet you there, all right?"

"Okay, I see them—I'll see you in a few." Then *click*, dial tone—she hung up. I stared at the handset and wondered if it was just a crank call; her abrupt good-bye's always leave me feeling fooled in that sort of way—*did that really happen?* I dropped the phone back into the charger and rose from the chair feeling dizzy. *How did she get here—why is she here?*

"I'm on break," I told Reg and Camille on my way out the door; they cringed without making a reply; they're not yet used to my being the boss—I'm willing to bet that they think I'm a creep for ratting on Mr. Ass-wipe—or they just think I'm a creep, period. That nerd used to let them get away with standing around picking their noses all day if it suited them, but I crack the whip and keep them busy cleaning and redecorating when the store is empty. *Say goodbye to Mr. Ass-wipe and say hello to Mr. Asshole.*

I walked out to the elevators and stood waiting. The doors opened, two people stepped out, but no Sammy. *Did she get lost walking the straight line from the front door to the elevators?* The mall is mid-week quiet; it's almost ten o'clock on a middle of winter night. The joint is a ghost town because there's a big storm churning up from the Gulf that's on a collision course with another storm coming down from the Great Lakes, so anyone who has sense is at home snug as a bug. The rest of us are either stupid or in need of keeping our jobs to pay the bills on time. With urgent concern, I leaned over the railing for a look-see if I could spot her; then the echo of footsteps coming up the stairway reached my ears. When I turned my gaze in that direction, I saw a small woman bundled in a winter coat staggering toward the top step.

"Sammy!" I called. The little face wrapped in a hat and scarf that turned to acknowledge my call was indeed hers, and a big smile cracked her face wide open.

"Guthrie!" she cried.

"Samantha—why did you take the stairs? The elevators are working," I scolded with laughter, tethered to relief.

"I hate elevators," she grumbled, reaching the top step.

"Okay, whatever," I laughed. As I went over to meet her, a couple of guys from security that I knew from conversations around the ashtray walked by; they acknowledged me with a *"How ya doin', Ryder"* as they glanced over at us with curiosity. I mumbled something slightly incoherent that she was my stepsister, and then I scratched my head while trying to imagine how she got here. "Well?" I asked, feeling awkward. Seeing her in this context is jolting; it seems as if I've lost my tongue—again the schoolboy with a crush syndrome.

"Well," she echoed with a laugh. "A well is a deep hole in the ground and water comes out of it," she sang the standard smart-ass reply that I had taught her when she was little and learning how to talk. I squirm whenever I think about the catalog of things I taught her—I certainly wasn't the best example to have around such an impressionable mind.

"Yeah, ummm, gee, Sammy, you're a lot smaller than I remember; I thought you were taller," I replied with an equally stupid comment—teasing her about her awe regarding my being tall the last time we met. She rolled her eyes at me with a laugh, and we fell together in an embrace. She planted her mitten-encased hands on each side of my face and pulled me down for a kiss. At first, our kiss was just a friendly peck, but it suddenly turned passionate once our hedonistic feelings came drooling forth and we started to slobber all over each other with an impulsive lack of restraint. Her hat and scarf unraveled from her head as my eager hands stroked her hair; she smelled like sweat, cigarettes, cold winter air, and an underlying hint of lavender; I wanted to devour her. When we parted from the embrace, the two security guys passed by again; they stared at us with moderately amused interest; I nodded acknowledgement to them, and scooped up her hat and scarf from the floor. When I turned back to her, she smiled with a psychotic grimace that stuffed whatever credibility I had into the dumper.

"I guess I can't say you're my stepsister after that," I mumbled around a smirk.

"But I am!" she snickered, clamping her hands over her mouth.

"Well—shee-yit, so ya are." I looked at her upturned face closely and noticed a fading bruise next to her left eye; my fingertips touched her face with tender concern. I have lost count of the number of times I almost pointed Delta Dawn toward Gloucester since I heard what that fucker had done to her, but she told me to stay away—*that hurt*. She ducked my caress with an exaggerated flinch; seeing this reaction, I became keenly aware of the damage done, and anger welled up inside of me—*I want to kill him*. "Sammy," I whispered.

"I really should go—Helena is waiting in the car—the weather really sucks out there—she was pissed at me for insisting that I needed to see you," she murmured, her body sagged with a sad lament that visibly cried for release.

"She's here too! What's going on—why are you here? Where are you going?" Too many questions all at once; Sammy gaped at me while her mouth fumbled for words and her hands flapped like a restless bird preparing for its first flight.

"We ran away from home—pretty fucked-up, huh?" she giggled, covering her face—but I wasn't sure if it was a giggle.

"For real?" I pulled her hands away from her face to see if she was laughing or crying; her face was red, but dry-eyed. She's tapped out—there are no more tears left because she's cried them already; the tender skin around her eyes appeared scarred by rampant emotions.

"Yeah, we drove Whitley's Caddy—Helena agreed to take me away—Preston won't notice it missing—" she burbled the explanation with excited hiccups of laughter.

"No shit—" I expressed with the lack of anything better to say.

"—he might not notice it gone until spring, so we left Helena's T-bird in its place at the lock-up. The guy who runs the storage place doesn't care which car is in there, just as long as he gets the monthly check for the space! No one trying to find us will be looking for us in Whitley's car—they'll be looking for the T-bird."

Upon my initial consideration, the logic was ingenious, but this odyssey sounded not only desperate, but it was wacky and not well thought out, if you're trying to hide from someone looking for you, the red Cadillac will stand out like a sore thumb. She continued the rambling, fragmented narration of their trip—the crappy weather in Buffalo foiling their effort to reach Cleveland yesterday—so this is their third day on the road. During the telling of the tale, her voice went from soft to something frantic; I couldn't help smirking while she ranted because her temper is just like Lenore's; standing here listening to her speak, the voice and the words together became music to my ears, but I didn't want to be on the receiving end of her wrath.

"Where are you going?" I asked again, trying to make sense out of why they chose to come this way if Helena was against stopping here to see me; it sounds like there was quite a power struggle between them all day long.

"I really shouldn't tell you, but we're going to Taos, New Mexico—we're looking for Dulcie—Helena thinks she's working in an art gallery out there—she found some letters Whitley kept in his desk—he knew where she was—"

"Sammy," I interrupted, "did Preston go after you again?" I needed to know.

"I had to go—I'm so afraid." She looked at me and then brushed her hair back from her forehead and she pointed at the fading bruise that appeared to have taken up most of the left side of her face. "This is a lot better now—you should have seen it after he did it to me. I had to go because he broke into the house Wednesday morning—he didn't get me this time—but he would have—he could have—thankfully, Sylvester had installed the locks on the garret doors so he couldn't get me—the police were looking for him when we left town, but they couldn't find him. I had to go—so I asked Helena to take me as far away from home as possible." While she gibbered along with her story, her entire face contorted by the involved effort to fight back tears, and then she collapsed against me, her little arms encircled my waist as she hugged me tight.

"I'm so glad to see you, Guthrie!"

"Oh, Sammy—" I moaned, clasping her to my chest.

"No one can guarantee my safety—I had to go—so, I came here to tell you."

I didn't know what to say, so I hugged her tighter—it did little to make me feel better or change her situation, but it felt good just the same. *I should have been there!* If I had been there, I would have kicked his ass, even better, I would have killed him—the jail time would have been worth it just to solve the whole thing in one final act of violence.

"I've been worried—especially after you said you saw his tracks around the house the other day. When you didn't call—at first, I thought maybe you had to go to Maine to Jacob's funeral—it was logical, but you hadn't called to tell me the news. You'll think I'm weird, but I was afraid something happened to you—I swear I felt something—something like—like your fear, I knew you were afraid—I can't explain it. I nearly drove out there last night to see what was up. I can't tell you how much I have missed you—I wish you had called!" I stopped myself before I revealed too much of my fear. These last few days of silence, I began to feel a sick jealousy that I've cultivated lately about Hayden—*I was afraid that he finally got it together to tell Helena to piss off and moved in with Sammy.*

"Last I knew Jacob was still alive—but Helena hasn't been able to reach Sylvester—I'm so worried about him. She's so stupid—she left her cell phone behind, so no one can reach us—there seems to be something wrong with our phones at home; the answering machines aren't working at either house—we think Preston broke in and probably trashed everything looking for me! Oh, Guthrie, I gotta go! Helena said I could see you for just a little while—I only wanted to stop by to tell you in person, I didn't want to call—it's just something I can't do over the phone—I hate telephones," she sighed as her body drooped in a posture that was not exactly relaxed—exhaustion mixed with anxiety. We stood still, and the stillness helped her restive body to recover a semblance of composure.

"I must go now," she muttered into my chest.

"Let me walk you out to the car."

"Okay, you'll need a coat, it's freezing out there."

"Nah, I'm okay," I scoffed.

"You're just wearing a t-shirt! Why do you men all have to do that? Even Sylvester is weird like that—I watched him go outside barefoot in the snow to get the mail rather than taking the time to put on his socks and boots," she laughed. Her cheeks became tinted pink in a quick reaction to the memory, and her face brightened as she cuddled me with another hug. Hayden barefoot in the snow was a funny image; I had an idea he would do it without much fuss, but not with much grace. Her blush reminded me again about their past intimacy, and I wondered about in what context did she witness him do this act of being a man.

"I dunno—we're just stupid, I guess," I snickered as I guided her toward the elevator, and pressed the down button; she looked at me, frowning. "I'm taking the elevator, I'm an old man, is that okay with you?"

"Sure, whatever—you make it sound like you're decrepit—you're not *that* old," she sneered with a disgruntled grimace as she pulled away from me; I let her go, half expecting her to bolt for the stairs.

"Aww shucks," I grinned, looking down at my shoes and kicking the floor; I was playing with her, trying to keep her with me.

"Really, you're a good-looking man, so what you're bald and gray, who the fuck cares, shave your head if it really bugs you—most bald guys are doing that these days—you have a nice shaped head—I think you look fine—miiigh-tie fiiiinnnne," she slurred.

"Sam—" I sighed to feign protest—if she wanted to stroke my fragile ego, I'll let her.

"What?" She poked my spare-tire with her finger still enclosed within her mitten. "You could do sit ups to take care of that little roll there—lift weights or something—if you cut out the beer you'd have a six-pack in no time—I remember how you could make your stomach hard and let me punch it—I would whale away on you with all my might, you'd just stand there and laugh." She poked me again with a light punch, and then she looked me over. "You still have a nice ass; I'd wrap my hands around that and have my way with you if you'd let me," she murmured, leaning in real close.

"Sammy." I sighed, rolling my eyes to avoid an expression of shock as my hand self-consciously rubbed where she had jabbed me in the gut; sometimes the things that drop out of her mouth disturb me a little bit too much. When the elevator doors closed, I grabbed her and we kissed again. While her arms gripped me tightly around the neck, she murmured something, but I didn't hear what she said because my tongue swabbed the words out of her mouth. When the elevator doors opened after the brief ride, we parted and stepped out.

"I hate elevators," she muttered.

"I couldn't tell," I chuckled; that giddy feeling overwhelmed me again—*I've got it bad.*

"That's why I had a death grip on you, pal," she growled. The fierceness in her tone disturbed me—*did I push it too far?* The tone of her voice sounded just like her mother, and that irritated me in a strange way; sometimes it is hard to separate the two women in my mind, yet they are different—*so different.*

"Oh, well, I thought maybe you just loved me or something like that," I said, trying to justify my reasons for swapping spit with her twice in the last five minutes. *She wasn't struggling—or does she not fight off a man when he's on her—does she just let it happen?*

"Well, yeah, umm—I do, ya know," she sighed as if defeated.

"I love you too, Sammy." I put my hand on her shoulder.

"Yeah, I know, in some form," she said, walking ahead of me. I let my hand drop away, stung by my own words being repeated to me. I followed her through the mall entrance and caught her by the arm; she turned to look at me and smiled sadly. "I gotta go now."

"Yeah, I know—umm, call me if there's anything I can do—" I fumbled for something significant to say—a send off to encourage her or something endearing, but my brain became pathetically feeble in the department of encouraging and endearing things to say.

"What can you do?" She tipped her head with curiosity.

"I dunno—I want us to keep in touch—I've missed you," I said with a lame effort to express my feelings.

"I've missed you too. I'll call when I can—" she paused as she glanced over at the snow-covered Cadillac. "If Preston is looking for us—he might try to find you," she mused, wondering if she might have put me at risk for some kind of trouble.

"I won't tell him—or anyone who wants to know—anything. I haven't seen you—Samantha who? Oh, yeah, her—nope, I haven't seen her," I mocked innocence, but her blank expression wasn't receptive to my humor, typical—sometimes she gets it, sometimes not. Feeling like a goof, I looked down at the snow around my feet. "Can I see you again?"

"Why?"

"I want to see you," I plead. It was selfish of me to make this request, but I was having a hard time letting her go off into the night without a guarantee that I will see her again soon—preferably sooner rather than later because the nervous schoolboy inside of me might die if I don't have hope of seeing her again.

"Maybe someday, but not right now," she sighed with impatience.

I shivered in my t-shirt and stuffed my hands into the pockets of my blue jeans; I glanced at the Caddy; the car is still a beauty—not a winter rat—the ragtop is not going to hold the heat in this climate. Helena's vague shape seated behind the steering wheel watched us; I could see the orange glow of a cigarette ash brightening every time she took a drag—*she's smoking like a frazzled chimney.*

"You two picked the worst time of year to run away from home—we're getting a storm tonight, and it looks like it's coming sooner than predicted. Can I take you girls out to dinner or anything?" I asked, selfishly hoping to prolong my time with her. I could bail out from work, the fucked-up cash drawer can wait until tomorrow—let the big boss figure it out—it's not like he's paying me more to baby-sit this joint while he interviews new candidates for a job I don't want.

"No, we need to get back on the road. Helena wants to try to beat the storm," she said as she tucked the hat on her head and wrapped the scarf around her neck.

"Well, you should tell Helena that she's only going to drive into the storm if you do. You're better off staying the night in Cleveland—it'll be out of here by tomorrow afternoon." When I looked around in the snow-filled air, my eye caught sight of a group of women coming out of the mall; one of their shapes seemed familiar. I turned away from them once I felt satisfied that none of the bundled bodies belonged to my ex-wife or anyone that

I might have slept with in the last five years or so. "I wish I could go with you," I whispered.

"You can't." There was a hint of panic in her voice as her eyes locked onto my face.

"I know," I nodded. "Why did you come see me?"

"It's the closest I've ever come to Cleveland in my life—I had to stop," she giggled.

"Well, there's better sights to see in Cleveland to see than me, but whatever the reason, I'm glad you did," I said. Perhaps I made my remark too stern—too serious, but I felt *serious*, and judging by her attentive expression, she knows I'm serious. My feelings for her run deep into my being—seeing her tonight meant a lot to me—the fact that she insisted on seeing me because she was in the area meant something. *I mean something to her.*

"You *are* in love with me," she said with a song of amazement trilling her voice.

"I'm afraid so—you could make an honest man out of me—I can't think of anyone else these days." I confessed to my dilemma with a hint of discomfort as I began to shift uncomfortably on my feet—it is fucking cold out, and I wished for my coat. I clenched my teeth and muscles, refusing to allow even a minor tremor to shiver.

"I'm sorry, I shouldn't have come here," she sighed with exasperation.

"It's all right. It's the best thrill you've given me yet," I laughed.

"Guthrie," she sighed, reaching up to caress my face, and I pressed my right cheek into her mitten, kissing the fuzzy palm. "I gotta go now, goodbye."

"Goodbye," I bent down to kiss her, but my mouth slid off her lips to land on her cheek that she purposefully turned toward me. I gave up the kiss and hugged her instead, but she broke away from me with a gentle push to let me know that she wasn't in the mood for any further fondling. I let her go, feeling rejected. I walked her to the car parked at the curb and opened the passenger door. "Hi, Helena," I nodded, peering inside just as a huge snowflake plopped into my eye. "What the fuck!" I laughed at the icy varmint's assault.

"Hey, Guthrie, watch out for those snowflakes, they're big enough to put yer eye out," she laughed. She turned on the windshield wipers, and the heavy snow full of moisture from the Gulf of Mexico slid off onto the curb—I jumped back to avoid it; I knew the evil witch did it on purpose.

"Call me," I said, kicking at the snow with my sneaker in mock humility.

"What do you want me to call you?" Sammy laughed at one of our old jokes, once again reminding me that I played a large role in her growing up.

"Just Guthrie—that's easier," I muttered. "I'm glad you're all right, Button's—it was good to see you—please, don't hesitate to call me if you need anything."

"Yes, it was good to see you too," she squeezed my hand that I extended, begging for one last touch.

"Take care driving, I don't need to point out that the roads suck," I said to Helena; she nodded and saluted me. I closed the door and mouthed the words *I love you* as the car rolled away from the curb, and Sammy mouthed them back, smiling and waving at me.

I stood on the snowy sidewalk, lit a cigarette, and watched the Caddy's elaborate taillights disappear around the corner heading toward the highway. An angry kick at the snow bank soaked my sneaker as my frustration got the better of me. It's so unfair that Sammy no longer feels safe in her home—a place of sanctuary for all of her life is now unsafe because of her spouse—the man who took vows to love, honor, and cherish her. He failed to meet his obligation; he has chosen to do harm—to hate. It was never about loving her, he's just a predator—he used her, he took advantage of her disability to get at her money.

I continued to stand out in the cold—smoking, thinking—and worst of all feeling. My feelings for Sammy confuse me more than ever after this brief visit. I felt safe from them with the distance between us. The phone calls to say hello and catch up on the happenings in our lives seemed safe enough for us to maintain a proper perspective. But right now, I feel like I just took a swan dive off a cliff—I'm hoping for water below, but chances are there are spikes of iron standing at attention like the maw of a biblical beast waiting to impale me.

If Sammy had said *let's go* to my wish to go along for the ride, I would have willingly left everything behind. Then I'd get her into a hotel room and screw her lights out, but her attitude said *no* to all of my longings. Sex is the last thing on her mind right now—*raped and beaten by her husband.* I kicked the snow again. *What the fuck is that shit all about?* I wanted to find that asshole and kick in his head. As dishonorable as I've been in my life, I've never raped a woman—if she said *no*, she meant *no*, there's no teasing about it, women are not that confused about what they want. I'm glad she got out of there—he's getting bolder—the next time might be the last, I know he will try to kill her the next time, that's the natural progression for sick fucks like him.

I squinted through the heavy snow, wishing to see the red convertible grinding and sliding through the snow-bound parking lot, the headlights flashing at me to stay put—but it didn't and it won't—the longer I waited the less likely it was going to happen. Now I wish that I had gone with them. If anything, I'd go along just to make sure they were going to be all right; two women on the road in shitty weather is asking for trouble.

Sammy had felt like a child in my arms; her heavy suede coat with soft, wooly lining was just like a protective padding around her fragile shell. She didn't look well—pale and thin—there was something odd about her eyes, something that looked like pain—*she is in pain*—pain from the rape and the beating she received, but there is a pain that runs deeper than physical discomfort. Anguish and fear layered her face with alternate coats of emotion; emotions that she couldn't articulate. It must be so hard for her to be away from home; it was always difficult for her to travel, and she's forced to rely on Helena to look after her—*holy shit, if that isn't the blind leading the blind!*

Helena's only shining moment in her life was the night Sammy was born. After that, she became inept, fucking up everything right and left, and she has the nerve to blame everyone for her failings; but the blame is all over her—blame is sticky like bubblegum all over her face. She always had to blow the biggest bubble, but lose interest, lose control, and then boom. She can't get it off, and won't because she's too damn busy pointing a finger at the one she felt held the needle to prick her bubble—Dulcie, Whitley, Lenore, me, Sammy, Shep; now Hayden must be catching her latest fall-out because she's abandoned him. He does love her in some form, but I think he's got it all wrong in his head—he's in love with Sammy. *I won't fight him for her if he wants her because I know he's the better man.*

Now sufficiently chilled to the bone, I crushed the spent cigarette into the ashtray and went inside. On my way back to the store, one of the men who saw me kissing Sammy earlier muttered something that sounded like *"Way to go, Ryder."* I smiled to myself thinking about how the kiss had quickly erupted into passion; I nearly sucked the girl's face off because I do love her—love her in more ways than I can explain, let alone justify.

Damn, I let her go! But what else could I do?

~

"Don't cry, Sam—please, don't cry," I pled to the heaving body on the passenger side, but this only made her wail louder as she continued sobbing with miserable gusto; anger flashed through me with enough heat to cause the end of an ice age. *This is just perfect, thanks a lot, Guthrie, you jackass, what the fuck did you say to set her off? Why did I agree to stop to see him? Because she pitched such a fit about seeing him that I had no choice*—Every time she saw a sign for Cleveland she made a ruckus—*"Cleveland 50 miles, Cleveland 40 miles, Cleveland 15 miles, Cleveland 3 miles, Welcome to Cleveland—Pllleeeazzzzzeee, we must stop—I want to talk to Guthrie!"*

Arrrgh! I was ready to kill her, but I had my hands full keeping the car on the road. I did not want him involved in our business right now, he was libel to fuck things up for us—although I couldn't imagine in what way, just the thought of him made my ass itch. I can't believe we wasted so much fucking time trying to find this goddamn mall out on East Bumfuck Road, Cleveland, Ohio. *I can't believe this weather—we shouldn't be out in it.* It was all I could do not to go foaming at the mouth crazy, pull over, and run screaming into the night. Suddenly she stopped, as if someone pulled the plug on the Sammy crying machine.

"This is what Guthrie would call *whatthefuck* weather!" I laughed, trying to get her to engage me, but she only moaned in reply. "Sammy, listen to me, this weather is really bad, and the roads are only going to get worse, I'll get us killed if I don't stop soon—I want to find a hotel, okay?"

"Okay." The muffled reply came from the passenger side. I glanced over at her; it seemed like she generated her own shroud of darkness, I could hardly see her over there.

"Are you okay?"

"Fine—I just—I just want to go home," she hiccupped.

"Well, sweetie, we can't right now—we need to hole up for the night. Tell you what, after we're settled in someplace, we can talk about going home if that's what you want to do," I offered. Truthfully, I was relieved she made the suggestion—going home might not be a bad idea; this cross-country trip can wait for better weather. I should have taken her to Deer Isle for a few days until the police caught up with Preston. *Why did I let her talk me into this bullshit trip? She was right, it is what you wanted to do—she gave you the excuse to do it.*

"I'd like that very much," she sniffled and then blew her sloppy nose into a tissue.

"All right," I sighed, letting my right hand release the steering wheel from the death grip I had on it to pat her shoulder. I could sense her body sitting over there, crushed into the seat—she's there physically, but where is she? She's so lost inside herself these days; it's been like riding alone. Ever since her confession bomb about sleeping with Sy, she became quiet, but we were doing all right in spite of it; I got over being mad—but I have not forgiven them—especially *him. What the fuck, Sy!* Had I known what I know now, everything about their relationship that ever bugged me would have made sense. Over the years, they always annoyed me—their closeness, the attention they paid to one another—all right under my nose! During Sammy's infamous wedding day, I saw her kiss him in the alcove behind the curtain—they kissed on the lips. At the time, I thought it was strange, but then my sister is strange, and Sy is used to her being strange. When I think about that day, the two of them squeezed into the downstairs powder room, she tending him while he upchucked his guts out, I wonder what they were thinking—*did they feel regret?* And when Whitley began to question her about who she had sex with, I defended her privacy—then Sy kneeling at the toilet began to hurl with such a guttural racket, he disrupted our conversation. It was as if he purged his guilt with every heave-ho—he's the rare bird who would fuck a girl and still respect her in the morning, but he wouldn't respect himself.

Three years—they had an affair for three years—doesn't that mean anything to him?

I still can't wrap my mind around what must have run through their minds when my return from Berkley forced her to make him choose between us. How could he be intimate with her for all that time and then turn away—*but has he turned away? Apparently not.* Now I know why he's been different since I came back from New York—I had sensed something wrong with him, but I kept my guilty conscience wrapped tightly around my brain, blocking out any insight about why anything was *wrong—he already knew, but said nothing.*

"*I know that he does love you immensely. If it were me, I would feel flattered if someone loved me that much.*" Her words. *Does he still love me?* His insistence that we should get married really puzzles me—then he said "*we'll have to move on*"—so, I guess it is over between us—*isn't it?*

I'm worried about him—*what's happened to him?* I have tried calling home and Deer Isle every night, but there has been no answer. And after a few unsuccessful combinations that pissed off the recipients of my wrong numbers, I finally got his cell phone number right; he isn't picking up his cell phone either—I can understand if he has it turned off in the hospital, but why hasn't he responded to my messages? He's had plenty of opportunity to call us at the hotels—I can't believe our timing has been that far off to keep missing each other—*something isn't right—maybe Preston got him—oh, shit, what if he's dead? Oh, thank god, there's a vacancy sign!*

A hot-pink neon roadside sign for a motor inn emerged like a beacon through the heavily falling snow. With sickening slowness, I slid into the parking lot and came within inches of taking out a newspaper stand outside the front door.

"I found a place, Sammy—I'm going to check in, all right?" I said to the quaking body leaning against the passenger side door.

"All right," she replied tearfully.

I wanted to cry too—to cry about everything.

෪

After figuring out the messed up cash drawer, I left work after eleven o'clock and headed for home. While driving on the highway at a crawl, I noticed a cheap motor inn and spotted the distinct profile of the Caddy in the parking lot; even with nearly four inches of snow on it, I couldn't miss it and I was only half-heartedly looking for it. I pulled in quickly, crossing over from the left lane and pissing off two lanes of crawling traffic. Delta Dawn came to a rest at the office door. Shaking off ruffles of snow, I entered the lobby, and met the mild gaze of the scrawny ethnic guy behind the counter. "I need a room, got any vacancies?" I confronted him with my lack of humor to avoid any small talk about the weather.

"I've had a lot of people seeking shelter on a night like tonight, but I do have a few rooms left—would you like smoking or non-smoking?" the clerk smiled. I found his excessive politeness irritating because my frame of mind was in no mood for niceties.

"Smoking if you've got it," I grunted, plopping my credit card down—*I guess I'm running away from home too.*

"The bar closes at two o'clock." He gestured toward the lounge across the lobby. I glanced in, but I didn't see the girls in there; just a knot of guys clustered at the bar watching some sport on the television, and a few wide-eyed couples at the candlelit tables for two trying to mellow out from their hair-raising experiences in the storm before retiring for the night. I'll keep it in mind, a beer before bed would go down nice.

After a brief examination of my room, I took off my coat and hung it up. I didn't know what to do about finding the girls; I didn't dare ask the clerk to ring their room because I didn't want Hajji Baba at the desk to become suspicious about my intentions. I stepped down the hall to get a soda, just to waste time so I can think about what to do. As I passed by each room, I thought about the two women in their nightgowns munching on cookies or chips, drinking sodas, their tired eyes mesmerized by the box after a long day driving—chances are Sammy's drawing. When I turned the corner to go back to my room, I collided into someone small wearing feminine flannel.

"Geezers!" The flurry of arms and flannel exclaimed along with a plastic clatter of an ice bucket and a tinkle of coins; then she came to rest with her back pressed against the wall with her hands crossed over her chest.

"Ho there, Sammy, it's just me!" I laughed, surprised by my luck to have found her.

"Holy shit, Guthrie, I think I peed a little—you shouldn't be lurking around, scaring people like that—what are you doing here?" she gasped.

"Getting a soda," I shrugged, grinning sheepishly as I knelt down to fetch the things she dropped. She watched and waited, and when I found her last quarter and gave it to her, I stood up, making old man groans in concert with my knees popping.

"You followed us," she said accusingly, clutching her coins and bucket in tiny white-knuckled hands.

"Uh, no—I just got out of work, and along the way home, I decided to check-in cuz the roads were crappy—and I happened to spot the Caddy in the lot—listen, I—I feel you need to have me along to look out for you. I'm afraid that something might happen to you two out there traveling by yourselves. I'll take a few days off from work to drive you there."

"Jeez, Luiz, Guthrie—Helena and I have gone to thousands of places without a man; we can take care of ourselves," she groaned, but her sarcasm resonated as false. I know when she's been spoon-fed information; her words based on Helena's sentiments rather than her own.

"Would it matter to you if I would feel better?" I scowled at her just so she'd understand my sincerity.

"No, you can't," she said, shaking her head; her soft dark hair swung freely around her face, a strand became caught on her chapped lips, and her hand flicked it away.

"Sleep with me," I blurted out; I didn't mean to say it, but I wouldn't take it back.

"Oh, Guthrie," she giggled, covering her mouth with her hand like she would when she was little, usually in reaction to my saying something *naughty*. I guess I am being naughty.

"Well, it was worth a shot," I muttered. "I've got nothing to lose."

"Guthrie!" she cried, walking away, apparently not only annoyed with me for making the suggestion, but also annoyed with her feelings.

"Aren't you gonna get your soda and ice?" I asked, teasing her a little bit.

She stopped with an irritated stamp of her little feet, and looked back at me. I studied her standing there; she wore a flannel nightgown with a matching bathrobe dappled with Pooh Bears and Piglets floating on a white ground. Fuzzy pale blue slippers that looked like they've seen better days peeked out from under the ruffled hemline—she always liked fuzzy blue slippers. She went into the snack room, got two sodas and ice without saying anything to me, and then I followed her down the hall until I stopped at my room door.

"That's your room?" she asked.

"Yup."

"Jeez, Luiz," she rolled her eyes. She opened her room with the key card three doors down from me and walked inside; the door clattered shut behind her. I could hear her muttering to Helena, and Helena's exclamation, *"Whaaaat—he followed us?"*

After a brief consultation or explanation, I wasn't sure which, the door opened again. "I'll be back—maybe—don't wait up." She closed the door. "Okay," she said, coming to me.

"What?"

"Are you gonna invite me inside?" she asked, leaning against the wall by my room as I opened the door.

"Okay." I studied her slim shape swaddled in flannel—*damn, who would' a thought a Pooh Bear nightgown could be so sexy?*

"Got any cigarettes?" she asked, leaning against the dresser; the mirror at her back allowed me to see a complete view of her—I noted how her flannel-covered fanny set perfectly on the edge was shaped like a little ripe peach.

"Yeah." I fumbled out the pack from my shirt pocket and gave her one along with my lighter. The only light on was over the entryway; she was caught in its influence—I was not, my image in the mirror hung in the dark—I didn't need to see me, I knew that I ogled her like a lecherous troll. "You don't have to do this," I said, watching her light the cigarette, the glow of the lighter revealing the quiet tension in her face.

"Do what?"

"Sleep with me—I was just kidding before, you know," I said, opening my soda and knocking back a swallow from the can; I wished it were a beer.

"I don't think you were kidding," she said, dragging off her cigarette. "Maybe I want to." She delicately took a sip from her soda. During the long silence that followed, both of our cans fizzed quietly as if having their own private discussion.

"Maybe you don't," I pointed out.

"I didn't say that."

"No, you didn't." I lit a cigarette and squinted at her through the smoke. "But considering what you just went through—I can't imagine how you must feel—but usually, a woman who has been raped doesn't really feel like having sex with anyone right away."

A twitch ran through her entire body in reaction to my statement, but her eyes did not waver from my face. "Guthrie—do you want me?" she whispered. I refrained from flinching in reaction to her direct question; it seemed as if her dark eyes could bore into my being and drag out the truth; her gaze reminded me of Lenore.

"I've wanted you since we met at Whitley's funeral," I said, admitting to my confused lust. Her resemblance to Lenore threw me a curve that I hadn't expected—and then her flirtation with me the next day only encouraged the fantasy to grow; I'm at the point of no return no matter what happens here tonight. We stood smoking in silence, looking everywhere else but at each other. I crushed out my cigarette first; I noticed that she always smokes hers down to the filter.

"Maybe you should go back to your room now."

"Can I sleep here with you?" she asked, peering at me with wide eyes, and a wrinkled brow; she looked like a child afraid of the boogieman under the bed.

"Why?" I demanded, annoyed with her treating me like a yo-yo.

"I just want you to hold me—we don't have to have sex." She stepped up to me, but stopped short, just out of reach.

"No, we don't, but I can't promise you that I won't try," I said with a smile tugging on my reluctant lips. At the same time that I desired her, I felt revolted by my thoughts.

"I want you to."

"I have no idea why," I muttered, now feeling reluctant to do anything.

"Oh, Guthrie," she sighed with a whisper that quivered close to a sob.

"I'll shut up before you change your mind." Laughing, I shook my head and raised my hands in a vague motion of surrender.

She put out her cigarette and moved away from the dresser; she studied the beds with a thoughtful expression. "Which one do you prefer?"

"We can push the two beds together and make a bigger and better bed—an extra-large love nest should things get really hot 'n heavy."

"Oh, Guthrie, stop!" she giggled, stepping within reach.

"Oh, Sammy," I sighed, sitting down on the edge of the bed, almost missing it, I hadn't touched her yet. "You're so beautiful."

"Am I?"

"Yeah, very beautiful."

She stepped closer, placing her hands on my shoulders; she stroked my face with sensitive fingers that examined my features before she bent down to kiss me. As she applied her lips against mine, my hands gripped her hips. She straightened and stepped back from me, and I let her go. She pulled off the nightgown, tugged back the blankets and slipped into the bed near the window. With just the slightest hesitation, I undressed and slipped into the bed next to her. While I pulled the sheet and blankets around us, she snuggled close to me, laying her head on my chest, and I closed my arms around her, sighing, loving the feel of her body against mine.

"This is nice," I sighed.

"Yes, it is," she agreed. "Sorry I didn't get to shave my legs; I wasn't expecting you."

"That's okay, with all the hair on my legs, I haven't noticed a thing," I lied; I was content with feeling the bristles on her shins grating on my calves; this intimacy felt special, as if I have been married to her for years.

"You're being too polite."

"Maybe so," I sighed.

With an uncertain delicacy, we began to maneuver under the covers, trying to work each other up, our hands and mouths busy with tender explorations, but our self-consciousness baffled our urges just like that day in Boston; being naked didn't give us free license to do whatever we wanted.

We lay on our backs, staring at the ceiling—I was ready to have a cigarette, but not for the cliché after sex reason—this was pure frustration that begged to be appeased with a smoky pacifier.

"I know what I want you to do," she laughed, sitting up, and I froze, feeling anxious. "I want you to jump up and down on the bed," she whispered in my ear.

"You want me to WHAT?" Repeating my performance with Lenore for her look-alike daughter is not what I want to do. "No fucking way, Sam—I'm not going to—" I nearly bolted out of bed, but she grabbed my arm.

"Oh, come on—just play with me a little—please—for me?" she giggled, scrambling out of bed, clapping her hands with girlish glee—a little naked cheerleader.

So I did it—for her—I felt very silly at first, but soon enough my self-consciousness was gone and I made love to her with my entire being. In the midst of our clambering around on the bed to satisfy our desires, I seriously thought I was going to die, but if I did, it was worth blowing out my brain with a stroke to feel like this. It wasn't just about sex—it was my emotional connection with her that made the act so intense. Afterwards, I slept the sleep of the dead.

∾

After Samantha left to be with Guthrie for the night, I tried calling Sy, but there was no answer at home or at Deer Isle, and his cell phone ceased working as a recorded message let me know that the number is currently unavailable. I called his office to see if the secretary could get a message to him, but she never remembers to turn on the voice mail—so typical, he's too kind-hearted to fire her incompetent ass and get a real secretary. I feared that he had gone out looking for us—or worse, that something dreadful had happened because of our departure. I thought about calling Jack, but quickly decided against it; I didn't want deal with him. That should be Sammy's call to make; he's not rude to her.

I paced the floor and wrung my hands like a worried mother. I worried about Sam being with Guthrie—*what the hell are they doing? Use your imagination—they're fucking—simply fucking for the sake of fucking each other*. I felt irritated, like being the only sober person at a party full of drunks.

After popping a sleeping pill, I fell asleep, and began to have restless, vivid sex dreams in which I was still with Shep, but he became ugly with hate, so I left, just like I knew I would. Then when I saw Sy, I was relieved, but he became grossly deformed by the time he reached out to hug me. Thankfully, I woke up to Sam shaking me awake.

"Hey—I thought we were going to get an early start—what are you doing still asleep—we're ready to go," Sammy laughed.

"*We* are?" I looked up and saw Guthrie leaning against the wall outside the room. "Close the door!" I moaned; my real nightmare had just begun.

"All right—stay out here, I'm closing the door—she's being modest," Sammy giggled as she slowly closed the door.

"No problem," Guthrie replied. They got all kissy-face, and their loud smooching made me want to puke. When she finally pried her lips off his, she closed the door, nearly snapping it shut on his nose.

"He's not coming with us," I grumbled, throwing aside the blankets, my feet searched the floor for my slippers.

"Why? He says we need him—most of all, you will need to have someone to share the driving—you can't do it alone—what if something happens—what if Preston finds us—Guthrie will protect us from anything bad happening—if the car breaks down, he can fix it—he's handy that way," she exclaimed with a cajoling tone.

"No—we can't."

"You're just jealous that he's in love with me and not with you—just like you were jealous of Lenore—you're just jealous!" she cried.

"Oh, yeah—he's such a prize," I grunted, getting out of bed and tottering into the bathroom; my legs and back are stiff from driving and sleeping in crappy hotel beds for the last three days. "First, I'm going to get dressed; second, we're going to find a place to go have breakfast, and then we're going to hit the road, okay?" I called out after I finished peeing. When I opened the door, I came face to face with Guthrie's chest. "Shit!" I shrieked.

"Sure, we'll go have breakfast, but after that, I want you to sit tight, let me go home to pack a few things. I need to call my boss and let him know I'm taking some time for a family emergency—if he doesn't like the short notice he can fuck-off. I know you don't want me to come along on this little adventure to New Mexico—but we have Sammy to think about—you can't take this on by yourself. In my honest opinion, it would be for the best to turn around and go back to Gloucester," he said, using an amiable tone that could have paved the way to making me agree with him. Granted, it was on the tip of my tongue to cave-in with a whole-hearted *"Okay"*, but I suddenly became possessive of Sammy—protective. Plus, the thought of being trapped in the confines of a car for eight hours or more, listening to cutie-pie-hoochie-coochie was so repulsive I could already taste bile in my mouth.

"You've got to be kidding—no—you are just coming along so you can get laid every night—you got some last night and that's it—we're leaving, and you are not coming with us," I grumbled, remaining firm in my resolve to get rid of him.

"Oh, come on Leeennaaaa—it isn't about sex—he is worried about us—what if Preston does find us—he will kill us both and all of this will be for nothing," Sammy wheedled at first, but her voice became more shrill with the mention of her husband.

"So he's going to be our watch-dog?" I laughed.

"If you want to think of it that way to make yourself feel better, then please feel free to entertain that thought," Guthrie laughed. "If I'm a watch-dog, then maybe I can get some doggie-style sex," he winked at Sam; she giggled hysterically behind her hands clamped over her bright pink face.

"You're a pig, Guthrie," I groaned. *Ugh, I didn't need the visual—I can't go there—too late—been there, and it wasn't a good image.* "All right, go do what you gotta do," I relented to his request just to get rid of him.

"Well, now, that wasn't so hard was it?" he said, pleased with himself; he didn't seem to care that I called him a pig—I guess he's been called worse.

Unfortunately, my arrival home overlapped with my ex-wife's departure for the day. She circled me in the foyer like a buzzard looking to see if a carcass was dead or alive. Then she questioned me about my whereabouts last night, and gave me the *"Why didn't you call?"* routine. I told her nearly the truth, naturally leaving out the part about getting my lights fucked out by a girl half my age. Then I wondered if she could smell Sammy on me; I reeked, and I didn't get a chance to shower because the girl jolted me out of bed in a panic to get on the road to somewhere fast. The roads still suck, and it wouldn't be a bad idea to hang around town until after the storm blows through and the road crews get a handle on the slop, but we can deal with that later.

My ex-wife, however, didn't believe my excuse, especially when I started to tell her that I was going away for a few days. I should have kept my mouth shut; she lit into me with a ration of shit as if we were still married. While listening to her ranting, I began to wonder if she was having issues with the reality of our divorce—maybe she isn't over me, or some such crap. When I reminded her of our legal parting of ways, she stormed out of the house in a torrent of tears. *Jeez, Louise, get over it—the divorce was your idea!*

With her gone, I quickly packed a few necessary odds and ends—clothes, toothbrush, razor, and then my sketchbook. When I threw the suitcase into the trunk of the car, I wondered about the car situation—*should we leave the Caddy and just drive my car?* The Super 88 has plenty of room in it for me and two little women; they could sit in the back; I could be their chauffeur—it's more reliable than the Cadillac that hasn't been driven over thirty miles or thirty miles per hour in nearly twenty years. *What were they thinking?* Was Sammy looking to make a jab at Preston by "stealing" his precious toy? It pissed me off seeing how that jerk had coveted Whitley's Caddy after the funeral; he drove it around with the top down, looking so smug—*what a prick—I can't stand him—I still don't get why the hell she married him.*

When I returned to the hotel, I discovered that the Cadillac recently vacated the parking place where it had been nestled in a cove of drifted snow. It was stupid of me to leave them, but I didn't think Helena was crafty enough to agree with my plan to get rid of me, and then talk Sammy into leaving. *What if she left Sammy behind to wait for me?* I went inside and when I reached their room, the maid was already in there cleaning up—they had left together. The latest edition of the ethnic front desk clerk wouldn't give me an answer about the girls checking out. *"Are you a cop?"* he asked first before he made his final decision to be helpful or not. My honesty got me nowhere.

I left, fearing that I wasted too much time grasping straws, now I have to try to find them in a snowstorm. *Damn!* I made a right turn out of the parking lot following the Caddy's distinguishable tracks that they had left in the snow-clogged exit, and I cruised along, peering into parking lots for a red Caddy with a black ragtop and impressive tailfins. Eventually, I got onto the highway going west bound and hoped for the best that I would find them along the way—the roads were terrible, visibility sucked, but thankfully, everyone was going easy.

When a whiteout caused traffic to slide to a stop about a half-hour later, I began to think that they might have gone back east instead of heading west. Through a thin veil of blowing snow, I saw the unmistakable tail end of the Caddy sticking out of a ditch; I pulled over with my stomach raging with sickly panic.

"Sammy—Lena!" I bellowed into the wind that sucked my breath away as soon as I stepped outside. The blowing snow sandblasted my face and hands, for a moment, I couldn't see anything, and I was grateful when my knees bumped into the bumper and my hands touched the tailfin. Sinking to my thighs in snow, I slid my bare hands along the cold metal that was quickly being buried in a drift, I saw them huddled in the front seat, pale and wide-eyed; it appeared they were unhurt in spite of their nose-first plunge into a snowy ditch. When I knocked on the passenger side window, they look out at me, startled. Samantha started to cry as her face contorted into a mix of joy and fear. As soon as I dug out the door to open it, she wrapped herself around my neck, her body trembling against my coat—the girl is scared—I held her tight as the wind-driven snow buffeted us. "Everything's okay, Button's, I'm here now—let's get your stuff into my car; we'll call a tow truck to haul this one out; let's go find some place warm, all right?" I said to her, but the neck of my winter coat muffled her reply; her arms gripped me tighter, so I took that to mean *yes*.

Helena crawled out after a struggle with purses, multiple packs of cigarettes, a portable CD player, and CD's in a case; leaning on my shoulder, she put her mouth next to my ear, "I don't think I will ever be able to thank you enough—I thought for sure we were dead!"

"Let's get in my car," I threw my arm around her shoulders and helped them out of the ditch to my car. After they tumbled into the front seat, I went back to the Caddy, pulled the keys out of the ignition, and fetched their suitcases out of the trunk, dumping them into mine—all this easier said than done—the driving wind tried its best to smother and blind me with every step I made to accomplish the simple feat.

Feeling breathless, I collapsed into the driver's seat with a curse, slamming the door against the storm. I looked at the two of them cuddled together, shivering; Sammy jammed herself under my elbow with her desire to be warm. With practiced maneuvers, I rocked Delta Dawn out of the snowdrift that already started to form around the tires, and rolled onto the snow-covered highway without an 18-wheeler rear-ending us in the process.

"Is Taos warm at this time of year?" I asked the older of the two sisters; Sammy tucked in closer to me with a nudge, and I put my arm around her.

"No, even though it's a desert, it gets mighty cold there—but it's a dry cold—at least that's what Dulcie always said," Helena laughed, lighting a cigarette with a trembling hand.

"I don't want to hear any of that shit—cold is cold, dry or humid—hot is hot, dry or humid—whatever, it's gotta be better than here," I growled as I continued forward along with all the other idiots on the highway trying to ignore the fact that the road conditions were hazardous. I turned on the radio to listen to the latest weather rumor making the absurd claim that we'll pass out of the worst of the *whatthefuck weather* into sunshine in another ten miles. *Oh, we'll see about that.* At the rate we were going, I figured we'd see sunshine in about an hour.

15

Keeping a Barstool Warm in Iowa

Initially, I came home to give Lenore an ultimatum—*"This is it, I want you to leave him, pack up Sammy and move to New York—if you don't, that's it, we're done."* But I didn't go there—Lenore has to decide for herself what to do—I know all too well that my happiness isn't her priority. When she said it was my fault that Sammy caught us, I accepted the blame without a fight. We both knew that once the little tyke started toddling around that she was on a collision course with our secrets. I willingly admitted that I was careless on purpose because I was fed-up with denying everything—*"I'm sick of pretending to be 'Just Guthrie' for the kid's benefit."* But I stopped the rant right there to avoid another fight; thankfully, I have learned when to pick my battles, and have the right terms for peace ready to defuse her wrath. It was imperative to soften my approach to this delicate subject—so I tried the less threatening *"Plan B."*

"Lenore, about this job I'm taking in New York—" I started to say, but she slipped out of bed and began to search for her nightie in the darkness—as expected, she was having none of it. She was fine as long as her legs were wrapped around my waist, but now that I'm done, she's done. But I wasn't done—as far as I was concerned, we weren't done. "I want you to come live with me." I sat up, grabbing her by the arm to stop her.

"I can't," she sighed, jerking her arm out of my loose grasp. I could never hold her tight enough—*she was always escaping me.*

"You can bring Sammy—I found a great apartment in a Brooklyn brownstone; I picked it because it has two bedrooms—" I begged out of desperation.

"I can't do that—she's Whitley's daughter—I can't take her away from him."

"Is she?" I asked. Sammy's origin always nagged in the back of my mind.

"Of course she is! Guthrie—we've been over this before she was born, and a thousand times since then—why don't you believe me?" she flared. Her anger was always close to the surface, ready and available to do battle; any false move on my part right now had the potential to ruin the mutual peace we shared only moments ago.

"I can't believe you did it with Whitley just to have a kid—why did it have to be his?" My anger rose up with the sour disposition of bile.

"Because he's my husband—and I wanted to have his baby—last I checked it wasn't a crime for me to have a baby with my husband," she sneered.

"What if I want to have a baby with you?" I challenged her.

She smiled with a girlish dimple deepening in her right cheek; her fingers strolled across my chest, petting me, and playfully tugging on the hairs; that smile, it was a cunning smile, specifically meant to placate me—yet it frustrated me.

"Maybe we will—we'll know for sure in a few short weeks," she whispered.

"Lenore!" I cried with a mix of shock, annoyance, and misdirected happiness.

"I'm trying again—I would love to have another baby—Sammy needs a sibling—a brother or maybe a sister. Do boys run in your family?" she asked, leaning against me.

"I'm the only child in my family. Margie's family were all girls, shitloads of sisters and cousins that were tight as sisters, but I know nothing about my biological dad," I answered, feeling giddy and almost sick—we hadn't discussed having a baby, and she went ahead and decided for us without consulting me. Does this mean that she's fucking Whitley to cover the bases—will she know for sure if it is mine?

"We'll have to wait and see," she promised. *I'll never know if she carried my child because by the next day she was dead—*

"*—a penny for your thoughts big guy.*" Millie's husky voice reached in to yank me in another mental direction; my mind is busy traveling through the past tonight, and has yet to find rest after a long day on the road. *Millie Geritz—well, that's a donkey's age ago!* I can still remember the smell of that strong herbal tea she used to brew in my kitchen, and the wafting scent of patchouli that covered the incriminating odor of pot on her gauzy clothes.

"Hey, sorry, I didn't mean to space out on you like that," I chuckled, trying to set aside the haunting thoughts of my last night with Lenore. Millie stood at the foot of the bed, carelessly wrapped in one of my shirts; a purposefully contrived posture to inspire me to draw her or to fuck her, it didn't matter which, she's always willing to do both. With greedy eyes, I noted the soft swelling of her right breast with the dusky pink nipple almost completely exposed, and her thick blond hair spilled over her left shoulder like a shimmering scarf. It was funny that with all this classic and titillating beauty to admire, I decided that I liked the way her small hands cradled a mug of tea instead. She had wonderful hands; they were slightly pudgy, child-like, pretty, little hands, very delicate—I loved feeling them on my body—she knew how to give great massages.

"Worried?" she asked, arching her unusually dark eyebrows. When I first met her, I didn't believe that she was naturally blond with those black arches over each pale green eye, but she is blond everywhere else; it was one of those genetic flukes—she said it was something from her mom's side of the family.

"Nah, just thinking," I said, clearing my throat as I smiled at her. "Ummm, do you think your roommate knows about us?" I inquired just to follow through with her train of thought. She'd like to believe we are *in touch* or *on the same wavelength,* but we're not—we're still strangers who regularly come together to have sex because we enjoy doing it with each other.

"So, you are worried! Believe me, Georgia has no clue—she's got enough on her mind thinking about Bailey and Eugene," she laughed, rolling her eyes.

"That kid, Eugene, has a bad case for her—I don't know too many young men willing to pose nude in a figure drawing class to get a girl's attention," I laughed, amused and annoyed by this discussion. No matter what she said, I didn't think her roommate was clueless; she and another student of mine, Katharine, were eyeballing me in the back stairway of Smith Hall last week—they're not stupid. Millie takes no pains to hide the fact that we're intimate in some form. Whenever she greets me, she hangs off my body like a monkey in a tree, and while she frisks my pockets for smokes and a lighter, she makes a point to grab my crotch and pinch my nipples in the process; her sexual playfulness seems non-stop. *I'm going to be so fired.*

"It's more like he'd rather she didn't have to look at some other guy naked—he's very protective of her—I think it's sweet," she said, easing down onto the edge of the bed beside me and crossing her bare legs. It annoyed me when Millie admitted to having a crush on Eugene Riley—but I can't blame her; compared to being fucked by me, what girl wouldn't want to tangle with him? When the blatantly naked Eugene Riley stepped up onto the model stand for the class to draw, it seemed as if all of the oxygen was sucked out of the studio; that kid has well-put-together anatomy—and he knew it as he stretched and held his lithe body in poses for their drawing pleasure. I've heard enough about the love triangle going on in the background of Millie's life that I can put a tune to it—she's obsessed with the fucked-up soap opera of two boys playing tug-of-war with one girl.

"Ah, to be eighteen again!" I lamented with a laugh. My eyes skimmed over her face. *What have I gotten myself into with this girl?*

"Listen, Guthrie, we're just having a good time—I'm not into tying you down. If you want out, we can stop at anytime—there were never any strings attached, and I'm not with you to get an 'A' in figure drawing," she said with a laugh, setting the mug on the nightstand. As she bent toward me for a kiss, the shirt fell open, and my hands wandered toward her full breasts.

"Why are you here with me?" I asked with a half-hearted laugh, avoiding her mouth, teasing her for an answer before I let her have her way with me again.

"When I see something I want, I go after it," she murmured as she kissed me; I let her. I never had to instigate anything, she did it all of her own accord—she came on to me that first day of class, the only thing I did was show up for work. It was nice for a change, no pressure—I was not in love, just interested—that was the beginning and the end of it.

Once again, my mind shifts from one past to another, and now I have returned to the present, thankfully leaving the memory of screwing Millie Geritz in my flat on Clark Street in Syracuse over twenty years ago. It's our second night on the road to New Mexico, we have landed for the night in a motor lodge in Coralville, Iowa, and I felt the urgent need to ask Samantha Ryder the same question I had asked Millie on that particular morning—*"Why are you here with me?"*

Sammy sat quietly on the bed beside me, focused on her pencil's travels over the smooth paper surface. My self-doubts have snuffed out my desire for sex, and she hasn't instigated anything since our night spent together in Cleveland. She turned her attention toward me in that unnerving indirect way with her eyes half-closed; she's not with me, yet she is more with me at this moment than ever. It's as if she has another sense beyond seeing and hearing; she's absorbing my words through her skin, digesting them, and eventually an answer will come. She sighed and her eyes opened wide.

"So few people hear me—no one lets me think—so few I am able to hear—so few reach in and take hold—so few who I can touch."

My body flinched with a jolt; when I opened my mouth to reply, she touched my chest with her hand, letting me know she wasn't finished yet. After a moment of silence, she lay down with a sigh; our bodies combined for comfort rather than arousal.

"Whitley and Lenore could make me hear them—they loved me, they were two extremely selfish people, but I made them less so. I was the one thing in their lives that joined them. Helena tries, but she barely scratches my surface. Preston is no good at it—his love was all a dog and pony show. Sylvester is different, I not only hear him, but he hears me because of his quiet; it's as if he can tune his soul in to mine—he can touch me—deep in my heart. You're a lot like Sylvester in that way. I love you, Guthrie. You are special to me because you were always able to reach through and take hold. You let me think, you wait for me to say what's on my mind—even if it is the most despicable thing that I can say to you, you take it. Like when I saw you at the funeral and cried out *"Oh-my-god, you're bald!"* I mean, how awful of me—no filters—Lenore always got on my case about that shit—if you haven't got anything nice to say, don't say anything at all—" she went on and on and on. I pulled the pillow over my head—I try forever to get the girl to talk, and now she won't shut up. Then she sneezed.

"Do you feel okay?" I asked, not to change the subject, but she looked wrung out; she sneezed and hacked through most of dinner.

"I've got some crap running down my throat, it feels a little sore, and I have a teeny bit of a headache."

I felt of her forehead with my hand, "You feel warm."

"Fever warm?"

"Maybe, come on, tuck in, let's get some shut-eye," I reached over to click off the lamp. In the darkness, imposing worries about our budding situation perked inside my head.

"I don't want to be without you ever again—I feel safe with you," she whispered.

"I'll be here for you—I promise; I will protect you with my life, and I will love you until the day I die," I swore this solemn oath and kissed the sweet curve of her sleepy forehead.

❧

Sammy fell asleep with the greatest of ease, but I couldn't; so, with as little disruption as possible, I got out of bed and began to get dressed in the dark. She woke up, muttered something incoherent that I translated to mean, *"Where are you going?"* and I told her that I was going down to the bar for a beer. *"Okay,"* she buzzed sleepily into the pillow, and without much fuss, dropped off to dreamland.

Once in the haven of the smoky bar, I had more than one beer, I reached the bottom of a pitcher, and while I sat ruminating about getting another, I noticed Helena standing at my elbow.

"Hey, Lena, care to join me?" I asked, curious about her being there; she looked three sheets to the wind—the self-inflicted kind.

"I've already had my share—I was about to turn in when lo-n'-behold, I find you keeping a barstool warm—did she give you the boot?" she smirked as she eased onto a stool beside me.

"Nah, I couldn't sleep, I'm just here trying to get inspiration—thankfully, Sammy's out like a light already, she's pretty beat," I smirked into my beer.

"I bet she's tired—I can't believe you're not dead to the world right along with her, between driving all day and getting laid after dinner. What's your problem? You're sucking down beer like water," she poked my arm with her finger.

"I didn't 'get any' tonight, but that's all right—I think Sammy's coming down with a cold—she's got a headache."

"Wow, she's using that 'not tonight, honey' excuse already—so much for bliss," she snorted, then lit a cigarette.

"It wasn't her, it was me. To tell ya the truth, Lena, I've got a big problem—I'm sleeping with a woman that I have believed for years to be my daughter—she's a dead ringer for her mother, who was—by the way—the love of my life—and get this—the girl has always fantasized about being with me. So now, I'm fifty something and she's not yet thirty—that's worlds apart on the age spectrum—how fucked-up is that?" I laughed. "It is pretty fucked-up if you ask me," I growled, not waiting for her to answer.

"Well at least you love each other, right?" She scrunched her face at me after getting smoke in her eyes. "At least, the view from where I'm standing in my size eights it looks like you guys do."

"Yeah, we do," I said, surprised that she was willing to admit it. "But, do you know who she's really in love with?" I leaned back and pointed at her with a perceptive finger.

"No, who—Beethoven?" she laughed with a bray of sarcasm. I chuckled too because we've listened to every Beethoven CD Sammy possessed on our way here.

"Your man, Hayden—and I'll bet you five bucks he's in love with her," I said, keeping my voice low to soften the blow for her.

"Yer on, pal!" she barked, extending her hand to shake on the bet.

"You don't think he's in love with her?" I asked, curious about her opinion.

"No—I don't think he's in love with her," she sputtered, letting her hand drop into her lap. "I don't know—maybe he is—" she wavered, and then she heaved a deep sigh.

"You really do have ass-up-head syndrome," I laughed.

"I have what?" she giggled at first, and then scowled with mild annoyance.

"It's a little joke Sammy and I always had about you when she was little; she always messed up head-up-ass—never mind." I waved my hand as if swatting at my words. "Forget it—forget I said anything."

"Fuck you, Guthrie," she grunted with mirth and punched my arm. I laughed with her—*boy is she toasted!*

"No thanks, I'm tapped out—"

"You're a pig," she burped, leaning on my arm, and resting her chin on my shoulder.

"Yeah, well, I've been called worse," I snickered, amused that she was so sloppy drunk that she was actually hitting on me, albeit half-heartedly, but hitting on me nonetheless.

"I hate you," she grunted, backing off.

"You used to be in love with me," I said, taking a sip from my dwindling beer.

"I never was!" she exclaimed, as if shocked that I knew her deep, dark secret.

"Yeah, whatever—I don't feel like playing a verbal tennis match with you."

"You're such an asshole!" she shrieked. The bartender glanced our way; I waved at him that it was all right; he shrugged, and turned back to the NCAA playoffs.

"What's the matter with you?" I asked her.

"You knew!" she shrieked, slapping my arm with the back of her hand—real hard.

"It was obvious," I shrugged with an audible *what's the big deal* noise. The bartender looked at us again, but seemed satisfied that we were just playing.

"I was a kid—I didn't know any better," she grumbled.

"We were all kids once," I agreed.

"It sucks to grow up," she mused with a sigh.

"It sucks to grow old." I applied the same wisdom from my barstool—tonight I feel ancient—older than Biblical dirt.

"You look good, Guthrie—" she muttered, looking down at her hands folded in her lap.

"Yeah, right, at 2 AM and after three to four drinks anyone looks good!" I laughed, stretching, wondering if I finally felt tired and could call it a night.

"You're so vain, mister," she giggled. "You haven't changed a bit!"

"Yeah, well, that was a long time ago; Lenore got the best years out of me," I sighed—*Nope, I'm not ready to go to bed yet.*

"Forget Lenore, Sammy loves you—let her love you, her love is probably the purest around because she isn't like the rest of us—fucked up old us," Helena said softly as she caressed my back with her hand. I rounded my shoulders in response to her hand rubbing me between the shoulder blades; the compassion of her physical contact felt comforting, which seemed odd coming from the ice-princess—*she's really shitfaced.*

"You really don't think she's in love with Hayden," I wondered aloud.

"Sy replaced you after you left; she discovered him through the bushes—she'd sit with him every day and draw his hands." She said this as if offering a bit of history that I haven't heard before. I have heard this story twice already—Sammy and Hayden told me their versions, every story has a different point of view that fascinated me, and both of them carry the weight of the significance of their first meeting: the spark of friendship that grew into a flame of enduring love. Sometimes you can be too close to someone and not realize how much you really love them—you love them without question—without being conscious of the passion because it's just there. Then one night comes along and you're fucking each other stupid just because it feels right at the time; then you agonize over the consequences afterwards in spite of the rightness of the moment. That fine line between right and wrong can drive a man insane. I can sympathize with Sylvester Hayden's indecisiveness and his weakness.

"His hands are not the only thing of his that she drew," I laughed. I also imagined she has a collection of more intimate drawings squirreled away within the hundreds of sketchbooks that she has filled over the years—things from the moment, things from memory; her mind is a treasure trove of things best left unrevealed.

"What do you mean?"

"You know, the drawings above her drafting table—she has a collage of him—his hands, every angle of his face, and his aaasssssss," I slurred with purpose.

"Shit! You're right, that is his ass—that bitch!" she snarled.

"Put yer claws away, Lena—it's unbecoming," I winced. It was amusing to see the realization creep across her face; she had seen the drawing and didn't make the connection—well, how do ya like 'dem apples, she didn't even recognize her lover's ass prominently displayed above her sister's drafting table.

"If they are in love with each other—then why are they with us?" she frowned as she propped her sagging head onto her hands supported by sliding elbows resting on the slick polyurethane surface of the bar.

"Fantasies. After years of cultivation, their hearts remained loyal to the dreams—while we were gone, they shared a bond together. Our reappearance only separated the natural progress they would have made on their own had we stayed away," I offered the explanation that has rolled around in my head for weeks, it felt good to articulate it—it sounded less crazy.

"Where does that leave us?" she asked with a sigh.

"Alone," I belched.

"I can't believe it—they've been there right under my nose, every time they were together—I've always been the third wheel and never knew it."

"I spotted it the minute I saw them together the day of Whitley's funeral."

"You're full of shit—goodnight, Guthrie," she got up and patted my shoulder gently.

"Full of beer actually—you've just been too close to them to see it—whoa there, wait—don't go yet—sit your ass down—enough talk about me, I want to hear about you—so, what brings you down here to this fine establishment at such a late hour?" I had to ask, and couldn't help but wonder if she came here looking for love and ended up tying one on instead.

"I couldn't sleep worth a damn, so I had a hankering for a decadent sweet—a hot fudge sundae with Spanish nuts and whipped cream seemed to be the cure for what ailed me. Instead of cheering me up, it made me feel more blah and pathetic. So, I moved from the restaurant to that little corner table right over there, and ordered a gin and tonic—and another—and then another. You know, I can't stop thinking about Sy's poor cat being up to her furry armpits in dirty kitty litter and starving to death. I haven't been able to reach him, I'm worried—he's—he tends to be depressed—his father's been ill, you know—he's expected to die any day now. It's obvious why he can't

get a hold of me—but I don't think he's getting any of the messages; I don't think he's checked for messages. I'm afraid something bad has happened to him." It was touching to see the way she bit her lip, and struggled with tears generated by worry.

"Ohhh, he's fine—guys are like that—once you've landed for awhile, he'll catch up with you." I scoffed at her fears; not meaning to minimize them, but to reassure her that he's a big boy—he can take care of himself all right. Sam's worried about him too; she fears that Preston will go after Hayden for revenge. My personal theory figures the cops snagged Hayden for questioning regarding the disappearance of the two women because there is potential that their unannounced departure could get messy for those left behind wondering what became of them. Without a doubt, Preston is crazy enough to spout off demented accusations for the sole purpose of covering his ass—but I will keep these notions to myself—the girls are scaring themselves enough already with their own imaginations. Whatever the situation is in Gloucester, I believe Hayden will handle it just fine—he's not stupid.

"I don't know who else to call, without my cell phone, I have no telephone numbers at my fingertips to call anyone to check in on Daisy, or ask what happened to Sy—"

"Speed-dial, shit—you know, I can still remember my home number in Cleveland when I was a kid—no wonder we have so much Alzheimer's going on in this nation, it's shit like fucking speed-dial that's screwing up everybody."

"I even tried calling Sy's office in the middle of the day during a pit stop, but the phone rang off the hook—once again, that old bat, Mrs. Beebe, didn't turn on the voice mail. But when it occurred to me that it's spring break, I wanted to cry—Sy and I had talked about going somewhere south—taking Sammy with us, of course—I had hoped for Key West—but then everything went higgledy-piggledy, so we planned to go nowhere."

"Listen—I'm sure he's fine—"

"I should get some sleep—and so should you," she said, putting her hand on my shoulder as she stood up with unsteady grace.

"I will—when you get older, you'll find that you don't need as much sleep."

"Is that so?" she slurred.

"That's so," I smirked.

"Well, no matter how old I get, I will always need my beauty sleep—I recommend that you go to bed soon—we have a big day ahead of us if we're going to try to make it to Colorado by tomorrow."

"Okay, I can take a hint, if I got more sleep I'd be less ugly—goodnight, Lena."

"Goodnight, Guthrie." She kissed me on top of my head and she giggled. "I've wanted to do that for a long time."

"Yup, I'm sure you have," I sighed, rolling my eyes. "All the girls want to kiss Ole Guthrie on top of his baldhead."

"Shut up," she cried, hugging me around the neck.

As I watched her wobble away, I felt more miserable now than when I first came in here. I signaled for a second pitcher and lit another cigarette. *This is going to be a long night.*

16 *Under the Table*

The last thing I remember seeing was the underside of the dining room table—it's not often that an adult has the opportunity to see the underneath regions of tables, and this one happened to be fascinating. In spite of the pain, I forced myself to turn over onto my back to study its aesthetic spirit. Sammy had spent a lifetime making a mural on the unfinished surface with her pencils, and emerging from shadowy cross-hatching were familiar portraits of faces and hands. One embellishment was of vine-like claws clutching a small human heart, and then twined within an art nouveau organic framework there was an elaborate script of my name, and there, in almost insignificant script it read, *Samantha loves*. Her declaration correlated with where my knees have been night after night for many years. I slipped into darkness buoyed by this lovely message.

Awareness seeped in with the consistency of a dark gray twilight as my senses were tickled by the septic-antiseptic odor and busy sounds of the hospital. Dull pain gnawed on my body in various regions. Voices at my bedside know I'm awake, they ask me questions, but I'm not yet ready to open my eyes to reply, I sought bliss in sleep. Eventually, curiosity got the better of me, so I finally opened my eyes, and peered through a thin field of vision at a nurse smiling down at me; she greeted me with the good news that I'm lucky to be alive. My consciousness crept away after that, the pain was too much to talk about; it was for the best that I slept. Later on, when I emerged from sleep, I learned that she had meant that I'm lucky because I had a strong enough will to drag myself out of the snow to call for help. The seductive powers of hypothermia would have killed me if I had remained lying in the snow feeling sorry for myself through the cloudless night when the temperatures plunged into the teens. Upon consideration, freezing to death would have been a kind way to escape my present misery, so I've been taking full advantage of the painkillers that my caregivers offer me, and I sleep a lot, when they let me. From Jacob's recent experience, I learned that one does not come to the hospital to rest, even when one is dying. But I'm going to live—*that's great, wake me when it's over.*

Other than remembering what I saw underneath the table, I don't remember much beyond the journey I made from the front dooryard to Helena's cell phone on the dining room table. I don't even remember the paramedics scraping me off the old wide planks to cart me away.

With consciousness, I became aware that my face felt immobile, just like a mask. My first trip into the bathroom with the assistance of the nurse gave me a glimpse of how bad I looked, but it wasn't until the next day that I could actually spend time closely examining Preston's handy-work. The mirror above the sink revealed a road map of stitches with colorful islands of swellings and bruises. I didn't recognize myself—I looked like a monster; they had shaved my hair off to accommodate the stitches in the three places on my scalp that correlate with the fine fractures in my skull. I've been told that the total number of stitches on my head and face is fifty-eight; most of them are on my scalp.

My first actual conversation with the doctor gave me the checklist of my many injuries. My nose is broken, but it should heal fine without medical intervention. Thankfully, I still have all my teeth intact, although some of them feel loose. I found out that the blood that I had tasted in my mouth was not from internal bleeding as I had feared, but from a cut inside my cheek that required stitches—*oh, drat, that's another four stitches, so sixty-two total.* My jaw has several minor fractures on both sides; I can eat and talk, but it's painful—I'm reduced to eating my food pulverized into mush—basically, I'm eating lukewarm baby food. The orbital rim below my left eye has fine hairline fractures that radiate in three spidery fingers down my cheekbone. The numbness that I'm experiencing in various locations of my face is due to nerve damage. The doctor said most of the feeling will come back once the swelling goes down, but there may be areas that will recover sensation later, up to a year, and in some cases maybe never. My right shoulder was dislocated, and my arm is broken in two places. The shoulder was quickly popped back into place; thankfully, the ligaments were only stretched and not torn; my arm was repaired during a surgery a couple of days ago, which I vaguely remember, now there are several tiny titanium screws holding the broken pieces together. My left hand is lightly bruised from clocking Preston; it's almost better now. I also have three broken ribs and four with minor fractures either caused by falling down the stairs or other blunt trauma, such as making an acquaintance with Preston's foot wearing winter weather SK's. I am grateful that my spine came through without a dent or a crack; most of the pain there is due to muscle strain and bruises. The good news is I'm fortunate that my internal organs had not received damage, but I have plenty of bruises in places where it could have gotten nasty had Preston persisted, and had I not rolled up into the fetal position while he worked me over. So, it seems I'm lucky that my injuries are survivable—but it's unfortunate that I have them all at once—so I'm going to be here for a while.

Since my arrival, and subsequent awareness, I've had many visitors; Carrie has come every evening with her brother Rick in tow; they have been taking care of cleaning up the mess Preston had made after he kicked the crap out of me; apparently, he also trashed the carriage house. She also kindly found one of my many pairs of spare glasses—*the better to see myself.* Of course, they've been taking care of Daisy—my cat had survived Preston's assault by slipping out the front door that he had left wide open—she never enjoyed his company anyway. The paramedics had found her inside Samantha's house crouched beside me, but she took off, not wanting any part of them. Carrie said she had a time catching her, but they are now getting along famously. It seems the fluffy brat has been spoiled rotten with dinners comprised of poached salmon and sautéed chicken livers, and she likes sleeping on Samantha's bed best of all.

Various colleagues and students from the university have streamed through to pay their respects as soon as everyone returned from spring break. Jack has been vigilant at my bedside, and so have the police; they naturally have questions. Apparently, the police had caught Preston inside the carriage house, and he's been retained without bail; he won't be going anywhere for quite a long time. Jack says Preston was high on cocaine when he attacked me, so it seems there's more to the picture of the man.

So far, no one has been able to determine the whereabouts of Helena or Samantha; considering what he did to me, foul play is the logical explanation—so I've been told to expect the worst. Helena's car is nowhere to be found. Preston claims that he knows nothing about their location. Jack expects the bodies of my two most beloved women to be given-up by the ocean any day; the search up and down the local beaches continues daily after high tide. They can assume the worst-case scenarios if they want to, but I don't believe the girls are dead—wherever they are, they're together. There is a part of me that believes I know them both well enough that I would feel their loss within the core of my being. While considering the message on the answering machine at Deer Isle, it is clear to me now that Helena got scared, and took Samantha somewhere after Preston broke into the house and menaced her through the garret doors—I hold off grief with hope that they got away.

Ten days after my misadventure, I am well enough to go home. I eased myself into the empty carriage house, and the expected loneliness. Daisy ran to me with her fanned tail straight up as she mewed for attention; I bent down with the effort of an old man to scoop her up with my one good hand, and cradled her within the crook of my elbow like a baby. She tolerated this for only so long before her fuzzy bedroom slipper feet began to skitter against my chest; she launched herself toward the kitchen with her tail crooked in that typical sassy-little-shit manner.

The house looked better than I had imagined; I felt grateful for Carrie and Rick's efforts to fix it up for my homecoming. I picked up the new cordless telephone Rick had installed to replace the one Preston had destroyed; there were no messages on the answering machine. It was unfortunate Preston did a tap dance on the old answering machine, the tape inside may have had a clue telling where the girls went; Jack and I both think he may have heard it and won't tell just to be an asshole. *Maybe Helena will call tonight—I'll wait.*

After feeding Daisy, and opening a snack-pack of chocolate pudding for an easy lunch, I propped my healing body on the sofa with pillows, not willing to attempt the stairs just yet. My stitches came out this morning, but my face is still puffy on the left side where the worst of the damage is located—I'm looking less like a monster, but certainly not myself. At least my hair is

growing back quickly, so I don't look too much like a concentration camp victim—my diet of pulverized food has created a wasted-away look to my frame—I had no weight to spare before this event. It will be many weeks before I will feel back to normal; in the meantime, I'm to rest, and not over-extend myself.

Daisy hopped onto the sofa next to me, I scratched her chin and behind the ears until she settled down into the shape of a puffed pastry covered in coconut on her blanket. Lulled by her steady purring, I slept, and dreamed uncomforting nightmares of the ilk that have plagued me since my return to consciousness. Preston has turned into an unspeakable hulking beast, tearing into Samantha, raping her, crushing her, ripping her apart, but I am unable to move to help her because he has dismembered me, and somehow I've been left alive to watch with horror while he devoured her with his powerful jaws oozing blood and drool. I woke up weeping. As I slowly calmed myself, I took comfort in the soft darkness; the moonlight reflecting off the fresh dusting of snow outside filled the living room with an eerie blue light; I could see well enough without turning on the lights; I was relieved to be home—grateful for privacy.

The unfamiliar ring of the new telephone startled me into a second awareness, and I fumbled the phone to my ear, but it continued to ring until I pressed the TALK button after a bit of confusion regarding how to answer its plaintive cry.

"Hello," I mumbled; my mouth still feels slightly misshapen by abuse, but I am getting better at articulating what I need to say.

"Sylvester, is that you?" A voice drifted like a strain of distant music into my ear, and I immediately recognized the soft tone.

"Samantha—where are you?" I asked breathlessly, struggling to sit upright.

"I can hardly hear you, where have you been? Oh, Sylvester—you sound terrible!" she cried with a familiar edge of frantic that I know well.

"Shhh—it's all right, dear heart, it's a long story—be calm," I wasn't prepared to talk to her, her delicate voice echoing inside my ear in clear pip-ing notes threw me off balance. "Please, tell me where you are," I begged to hear news to put my mind at ease.

"I'm feeling better—I'm with Lena and Guthrie, I'm safe—where have you been, you don't sound right—what's wrong—did Preston hurt you? I have been afraid that he went after you—Guthrie, go get Lena, it's him—it's really him, he's at home!" Samantha shrieked with a confused mix of excitement heightened by the days of worry that have plagued her mind since I have been incommunicado.

"Where's Lena? Let me talk to her." I pressed because I didn't want to tell Samantha what had happened.

"She's sleeping—Guthrie's gone to wake her—we've all been sick with the flu or something, but we're getting better—and the weather has been so dreadful. Oh, Sylvester—I was so afraid something bad had happened to you—I've been having such awful nightmares—please tell me you're all right—you sound so wrong," she continued without replying to my question, her voice wound tight by a choke-hold of tears.

"I'm all right now—Preston is not going to hurt you anymore—you can come home—where are you? Please tell me where you are," I plead to her. I hadn't thought that they would go to Guthrie. It makes sense that Samantha would think to go to Cleveland; it's as safe a place as any, no wonder there isn't any sign of the car.

"No, not yet, we can't come back—we just can't, we're so close—wait, here's Lena! Oh, Lena, he sounds awful!" Sammy sobbed. My heart ached, knowing that the poor thing will be horrified once she hears what Preston had done to me—and to her house. I could hear her weeping in the background, and then Guthrie's low voice rumbling comfort; I imagined him holding her, his bulky arms cradling her diminutive being against his massive body—*she left home seeking protection, so she went to Guthrie.* I instantly felt better knowing that she was with him; he would never let anything happen to her.

"Sy, are you there?" Helena's voice came on the phone. I heard a distant door close; Guthrie must have taken Samantha away so Helena could speak to me in private.

"Helena, where are you?" I asked, but she left me hanging until after I told her everything. She listened, she cried, and she told me that she was sorry—sorry for everything—sorry for being unfaithful. I told her that none of it mattered, I told her that I loved her—but when she only sighed in response to my declaration, I felt desolate and abandoned all over again.

"Do you love Samantha?" she asked.

"Oh, god—" I choked. The question was so out of context it shocked me. "We can talk when you get home," I mumbled. My emotions are far too exposed; Samantha's declaration inscribed underneath the table has become etched in my brain—*does she still love me?*

"I need to know," she demanded softly, her voice almost a whisper. "Sammy told me everything—don't try denying any of it—please tell me, I need to know," she persisted.

"I love you," I sighed, tears prickled my eyes. "I really do love you."

"That is not what I asked." Her voice firmly pursued for the answer she already assumed.

"I do love her—of course I do!" I cried, feeling desperate. "But please understand, what happened between Samantha and I happened a long time ago. I took advantage of her innocence, and I always felt bad about it, but I loved her—purely loved her—I never meant her any harm. What happened between us recently is unpardonable—I won't use the stupid excuse that I was drunk, I knew what I was doing—I made love to her to hurt you because I felt betrayed. It was wrong that I used her in that way—I hope she will forgive me, and I hope that you can forgive me—please, forgive me—I have felt awful ever since." I stumbled through my explanation, but it felt inadequate and forced under duress. I felt sick and leaned forward, putting my head between my knees, and I gasped for air; tears fell from my eyes and splashed onto the floor at my feet. After awhile, I became aware of the silence on the other end of the line, and it led me to believe that she had hung up on me. "Helena!" I exclaimed in despair.

"I have already forgiven you," she said at last. "You must forgive me—I'm the one who treated you like shit. When I think about how I've behaved, all the awful things that I've said, how I've nagged you—I'm so sorry," she said, her tone beseeching, yet hopeless.

"Marry me, Helena," I implored without pride.

"Oh, Sy—I don't know what to say!" she exclaimed, stunned upon hearing my proposal.

"Just say 'yes'—please, it's what I want," I murmured, the pain in my ribs was breathtaking as my left hand flailed for leverage to help raise me upright again.

"I—"

"Helena, do you love me?"

"Yes," she replied after a long pause. "I have loved you."

"Then why—why not?" I asked, puzzled by her meaning.

"It's impossible, Sy—I just can't commit to you right now—not after what I've done, or how I feel right now," she sighed. "I don't expect you to understand."

"How do you feel?"

"I don't, I don't feel anything. I can't say what you want to hear—it would be a lie!" she cried with the tingle of frustration in her voice.

There was a long pause between us—barely breathing—there was nothing left to say.

"I understand—we will talk when you come home," I continued at last.

"Yes, we will," she replied.

"When are you coming home?"

"As soon as I find Dulcie—I'm so close, I can't come home now."

"Where is Dulcie?" I inquired with curiosity about this strange quest in the midst of a family crisis—yet it's a typical mode of operation for her to follow the beat of her own drummer no matter what else is happening around her, and it's typical of her to drag along anyone else who happens to be around at the time.

"I'm not sure yet—her last known location is in Taos—please understand I have to do this—I have to try to find her," she said with a strained plea in her voice.

"Where are you now? I need to tell the police where you are so they will stop looking for you—they're expecting your bodies to wash up onto the beach any day now—I've known all along you were together, and that you were all right—I hadn't given up hope."

"We've been in Colorado Springs for almost a week now, we've all been so sick—the flu double duty—the pukes, shits, sore throat, fever, head cold—Sammy's better, I'm better—Guthrie still has it in his chest, but he's finally feeling better—he had it the worst out of all of us," she sighed. "It's been awful—and the weather sucks, the snowstorms out here are unbelievable!" she then hacked with a barking cough that rattled my ribs hearing it.

326

"Come home soon, please, Preston is in jail—it's safe for Samantha to come back," I said after she finished blowing her nose.

"Oh, Sy, I'm so sorry about what happened to you—it's so horrible—I tried to get in touch with you—but I guess we just missed each other on that day—I'm sorry that I messed up and didn't tell you Sammy was with me," she cried. "I'm sorry about Jacob," she added softly.

"I'm all right now—I'm home and on the mend."

"Oh, Sy—I can't imagine!" she groaned.

What can't she imagine? What I went through or how hideous I must look with my scars and bruises. I sighed, feeling bad that my life with her has conditioned me to believe that she'd be embarrassed to be seen with me like this.

"Tell Samantha that Jack really needs to talk to her. And also let her know that Carrie's brother, Rick, has taken care of fixing the broken windows, he's been locating old glass panes at salvage yards to replace them—I know how much she loves the old glass, I asked him to do what he can to make them right," I stopped, and sighed, feeling exhausted by this conversation. "Please—let me know when you get to Taos."

"I will," she sighed, her voice sounded as tired as I felt. "Listen, I'll talk to you tomorrow night, all right? We're going to try driving there in one day—it'll be a push, but Guthrie is sure we can do it in one day—weather permitting."

"All right—please tell Samantha I'm all right."

"Goodnight," she muttered, without acknowledging my last request, and I wished her the same. It didn't matter if she told Samantha what I said or not, just saying it granted me a brief sense of peace.

After we severed our connection, I lay prone on the sofa, my wounded determination crushed by fresh despair, and I longed for the bliss of oblivion. My love for Samantha bit into me, its jaws clamping onto my heart and it refused to let go. Without realizing that I had fallen asleep, I believed that I saw her. Overjoyed, I cradled her sweet face within my hands as I once had while I beheld her as my lover. In this sweet dream, I told her that everything was going to be all right, and she kissed me with the softest kisses, gently caressing my wounds with her lips. She said something, but she didn't speak it out loud—I only felt it—*I love you.* I told her that I loved her—loved her more than life itself. I grasped the dream. It felt as if I slept with her in my arms, and I swore I could hear the lull of her quiet breathing; but I didn't dare open my eyes, because I knew that it was only Daisy's soft purr. *Why spoil it with reality, this is the happiest I've been in days.*

17

Taos

On the twelfth day of our departure from Gloucester, we arrived in Taos, New Mexico. The cloudless, late afternoon light dazzled our tired eyes with the promise of rest for the weary; we heaved sighs of relief—*we're here at last.* Now that we're here, the incomprehensible idea to bring Samantha this far to get her away from Preston still doesn't make sense, but we're here in spite of every sensible reason why we should have just turned back home. The reality that I'm this close to finding my mother is a phenomenon that I never believed possible.

As we drove along the main drag, my gaze through the backseat windows wandered over the shops and galleries lining the street, and I was surprised to see a sign that read: *Ryder-Tate Gallery.* The adobe storefront in the legendary Taos Plaza with its windows gleaming in the waning daylight beckoned to me—almost daring me to yell, *"STOP the car"*, but I didn't. I stared through the rear window with disbelief—*Ryder-Tate Gallery*—the hyphen much like the thin thread that held them together while they lived under the same roof in Gloucester. *Did Whitley help her buy it? Were they partners in this venture?* I harbored these questions in silence, wanting to process the significance of the gallery later when I was alone.

After much bantering in exhaustion-toned voices peppered with the hacking leftovers of the flu, we finally checked into a historic inn that Guthrie grunted was too pricey for his taste, but Sammy insisted that we deserved to pamper ourselves with a finer establishment after the hard push we made to get here. Naturally, I agreed with Sammy—my agreeing had nothing to do with annoying Guthrie—I felt ready for luxury.

Our two rooms were situated in a pleasant, low-slung adobe bungalow set off by itself in a secluded courtyard; the front doors and window sashes have been painted that renowned Taos Blue. Each room was charming, and simply furnished with local antiques and stone hearths. After dinner, Guthrie brought in a load of wood to build a fire in their room; he also set up logs and kindling in my room should I chose to indulge in a fire before bed, which of course I did after I left them cozy like two hibernating bears in front of the television. They looked beat; Guthrie lay sprawled on the bed dozing, and Sammy lazily scribbled his shape in her sketchbook.

Once I settled behind my closed door, I hoped that I didn't hear any hanky-panky through the wall now that I'm out of sleeping pills. I've noticed that they didn't seem as touchy-feely anymore, and wondered if the sickness had affected their physical relationship. There's nothing more cooling for a hot relationship than to witness the object of your affection in the throes of diarrhea and the pukes.

Squirming with impatience to get through this night, I telephoned Sy for something to do; we talked for a bit about nothing. I didn't tell him about seeing the gallery with the mated name of Ryder-Tate. The idea that my father and mother were in a partnership was so bizarre; the secrecy irritated me. *Why didn't Whitley tell me? Maybe he didn't know.*

I couldn't trouble Sy with my familial puzzle; he sounded wretched with loneliness, and I felt horrible for not being there during his time of need. While he murmured and sighed about his aches and pains, the call waiting blipped. *"Hold on,"* he grunted indelicately. Seconds later, he came back to tell me that Sammy was on the line. From my end, I could hear the pleasure in his tone because she had taken it upon herself to call him. To ease his dilemma, I let him go.

After hanging up, I felt worse—I only dragged him down with reminders about the sorry state of our relationship. While watching the embers in the hearth wink out, I caught myself nodding off in the chair, and felt compelled to drag myself to bed, but the motion from chair to bed woke me up. Trying not to think of anything was next to impossible, and so, without a sleeping pill within reach, I slept lousy in the downy allure of the old four-poster bed, caught in-between the discontent of the past and the immediate worries awaiting me the next day.

When I got up this morning, I pulled myself together early and left without rousing the exhausted couple in the next room because what I needed to do I had to do alone. After picking through a light breakfast that I wasn't hungry for, I wrapped myself in the tawny wool cape I had bought in Colorado Springs just before I came down with the flu, and took a stroll along the Plaza sidewalks like a typical tourist, peering into windows of interest—all but the ones belonging to the *Ryder-Tate Gallery.*

During my self-conducted tour, I treated myself to trinkets—especially jewelry, silver bracelets and rings encrusted with turquoise, necklaces of liquid silver shot through with beads of brilliant greens and reds, and another necklace strung with fetishes of carved animals made from semi-precious stones. Then, I wasted more time buying clothes at an affluent boutique consisting of blue jeans, a wool sweater, and finally a pair of suede boots. After this most satisfying binge, I left the last store wearing all of my acquisitions, and carried off my discarded New England clothes in the shopping bags. For the first time in a long time, I actually felt pretty, in spite of the streaks of white layered through my dark brown hair; with all the recent bullshit in my life, I forgot to go to the hairdresser for another color rinse. During a vain debate in the dressing room in which I considered paying a visit to a local drugstore for bottled color, I wondered about how I would look once my hair turned white like Whitley's—or will my hair be more like *hers—whatever Dulcie's looks like.* Based on the memory of my mother, I pegged the former New York fashion model to feel compelled to color her hair—and I figured she would have had a face-lift to stave-off the effects of aging—if she's still here in Taos, the desert environment would not be kind to her skin.

As I continued with my walk, I wished Sy could see me now. It was easy to envision us here together; we'd walk arm in arm in that lazy manner we have, moving together with the familiarity of a couple in a longstanding relationship. He was always good to me; he'd attend to my whims, and listen to my steady commentary with his quiet presence. *"Oh, look at that—isn't that a nice O'Keeffe poster of 'The Lawrence Tree'? It would look so nice in my study between the windows—will you let me paint the walls—you know, with that new suede paint? It will look so beautiful there with a pale adobe wall."* Ah, but he'd never let me paint the walls, he wouldn't say it, but I knew he wouldn't allow it to happen. With an internal wince, I missed him, and wanted him with me more than ever, but I shoved his presence away to spare myself the pain because things will never be the same between us— *never again—it's really over between us.*

I stood on a street corner and made an audible moan that caught the attention of people passing me by. I smiled at them, feeling foolish for making such a mournful noise on a day in which a pristine blue sky dominates the senses of anyone outside. To avoid further scrutiny, I peered inside a window of the shop next to the *Ryder-Tate Gallery.*

What a fucked-up mess everything is! Me, Guthrie, Sammy, Sylvester, Whitley, Lenore, Dulcie—Merry next Christmas—I'm stalling. I need an entrance strategy.

The Taos Blue painted doorway of the Ryder-Tate Gallery beckoned to me with the same teasing wink as the windows did yesterday. When I walked through the door, I entered my expectations and left behind my apprehensions. It had to be the bravest thing I've ever done in my life, but at the same time, it is the most selfish. Without warning, I'm forcing my way from a woman's past into her present—a woman who had forsaken me out of selfishness. *This is my bittersweet revenge.*

But my forward momentum stumbled when the person who greeted me wasn't Dulcie. She was someone younger than I had expected, a perky artsy-fartsy type normally found in galleries; tall, thin, spiky dark brown hair, granny glasses, standard black dress, tons of silver jewelry encrusted with turquoise, and a scarf loosely draped around her neck. She remained perched on a stool at the counter with a cup of coffee in her hand and the morning paper spread out before her, her greeting was pert and genuine, while mine was subdued and guarded as I tried to cover my vexation with a lack of emotion. *Of course, she would have hired help—why should I expect a woman who is almost seventy to be fuss-farting-around working in a gallery?*

I looked around the gallery with vague interest because I had practiced for years how I wanted to greet my estranged mother—during the formative years it went something like, *"Dulcie Tate, I presume?"* But I had revised it away from the juvenile greeting to more dramatic entrances constructed with varying degrees of bitterness. I often imagined that the stormy meeting would culminate with her accepting the blame for everything that ever went wrong in my life because of her absence. I imagined falling into her long, elegant arms after finally relenting to her plea for forgiveness. But her not being here in the flesh foiled everything—*I'll have to come back*—or get up the nerve to ask the gallery attendant where I can find her.

It became an effort to focus on the artwork in front of me as I struggled with tears of disappointment. Blinking them away, I took my first step toward a wall to acknowledge the paintings and drawings that Whitley had made during their years together. Seeing them was like unexpectedly stumbling upon long lost friends; their sudden disappearance from my life occurred not long after my mother's departure. When I initially went snooping around in the garret with my small hands clenching a flashlight, I found he had only set them aside with their faces turned to the wall as the emergence of newer work took over the easel and drying rails—because of Lenore. After my mother left us, I saw how the repressed drawings of his young lover that he coveted in clandestine sketchbooks became dazzling paintings of flesh, water, and sky. With delicate, pastel colors and flowing brushwork, Lenore blossomed unlike any canvas manifestation; her small breasts and hands were like the buds of water lilies on the shimmering surface of a pond. They made the abstractions of Dulcie's body appear wretched in comparison; her figure dissolved into the turbulent atmosphere of moody monochrome brushstrokes—blustery squalls like the emotional weather of her relationship with him. I remember how I wanted to destroy the new paintings—I wanted to rip that bitch to shreds—but I couldn't because they were beautiful, and Lenore was always nice to me.

The paintings of Dulcie had been unaccounted for in the appraiser's last inventory following Whitley's death. I desperately searched the garret for them in the place where they had been, but they were gone. Whitley kept meticulous records when it came to reporting his income because his accountant was such a stickler, but the undocumented departure of these pieces bugged me. After the first month of puzzling over their whereabouts, I threw up my hands in frustration with the catalog project. As I perused the documentation Whitley had left behind, there were indistinct notations that they may have been *sold*, but not to whom or even for how much. Now I wonder if I had mistaken the solitary cursive letter to be an *"S"* instead of a cursive *"G"*. *Had he given them to Dulcie as a gift?* Other gifts to family, friends, and institutions were always documented with a paper trail of some sort—a letter, shipping receipts, or an acknowledgement of arrival from the intended destination. But these had nothing.

She's my mother, why did he get rid of everything—why didn't he save something nice of her for me? While I contemplated the paintings, it occurred to me that Whitley must have sent them to her to purge himself of her existence from his studio—*or had she asked for them?* But why would she ask for these dark tokens of his estimation of her? They were only a dedication to his regrets that her presence inspired within his heart. I never liked them—I always thought they were horrible depictions of my beautiful mother—tall, leggy, and thin like Edie Sedgwick in a 1966 *Vogue* magazine that I have preserved for all these years because it was *hers*. Long before I was born, and just before she caught Whitley's roving eye that claimed her as his, Dulcie lived in New York working as a fashion model—the photo collection of her modeling days that I loved flipping through for fun had vanished along with her. The longer I studied the wall dedicated to Whitley Ryder, my visual vocabulary as an adult appreciated the paintings more than when I was a child—they were gorgeous, lush surfaces, flesh and fabric, light and shadow.

Memories of my mother rattled like loose change in a pocket, but all the brain noise fell silent when a muddy potter's wheel and stool pulled me back in time. It stood in a corner on a low-rise pedestal with a spotlight trained on it, revered like an artifact. There was a tattered Christmas tag tied to one of the stool's legs, its faded message on display: *To my darling Dulcie—living with me will probably cause you to want to 'throw' something—Ho-ho-ho, Merry Christmas! Love, Whitley.* When she first met Whitley, she was studying ceramics at an art school in New York. When she moved to Gloucester, he gave her the potter's wheel to encourage her to continue making art, and he put the kiln in the barn so she could fire her creations. I remember watching the wheel spin, and I loved how her long hands turned lumps of clay into elegant shapes. She let me play with it sometimes, my little feet kicking the turntable beneath to get it going; I hollowed out numerous lumps into blobs that were vaguely bowl-shaped, I could never manage to get up enough speed to make anything very good.

A spark of realization caused me to turn around to face the rest of the gallery once again—*she's here*, but she's here in another form, a form that I hadn't expected. The Taos Blue bowls, vases, dishes, and tea sets accompanied by colorful mixed-media hangings, collages of watercolor-stained paper, and ceramic panels encrusted with river stones and incised with designs—they are all hers. These art objects spoke of a simple life, one that is content, and they expressed the artist's appreciation for the complexity of even the smallest elements of nature.

"Would you care for a cup of coffee or tea?" The gallery attendant inquired with a friendly air that drew me to her; at this point, I welcomed her attention.

"Yes, please, a cup of tea would be nice—" I smiled. Upon approaching the mosaic-tiled countertop, I let my hand caress the surface, the design could only be hers, the colors and shapes are now familiar like the penmanship of a loved one. "Can you please tell me—is Dulcie Tate here?" I asked when the attendant poured hot tea into the cup and saucer she set out for me.

"She's at home this morning—it's kiln day—is she expecting you?" The young woman asked, adjusting her glasses that had slipped down her nose.

"No—I didn't make an appointment—I didn't know for sure if I was going to make it here," I replied brusquely, too preoccupied by my disappointment to want to chat with a total stranger about why I'm here. I had hoped to find Dulcie tucked away in a back room or upstairs in the open loft studio visible above—or at least somewhere accessible—home could be Taos or home could be Mars for all I know.

"I see—I can call her if you'd like to set up a time to meet with her."

"No—no, don't trouble her—as I recall, kiln day can be hectic," I shook my head, unable to look at her because I felt too prickly to be nice to anyone willing to accommodate me.

"Have you come a long way?" she prodded with bright enthusiasm, attempting to put me at ease, but it became apparent that my shitty attitude was worming its way under her skin.

"Yes, Gloucester, Massachusetts," I answered, perhaps a little too conceitedly.

"Oh—are you a collector?" she asked, with a hint of suspicion in her voice that annoyed me with its tremor of doubt.

"No, I am her daughter," I said with an affected haughtiness that I used to portray a privileged New England upbringing—my manner conscious of the artwork surrounding me—artwork my parents made; their combined effort produced me—*their daughter.* The woman reacted with a double take and a shudder.

"Helena?" she asked with a nervous flutter in her voice as she came away from the counter separating us.

"How do you know my name?" I asked warily as I studied her; my scalp tingled.

"I'm your sister—my name is Sophie," she said softly. Her hands made an awkward motion as if longing to do something other than hang in the air with nothing to do, and then she pushed her glasses into place again. This is a gesture all too familiar to me—they're new glasses, and they need to be adjusted to fit the narrow, straight bridge of her nose—a nose just mine. She wore rimless glasses with feather-light contemporary lenses, not the bottle-bottom spectacles in heavy plastic frames that I had to deal with most of my life. It's funny, ever since my eye surgery, I still catch my hand wandering to my face looking for something to do, but it falls aside as if at a loss—pathetically confused that it has no purpose.

"No, shit—" I blurted out with a laugh. "My sister—are you a half-sister?" I asked, while visually taking her in, and recognizing our physical similarities; she's tall like me, with dark hair and dark eyes, pale olive skin, and high cheekbones. We stared at each other as we wavered with uncertainty on a tightrope of emotions.

"We're full sisters—Dulcie was pregnant when she left Whitley," she muttered as if with shame. I dropped my shopping bags, and we fell into each other's arms in a clumsy hug that felt halfway honest, but a little bit contrived—*how are we supposed to react?* We awkwardly parted from our embrace and stared at each other with edgy amazement—so many questions to ask, both speaking at the same time, stopping, starting—*"You go", "No, you go."* From my perspective, it became clear that Sophie was the reason why Dulcie didn't want me—she couldn't support both of us—she didn't want Whitley's help because she didn't want to feel obligated to him—most of all, she didn't want to be dragged back to Gloucester. She hated it there, she hated the ocean, she hated the fog, she hated the rain, the wind, the

Nor'easter storms, and she especially hated it when the hurricanes buzzed the coast. And she always complained about being sick—colds, allergies, flu, bronchitis, she even had pneumonia once.

"I never knew about you. He didn't know about you, did he? If he did, he never told me," I said with a gravely rasp leftover from the flu.

"No, she never told him," Sophie said, shaking her head. "A letter from him tracked her down at Gram's house not long after I was born—he wrote asking if she needed anything, and she pretty much told him to fuck-off." We chuckled with mutual amusement over our mother's bristly demeanor. "Tell me—what led you here?"

"It's a long story," I laughed. "After Whitley died in November, his paper trail led me to believe that Dulcie lived in Taos—so, I made up my mind to find her—Samantha and Guthrie came along for the ride," I shrugged through the half-truth, I didn't feel like discussing the Gloucester soap opera.

"Wow—a whole family that I've never met!" Sophie exclaimed with a sigh of awe.

"Yup, they are my family," I grunted, trying to hide my disgust with the situation between my stepbrother and half sister, yet I smiled because they are my family, our history together binds us with a dedication that can only be love.

"Whitley called last year—I happened to be at Dulcie's house that day, and answered the telephone, but I had no idea it was *him*. He just started chatting me up like we were old friends, I never saw her move so fast when she blew out of the studio with her hand out for the phone—like she was expecting him. They talked for hours. After she hung up, she cried because he was so—well, you know—*Whitley*. Just talking to him reminded her that she still loved him. She said he called to say goodbye. It was sad realizing that I didn't know him—he didn't even know who he was talking to—I always wanted to meet him."

"Did they talk often?" I asked, curious about their contact.

"I really don't know; she was always secretive about him—and angry. After the call, she received a check a few days later and the letter with it told her: *'This is money I've kept in an account under your name—I want you to have it, so don't you dare rip up this one! If you do, I'll have to put you in my Will and I don't think you want to deal with Jack!'* I guess she didn't want to argue with him about it, so she deposited the check, and bought this place shortly thereafter. The entire time she went through the process she cursed his name—"*He hasn't changed a bit!*" Sophie laughed. Her laugh reminded me of Dulcie's, but her smile was more like Whitley's generous grin in the way that it lit up her face with pleasure.

"He never changed a bit—to his own detriment sometimes," I muttered with a smirk.

"I think she appreciated the gesture, although she was doing well enough selling her things from home and through a couple of galleries, but she really needed a place of her own to showcase her work. After she bought it, she didn't want to manage it, so she put it in my name—my middle name is Ryder—Sophie Ryder Tate. I figured that if I called it Ryder-Tate, it gives him half credit for the gallery coming into being."

"He would've liked that."

"I always believed Whitley was overshadowed by the big names and neglected by the critics during his lifetime."

"Of course he was neglected, he didn't 'kiss the ring'—he always liked being on the fringe doing his own thing. I wrote my dissertation about the 'family connection' with Albert Pinkham Ryder—Whitley always made a huge deal out of our relative in one breath, but in the next he'd say he was just another man who happened to paint some nice paintings in his lifetime—one big poof and it'll be gone—none of it matters," I laughed. I looked back at the wall dedicated to Whitley. "I've been looking for these paintings—when did they come here?"

"The crate arrived unexpectedly at the Howard Gallery where she used to work back in the 70's—Whitley gave them to her so if she ever needed cash, she could sell them. Oh, she had quite a fight with Mr. Howard about them—he was such a jerk. He really wanted to buy them from her, but she told him they were not for sale. She figured if she ever needed the money she'd sell one to him, but she never did; she held on to all of them. I hung them in the gallery after I heard the news about his passing—so the walls at her house are barren now, but she likes them here better—it's our Whitley Ryder memorial wall," she laughed again. It was a nervous laugh; she's still in shock from meeting me like this, but she's also thrilled with the opportunity to talk to me; almost as if she has looked forward to this moment all of her life—*had I known about her, I would have felt the same way.*

The more I look at her, I can see our similarities crisscross, meld, and then go in separate directions—I grew up without my mother, she without her father—worse, without her father ever knowing about her existence, and she worshipping him from afar.

"The drawings came last October. She loved these best because they are the ones he made when they first met—before—" Sophie continued.

"Before I came along," I laughed bitterly.

"Oh, don't say it like that—Dulcie always said he loved you—he was thrilled when she got pregnant—he became very protective because she was sickly, and he was so kind to her—he even stopped painting to take care of her." My sister's expression appeared so awestruck; her outlook innocent of the bitterness that plagued me all my life.

"I remember hearing something like that—I think Gram mentioned it," I murmured while staring at a gesture drawing made with an ink brush, oriental in its simplicity—the perfect line defining her protruding belly, her hand resting upon it, splayed fingers curving around its roundness. He had made similar drawings of Lenore during her pregnancy with Sammy. "I always thought he must have resented me—he's—he was always so selfish."

"Yes, he was that too—but Dulcie didn't want him to know about me! After she caught him with that other girl, she wanted him out of her life completely—and she was afraid that if he ever knew about her being pregnant, he'd drag her back to that drafty old house in Gloucester, to the cold and damp that she couldn't stand. She hated herself for leaving you—and after she heard that he was dying she felt guilty for not telling him about me when they last spoke—she even said it was stupid—believe me, we had our share of nasty arguments about it—but sometimes it's difficult to undo a wrong. Truthfully—I came close to going out there by myself about ten years ago, but I chickened out—I got married to the *'man of my dreams'* and then went through a messy divorce a year later—I wanted my *'mommy'* after going through that shit," she said with a quirky smirk. We laughed together—our life parallels seemed ridiculous.

"Can you tell me, please—how is Dulcie?" I asked with timid desire; I have feared that with her age tipping toward seventy that her health maybe in decline, and it would be just my luck to find her after it's too late to enjoy her—*like Sy with Jacob.*

"Oh! She's well, very well—she's Dulcie—a survivor and more. I don't think you'll ever comprehend the choice she made back then—she was so sick—Gram had to take care of me after I was born because Dulcie nearly died," she said with a frown. "This—your arrival—will be hard for her, as you can imagine," Sophie murmured thoughtfully.

"Yes—it's been hard for me—the journey here, and my life without her," I sighed, but I no longer felt resentment, nor any selfish satisfaction to make it difficult for her, or to outdo who had it tougher. The cost to maintain the desire for revenge has drained away my energy to play such games.

"It was hard for me growing up without a father—I can only imagine how hard it was for you—because of the way she left," Sophie sighed with sadness. "Gram's still alive—she'll be so thrilled to see you!" she exclaimed, grabbing me by the elbows.

I let out a hoot of laughter upon learning that my infamous grandmother was still alive—I had only met her once when she came all the way from Abiquiu, New Mexico to see Dulcie and me when I turned four years old. As I remember, she was a half-breed holy terror, and gave Whitley a migraine, causing him to slink into the garret to hide. Dulcie gave me the task to carry a tray with a cold compress and tea upstairs; it became my job to look after him during Gram's month long stay. I knew that he loved it when I came, and once I got there, he didn't want me to leave. He'd lie there with the compress over his eyes, talking to me; half the stuff he said was over my head, but I would listen to him anyway—just to listen—and I'd stare at the marvel of his paintings, trying to comprehend the broad expanses covered in washes with perplexing thick slashes of color. When he finally stopped, I would sneak away after I knew for sure that he was asleep—*he did love me.*

When the door opened behind us, we both started like spooked horses on a windy day, and craned our necks to see who dared to intrude on our conversation just when it was getting interesting. I immediately recognized Dulcie's willowy figure framed in the doorway. Her exquisite posture distinguished in black garb, a wide-brimmed hat, wool cape, and a skirt that swept the floor around her ankles; a long steel-colored rope of braided hair hung over her shoulder. It was apparent that she knew me too as she strode across the room; her expression a road map of curiosity and questions. Without a word, we enveloped each other in a tearful embrace.

"I had a feeling about this day—actually—it started last night—I must've heard you come into town." Dulcie started to say as she stepped away, and removed her hat, self-consciously patting her tight silver hair. "When I got up this morning, there was something special about the sky—you know me—I don't go for any of that mystical bullshit, but there was something in the air making my hair turn into a bushy-tail. When I went out to check the kiln this morning, the temperature wasn't right, so I took it as an omen, changed my clothes and came here. I knew your curiosity would eventually lead you here. I'll bet he left clues for you to follow."

"I guess you can call them clues—though half the time I didn't know what I was looking at—I'm so dense sometimes—he should have known better than to be so vague."

"Yeah, well, vague was Whitley's style," she smirked.

"Even in his artwork," I pointed at a beautiful dusky image entitled, "*...come in out of the darkness*".

"I hope you know how much he loved you," she murmured, caressing my hair.

"I never knew if he did," I replied, denying what I knew to be true. "At least, not while he was alive." I stepped away from her to ponder what I just said.

With my focus centered on my mother's abandonment, I never gave Whitley much thought—to me, he was an egotistical, first-class asshole. "No—I never knew that he loved me—I guess he never got around to saying so—sometimes he was so inept!" But in his subtle way he did tell me—the braces on my teeth, nicer glasses, then my contact lenses, and the big wedding when I married Shep—even that shitty T-bird—I just refused to see these efforts as tokens of love—I didn't think he was capable of love for anyone but himself. Lenore always said he was passionate about too many things at the same time, even his love for her—it was intense, but there was always something else distracting his attention away—a painting, an idea, booze, or another woman—temptations. I always thought I was stuck in the middle—between Guthrie and Lenore, and then Samantha—I even thought Sy came between him and me.

I'm so much like him, it's no wonder we never had much to say to one another after I reached a certain age and my nascent personality became a thorny obstacle between us. I shoved him away every time he tried to get close—every time anyone gets too close; Shep and Sy are victims of my misery. Even Sammy when she needed me after Lenore died and Guthrie left—but instead, she made her way to Sy seeking friendship, seeking love—he accepted her friendship, he loved her—*he still loves her.*

"I knew that he loved you very much—but he was never consistent about showing it—little girls mystified him—he wanted a boy, but when you were born you should have seen him fuss over you! He'd stand by your crib listening to you breathe, just making sure you were alive. You were his first-born—he loved you, honey, and I loved you too. Leaving was a hard choice to make, but I couldn't stay there anymore. When I told him that I was leaving—he begged to keep you—I suppose he expected me to stay rather than give up my daughter. I left you behind because I knew that he'd take care of you—I knew you'd be safe—I didn't know what I was getting into when I walked out the door that day—and I had Sophie to think about. I worried that you would hate him because I left—it would have broken his heart if he thought you hated him," Dulcie sighed. "Will you ever forgive me?"

Finally, I'm hearing the words that I wanted to hear for years. In all the time that I spent dreaming and plotting this moment, I never thought it would be like this. The bitterness that had cramped my entire being loosened its hold as I put my arms around my mother to hug her again, and she clasped me tight in return. Our coming together was better than I ever imagined—even better than I ever rehearsed. But the joy I should feel is laced with a fresh grief. From the perspective of a child, I thought I was the victim. From my solitary point of view, I only saw one side of the story—mine. While growing up without my mother, I felt justified to blame Whitley for her being gone, and I relished in doling out unforgiving antagonism to punish him. With a transformed vision born on the shoulder of my mother, I can see how he fumbled to make me happy, and how he suffered in the shadow of my disdain. *The story wasn't just about me.*

18

Zig-Zag

Why—why does he always do this to me? Two days later, Sy did the one thing that always drove me nuts—*he followed me!* I couldn't believe it when he called at noontime from the Denver airport and said that he was renting a car and driving to Taos. *"What are you, crazy? Do you realize how far it is from there to here? It's like 300 miles—you're in no shape to travel!"* I cried. He balefully muttered an answer, I didn't quite hear it, but whatever he said couldn't have been too nice because I distinctly heard him laugh that stupid laugh he uses to antagonize me when he thinks he's being funny. *"Well, fine, come then, I can't stop you!"*

After hanging up the phone with a frustrated bang, I considered all the times that he followed me somewhere; he never followed me when I traveled alone—*Sammy!* He only did it when I was with Sammy—*he wasn't following me to check up on me—he did it for Sammy.* It is a known fact that he became a cushion between us, softening our frustration with each other—his arrival always perfectly timed to intersect with my desire to throttle my sister. He'd appear in the midst of Christmastime shopping sprees, and I'd willingly let them go off together, linked arm in arm, quietly interacting in soft language and smiles. From the time she was a child to an adult, I'd find them later, tucked in a corner of the bookstore reading—he would be propped in a chair, and she'd sit at his feet with her back leaning against his bony shins. She'd read aloud to him from a book of poetry or a Greek play, fully engaged, her voice clear and unhindered by self-consciousness, and he'd sit with his eyes closed, listening to her read to him, his face exhibiting pride because he had taught her how to read. *I saw all of this, yet I didn't really see any of it to comprehend them—he really loves her—Sammy is the real reason why he's coming here.*

As soon as I made the connection, I nearly danced a jig, but the joy was quickly snapped away when it hit me that Sam is still in bed with Guthrie every night; my liberation sputtered and turned into a fresh anxiety. *Oh, crap!* Sy's last place of firm footing has broken away and he has no idea that it's gone; with his body barely healed, I feared his spirit might take on another kind of wound from which to recover. *I should have told him. Oh, Helena, since when have you ever been considerate of his feelings?* Since when have I ever gone out of my way to spare him any embarrassment by warning him to zag when I knew he was going to zig? It looks as if I wanted to hurt him on purpose, but I don't want to hurt him, I never meant to—*at least not this time.*

In spite of his marriage proposal and declarations of love, I am even more certain that his heart does not pine for me. If an outsider like Guthrie coming into a situation from the outside can see the evidence, then it must be so. *If Guthrie knew, then why is he screwing Sammy?* Because, as he suggested in the bar the other night, she looks enough like Lenore to ease his years of grieving, and for her, it's a fantasy—but it seems to be coming to an end in his mind; now he needs to come up with an exit strategy to set things right. Maybe Sy's arrival will set him free—that all depends on Sammy I guess.

I lit a cigarette and huffed with a frustrated exhale, a sound much like one made by an irritated cat.

"So, that's your man-friend," Dulcie smirked, peering into the kitchen. I knew she was lurking around out there, eavesdropping because after she handed off the telephone, she tiptoed away on the pretense of giving me space, but the curiosity would have killed her if she went more than two feet away from the doorway.

"Yes—he's on his way here—he should arrive sometime late tonight—barring bad weather, of course," I replied after taking another nervous drag off my cigarette, the idea of him becoming stranded on a middle of nowhere piece of highway put me on edge.

"Bad weather happens in March—especially on 64—I hope he's a good driver," she laughed with a nod as she glanced outside. "But I don't think that's a problem tonight—the sky over there is perfectly clear—there is no need to worry—it's such a warm day—I expect tonight will remain balmy."

"He is an excellent driver—but he has a broken arm, broken ribs—I don't know if I like him driving with only one good hand," I muttered. Taking an anxious glance over my shoulder, I looked for Sammy to appear, but her *Sylvester radar* must be off. There hasn't been a peep out of her yet this morning; however, Guthrie is up. The distant sound of an ax splitting logs out back has been going on continuously for nearly an hour. I wondered if they had a fight—*whatever it is, there's something going on between them behind the closed door, and it ain't sex.*

"Well, I'm sure he'll be fine—men tend to be single-minded to the point of stupidity when they are on a mission, and there's no fixing that behavior!" she laughed. I knew she based her remark on a wealth of experience, she was married twice since her split from Whitley, and divorced both men—"*They were good men, but they drove me crazy.*" Yet another explanation of my makeup—it isn't just Whitley. "What kind of accent is that?"

"Maine, ain't it a beaut?"

"Lordy, it's thicker than a Boston Kennedy—he has a nice voice tho', I can't wait to meet him—I'm sure he's a good man since you've been with him for so long." She patted my shoulder with an assuring manner, but I saw the crease of concern forming on her brow.

"That's the problem, he is a good man," I agreed, stifling a moan.

Dulcie's eyes narrowed into thoughtful notches while lighting a cigarette on a match. "If he's so good, then why, pray-tell, are you not thrilled about seeing him—you've hardly told me diddly-squat about this *man* of yours," she said, puffing smoke; she then shook out the match, and tossed it into a ceramic ashtray (one of her design and much prettier than the oak leaf ashtray in Gloucester). I watched her through these motions and expressions, and found it funny how we have the same gestures—so funny it's disturbing. Being with her these last two days, I have learned more about myself—more than I want to—the sad thing, I'm also learning how much like Whitley I am, which she has gladly pointed out to me several times.

"I'm not thrilled—that's the problem—things have happened, things have changed between us." I kept my reply vague on purpose, hoping she'd take the hint and back off.

"Oh, the thrill is gone—you've been together for a long time—it could be just a little mid-life itch," she chuckled with a wink. "Men get that way as they age, it's a phase—only—your father was always in *the phase*—he was never satisfied with anything."

"It's not Sy—I've had the itch—I can't explain it—I love him, but I don't love him enough. He knows what I've done—he says he loves me—but—right now, it's just convenient for us to stay together," I sighed. "He wants to get married; I told him 'no' twice."

"Well now, this *is* interesting," she cocked her head curiously, and gave me that familiar scrutinizing squint. "There's something you're not telling me."

"He's in love with Sammy," I whispered for the dramatic effect.

"Now that's something I didn't expect—just like I didn't expect Sammy and Guthrie to crawl into the same bed together the other night—it's no wonder you're in such a tizzy, girl—what the fuck?" she sighed, rolling her eyes. We both stood inhaling and puffing, and listening to the steady thunk-crack of Guthrie's distant log splitting.

"There's a man out there with a lot on his mind," Dulcie mused after a long silence.

"Yeah—he knows that Sy and Sammy are in love with each other—he's out there trying to come up with an exit strategy," I muttered.

"Maybe he wants to keel over and die while chopping wood—that would suck—he's a mighty nice hunk o' man," she growled. "By the time the ambulance got here he'd be dead."

"That would be an exit strategy—but I don't think he's trying to kill himself by chopping wood all morning; he's an ox—Mom, this is awful—what are we talking about?"

"Exit strategies—you need one and Guthrie needs one—why don't you go out there and jump his bones before Sy gets here and the whole thing will be solved," Dulcie laughed through her exhale. "Oh, never mind—I can tell by the look on your face that you have no interest in him—so forget it, I'll jump his bones and that will be that!"

"Dulcie—I will forget you said any of that," I grunted. "Guthrie Ryder would never give me or any woman the time of day—Lenore is who he wants, but she's dead—Sammy just happens to look like her."

"Ah, yes, Lenore—your father made such a fool out of himself over her—it served him right to bring home his child bride and have her fuck his stepson," she said with a humph. "Hey, you—just a second ago you called me Mom—it was so nice," she pouted.

"Fuck off—Mom," I laughed.

"That's my girl," she snickered. "I bet you talked that way to your father too."

"You bet your ass I did—that asshole."

"Yup, you got that from me—you're my daughter, through and through."

⟅

A haze of cigarette smoke curled within the blazing terrace lights; in spite of this toxic fog, the steady luminescence will show Sy the way down the driveway lined with mature cottonwood trees; and so, the welcoming committee, Guthrie, Sammy, and I waited like a trio of chimneys reclining in Adirondack chairs. Sophie had gone to bed hours ago because she has to open the gallery in the morning. Dulcie had gone to bed around midnight, but when she pushed open the screen door, this signaled his imminent arrival. I had figured she'd be at the door to meet him before we were aware that he was coming, she always had a damn good maternal sense of hearing that picked up any sound that was out of the ordinary or anticipated. If I made a peep in my sleep, she would arrive at my bedside, a whirlwind of silk kimono and dark hair. I swear she could hear Whitley's Caddy from a mile away, so by the time he crept up to the front door, she'd be there to nag at him about whatever crime that made him late, and he'd placate her with promises she knew he would never keep. Within seconds of her appearance, headlights turned down the lane. The three of us rose to our feet to join her at the edge of night as the car rolled to a stop—I braced myself in the dusty light for the wait to finally end.

When his familiar shape wearing a familiar tweed cap and leather jacket stepped into our midst, I hesitated because I didn't recognize him—*poor Sy, he looked awful!* Even though he had told me with vivid language what to expect, I have no imagination with which to prepare myself, I could never visualize anything without the actual physical reference in front of my nose.

My initial fears that his face drooped like a stroke victim's from the nerve damage were assuaged, but instead, he appeared out of sorts due to swelling and discoloration. His hair is shapeless like a grown out boot-camp buzz-cut; he looked so odd with such short hair; I have always known him with a shaggy mop that looked perpetually stuck in an in-between stage of growing out. Every year he'd go somewhere to have it pruned to keep it out of his eyes, but he never maintained a sense of style; he'd wash it, comb it back, and let it fall where it may while it air-dried. I used to nag him for years about his hair as if he was an embarrassment, but to no avail—bottom line, he didn't care about his appearance—although in retrospect, my nagging brought him *some* attention as he either teased or ignored my repetitive tirades concerning his shapeless hair. All of my efforts to change him to fit into my ideal were for nothing; it's time to let him be, none of it matters anymore.

After our initial greeting in which we hugged with tepid awareness, I stepped back and watched his response to Sam—and hers toward him. It looked so natural to see how he cupped her tiny face in his one good hand, and then the poor puffy-looking fingertips protruding from the cast of his other hand tenderly touched her cheek. She then rubbed her face into the open palm of his good hand like a cat leaving its scent on him; only she left the traces of happy tears. They leaned into each other and hugged, rocking together in a gentle swaying motion like a slow dance. Neither one said anything during their long hello, but everything left unsaid appeared understood between them, just like it has always been—I knew all along—*I knew, but didn't care to see.*

Without turning my head, I dared to sneak a peek at Guthrie to see his reaction; he stood with his arms folded across his chest, his gaze focused on the ground at their feet. I noticed a strange little smile quirked in the corner of his mouth, and whenever it faded, he'd jerk it back into place with an intentional spasm. Then just beyond the ridge of his shape, I caught a startled expression from Dulcie—as if she didn't believe what I had said earlier in the day, so now she's giving me the classic *"Well, I'll be damned!"* look; my glance bounced away unwilling to acknowledge her curious expression. It was too bad that Sophie missed this—I would have appreciated hearing my sister's reactive—*"What's up with that?"*

As the excitement of his arrival wound down and the night turned into the wee hours of the morning, Sy's rude awakening about Sammy's relationship with Guthrie came when they went to bed. He wished them goodnight without batting an eye, but he blinked as if bedazzled when the bedroom door closed behind both of them. The final nail in his coffin came when Guthrie did not come out. He sat speechless; his face turned into a pale, gaping wound of distress. Although his gaze purposefully avoided the hallway, it was difficult for him not to look down the inviting entry as his sight line faced toward their closed door.

Dulcie followed their departure a few awkward minutes later, and then Sy trailed behind me to bed; of course, our long relationship naturally dictated this arrangement. We lay down together, flat on our backs in the darkness, neither one of us bothering to undress. After an awkward period of just our breathing, he turned over onto his side; his finger touched my hand draped on my stomach.

"Tell me how it happened," he inquired.

"How what happened?" I pretended that I didn't know what he wanted, just to make him squirm on purpose; he should know better after all these years.

"Samantha and Guthrie," he sighed, lying down on his back again as if my reply with a question deflated him.

"It just happened," I snickered, feeling a little mean. A petty part of me wanted to torment him just for the entertainment value of getting him riled.

"It happened just like that?" he asked, his voice full of low-voltage tension. He's too tired to get riled, but not too tired to interrogate me until I go insane and tell him everything.

"Yup, just like that," I snapped my fingers for the effect, making him flinch.

"Lena, there's got to be more to it than that."

"You bet your bippy, it was in the making while he stayed with us in Gloucester—she told me that's why he had to leave. She hopped into bed with him the minute we arrived in Cleveland," I explained in simple terms.

"I see," he replied with a stoical tone. I wanted to smack him for feigning curiosity as if it didn't matter to him.

"What's the matter, are you jealous?" I teased, to call his bluff.

He made a funny noise that sounded like a mixture of a scoff and a gasp. "I'm just concerned—he is a little old for her." As soon as he said it, he let out an exasperated sigh because he knew that it was the wrong thing to say.

"Oh, is he? And you aren't?" I crossed my hands over my mouth to suppress laughter.

"Yes, I am—" He spoke in that manner I know so well; just by the tone in his voice I knew his expression—his mouth has turned into a sulking thin line, and his ears have bloomed red—soon enough the veins in his temples will start to pulse their way to the surface, but not yet.

"I never had any business being involved with her—" he sighed and sat up. "I just think he's being foolish." He spoke with a grasping-at-straws sound to his words, but no matter what he said to cover-up his distress, his jealousy remained exposed.

"I see," I said thoughtfully, wanting to make him suffer a little. "So—do you feel foolish?" I asked with poignant timing that might as well have been a knife in his back. He stiffened in reaction, and without making a reply other than a noise of disgust, he rose from the bed and stalked out to the bathroom. Now I'm certain that the veins in his temples are bulging.

Taking advantage of his being out of the room, I changed into my nightshirt, and plopped back into bed; with my heart pumping from a pulse full of nicotine, I longed for a sleeping pill to knock me out. With overly keen awareness, I listened to his familiar bathroom noises—pissing, flushing the toilet, running water, and scrubbing his teeth with a toothbrush. Then after a gross ordeal of honking and spitting to clear his sinuses, he emerged from the bathroom wearing his t-shirt and boxers, and sat on the edge of the bed with his back to me. I felt sorry for him—I felt sorry for being mean to him—sorry for everything I've ever said to berate him in the past.

"I'm sorry," I said, touching the slouch of his defeated back, its familiar curve knew my hand, but he quickly shrugged away from it.

❧

"Are you all right?" Helena asked; her long, thin fingers timidly brushed over the surface of my t-shirt—it was evident that her nervous hand didn't want to imply intimacy. It seemed as if these weeks of distance, tragedy, and revelations has suddenly caused us to be strangers.

"Fine," I answered after clearing the wretched emotions caught in my throat. Helena's coolness toward me is confusing; her gaze takes in my battered appearance with a sense of sympathy, but she can barely look at me; her greeting kiss winced from my mouth as if I caused her pain.

The development between Samantha and Guthrie disturbed me in a way I can hardly grasp. It isn't quite accurate to call it jealousy—at least, not as I would normally identify it—there is a protective feeling toward her that has always been present throughout our long relationship. Within this feeling there lingers a crushing sensation of disillusionment—I had felt the same way when she started to see Preston, and then again on her wedding day. Questions like, *How could she?*—and—*What does she see in him?*—echoed in my mind with a disquieting tremor of emotion akin to shock.

Helena knew, but she didn't tell me, she left me unprepared as if with the purpose to hurt me. Confusion soaked my mind; emotions trembled with nowhere to go. Samantha's warm greeting groped into my being, arousing physical memories; her tender kisses crossed over my ruined face with sweet touches, leaving damp impressions that my skin absorbed with greedy delight. I made a complete fool of myself by intimately sniffing her neck where the heady scent of lavender lay in wait beneath her hair, but to my dismay, I was barely able to sense it because of the swelling inside my healing nose—*oh, how I longed for a clear breath to suck in her sweet essence!*

Guthrie stood like an emotional wall, as impassive as stone; he couldn't look me in the eye when he shook my hand in greeting—*"Long time no see, Hayden,"* he joked. He watched Samantha perched at my side, her arms wrapped around my waist, unwilling to let me go, all the while murmuring, *"Oh, Sylvester, I'm so happysohappyso happy to see you again!"*

"I just don't know what to think," I muttered with a sour taste in my mouth. "I guess I should have expected it because they were so close while he was in Gloucester." Which is true, I noticed the attention she paid him—even in front of Preston. And I haven't forgotten her childish proclamations she had made long ago about him returning one day like a glorified knight in shining armor—coming home for her. *Why do I feel betrayed? It's been over between us for years—because you love her—you never stopped loving*

*her—you're a fool, a foolish man who lives in dreams—always longing for
something he can't have—never acting on the reality of the situation when
faced with a choice. Well, Doctorsylvesteraloysiushayden, you have another
title to follow behind your Ph.D.—now you are, from here on in, dubbed
F-O-O-L.*

I slipped into bed next to Helena without expectations, even though my
healing body longed for the touch of someone other than a clinical hand.

"What do you think of it?" I asked.

"I try not to think too hard about such things—when I do, I get too
fucked-up," Helena laughed, she turned over onto her side, facing away
from me, her awareness of my being beside her clearly disturbed her. "I need
to get some shut-eye—goodnight," she sighed, pounding the goose-down
pillow into shape with her fist and settled into the hollow she prepared.

"Helena—I want to marry you," I declared to her back as my hand
caressed her arm, my entire body yearning as I pressed close to her—I felt
mildly ashamed of my desperation.

"Cripe!" she exclaimed, jolting upright.

"What?" I exclaimed, surprised by her sudden motion.

"Let's not get into this right now—it's past three in the morning!" she
whispered fiercely. The mercury vapor light mounted on the barn behind the
house dimly illuminated the night through the window, its glow allowed for
an unobstructed view of her horrified expression.

"When are we going to get into *this*—tomorrow, next week, after you
get back, or next year? Please don't leave me hanging, Helena." Although
anger flared within me, I kept my voice low, as I remained conscious of the
sleeping household.

"I thought I made it clear before—*no* means *no*," she murmured, dropping her gaze; her hand fumbled for mine and she squeezed it hard. "Listen to me—I've decided that I'm not going back to Gloucester, I'm staying
here."

"What?" The shock of her words shivered through me. "Why?"

"I can't leave—I don't want to go back—I have found my mother, and I
discovered a sister that I never knew I had because my fucked-up possessive
father would have taken her away from Dulcie if he had found out about
her. Being here with them is what I need now, more than I need you for a

husband," she whispered with inflamed impatience. As I made a nonverbal protestation in reply, she frowned, and set free my hand. "I can't marry you—because there's more going on here than what's happening to me, and to you and me. You need to settle something within yourself about Sammy, and she about you—and then there's Guthrie in this mess," she continued with a gentle firmness that I've never heard her use before.

"I've always loved you, Helena," I affirmed, but the uncertainty in my voice gave away my misgivings, and I knew she heard the subtle hesitation.

"I know you have," she answered with more conviction than I expressed in my words. "I always knew—and I was always grateful for that—it's not as if I never cared about you—I do, but I can't stay with you—I can't marry you—and it's not fair to leave you hoping."

With nothing more to say, we lay apart in silence. I listened to the rhythm of her breathing as it changed from the tension of wakefulness to the gentle exhales of sleep. Time passed while random thoughts were fitfully churned by the beating of my heart; I don't know if I slept. I stared out the window, eventually, my tired eyes perceived the subtle shift of the light that grew in intensity with the rising sun, and I witnessed the moment when the mercury vapor light shut off. I looked at Helena lying beside me; she appeared to be dozing in a state of half-awareness, because her brow furrowed as if she knew that I watched her. Soon the perplexing disappointment crushed shut my eyes against the painful daylight shining through the thin muslin curtains. Just as I drifted toward much needed rest, I felt her rise and leave the room. Left alone, I fell into a deep sleep—it no longer made sense to follow her anymore.

Immediately after Helena found Dulcie and Sophie, she was sporting a spiffy personality transplant and a sickish-sweet attitude adjustment—she was so changed I wanted to ask, *"Who the fuck are you and what have you done to Helena?"* But who am I to question it, right? The girl found her mom and a sister she didn't know she had—it made the hellish-bullshit trip worth it just to see her happy.

Dulcie and Sophie have been gracious hosts, yet thankfully informal. It was nice to be in a home again; just having a stocked refrigerator to stand in front of and contemplate the contents is a reality that is normally taken for granted until you go without it for several days.

In spite of the creature comforts, I quickly turned my concern to Sammy because she regressed into a child-like shyness as she clung to me like a shadow. I lie in bed with her beside me every night—if she got any tighter against me, she'd be wearing my skin. Now I know Dulcie and Sophie both thought it was weird that I was sharing a bedroom with her, and I went in with the attitude that it wasn't any of their damn business what went on behind the closed door. Even though I'm sleeping with her at night, the physical nature of our relationship is over, and has been since that night in Cleveland—sleeping in the same bed is a habit I'd like to break as soon as possible. Frankly, it's not a hardship on me, it only confirmed two things—number one, I am getting too old for this shit, and number two, I have finally gotten over the madness that gripped me since I first laid eyes on her back in November. Well, sort of—it's complicated.

When Hayden arrived a few days later, I stepped aside to give them room, hoping that she will initiate the first move. Truthfully, I think we were all anticipating passionate grappling to erupt, but no, nothing like that happened. While I watched their reunion, I saw how her silence spoke to him, and I found it interesting how he reacted with practiced responses. It's plain to me that they love one another—*what else could it be?* During the ensuing days, I perceived an edgy disappointment emanating from the trio who viewed their quiet interaction through sidelong glances, and then they perked their brows at me for my response—I pretended not to notice their curiosity. The expectation that Sammy would eventually seduce Hayden was the unspoken bet—but it was a good thing no one put money on it; he was the epitome of a gentleman when he resisted temptation that day she kissed him—and she followed his lead. And so, they enabled the denial of their truth, and continued their relationship within their set comfort zone.

The women were inside cooking dinner while Hayden and I stepped out onto the patio behind Dulcie's sprawling adobe to smoke cigars. He lounged in a chair as if without a worry in the world—but I knew that he was only pretending to be relaxed around me because my being with Sammy is giving him a major bug up his ass. We haven't said much to each other all day, mostly because Sammy has kept him preoccupied with her constant

attention. It makes me feel good to see her happy again, she's been so subdued since the flu laid us low in Colorado. Although my influence moves
her through the day-to-day events, things are different between us now, her
reactions to me are like familiar beaten paths—she's only going through the
motions. Part of it is my own fault because my internal struggle with the
logistics of our relationship continues to mar the emotions I've associated
with her since Whitley's funeral; everything that I had convinced myself to
be right about our relationship now feels wrong. With Hayden in the picture, it is clear that I need to know one thing—

"Are you in love with Sammy?" I got right to the point.

"What?" he jolted in his seat, choking on cigar smoke.

"Easy there, Hayden, I have no quarrel with you." I forced myself not
to laugh at him because he appeared so jagged by my question. With a stab
of guilt, I flinched upon seeing how the color suddenly drained from his face
when he shot out of the chair, and I feared that he might stroke-out. Now
that he stood with his back to me, I lost contact with his facial reactions, so
I rose from my comfortable chair to join him as he wobbled over the stone
slab path. "Listen, I know there's a history between you two, and I need to
know where you stand."

"I—I understand why you might think that way—but what happened
between us was such a long time ago," he murmured, standing with his head
downcast as he leaned on the garden wall with his good hand. He managed
to balance the cigar in between the swollen thumb and fingers that stuck
out of the cast, and kept it elevated above his heart to keep the pain from
pounding too much. He's paying in spades for making the trip when he
should have stayed put—no, he couldn't sit around in Gloucester, he needed
to be here, he needed to see her—*or them*—whatever, he needs to settle
something in his mind one way or another.

"Well, Hayden, the way I see it—it was not that long ago, you two
had a recent event—that's the one I'm thinking about—two people like
Sammy and you do not just pick up and do the wild thing for no reason."
I maintained a mild sense of humor about it, and this time I did laugh,
hoping to ease him. I didn't want him to think that I intended to knock
him into the year after next—he was already there courtesy of Preston
Ackerman.

345

"I'm in love with Helena," he muttered at his feet as if checking to make sure he didn't just step in some shit. I grunted and he looked up at me, scowling.

"Yeah, well, I'm in love with a dead gal named Lenore, so I slept with her daughter who happens to be the spittin' image of her mother—that doesn't make it right," I chuckled. His devotion to Helena in spite of her faults would be admirable, if I didn't know better. "Listen, we all have fantasies Hayden; sometimes the reality is the shitty part. I do love Sammy, I love the shit out of that child, but that's the key—she's been a child to me, and that's the reality I'm having a hard time with. Truthfully, I want her to be happy, and as long as I make her happy, I'm wherever she is," I paused and thought about what I could possibly say next to persuade him that I have chosen to discuss this with him because I want to see Sam happy. "I watch her with you, and I can see that you make her happy—" I said, easing myself onto a stone bench by the wall; I ached all over from splitting wood yesterday, so it felt good to sit.

"I do?" he asked as if amazed by this piece of information—*can he be that unaware?*

"Glory, yes, she's been all over you since you got here—playing nursemaid, loving you up with massages, petting you—making a total fuss over you. I'm not jealous—how can I be? I knew way back when I stayed with her in Gloucester that there was something special between you two—it's not surprising—I mean, there ought to be after all the time you've spent together." I paused; even though he wasn't looking at me I could see his posture take each word in, he appeared to be in pain. "I'm just tellin' you what I see—that girl is in love with you—I've known it all along."

"She's not a girl, she's a woman," he corrected with a flat tone that thinly disguised his irritation with me.

"Yes, she's a woman, and that's the difference between us—you can see her as a woman—I can't." I measured each word carefully so not to spill their content.

"What are you going to do?" he asked; his eyes grew wide with curiosity.

"I love her, but I'm not going to marry her—." After saying this much, I decided to shut up; I wanted him to digest the information that I've given him. How do I make him understand that my relationship with Sammy is based purely on devoted emotions? Love—yes, love, but not the love that they have for one another. "I won't stand in your way, if you know what I mean," I muttered with an awkward sense that he picked up as he regarded me with that puckered look he gets while he's thinking things through, and trying to figure out what he's going to say next.

"I can't," he sighed, lowering his head as if in shame.

"Can't what?" I asked, frustrated. Now I can completely understand Helena's impatience with him.

"Change—I guess," he sighed, slumping onto the garden wall, his posture withdrawn—sort of like Sammy just before she shuts down.

I studied his marred face—Preston really did a number on him. Even though a plastic surgeon did the work to minimize the physical scars, the emotional scars will live with him for years to come. He's a mess right now, and I just contributed to that soup-pot of crap swilling around in his guts—I should have left him alone.

Suddenly, he shifted his stance at the wall; I knew by the subtle cues of his motions that he intended to unburden his mind, and I hoped the girls left us alone long enough to conclude the conversation. Inspired to avoid interruption, I moved from my seat on the bench, and he followed, apparently for the same unspoken reason. We casually walked away from the house to go lean on the paddock fence under the cottonwood trees where the two horse buddies stood head to tail swishing the flies that the spring sunshine aroused. Their large brown eyes gazed at us with lazy interest; they're a pair of aging wild ones that Dulcie started to feed when they turned up in her yard one day looking for a drink, they stayed for almost five years. They're not broke for riding, but they are perfectly content to act like a couple of big lazy dogs. And like dogs, they enjoy having their ears rubbed, and so my fingers massaged the closest velvety ear. The rapture exhibited on the beast's face was so universally recognizable it was sweet, its eyelids drooped at half-mast and the lower lip flopped loosely in equine-ecstasy.

"Helena is not coming back to Gloucester," he said softly.

"Oh, really? I hadn't heard about that," I hissed, feeling sympathy toward his recent rejection, now I feel really stupid for bringing up Samantha—*but I need to know.* He nodded to acknowledge my sympathy, and drew deep from the precariously balanced cigar.

"She's happy here—she's found her mother, her sister, and today she's starting to make pottery. For the first time in her life, she feels like she's found her niche—she's happy. She's going to resign her position at the university. She's given me Whitley's catalog to finish—I can't tell you how many projects she's left unfinished; they're all collecting cobwebs in a file cabinet," he said, scowling at the sun. "I suppose you're thinking that if I really loved her, I would drop everything to follow her—but it's not that simple. I don't want to leave everything that I worked hard for; I'm not ready to give it up to follow her—so—I guess it's over between us for good." When he finished saying his piece, his frame trembled; he grasped the top rail of the fence to steady himself while he pulled smoke from the cigar.

"Niches are hard to find," I agreed lamely; at this point, I guess any excuse will do. He looked at me with a raised eyebrow, and then sighed. My unintentional barb hit a sensitive spot.

"I know—what I just said seems to minimize the tragedy—you have yet to understand the tragedy—for years, Helena's been the love of my life, and I'm just figuring out that it was all for nothing. I need time to get over this—and I don't know if I ever will."

It was amazing that he didn't crack; he leaned heavily against the fence, and drew in smoke from the cigar, savoring its richness; he suddenly looked unburdened, his shoulders came up, and his back straightened.

"You have nothing to worry about, Guthrie—there is no competition with me for Samantha's affections. She does love you—I know it because she told me once a very long time ago. She always hoped that you would come back someday—she told me once that she wanted to marry you," he said with a smirk that looked painful for him to make, but there was a hint of mirth to its composition that displayed a twisted sense of humor—*or is it an unhealthy irony?* It's so odd to me how Sammy and Hayden remain fixated in their long held beliefs—her adolescent fantasies about me are a gospel he will not dispute, and her assertion that he loves Helena has her determined not to interfere with their being together. *Now what?*

"Well, for one thing, you're right about that—she does love me, however—I do question the reason why she has a drawing of your naked ass over her drafting table," I laughed, feeling slightly sick to my stomach. *What did I expect him to do? Did I think he would feel grateful that I'd be willing to step aside and let him go for it?* "I'll take her now—that is if you're done fucking her yourself—thanks for keeping her warm for me, man—I really appreciate it—you're the greatest friend a guy could have."

"I've seen that drawing," he muttered, his back stiffening; a peculiar noise seemed stuck inside his throat, he coughed, and his face squirmed with withheld amusement. "Chances are, it's just another drawing in her collection—I can't imagine it means anything more than that," he shrugged. "How did you know that it was me?" he inquired after a meditative silence.

I stepped back, put on a thoughtful face, rubbed my chin, put my hands on my hips and chewed on my mustache, looked him up and down, walked around him, and then laughed. "Yup, it's your butt all right—it was just a simple process of elimination—it's definitely not mine."

His priceless expression and the ensuing silence said a thousand words and then some. With a chuckle gargling in my throat, I walked away so he could be mortified alone.

19

Islands in the Sky

I feel funny—restless. Ever since our arrival in Taos, I've felt out of sorts. *I feel wide-awake*—it seems as if I've been asleep ever since—well, I don't know when—since Cleveland? I guess. Everything feels too complicated— more than necessary. My talk with Jack about the divorce, the details about Preston's arrest, and his mandatory rehab for cocaine addiction was a long disturbing conversation in legalese that I'd like to forget, especially because of the associated memories that can still make my stomach flutter with a queasy fear sensation—*it makes me want to scream! I fear that if I start screaming now, I wouldn't be able to stop—so I won't scream.*

Sylvester's being here has made me feel restless in a happily uneasy way that is both pleasant and distressing. Although I am very glad to see him, seeing him has made me feel bad—*it's my fault.* I have kissed each conspicuous red scar and each faded bruise as if to make it better. It's too bad that his hair had to be shorn away—I always loved how his man-smells collected within its texture—but no matter, he still smells the same, he's just as fascinating to look at, and I love him all the more. During my examination of his being here with us, my intense curiosity discovered that when I stroked his head against the nap, the softness felt exquisite to touch. And then, while petting it in the smooth direction, I loved feeling the curve of his skull beneath my hand—I'm in awe of its structure, yet too aware of the fragile nature of its matter. He had to assure me that it didn't hurt when I touched his head.

The day after he arrived, I spent precious time doodling all over the surface of his cast with magic markers; creating special designs that are medicinal in my mind's-eye, an organic geometry made up of feathery waves and curling spirals depicting his bones healing. He sat with patience watching the chisel-shaped tips leave their delicate trails—and then laughing, he proclaimed that he would have to save it as a work of art. I joked that it would sell for millions of dollars someday; he smiled as if pleased with the notion, and then told me that it would be priceless, he would never sell it.

I could tell that although he found my attention endearing, he felt uncomfortable—and it seemed that we were being watched by the occupants within the whitewashed walls—*because they know. They'll never understand the meaning of our relationship, nor will they understand how much I love him—and he feels ashamed that they know about what happened a long time ago—back when we shouldn't have—oh, Sylvester, I know I said that I wouldn't tell, but I did—I'm so sorry. Whattodo-whattodo-whattodo—what to do.*

I tried to stay away from him—to leave him alone—but I couldn't because my heart wouldn't let me—it made my head hurt because I wanted to be near him all the time. When I saw him napping in the lounge chair on the patio—his shirt unbuttoned, his winter-pale skin exposed to the warm desert light—he looked so frail, and so alone. When I quietly eased myself onto the edge of the cushion beside him, the sweet smell of cocoa butter sunscreen mixed with the heat of the spring sunshine enticed me to touch him, so I gently placed my hand on the faint bruises that marked where the broken ribs are still mending. Startled, he opened his eyes unaided by his glasses, and then he smiled.

"I'm okay, Samantha," he said upon recognizing my shape, and he touched my thigh with affectionate fingers.

"Oh, Sylvester, I'm so sorry," I whispered my regret, my hand caressing his flesh that always interested me—his tactile existence—his life—means so much to me. It makes me sad that I was the catalyst that caused his pain.

"No, don't be sorry—it's not your fault," he murmured, crumpling his brow at me. I kissed his mouth, and with a soft moan, he turned away from my lips.

"No, Samantha—" he said firmly. He suddenly seemed distressed by my attention, and anxious that someone might be watching us as he glanced toward the house.

"I'm sorry," I repeated after groping for words to express my feelings, but I found none to apply. He squeezed my hand as if to give me reassurance.

"It's all right, please don't go—sit—so we can talk," he sat up, sliding his long feet to the ground, moving with stiff care—his body still hurts—he winced and grinned. "I'm okay."

He doesn't have his glasses on—I need him to see me, so I plucked them from the place where he had left them on the table and carefully perched them on his face. Once his vision sharpened behind the lenses, he cringed—he could not look at me—he could not look at our reality.

"Oh, Samantha," he sighed, shaking his head, he held my hand, and lightly caressed it.

I stared at him, taking in his being there beside me—my mind's eye seeing us surrounded by sunshine, I am filled with its yellow light, and there he is, blue shirt, blue eyes, haloed by a pale blue aura—we're sitting together in our silent impotence, magnetically opposed even with our hands linked, unable to communicate in spite of all that we needed to say. I quickly shut off the internal vision I had of us, and my body began to rock with nervous compulsion as I murmured a restless excuse and abruptly launched myself from my perch beside him, leaving him alone. Although he stood up and uttered my name as a soft protest, he stayed where I left him—he won't call me back because of Helena—he won't follow me because of Guthrie.

Whattodo-whattodo-whattodo—what to do. Restless—I am restless—I need to move on. I lie in bed at night, my legs twitch with spasms, disturbing my sleep—disturbing Guthrie—although he says not. Restlessness will take me somewhere else instead of leaving me stuck in one place—for once in my life, there are no routines. I have become addicted to the willy-nilly events of traveling, and seeing things that I've never seen before. My eyes can't get enough of seeing the raw, eroded bands of ochre, rose, violet, and turquoise earth streaking the undulations of hills, and the sky—*oh, the sky—it seems to be a different color here than at home—the land meets sky and vibrates—I must see more! Restless-restless-restless-whattodo-whattodo—it's time timetimetime—it's time to go.* When I told Guthrie that I wanted to go see Yellowstone, there followed a sigh of relief in the bright white adobe household; it seems as if the restlessness of my making has infected everyone, and my leaving will put them all at ease.

Guthrie and I left Dulcie's house the next day to explore the wonders of what April Showers can bring to such a dry world. We wound our way along a recommended scenic route that led us through changing landscapes—brilliant orange and pink painted deserts with purple buttes and red mesas; then dense green forests with white cascades cutting through rock, and solid blue mountain fortresses capped with snow. As we sped along the highway, the distant mountains that already appeared enormous and unreal grew to an unimaginable size once we reached their roots, our necks hurt as we cranked back our heads to see their tops. On flat lands, we witnessed far away storms with lightning shooting from the sky to the ground, and dark curtains of rain blotting out the landscape as the storm crept across the horizon. One night, we stood on the shoulder of the road and watched how the distant sky was illuminated by sheet lightning laced with jagged bolts and crackling with red and green fires. *Remarkable.*

Seeing this world shook me from the dream I've been in for years, and my sketchpad filled with new shapes and new ideas. I became anxious to paint again, and bought supplies along the way, but I have not touched them because all of it is so stunning, I can barely comprehend the beauty. I took pictures with dozens of disposable cameras and spent a small fortune at several one-hour photo-processing places along the way—most of the pictures were disappointing and limited, they failed to capture what I thought I saw out there.

Guthrie drove tirelessly, his body relaxed behind the wheel of Delta Dawn. He sang or whistled, keeping me company while I examined the world from the passenger side—he seemed content with my quiet. The endless loop of music softly haunted the air around us; Beethoven supported by Copeland and a mix of muscular themes from famous Hollywood Western's.

At the Grand Canyon, only a brownish-green shard of the mighty Colorado River was visible from where we clung to the rim, buffeted by a bitter wind that nearly froze our noses. While I stared out at the vastness, humbled and breathless, the blue sky arching above the dusty red landscape made it too surreal. After a long contemplation from my chosen perch on a rock, I couldn't grasp any of it enough to move my pencil. Out of desperation, I concentrated on a dead tree that braced itself against the red and blue division, its weathered bone whiteness like a stark cutout. I made a few lines behind it to indicate the world beyond, then shaved off graphite dust and blended it with my fingers for the sky to be in contrast with the tree, but that was all I could say about it. I felt negligible standing on the edge of so much geological time—just like that dead tree; there was a sense of anguish in the way its earthbound roots clung to its place in the world—*familiar, familiar, familiar life.* Time will erode the last memory to which it clings, and from there, it will fall to its final resting place.

Feeling insecure, I turned through the pages of sketches and came upon Sylvester's hands and his steady gaze. Then I sought solace while looking at the abstract slices of his bodyscape that I've drawn from memory—the curves of his neck and collarbone, the wing of a shoulder blade, the subtle protrusion of his hipbone on the intimate ridge of his pelvis, and the turned-under curl of his pinky toe. Closing the sketchbook, I leaned against the sturdy form of Guthrie, his strong arms enfolding me into his reassuring protection, but he ruined my quiet feeling when he tried to talk to me about Sylvester; a warm sadness bloomed inside of me and the cold canyon wind fanned my persistent restlessness. I knew that I needed to keep moving to find what I'm looking for—I haven't found it here. An hour later, we were back in the car, wending our way toward Utah on an asphalt ribbon woven through the desert—a trail of wonders that lulled me into a trance, helping me to forget everything I should remember.

When she came to me and said, *"Guthrie, I want to go to Yellowstone,"* I was ready to bolt within the hour because I couldn't stand her nervous twitches and restless pacing between Hayden and me anymore, but we left the next day, taking the proper time to pack and say goodbye to anyone who cared. Hayden carried his disappointment like an anvil had dropped out of the sky and landed on him. I wanted to wring his stupid neck because he did nothing to stop her. Although it practically burned the tip of my tongue to invite him to come along for her sake, I knew that he was physically in no shape for such a grueling trip, pain perked with every movement he made, sitting still made it worse. Even if he was able-bodied, the situation might introduce a dynamic that had potential to become unsavory for one of us should she suddenly decide to choose one over the other for a more intimate companionship. So, we left Hayden behind in the care of a troupe of women who will eventually have to shuffle the wounded old bird out the door once he's ready to fly again.

When we first set out, I thought—*well, heck, this is easy-peasy, Sammy and me traveling together, how hard can it be?* She's quiet, she listens to music, she likes to read maps, she looks out the window, she draws—but no, the reality on the road sucks—she's a pain in the ass, her music is driving me bat shit, she's a crappy navigator, she wants to stop every few feet to take pictures, she has to pee at every rest stop, and she's too dang quiet. She's been virtually silent since our departure from Taos; I had hoped for a change once we reached the Grand Canyon, but nothing happened. Her constant silence disturbs me, and when I have spoken to her, she connects with me in brief conversations that make me feel as if I'm interrupting her train of thought. She's not belligerent toward me, but she isn't herself. It is different dealing with her now than when she was a child, but back then I was Lenore's relief; earlier in this escapade, I was Helena's liberation—now I'm alone. Unfortunately, with every mile I drive, there is a distance between our closeness, it has grown wider and deeper, and my frustration with her has grown into a giant rock formation rising from the center of the distance that she has created. I could yell my head off sometimes, but I don't. It wouldn't make a damn bit of difference if I stamped my feet and threw a shit-fit, those black button eyes would stare back at me and not comprehend why I'm behaving like an asshole. Well, she did warn me that I'd want a spot in line to throttle her one day—so, I take lots of deep breaths, smoke copious numbers of cigarettes, and drink a pitcher or two of beer at the hotel bar before turning in—whatever works, I guess.

While she sat on the hotel bed surrounded by sketchbooks and the scattered implements of drawing, I became nosy, and paged through the hundreds of drawings for clues pertaining to her state of mind, but the only blip noteworthy were the entries when Hayden arrived in Taos. The sketches that she made of him were painfully honest with the injuries prominently fracturing his surface—deformed and beautiful at the same time. It's clear to me that she feels something for the man, it can only be love, but I don't know if she can articulate it in a way that could be fulfilling in a long-term relationship for both of them. Even with me—she claims to love me, but there's an emptiness in her silence that I can barely stand. I have to wonder if the silence is what prompted Hayden to follow through with his fantasies about Helena. When I finally spoke to her about him while she sat on a rock overlooking the Grand Canyon, I watched her face flicker with a spark of delight, but then it quickly dimmed, the bright light of pleasure snuffed out by sorrow. It is perceptible that she feels horrible about what happened to him; she started to rock and murmured a mantra, *"I'm sorry for Sylvester— why did Preston have to hurt poor Sylvester—I'm so sorrysorrysorry so sorry for Sylvester."* It breaks my heart when she shed a few precious tears signifying her grief. *"He loves you!"* I said, gripping her by the shoulders to force her to stop rocking. She stared at me, blinking, and then made her reply, *"Yes, he does,"* she said, and then she said nothing more, shutting down, closing up her face—even to me.

After the grand tour of the Grand Canyon, we arrived in Moab, Utah. The first day we spent hours hiking at Arches National Park; Sammy was in silent awe of the red rock world with its bizarre formations that inspired her eyes; the fiery stone façades with their drip pattern of black glaze that the guidebook called *desert varnish*—this dark stain marks the oldest part of the rock where it hasn't broken away for centuries. She spent the evenings repeating what she saw with a pencil point and watercolor washes filling sketchbooks with new visions—visions of holes filled with sky. She fell in love with the land and sky, the sky through windows in the rocks, and things far away that are so big they look as if they are nearby.

At a place named the *Island in the Sky*, I peered out into forever from the edge of a cliff; I felt even more insignificant here than at the Grand Canyon because it was empty and quiet. Sammy sat busily sketching, her pencils, erasers, and fingers molding an image on the paper surface; her interpretations of the rocks, horizon, and clouds possessed a dreamlike quality. In the less complex drawings, the subtle bands of values signifying sky and land were luminous, and my eye swore that it saw color in the graphite; my mind accepted her deception without a doubt. Normally, I could sit all day watching her work, but I have become weary, and I long to pause in this journey we've been on—I want to start over again. I longed to go back to that night in Cleveland. Not for the sake of recapturing the passion that we shared, but to take it all back. What if I had not slept with her—what if I had kept my mouth shut, and sent her back to her room with her ice bucket, soda, and Winnie-the-Pooh nightgown intact. *If only I had talked them into going home. Well, you didn't, jackass—so stop thinking about it. I think way too much.*

"On that day—when you and Lenore argued—why did you come back?" Sammy's words came out as if she pulled them from the blue sky while she stared at its infinite expanse where it seemed that we could perceive the curve of the earth.

"Love." I made my initial reply with the simple term, but it wasn't that cut and dry; my head staggered to gather the past so readily at hand and suddenly I was there, recalling the sun-filled bedroom, Lenore's harsh words spouting denial. Sammy was in the midst of us, wide-eyed, sucking her fingers, taking it all in—*never forgetting*—her little brain, a trap for information of incidents, knowledge of encounters, memories of events, the recollection of feelings—she gathered all of it and made colorful pictures inside her head. "That's what I believed at the time—I left the house swearing that I wouldn't come back, but I only got as far as the beach where I stood throwing rocks at the water until my arm nearly fell off. I couldn't bear leaving town with bitterness between us—I wanted a bridge back. In spite of what she had said to me, I had to come back—but now, when I think about it, it wasn't just love, it was selfishness—it was a desire to control—because I wanted her for myself. And it was fear—I feared losing that connection—not only with her, but with you too." My words tumbled out as if I had them rehearsed—for some reason, they came easy today, perhaps because from where I stood on the rim of this canyon, my desolate feelings are close in genre to the ones I had on the beach on that particular day. I wondered if she sensed this. I picked up a stone and hurled it at the pristine world out there, that empty expanse is as close to the vacant ocean I can get out here—only there is no satisfying splash—I didn't even hear it hit the ground.

"Did you love me then, Guthrie?"

"I loved you back then—my love for you is probably the most honest love I ever felt in my life. I want to protect you, and keep you safe—like a father protects his daughter, sometimes that feeling is hard for me to reconcile—cripe, girl, what do you want from me?" I sighed, feeling hopeless; she has pierced into my daily emotional struggle by questioning me this way.

"Just you—just your love."

"I'll die long before you." I spoke as if reminding her of our immortality—but I reminded myself as well—I understood Hayden's sentiments about being older—and feeling foolish.

"Yes, perhaps, but why should we deny ourselves the years we may have? We can walk away from this place, get into the car and die in a horrible accident on the highway an hour from now," she said, squinting at the horizon.

"Who will take care of you after I'm gone?" I asked, squatting beside her.

"I can take care of myself—let me worry about that when the time comes." She fell silent, her gaze looking out, capturing forever in her eyes, and once again, she became lost in the vastness ahead of her, then her pencil became busy; the importance of our conversation suddenly minimized by her desire to interpret what she saw out there. *I will worry.*

During the days that followed, her drawings turned into paintings, and then the watercolor pans eventually changed over to a pallet of oil paint and the familiar scent of linseed oil drifted on the breeze. The hotel room quickly became too small for our altered mode of operation, so I scouted around and eventually relocated our home-away-from-home to a campground that had housekeeping cottages and a breathtaking view of the La Sal Mountains that pleased her discerning eye. Every morning, I would set up the traveling studio wherever her little heart desired, and broke it down by sunset. As her prolific output became cumbersome for the cottage, I found a storage space to rent where we could store the finished paintings at the end of the day, and it offered me a place where I could prepare stretched canvases per her instructions, and build crates for shipping out her finished work to the Kramer Gallery. By the beginning of our second week, I sent the first shipment of eighteen cured oil paintings and a portfolio of more than fifty watercolors to Boston.

Throughout this prolific time, she moved through the day as if on autopilot, I did what I could to guide her through basic hygiene and making sure she ate and slept, but her constant silence became even more unnerving—

she wasn't just *Silent Sam*. I had no clue what brewed behind those black button eyes, so I watched and waited, wondering when she will come out of it. Then one morning at the *Island in the Sky*, she threw down her paintbrushes in frustration.

"I'm just copying," she cried out, kicking the ground, and stomping on the brushes.

"What's the matter?" I jumped with a start as if her outburst woke me up from a light doze, and I watched in stunned disbelief as the wooden pallet loaded with the day's paint sailed from the cliff and briefly soared like a Frisbee before it plunged out of sight. *Oh, shit.*

"Damn it! There's no difference—whether I'm copying from a photograph or from nature, it's all the same—it's just me copying from something in front of me," she growled, rubbing her face with her paint-stained hands, smearing turquoise sky and ochre desert on her cheeks and forehead; a streak of titanium white flowed into her dark hair. "Ohhh, fuck-fuck-fuck-fuck-fuck, this isn't what I want!" she shrieked as her foot lashed out at the easel, and the large canvas tumbled over backward; I managed to catch it before it hit the ground.

"Easy there, Button's," I expressed as calmly as I could because my guts were in a rage.

"I want—I want—I want something that is mine—something only I can see—something from here!" she growled, her hands clutching her chest as if she might pull her heart out; suddenly, she roared, and her fists violently flailed at the painting.

"No, Sammy, don't start destroying stuff!" I exclaimed, scrabbling to hold her back from the easel to keep the painting safe from being pitched off the cliff—for all I know this thing could be worth a million dollars someday. "Come now, this work is beautiful, it's so much better than copying pictures from museum postcards—this is more you than you think—it's not emulating anyone's style—" I tried to reason with her, but her entire body kept writhing against my force. "Easy—easy, now!" I pulled her close, holding her tight against my chest until she finally stopped struggling. Once she calmed, I let her go, and she sat down with a deep sigh.

"But you don't understand, it's not mine—I'm just reacting to it—I can barely grasp it—it's so big here," she sat staring ahead at the horizon, her body lightly rocking in place. "What I have inside my head is much too big—I don't think I can ever paint it. It's like music—sound—like Beethoven, his music trapped inside his head—he wrote it to let it out, but he never heard it played by anyone to his satisfaction—no one understood. I can't see what I want out here—what I want my work to become, it's sound, but in color, it's music, but made with lines—I'll never see it—I might as well be blind like Beethoven was deaf!" she cried, clasping her hands over her eyes. She fell silent and I left her be so she could process her turmoil. I lit a cigarette while I waited for her to either explode or come away quietly—it was a toss-up, so I mentally prepared for both. When her hands finally fell away, her gaze turned toward me, and for the first time in days, I sensed her comprehending my being there.

"Don't worry Guthrie—I'll be able to take care of myself." She spoke as if she picked up our conversation right where we left off before this obsessive episode on the canyon cliff began almost two weeks ago to the day. I came close to weeping, though I did shed a few stray tears, the desert wind sucked them dry.

"Sammy—I will worry—even after I'm dead and buried in my grave, I will worry," I replied right where I left off with my feelings on that day.

"It's so beautiful here," she whispered. She stood up and walked up to the edge of the cliff and looked out at the distant cliffs and canyons, then she turned back toward me, her face etched with anguish.

"Oh-my-god, Guthrie, I feel like I've been asleep for a very long time—how long?" she asked, now mortified by the realization that a lot of time has passed since she was last fully aware of her surroundings—or of me. I didn't respond, I couldn't bring myself to tell her, but she knew; her inner clock understood the passage of time. My hand caressed her wind-whipped hair while she hugged me around the waist, and I kissed her when her lips clamped onto my mouth as if with revived passion—but I knew better—she kissed me out of habit now. *It's love in some form.*

20
Old Faithful, It's Time To Go Home

"Here's word from Yellowstone," Helena said, holding up a postcard from Samantha and Guthrie; the front depicted the classic image of Old Faithful sprouting its white bloom toward a faultless blue sky. It's been three weeks since they departed from Taos, and it's been nearly a week since we received the last postcard from Utah. She examined the now familiar heavy-handed penmanship printed in blocky capital letters that I could clearly see from where I sat at the kitchen table.

Dulcie leaned against the kitchen counter wearing a clay-spattered apron wrapped around her girlishly slender waist; she looked beyond Helena with a placid gaze that always scrutinized me anytime Samantha is mentioned.

"So, what's Guthrie got to say for them this time?" she asked, after a long drag off the cigarette between her fingers.

"This time he says: *"Howdy, y'all! We arrived in Yellowstone yesterday—there was a young bull moose grazing by the road that Sammy wanted to take home, but I told her 'no' because he wouldn't be happy in Gloucester. She's been doing fine these last few days—still quiet tho'. It's snowing out today—the weather has been hit or miss up here. We both wish you were here, love G & S"*—yeah, right, you wish—snow—no fuckin' thank you, I had my fill of that shit getting here," Helena chuckled. "Check it out, he drew a picture of Delta Dawn looking tired—I imagine he must be beat—I'll bet she's been a handful," she snickered in a suggestive manner. Dulcie peeked at the message as her daughter stuck it under her nose to take her turn reading it; she snorted without comment.

"It's been a long trip for them both," I put in, and then focused my attention on the Sunday crossword puzzle spread out in front of me. *What is number nine down? Five letters, third letter is an 'r'.* It is my genuine hope that they are content, but the postcards have so far relayed a hint of distress in the man writing them. The last time he called us, he indicated that Samantha's eerie silence and her tendency toward obsessive behavior was becoming problematic. It is evident that he feels alone in her company without the companionship of a third party to bridge the gap. I am concerned about his apparent inability to interact with her one-on-one—I know that a relationship with Samantha cannot hinge on physical gratification or selective attention. And I know he isn't the only one distressed—she must be feeling the loneliness too, especially if he has allowed her behavior to go unchecked, thus encouraging her to withdraw further away. When I had the opportunity to talk to her on the telephone, it troubled me to hear the change in her. Although she squealed with delight to hear my voice, her replies to my inquiries were monosyllabic and whiny like an overtired child—the symptoms are all too familiar to me. *"Just keep talking to her, Guthrie."* I offered for advice once he came on the line again. "I really hope they're happy together," I commented with genuine concern for their well-being.

"I hope so too," Helena sighed absently, flipping the postcard over to look at the photo and then back at the short note before she passed it to me to see. "You know, at first, I was against their relationship, but as I watched them—it only made sense—he gave Sammy unconditional love from the moment she was born. Whenever he came home, he enjoyed spending time with her—Sammy adored him—as soon as he walked in the door she was all over him like a monkey climbing a tree—having him home meant more to her than piggyback rides, teaching her how to talk, and how to swim. Out of all that mess with Lenore, they were the two most wounded by her death—they should be together." Helena said this with a wistful tone. Ever since she recaptured her bond with Dulcie, her tendency to over-dramatize is getting on my nerves. I have recognized the symptoms of her usual phase of possessive behavior—the heady feelings that are akin to being in love have swamped her senses with a complete immersion into a rapturous ecstasy—she's simply high on Dulcie. She had been high on me once—then before me she was high on Shep—before him—Guthrie? Samantha had told me how Helena used to have a crush on him. And of course, Whitley—all of her crabbing at her father was no different than her nagging me for nine years—it's all the same *me-me-me—do as I say, you're mine-mine-mine*—somehow I don't see Dulcie putting up with too much of that shit.

"She's certainly got him wrapped around her baby finger," I laughed. My observations of them in Gloucester and in Taos told me that much, it is perfectly clear to me that the man will stand on his head for her. "I can see Guthrie having to wrestle the darn moose to lead it home if she had persisted about wanting it—he won't deny her anything." *Nine down, the stellar virgin—of course, Virgo, so Orion—The Hunter—is fifteen across.*

"Oh, please, you should see yourself when she's around, I cease to exist the moment she walks into the room," Helena scoffed with a sneer.

"All right, so I'm guilty of looking out for her—someone had to—I was there for her after you left home—sure, Whitley catered to her—but he always made her more complicated than she really is—you do it too. Most of her frustration was because the two of you wouldn't let her decide anything for herself! At least I taught her about autonomy, which—as I understand it—was something her mother wanted her to learn." Scraping back my chair, I left the table to refill my coffee cup. After weeks of relative calm and acceptance, it surprises me to feel my heart racing with instant anger. Dulcie stood next to me, silent, watching—I waited for her to throw in her two cents, but she only flicked her ashes into the sink.

"I suppose you're right," Helena sighed, but this time, the escape of air had the tone of annoyance, her glare across the space between us let on that she was fed-up with my still being here. "I've never been very good about dealing with her—you know I can only take her in small doses—"

"I know she can be difficult—I completely understand what Guthrie's going through. The obsessive behavior, especially the *painting trance*—I saw that plenty of times. He made the mistake of caving in to the flow of it—that was the worst thing he could have done—I wouldn't have allowed her to sit on the edge of a cliff painting day after day until she became frustrated enough to want to pitch a painting into the canyon. I know she can be pretty stubborn and she's more independent than you ever imagined—I always tried to get her to think about what she was doing because once in awhile she needs the slightest nudge to redirect her when she gets stuck in a groove."

"So you redirected her into bed, perhaps?" Helena laughed with a snide attitude.

"That's rather unfair of you to say," I muttered, feeling the extension of her jealous claws pricking the tender swelling of hurt that still lay inside of me. Somehow, Samantha and I had managed to keep our sexual relationship separate from everything else—only at night did we allow it to happen—peculiar as it may sound, I believed she made it part of her schedule. "It wasn't always that way between us. Even after you and I were together, I continued my responsibility to Samantha because you couldn't handle her—believe me, it wasn't easy." I censored my resentment with an even manner that longed to be unleashed into rage. "The reason why I tagged along on your excursions with her was because I knew you couldn't do it alone, even Whitley knew you couldn't handle a weekend in Cape Cod with her—Guthrie can barely manage her—both of you were crazy to bring her all the way out here! She needs to go home—that was my reason for coming here—I expected to take her home. I know you couldn't talk her into flying, but I know I could—I would've promised her a window seat because I know her nose would be glued to the glass looking out all the way home—she'd love it, and she'd love it that I was with her—but I wasn't expecting to find her with Guthrie—" I sighed with irritation.

Dulcie started laughing, we both turned toward her mirth as if aghast that she overheard us. "You two should hear yourselves—jealousy all around." she exclaimed. "You're jealous that he had an affair with her, and he's jealous of Guthrie having a fling with her—I've never seen anything like it in my life—it's so funny, it's sad."

"Dulcie, please, we're—ummm—oh, shit," Helena lamely tripped over her thoughts, but gave up with a helpless shrug that exhibited refusal to confront her newfound mother with the ugliness of an argument.

"Jealousy has nothing to do with it—I want them to be happy, really—I—I want Samantha to be happy—she deserves it," I stuttered, feeling besieged by both women.

"Sorry, but I tell it like it is," Dulcie demurely chuckled behind her hand.

"Don't pick on him," Helena scowled at her mother.

Dulcie laughed at her as if savoring this disagreement between them. "I'm sorry, Sy—I won't bring it up anymore," she said, glowering at her daughter. I noted that they were both equally scrappy like a couple of snotty lapdogs.

"There is nothing to be sorry about," I said to be diplomatic, feeling confused and excited with a strange anticipation for a revelation.

"You know, Sy, there is a fact that you cannot see even with your glasses on—you're in love with Samantha Ryder. It's bad enough that you won't admit it to yourself, but the saddest thing about it is you haven't got the nuts to tell her how you feel—and I am willing to bet that you never said those three little words that speak volumes even to a woman whose emotions are a jigsaw puzzle with a few pieces missing. So here you are—the woman you really love is off gallivanting around, so you have chosen to hang around here, hoping that Helena will change her mind about you because you can't have what you want. I'm telling you right now that you're wasting your time, Helena's not going to find her way back to Gloucester—you know why? I'll tell you why—she won't stand for the competition with Samantha hanging off you!" Dulcie laid it out for me with her steady-as-she-goes manner that passes through like a freight train.

"Dulcie!" Helena clamped her hands over her mouth mortified by her mother's brazen claims on her behalf—even if it is a truth that they had discussed in private.

"It's okay, Lena," I waved my hand to show I wasn't miffed. Over the years, I have allowed many criticisms fired off by Helena to roll off me. Although Dulcie's comments were not the revelations I had expected, but they shook my core in a peculiar way. It was obvious to me that mother and daughter alike suffer from a selfish blind spot that causes them to fail to see the bigger picture—my sacrifice. I came here to take Samantha home only to let her go—again.

"Daughter, I can't sit here and be quiet anymore—I don't want this man throwing away his life because of some whimsy about you. He's a good man—it's so painfully obvious that he truly loves her. The poor thing turned white as a desert-bleached bone when the two of them went off to sleep in the same bedroom—I really felt for you right then," she sighed. "Why don't you admit it—you didn't come here because you felt it was your duty to take her home—you're here because you love her."

"Of course, I love Samantha—I—I do, I just do." My words jarred out of my mouth because of her explicit demand for me to confess my undeclared adulation. "I do love her." I said it again as the truth of the spoken words became more concrete than harboring the silent emotion. I have always known how I felt, but I crippled myself with some absurd wish for something that I can't have. I knew bliss with Samantha after years of pursuing Helena for nothing but rejection. Then after I obtained Helena to fulfill my latent desire, I lay in wait for Samantha to turn her eyes upon me for a jolt of unrequited love that felt more like heaven to me than lying in bed with the woman whom I professed to love for the rest of my life. "I do love her," I moaned into my hands as I sat down at the table again. Guthrie had given me a chance—he wanted to be sure—I perpetuated their departure with my insistence that my affection was no longer driven by passion.

"Sy?" Helena's hand perched on my shoulder, offering comfort.

"It's true—but now she's with Guthrie, I can't come between them. Before they left, Guthrie and I had a conversation—he told me that he believed Samantha is in love with me—I guess he wanted to make sure there wasn't any competition between us—I told him not to be concerned about me." I felt mortified by what I just said, and looked at them—their expressions equally startled.

"Jeez, Luiz, why'd you say that for? He was trying to fix you up with her," Dulcie exclaimed with heartfelt distress in her voice.

"I was so stunned when he started to talk to me about it—I only wanted to do what I thought was right! She's been in love with him for years, and he says that he loves her—what was I supposed to do?" I cried out, exasperated with myself—I had done for her what she had done for me when Helena came back—I let her go to fulfill her fantasy. My stomach decided it didn't like the breakfast I just ate as it clenched in an anxious knot—I wanted to puke my guts out—much like I did on Samantha's wedding day, ejecting my personal shame.

"Shit," Helena cursed under her breath.

"What?" I demanded to know what she was hissing about.

"Preston really scrambled your brains didn't he? If I hit you, will it knock some sense into that pointy head of yours?" Helena snorted, giving me a gentle cuff at the back of my head. I laughed because I deserved her reproach, and it seemed right that she'd be the one to dish it out.

"Leave him be, daughter, he's had enough abuse from us for one day," Dulcie sighed. "I'm sorry, Sy, but the truth has got to be told someday—Guthrie and Samantha need to know how you feel."

While I contemplated my quandary, a silence descended upon our trio in the bright kitchen; the whitewashed adobe walls filled the negative space between us with an awesome light—clean white light. During this uncomfortable stillness, it became clear that the two women couldn't look at me as I wallowed in my wretchedness, and I decided then that it was time for me to go home.

∾

Helena came along to see me off at the Albuquerque airport, I dreaded it, I really wanted to be alone, but she insisted—*"I'll worry,"* she said. I have no idea why she'd be worried.

"Take care of yourself, Sy," Helena said with a bright demeanor that I found plastic.

"I will—you take care—keep in touch," I muttered.

"I will," she smiled as she hugged me, and I hugged her in return. "I'm sorry," she sighed, clinging to me tighter.

"Sorry about what?" I asked, but wished that I hadn't. I released her, and she set me free from her grasp in response to my desire to stand apart from her.

"About us—I failed you—I used you for security, support, and any other excuse I could come up with, but it was never enough. You are a good man, you didn't deserve to be treated like that—I'm sorry," she intoned with sincerity and her tear-filled eyes threatened to flood her face with their release.

"Did you ever love me?" I inquired.

She opened her mouth to reply, hesitated and then sighed. "Yes, in a way I did—I had once hoped you were 'the one', but—it wasn't the love you expected from me—even in the beginning when things first started between us—it wasn't enough. I starved you while you smothered me—we were so wrong for each other," she laughed as she dashed the tears from her cheeks with two quick fingers.

"Who do you love—is there someone?" I dared to ask.

"Me, myself, and I—just like Whitley, only worse because I barely love myself, so how can I justify loving anyone else? I left Shep after being unfaithful to him, and I leapt to you without taking a breath should I happen to fall in between the lily pads. The second the luster of novelty rubbed off, you were just another male body I had gotten into bed with—can you believe I'm such a sicko?" she laughed. Her uncomfortable laughter fluttered from her throat as her admission to a lie revealed a truth I had suspected. "I need to swim on my own for a while. Dulcie will help me for a little bit, but she intends to kick me out of the nest. Oh, Sy, I'm rambling nonsense now, but before I shut up, did I leave out any other stupid clichés?" she backed away another step to create distance from me so that the influence of her tears wouldn't draw me in to comfort her.

"I think you managed to touch on all that apply," I forced a laugh, but it expired into the air with no ambition for humor. "I hope you will be happy here," I stated with mastered composure as I squeezed her hand with mine.

"Me too, it would really suck if I've made a bad decision—there's no turning back for me this time," she said, rolling her eyes.

"No, there is no going back to the way things were," I agreed and I meant it. "But you can always come home—Sammy will miss you." I knew in my heart that it was finally over between us, and I have no more illusions of affection for her clouding my judgment. I don't hate her, I'm not indifferent to her welfare—we are still friends based on years of knowledge—there is love, but no passion—not anymore, and I wonder if there ever had been passion beyond the infatuation that inspired me to desire her from afar. *Had I just loved a body and not the human being encased within?* It seems so—there was no loyalty in my heart once my mind began to construct dreams in a starry sky while I longed for the intensity of my feelings for Samantha.

Samantha. She does love me—her kiss by the pool in the Taos sunshine—even the kiss on her wedding day—every touch of her hand told me all I ever needed to know about how she felt about me—*she loves me.* Her declaration designed underneath the dinner table was a visual detail of her adoration; I have done close to the same thing anytime I have written her name, I take great care with my pen's pronouncement of her name. I love her—I still love her. Any doubts were inventions from inherent weakness—flaws in my character that I need to overcome. But it seems to be too late now. I turned away from her because I believed she deserved better—someone younger—or just someone other than me. *Had I ever expected it to be Guthrie? No and yes.* Long before I came into her life, her heart belonged to Guthrie; she waited for his return in her fantasies—*I don't know where I fit in anymore.*

"Sy—promise me you will look out for her—even with Guthrie there, he won't stop you because he knows she loves you, and that you love her. I know it's a bit icky that they had that one night stand in Cleveland, and we'll never understand why, but it's over—it's been over—yeah, he loves her, but he wants her to be happy. I want to see her happy, and I want you to be happy. What I said before that they should be together, I meant they need to be together because of what happened to Lenore—it was wrong when Whitley kicked him out—Sammy needed them both there—things would've been so different if he had come back," Helena said as she squeezed my hand. "Sammy needs you—she deserves your love—especially your devotion. You must continue to love her, promise me that you will always love her with all your heart."

"I will," I promised with steadfast assurance even though I was feeling queasy inside.

When my flight was called, I left Helena behind—it disturbed me how it was too easy to turn away, and forced one more backward glance with a wave, it appeared that she had done the same thing. Unfortunately, in spite of the relief that this part of my life has been resolved, the feelings that lie at the bottom of my heart will remain there to become a thick sediment, weighing down my spirit when I'm alone, causing sleepless nights without end. I'm thrashing in-between Helena's cliché lily pads, the temptation to let go of my nose to either sink or swim is a quandary left to consider—at least I can finally move on.

21 *Wild Horses*

After I made one last visit to the diner bathroom to pee, Guthrie and I left behind yet another out-in-the-middle-of-nowhere roadside motel and drove into the gray morning light. At the first intersection out of town on the Wyoming desert highway, he paused *Delta Dawn*. Together we looked both ways, and then forwards and backwards; it didn't seem to matter, all directions looked like rain—at least today is too warm to snow.

"Which way?" he asked, drumming his fingers on the steering wheel in a contemplative tempo.

"Turn left?" I shrugged with a non-committal opinion while looking down at the map—left or right look all the same to me. My fingertip lightly traced a small circle around the area of the Great Divide Basin—the Red Desert—Route 287—*we are here*—but here is a lot like being lost. We wore out that old joke long before we arrived in Taos, so I don't dare say it again for the sake of a cheap laugh—though we could use a good laugh—I can't remember the last time we laughed at anything.

Raising my gaze from the map, I peered over the hood of the car at the crossroad, and then the persistent gray horizon—so flat—soot gray and dust brown, nothing new, familiar colors—this is where we are at the present, from here we can go anywhere.

"Nope, right—we've already seen left," he coughed.

"Okay," I agreed, studying him. *There, there he is, my Guthrie!* He's relaxed and rested—content with a lit cigarette slowly burning between his fingers, a can of cola cradled between his legs—cola with a splash of something stronger, I know there's a bottle of Jack Daniels under the seat—he doesn't know I know. Feeling me watch him, he wordlessly offered a cigarette plucked from his shirt pocket; I took it, and pushed in the lighter knob on the dash. Coughing again, he stubbed out the remnants of his cigarette, grimacing in disgust.

As I lit the cigarette, I thought about how we should look after each other better, starting with cutting back on smoking or maybe, god-forbid, quit. The last time I made the suggestion back in Colorado just after we completely succumbed to the flu; he flipped out and accused me of being a nag—he was teasing of course. Without smoking, what else is there to do in the car during the span of a day driving? Smoking gives our hands something to do, at least for about five minutes. Then there is the eventual quest to find more when the supply dwindles to almost none. Until the time we roll into the next highway service station to stock up, we smolder with irritation. Opening a fresh pack is exciting; the cigarettes in their white filtered rows smell sweet—although the smell and taste never jive.

"So—where is this road gonna take us, Buttons?" he asked.

Where are we going? I consulted the map spread out in my lap—I love maps—flat whiteness with twisty little roads, bumpy landscapes highlighted with browns or greens, triangle trees signifying special places. What we really need to do is end this aimless trip and go home. *Can we go home?* Suddenly the map stopped making sense to me, and I didn't want to look at it anymore; raising my eyes, I looked at Guthrie. *Home has been Delta Dawn for weeks.*

At first, this trip was about my running away from Preston—running away to somewhere safe for a little while, now it seems we are running away from home at every crossroad whenever we consult the map to make our next turn.

Will we always drive—will we ever go home?

"Storm ahead." Guthrie pointed at the horizon, and then he glanced at me for a response. I stared at him, not wanting to look at the storm—I only wanted to look at him; I could do it for hours. It drives him nuts when I do this. I love looking at his face, studying his rough, unshaven jaw-line; I love the furrowed lines creased across his brow, the curve of his head, and the way his mouth hid within the perpetual frown of his thick mustache. Since he returned to me, I can't take my eyes off this man. *I do love him.*

"What?" His brow wrinkled with curiosity as he quickly glanced at me.

"Just thinking," I said my gaze remained on him; my voice felt rusty from the lack of use.

"About?" he encouraged me to elaborate. It bugs the shit out of him that I've been so quiet, he has to drag things out of me with endless questions; I listen without answering most of the time. I listen because I love hearing the low rumble of his voice while he talks to me; the range of softness and harshness, his laughter, his muttered complaints, and the normal speaking tone is music to my ears. I had missed him while he was gone for all those years—and I loved him—I had wished on countless falling stars for his return home. I miss him and love him now in the same way, although we've been together all this time, it seems as if the space between us in the front seat divides us with its silence. When I hug him, the silence is still there no matter how tight I hold on to him—I can't hold him tight enough to make it go away.

"I'm thinking about you—how much I love you, and how beautiful you are to me." I reached out to caress his bristly cheek with my fingertips, loving the feel of his coarseness, knowing that lying beneath his spiny shell is a man with a tender heart that loves me.

"Beautiful?" he laughed and coughed. "You're on drugs woman—I am not beautiful—men are not beautiful—you said so yourself once," he growled.

I laughed at his grumpy reaction. I remember our conversation, and instantly recalled the smells of the restaurant, my cold hands and nose, the smell of a winter day in my hair. I remember the smell of beer on his breath when he laughed about the notion of his *not being pretty*—he had already been drinking before he met me at the train station; several empty beer bottles rolled around under the seat when he drove me back to Gloucester. That day in Boston was so long ago, but not really that long—it's the stuff since then that makes it feel like years ago. "I said you weren't supposed to be pretty—or something like that—but you are beautiful to me," I snickered. "I'm not talking about physical beauty—it's more than that—it's too abstract to explain." I fumbled for the right words, but they remained as elusive as the images inside my head; my curiosity piqued by his objection to my admiration.

During my visual growing up, I found many men in works of art to be beautiful—beautifully portrayed in idealistic ways, in the same reverent manner as the women. I think Sylvester is beautiful—his handsome features, a result of a mongrel European lineage, are much like a portrait out of a classical period—his aquiline profile is noble like that of Augustus. Guthrie was always a godlike image in my childhood mythos; I always thought of him as being like Atlas—now he is tragic in a way like the famous marble of the *Dying Gaul*.

"You have funny ideas—abstract or not—but who am I to tell you how to feel about me—or anyone for that matter," he grunted with a chuckle.

"I love you, Guthrie—why is it wrong?" I demanded softly. His attitude troubles me, he's pretends there is nothing wrong, but there is something—ever since Utah—no, ever since Taos, maybe even before that. Somewhere between Cleveland and Taos, the origins of an internal conflict raged inside of him. So far, I haven't dared to ask what's wrong because I knew he wouldn't own up to anything *being wrong*, like now as my question hangs between us, his expression tense, his unspoken answer is swelling inside his throat.

"What the fuck is this?" He spewed, ignoring my question with a gesture at the smudged sky ahead. "Look at that rain—it looks bad." He crinkled his face with additional irritation inspired by the weather. Just the other day we stood on the edge of Hell's Half Acre in the rain and he cursed much in the same way about the shitty climate that plagued us since we came into Wyoming. I ignored that he just ignored me as I pondered the wall of rain that disturbed him. The storm itself is one of those weird highway sights that will never cease to amaze me; it looked like a tarnished silver sheet hammered so thin it has taken on a gossamer quality as it wavers in the wind.

"Wow, that sky looks Biblical," I acknowledged the severity of what lay in wait down the road.

"Nah—do you think I'm crazy? I wouldn't drive us into a Biblical storm! That's just a Manifest Destiny storm, to go there because it's our God given right to do it," he laughed.

"No—that there sky is more like *Star Trek*—let's boldly go into that weird shit up ahead and see what kind of trouble we can get into this episode," I corrected him.

Guthrie laughed hard; the muscular sound of his mirth made me squeal with delight as I clapped my hands together, pleased to have made him laugh. The car wavered in a sickening slide as we entered the wet gloom, but he skillfully kept it going straight. With a final chuckle, he flipped on the lights and wipers, and slowed down for the rain-soaked pavement.

I rolled up the window, leaving it cracked open enough to let out the smoke from my cigarette. The rain came in on my arm, and I rubbed the wetness into my skin, enjoying the cool feel of it. Closing my eyes, I listened to the rain beating on the metal body around us; it made a fantastic roar as we moved through it. When I was very young, downpours like this used to terrify me, but not anymore—no—I have different fears. This drumming sound consoles me. Within this car, I am safe from the things that have caused me fear; its familiar structure and Guthrie's presence soothe me into a sense of protected tranquility that I never want to end.

My mind lazily returned to our situation—how we haven't dealt with it—always dancing around the subject of what we're going to do or where to go next. *When are we going home?* We vaguely know where we're going right now; we have not discussed a plan as we drive from point A to point B every day, moving on from one place to another—getting somewhere before dark has been our ultimate destination lately. Every day, I sit beside him with the ever-present road map opened in my lap, smoothing it out to study where we are, and where we've been; not knowing where we're heading until we come to a crossroad and have to decide whether to turn or go straight—*or just go home.*

Since we left Yellowstone three days ago, we have stopped at several tourist traps to stretch our legs just long enough to forget about the road. We've done the tourist things like asking a park ranger or a random someone to take our picture while standing at a scenic point with a disposable camera purchased at the over-priced park gift shop.

As we mingled with the rest of the road-weary tourists, people would stare at us, perhaps wondering if we're a May-December couple or a father and daughter. Our ambiguous relationship depends on our posture of the moment. The various forms of walking together, usually holding hands, sometimes linked with our arms around one another—mine around his waist, his draped around my shoulders—we rarely walk apart, he hangs onto me as if afraid that I might disappear, and I hang off him fearing that I might become hopelessly lost.

Then we get back in the car and move on, leaving behind the curious stares and whispers—some are perceptive enough to express *she's not all there* as if this recognition of my handicap sets their mind at ease that the much older, big bald dude is only my guardian.

The windshield wipers slapped madly at the poor visibility; I looked at Guthrie again, he's concentrating on the road, his brow furrowed and his mouth grim. I can feel the tension in his body without touching him; I remained quiet so not to disturb him. He grumbled under his breath, uttering an occasional vivid curse at the SUV we're trapped behind. It has been pissing him off since we came upon its taillights in the rain, he's itching to pass it, but the storm is making it hard to see if anything is in the oncoming lane. I reached over with my hand and caressed his shoulder; he sighed in response, and settled back as if deciding it's not worth getting riled about it. He slid his arm across the back of the seat behind me, his fingers tickling my neck; I laughed and he smiled.

"Holy shit!" he shouted; his entire body suddenly returned to a defensive posture at the wheel because the SUV began to weave in the lane as if with indecision, its brake lights flickering. "What the fuck—pull over if you're gonna talk on the phone, you jackass!" He honked the horn for whatever good it would do. Tense again, he gripped the steering wheel with both hands and scowled through the windshield.

After putting out my spent cigarette, I looked out the window and saw a pale yellow plastic penis standing at the side of the road. I did a double take as we passed it by, and laughed.

"Hey, did ya see that?" I asked, watching it grow smaller in the side mirror until finally it disappeared in the storm.

"See what?" Guthrie growled, taking his eyes off the offensive SUV ahead to look at me.

"There was a pale yellow plastic penis standing out there trying to hitch a ride," I tittered girlishly from behind my hand clamped over my mouth—saying the word *penis* always makes me laugh, I know it's childish, but I can't help it.

"Nope—I'm too busy watching the asshole ahead of us driving and talking on the phone—there oughta be a law against that shit," he replied with annoyance, but smirking. He briefly glanced at me, and then turned his attention back to the road with a low snicker gurgling in his throat.

"Too bad you missed it, that's something you don't see every day—do you wanna go back so you can see it?" I looked back, but the rain on the back window obliterated the view behind us.

"No, that would be such a tourist thing to do," he chuckled.

"What an odd thing, it stood at attention about like so—cripe—I'd say it was over twelve inches tall, you know those things are always exaggerated to represent perfection." I held out my hands at about a foot apart to show him how big I thought it looked, but my hands wavered doubtfully as I parted them wider for the give or take an inch factor of distance.

"Hmmm," he hummed.

"What?" *What the fuck does that 'hmmm' mean?* I wondered. So, I ask him again. "WHAT?" I laughed, tugging on his arm.

"Don't do that while I'm driving," he coughed. "What?"

"I'm asking you what does that mean?"

"What?"

"That *hmmm*—you're hmm-humming about something, and don't tell me you're hmm-humming about *nothing*," I squeaked as I strained against the seat belt to reach him, I flicked the worn-soft denim of his shirtsleeve, and briefly stuck my finger into the frayed hole in the elbow. I stopped myself from continuing because judging the grunt that issued from his place behind the wheel, I just stepped into a debate that I don't really want to get into, and he's not going to let it go without pontificating about male anatomy—probably his.

"Perfection?" he asked his heavy brows rose as if with surprise, his eyes are so shocking blue they made his expression appear even more astounded. "Aesthetically speaking—as an artist—define penile perfection," he said while fumbling a cigarette out of his shirt pocket.

"Ah, jeepers-creepers-shut-yer-peepers, it's just a goddamn dildo—ar-rrgh—why do I ever open my mouth?" I shook my head, and looked out the window.

"Well, Silent Sam, at least you are talking, it's the most you've said in weeks," he said, teasing me while lighting his cigarette. "We might as well talk about anatomy."

"Whatever—it was just silly, seeing it out there, okay? Like seeing someone's shoes in the middle of the road, it makes you wonder how the fuck they got there. Did someone wander out into the road and get knocked clean out of 'em? What I'd like to know is how did a pale yellow plastic penis end up on the side of the road!" Laughter burbled forth, and I held my sides; I thought I'd just about explode trying to hold back a clamoring hoard of giggles.

"You want to go back and get it?"

"God no, you don't know where that thing's been!" I cackled. "Don't be such a tourist!"

"Been there, done that, not only did we get the lousy t-shirt, but we found this plastic pecker on the side of the road!" he mocked, grinning mischievously with the cigarette dangling from his lips. He made another attempt to light it because the first attempt didn't take.

"Do you think they were fighting over it? *'It's my turn—no mine'* and it slipped out of their hands and flew out the car window."

"Nah, I think a jealous husband got pissed that the little wife preferred the toy over him, and chucked it to get back at her—"

Our laughter burst into hysterical caterwauling, I eventually had to put my head down between my knees while I gasped for air; his hand patted my back as he inquired after my all-rightness. Wiping our eyes, sniffling, coughing, and eventually pulling ourselves together again—I can't remember when we last laughed like this—*it's been too long.* I reached over and caressed the back of his head. With smoke successfully puffing from his lips, he tucked the lighter back into his pocket, the expression in his eyes playful, his mustache squirming to mask his smile from me. The rain poured harder, the lightness of our laughter faded into the gloom.

"What's the matter?" I inquired.

"Nothin'." Guthrie grimaced through the windshield, concentrating on the taillights ahead of him; the SUV pulled over. "Good riddance!" he shouted as he hit the gas; we splashed past it.

That *nothing* didn't sound like *nothing*, that *nothing* has a whole lot of *something* in it. *What?* We continued on our way for a few heartbeats. I sighed—and then sighed again with growing annoyance, but he refused to cave in to my impatient noises. I can't stand his stubborn silence, it makes me crazy—he used to drive my mother insane when he acted like this. I stared at his impassive face, he looked straight ahead, but his eyes failed to hide his buried sadness—*sadness Lenore created.*

"Guthrie—are you angry with me because we haven't had sex?"

"Ummm, well, shoot, no—forget it—it doesn't matter—I'm not complaining or anything like that—" he mumbled around his cigarette. "I never know what goes on inside that little coconut of yours—and I haven't been in the mood anyway," he went on to say with a lilt of defensiveness, and then his face relaxed, his gaze seemed to focus somewhere other than the wet road and driving rain.

"Yeah, I know—" I replied, mystified by his rapturous expression. Shifting uncomfortably, he picked up the sweating soda can from between his legs, but it slipped out of his hand, spilling between his feet.

"Oh, fuck," he muttered, too distracted to be fierce.

Snapping out of my seatbelt, I fetched the soda can from off the floor and dropped napkins out of a paper bag from yesterday's fast food lunch to soak up the mess.

"Do you love me, Sammy?" he asked, his thoughtful gaze examined my being.

"Of course I do—I do love you," I replied with an excitable sigh. "I can't say it enough."

He grinned with pleasure upon hearing my answer, then shaking his head as if at a loss for words. I gazed back at him, smiling so much my face hurt.

Over the next ridge, we approached a brightening horizon, and we passed through the remains of the storm, arriving within minutes at a place where the sunshine lived, the blue sky full of shredded clouds, golden rays slanting across the vista. It was weird to see that the roads were dry as if no rain had touched this part of the landscape in days.

"Oh, look over there—horses!" I exclaimed, pointing out the passenger side window at a small herd traveling at a trot. We came to the Red Desert to look for wild horses—here they are!

Guthrie slowed down *Delta Dawn* upon seeing them approach the highway, and then rolled to a stop as a dusky gray stallion with a bluish cast to his coat came up on the shoulder of the road—there was no fence to contain them, no brands or halters to indicate that they belonged to anyone. The proud horse stepped in front of us and stopped, fixing us with a baleful glare like a crossing guard with a mission; then behind him, a colorful parade filed past. First came a matching pair of piebald mares, they appeared to be a mother with her yearling daughter. The elder's black and white barrel was round with an expectation not yet born, while the other had the gangly appearance of a bright-eyed teenager as she bounced her chin on her dam's ample croup while casting a nervous glance in our direction. Then along came a shy pinto that was nearly all white except for her red head and a wide red spot on her belly that spread up onto her sides like an apron, her mostly white mane and tail were streaked with black. She crossed over with a solid rust-colored foal following close by her side; the spindly-legged little one nearly blended in with her spotted flank. An immature male crowded behind them, bumping gently against the mare's rump, probably her off-spring from last year; he was dark chocolate brown, nearly black, with a single rivulet of white cascading from the crest of his neck to his shoulder, the marking was so random, it looked like someone had accidentally dribbled bleach on him. Last, came a golden palomino mare with a black colt sporting a startling white mane and tail, I gasped and cried out, "Oh, look at that one—I wonder if he will remain black like that or turn gray like his sire! How pretty they all are, Guthrie—isn't this wonderful?" He didn't reply out loud, he only nodded; he sat with his arms crossed over the top of the steering wheel, resting his chin on the cushion of his forearms.

As soon as his family was safely on the other side, the stallion followed them with a toss of his head and his tail rose like a flag. On their leader's silent command, all of them took off for the open range, their colorful bodies racing through the pale green sagebrush, kicking up a cloud of pink dust behind them. We sat watching them go without speaking; we moved forward after seeing the last of their rumps disappear over a rise on the deceptively flat desert, and then we turned our attention to the sky ahead of us.

"Now that's a Biblical sky—it's got Jesus rays and everything," I observed.

"You got that right, Buttons, it is Almighty sublime," Guthrie agreed with a hearty laugh.

We drove on, both of us quiet. I watched the sky change—the rays extended toward the darkness we had left behind. I looked back to see a rainbow spanning the highway; the fractured hues of white light manifested in the form of an arch shimmering upon the sheet of rain. I suddenly wished Sylvester could see this—I wanted to share so many things with him on this trip, it's just not the same to relay the beauty of Wyoming over the telephone. *I miss him.*

"Can we go home now?" I asked; my throat tightened with tears that came up in my eyes with haste. "I'm homesick," I declared.

"All right, we can do that—it is way past time to go home," Guthrie nodded in agreement, as he reached over to caress my hair.

"It is—while you were out to the bar having a beer last night, I called Sylvester—I hate thinking of him there alone without us to keep him company."

"Yes," Guthrie replied as if agreeing with me that Sylvester shouldn't be alone. His expression of rapture faded as his mouth gaped for something else to say, "Ah, shit," he said as he suddenly swerved the car over to the shoulder and parked.

"We really need to talk," he sputtered.

I stared at him; his expression looked so shattered, fear crept around on the lining of my heart with icy tiptoes.

"Oh, crap," he groaned. "Sammy—do you love Hayden?"

Upon hearing his question, a spark fired inside my heart, and I knew there was nothing to be afraid of, my heart's fire quickly melted away the accumulation of fear, replacing it with the warmth of joy. I smiled as I cupped his strong jaw within the palm of my hand.

"Of course I do—I have loved Sylvester for a very long time—I told you that before, remember?" I assured him.

"I remember," he sighed, settling back in the seat behind the wheel, leaning his head back, and closing his eyes. "He loves you—you know that don't you?" He opened his eyes, but didn't look at me; he stared at the cloth ceiling over our heads—our shelter from the storms of the world, but now it is containing the storms of our emotions so the world doesn't need to know about them.

"I know he does—oh, Guthrie," I sighed as I began to comprehend his private agony that he has hidden from me all this time—*a fantasy—it's only a fantasy*. Suddenly, he transformed into the tragic figure that has haunted my memories; my fingers brushed his arm, and then landed upon his hand, but he wouldn't close his fingers around mine. I crawled over the seat to hold him; our arms clasped one another—this is love as we have always known it.

"Take me home, please, take me home," I murmured into the warmth of his neck where I buried new tears.

22 *Full Circle*

We have come full circle. I drove all night because I didn't feel like hunting for a hotel in Altoone, Iowa nearly twelve hours ago, so at dawn when the Cleveland skyline crept into view, I never thought in my life that I'd ever feel so glad to see it ahead of me. But once I drove within the city limits, and drifted past a certain hotel where I had spent the night with Sammy, the oppression of memories diminished my relief. *Welcome home, Guthrie, your baggage is right where you left it.*

After I filled up the tank with gas, I decided to keep going. What's the point in stopping my momentum—why should I drive all the way to University Heights to lurk outside my mother's old house to see if my latest edition ex-wife's car is in the driveway? *I have no reason to go there.* There's nothing of sentimental value to retrieve, the things that I left behind when I walked out the front door on the last day of February are just things that once belonged to a man who no longer lives there, and he doesn't expect to be back. Any possessions from the past that mattered are in Gloucester where I left them a long time ago.

One stop I had to make was at Mike's garage on Route 20 where Whitley's Caddy had been towed. Mike is a real classic personality—thankfully, he doesn't change. So much has changed. I have changed. Mike is the first person I've seen in weeks who remembers me as I used to be—although we're not best friends, he has known me since we were little boys in elementary school. In recent years, we've spent many nights keeping barstools warm at Harvey's, swapping divorce stories and trying to pickup unsuspecting women. I knew that he didn't recognize me when he failed to hide the *Who the fuck is this?* expression on his face as he emerged from the shadowy depths of the garage's open bay. First, he looked at my car, and then looked me up and down before he cut loose with a greeting. *"What the fuck, asshole, if it weren't for that crappy car and that ratty fur on your lip, I wouldn't have known it was you."* Mike uses the word *asshole* as a term of endearment—he has a special set of words for the people he doesn't like. *"How the hell are ya?"* He inquired as he lit a cigarette. This is his way to ask without asking if I had cancer. His concern for my well-being was touching. As I lit up a cigarette of my own, I assured him that I was fine without committing to certainty—*I don't have cancer, at least, as far as I know.* It's understandable that he'd wonder about the worst because physically, I look like someone who survived a catastrophic illness rather than an extended vacation. I've lost so much weight I had to add two notches to my belt to keep my britches up. Sammy had expressed some uneasy worry about my rattling smokers cough when we were at the Grand Canyon—she thinks it could be a sign of heart failure. When I asked *Dr. Samantha* why she thought so, her lower lip quivered a little as she asserted her certainty that I was about to die. *"Because Whitley had the same cough."* Maybe I do, maybe I don't. What the fuck, ya can't live for-fucking-ever, damn it.

Mike accepted Sammy's check to cover the towing, repair, and storage that I had negotiated with him over the phone several weeks ago, and she added a "tip" to the total. When I promised to come fetch the car later this summer, he waved me off, *"Take your time, asshole, the li'l red darlin' has brightened up the place a bit."*

By the time I pointed *Delta Dawn* eastbound on 90, Sammy had fallen back into a deep slumber in the backseat, I let her—*it's better that way.* I'll be relieved to get her home, I'm physically exhausted, and emotionally burnt-out—and she's an unfortunate mess. She's mentally a wisp of the young woman she had been when I first laid eyes on her at Whitley's funeral—if she's found incompetent at that hearing in June it'll be my stupid fault for letting her get this way. The sooner I get her home, the better. I'll be more than happy to let Hayden take charge of her, hopefully, he'll know what to do—what doctor she needs to see to reverse my slapdash impact on her well-being. While he works on fixing her—I need to work on getting my shit together and move on.

My coping skills haven't exactly been the best in my life; the emotional rollercoaster that I've endured during our time spent on the road has been a personal odyssey that I never imagined. In a wretchedly slow progression, I have evolved away from the sensibilities that I started with in November. The fact that I'm not Sammy's father has become a vague disappointment that no longer makes sense, but when I recall her as a wee pink bit in a receiving blanket, I never considered myself as her step-brother. Whitley pegged it right when he said that I came to Gloucester twice a year to *"play house"* with his wife and daughter because along with the desperation that I felt to *be there*, there was the relief of distance once I left.

Thankfully, I haven't fucked her since that night in Cleveland, and I felt oddly glad that any subsequent sexual efforts petered out with very little drama—although for a minute in Wyoming I felt tempted, but it was brief, very brief. I had put a stop to our sharing a bed since we left Taos, and although she never quibbled about it, she has crawled into bed with me in the middle of the night, snuggling close, hugging me as if I were her personal teddy bear. That shit has to stop when I get her home—because when I get her home, I'm delivering her into the arms of the man she truly loves.

After I get her home, where do I fit in? Fucking good question.

The more I think about the impending future of our life in Gloucester, the more my head feels like it might pop off my body as jealousy rages in my heart. I can't sleep, I can't eat, and I heave deep sighs like a heartsick fool. *What do I feel?* What I feel for Sammy is an overwhelming unconditional love—I just don't know how to express it, let alone how to classify it. For a lack of a better term to describe our relationship, I am her friend—or her companion—which is the trendy term for a relationship that isn't a marriage. For as long as I live, I will love her and I will protect her with my life—this is the only way that I can feel at ease about being with her. After I get her home, I need to make a graceful exit because I know that Hayden won't do anything to consummate their relationship while I'm hanging around. Cripe, even if she threw herself at him naked, he'd courteously hand her back to me—*the idiot.*

That last day in Taos I wanted to grab the fool and shake the teeth out of his head—*"Are you really going to let her leave with me? You're not even gonna to try to stop us—I really should kill you for being such a dumbass!"* He did nothing more than give her a chaste peck on the forehead and wave goodbye from the driveway. If only I had insisted, *"Why don't you take her home sort out this crap with Preston, and then go to Yellowstone on your honeymoon."* If I had, it could've changed everything—she would've gone with him—but I didn't say it because as I drove away from Dulcie's house, I was a jealous fool clinging to the broken threads of a ridiculous fantasy. *I'm a stupid asshole, and he's a stupid asshole too.*

When I get back to Gloucester, I'm going to get him drunk—get him good and drunk to get that Helena bug out of his ass—I'll get Mr. Prim-and-Proper-Academic-New-England-Puritan so sloppy *"I love you, man"* drunk that he'll spill his guts about his true feelings for Sammy all over the place. I'll have him shouting from the rooftops tellin' the world.

As I eased through the lines at the tollbooth entering New York State, Sammy grunted and thrashed around in the backseat, waking up. Her hands gripped the top of the front seat to the right of my shoulder, and we grinned at each other through the rear view mirror.

"It's past noon—we'll make a pit stop at the next rest area all right, Buttons?"

"Okay—" the word drifted slowly from her mouth. "I want to go home."

"Yeah, me too," I sighed.

Home, I have to get her home. If I push myself, we can get there by tonight. Once there, I hope that she will settle into her familiar Sammy routines, and then start drawing in her sketchbook again. Ever since Utah, I've had my hands full trying to keep her from destroying her stuff during her combustible tantrums. It seems she's aggravated with the paper and pencils as if they are not cooperating with what she sees. Now, she's not drawing at all—at least not since we spent the night in Nebraska—she sat watching movies on television instead. That Eugene Riley chick-flick *Dandelion Wine* played in the middle of the night, and she stared at the screen with tears streaming down her face. I wanted to smack her to make her snap out of it, but I left her alone, afraid to ignite the flammable emotions within her. I hate to admit it, but her zombie-like quiet makes for a more peaceful existence. At least I can think—but when I think for too long, I have a knack for making the wrong decisions. If only I could empty my mind of everything—erase all memory, and forget all feeling. Lenore is dead; the least I can do is take care of her daughter in a manner that she would have expected from me. As for my jealousy, it can go take a long walk off a short pier.

❧

We arrived in Syracuse, New York by late afternoon. When I inquired if Sammy needed to pee, her eyes became bright with excitement and she announced that she had a craving for reading a specific book, and begged me to take her to a bookstore. It was the most she's said for nearly three days, and I knew by the set expression on her face that if I didn't do it, I wouldn't hear the end of it, and I was just too damn tired to object. After giving this venture into the city careful consideration, I decided to take her to the east side neighborhood where I used to live, figuring that it was a good place to start, and just as I was getting my bearings, I found *The Mabinogion Bookstore* on Westcott Street.

The shop hadn't been there during my time spent in the area; the storefront had been a fascinating old Five & Ten where silly things like a rubber chicken could be picked-up for a dollar. I always went in there to look around every Saturday morning feeling like a kid with money burning a hole in my pocket just to see the common place house-wares mixed with traditional toys—the sort of things not found in the big department stores or malls these days. It was too bad that the store was gone, but when I stepped through the door with Sammy in tow, the ancient wood floors that I remembered from over twenty years ago still creaked under my feet with homey familiarity. I felt grateful to the owner for recognizing their beauty, and had elected to refinish them rather than ripping them up or covering them with industrial carpeting. Breathing in the wood and book fragrance of the place, I gaped at a cluster of women near the cashier counter admiring a baby in a stroller; when they looked up to acknowledge our entrance, reminisces of the past crept out onto my skin causing an eruption of goose bumps.

"Oh-my-god, it's Guthrie Ryder!" One of the women exclaimed as a smile split her face wide open; she broke away from the group with her arms out to receive me.

"Millie," I exclaimed, completely stunned as I accepted her embrace. She had not changed a bit—older, perhaps wiser, but as pretty as ever. I recognized the other two women as my former students, Katharine and Georgia.

"Wow, this is a surprise—who would' a thought we'd see you here!"

"How are you doing?" I fumbled, feeling awkward like I always do when I run into people in an out of context situation. My hand instinctively reached for Sammy, and her fingers eagerly clung to me while she absorbed these people; her indirect gaze taking snapshots of their distinguishing features.

"Hey, what's all the hubbub, Bub?" An inquiry from the stacks drifted toward me as another familiar face peered around the corner, and I recognized the infamous Eugene Riley. Alongside of him stood a gangly teenager who could only be Alice Riley, the kid he had with Millie, and what a knock out she turned out to be! This girl is one of the few times that it is acceptable for a daughter to look like her dad and have it come out looking right, but the maternal-side dark eyebrows tagged her features as if in defiance of his strong genetics. I had to wonder about how she dealt with her father's fame; it has to be strange being the child of a famous Hollywood film star. What does that do to a little kid trying to define the difference between reality and make-believe? Essentially, she's grown up around the fact that her dad has a weird job, he makes gobs of money, and every woman in the world wants to fuck him.

"Jeez, Guthrie—look at you!" Millie exclaimed. "He looks great, doesn't he?" When positive sentiments echoed all around, I doffed my Boston Red Sox cap to expose my trendy 'bald-do'; I finally broke down and buzzed off the shaggy leftovers that I desperately held on to for years. Millie gave me a wink of approval—she always said that I'd look good bald.

"Hey, it's good to see all of you again—this is a surprise—ummm—I want you to meet Samantha Ryder—Whitley's daughter," I tugged on Sammy to come out from behind me. Although she practiced her typical shyness with strangers, she eagerly peeked at the baby in the stroller, making faces and funny noises; the infant stared at her with the confused expression of a babe new to the world.

"What is his name?" Sammy asked with timid interest, leaning closer to the stroller.

"Nathaniel," Eugene said, his paternal hands gently scooped up the little bundle in a blue one-piece sleeper. "Hey, li'l Peeper, what a big day for you, meeting all of these people, this is Samantha—say 'hi', wow, he really digs you—look at him look at ya, a flirt already, that's my boy! Do you want to hold him?" he laughed as he offered the little one to her. Her face brightened with a silent reply as she held out her hands for the child; she cradled him in her arms like an experienced mother, cooing and clucking in a high-pitched singsong language that held the baby's undivided attention. It was funny to see how the wee one was fascinated with the essence of Sammy; his blurry awareness at this point in life has been mostly tuned-in to his parents, but on this outing, he has discovered someone new who apparently understands him on a level that has pleased him.

"Oh, look at you, wee man!" Sammy cooed. It seemed as if she had forgotten all about buying a book to read while she examined a tiny pink fist that opened and closed like the spindly petals of a flower. The cheerful sound of her enchantment with the baby perked my curiosity. I have noticed this effect during our travels; babies and small children attract her, and in turn, they gravitate toward her, maybe because she's so childlike herself. *What kind of a mother she would be to a child of her own?* A part of me could imagine her as a loving mother, but there was a part of me that felt uncertain about the viability because of her autism, and her tendency toward distraction. With kids, a parent has to be constantly aware of every motion, every sound—to turn your back on them for a second could mean life and death because kids move quick, and in a flash, bang—they're gone. Like everything else in Sammy's life, we can find something to help her maintain her focus—some new trick, some new routine. With this thought, it bit into me how the cross-country trek disrupted her routine ruled by clocks with alarms.

"Where have you been—and where are you going?" Millie asked from her persistent location at my elbow; my heart stuttered over the memory of our time together.

"Well, we've been all over the place—it's a long story—Gloucester to Cleveland, from Cleveland to west of the Mississippi. We've been to Colorado Springs, Taos, Moab, Yellowstone, and all over Wyoming until a few days ago when we made our way east of the Mississippi, cut through Cleveland this morning—now we're on our way to Gloucester," I said, after abbreviating our journey. "We've been on the road since the last day of February—or something like that; I lost track about 5000 miles ago," I finished with a long sigh.

"Okay—that explains why you look so beat," she nodded. "It's good to see you—it's been seventeen years since I last saw you," she concluded, nodding toward her daughter, a living benchmark of passing time. I had noted that although Alice didn't ignore the group around the baby, she kept her eye on Millie and me; when I met her eye during my casual glance in her direction, she made a silly smirky-face.

"You should come stay the night with us—" I overheard Georgia say to Sammy; I had missed the context of the conversation that lead to this offer. I peripherally kept track of Sammy as she stood with her head together with the parents discussing the baby boy, but had no idea they were making plans. "Oh, Guthrie, Samantha says you've been driving since yesterday without a break—that's not good—we'd love it if you'd at least spend the night—get some rest before going home—there's plenty of room at our house," Georgia added to the invitation; Eugene echoed her sentiments with eager agreement.

"Oh—I don't know," Sammy looked up at me with heartfelt indecisiveness tearing her up inside. I understood her desire to stay on to visit with people who are outside of ourselves because being in their company brought about a sense of reality that we have been missing since we left Taos. For once, our feet felt firmly planted on the ground that isn't asphalt zipping away at 80 MPH underneath our butts. As I looked at her, I felt willing to do whatever she wanted to do, but unwilling to tell her what to do.

"I don't think Natty is ready to give you up yet, right li'l bud?" Eugene teased as he tickled his son under the chin; a toothless grin constructed by the contortions of a sleepy yawn bloomed with an elastic response. "Listen, we have a great place with lots of room. Katharine is coming over with her husband for dinner tonight—we're having a cookout—it's sort of a celebration because it's been a long winter up here. You guys look to me like you could use a home-cooked meal to send you back to Gloucester with—I have plenty of steaks marinating to feed everyone—I've gotten really good at cooking this past year," he winked at his wife. "Georgia was on 24 hour bed rest for the last trimester of the pregnancy, so I pampered her—catered to her every little craving—molasses cookies went a long way to appease this woman—I swear Natty came out smelling like a batch fresh from the oven on the day he was born!"

"Eugene does make awesome steaks, but he makes the best grilled asparagus sandwiches in the world—the spears from their garden are heavenly," Katharine exclaimed; a round of guffawing, giggles, and snorting radiated through our little group.

"Yes, I can grill asparagus for those who want it," Eugene laughed at Katharine's peculiar lust for asparagus. "Are you sure you're not pregnant?" he teased her.

"I'm sure," Katharine waved him off with a smile; she quietly stood by admiring the infant miracle with a distant expression of awe, her hand absently brushing over her flat stomach.

While everyone began to talk at once, and as Millie whispered in my ear that Katharine had lost a baby last fall, I stepped outside of myself to examine this group of people whom I haven't seen in years, and once again, I found that I have come full circle. Then something strange needled inside of me with omen-like foreshadowing—*this means something.*

"Guthrie—would it be all right if we stayed?" Sammy asked, smiling, her eyes shining with a delight that I haven't seen in such a long time; I decided to go with it—the sense of rightness in the situation granted me a sense of reprieve.

"It will be fine," I nodded. Hayden will still be there—along with everything else that awaits our return.

∽

"*Wherethefuckarewe—Walton's mountain?*" I growled during the drive that felt a lot longer than it should be to get somewhere. The road kept going up, up, up, and then we went down, down, down. When we finally arrived at the farm, I got out of the car and took in the view of the valley surrounded by the rolling flanks of forested hills and meadows dotted with livestock. The windmills turned with seemingly lazy revolutions, and the old Victorian farmhouse sprawled with feline grace, its cool porches laced with gingerbread beckoned to my road weary body—finally a place to put up my feet. "Wow, they still make places like this, huh?" I said with awe as I stepped out of the car to breathe in the sweet earthy atmosphere of tranquility. I peered over the car roof and caught sight of Sammy; she stood with her mouth hanging open, turning around and around, trying to take it all in at once. I began to laugh, she did the same thing at the Grand Canyon, and I had to hang on to her to make sure she didn't get dizzy and fall over the edge; but here, I knew that she was safe. When she stopped spinning, she looked at me, her smile beaming—"Look, Guthrie—kittens!" A litter of kittens tumbled out from under a lilac bush with their skinny tails straight up as they made a beeline for our feet. Sammy and Alice plopped onto the grass and became instant jungle gyms for the furry balls full of play.

"Want one?" Eugene asked with a laugh as he slapped me on the back.

"If she does, I won't have much choice," I grunted.

"Take two—one will get lonely," Georgia put in with a giggle. I rubbed my eyes, and pretended that I didn't hear that.

Years ago, Jonathan Wiley was one of my students while I was doing a teaching stint at Pratt not long after I abandoned my post at Syracuse. He became a frequent drinking buddy since we were neighbors in the same Brooklyn brownstone and often had time on our hands in the evenings— it was almost scary how much he could drink in one night. Upon seeing his familiar tall, rangy figure beside Katharine Tierney, I felt another hit of omen-like weirdness that something was going to go down real soon in my life. "Well, if it isn't Jonathan Wiley—somehow, it makes perfect sense to me that you would marry Katharine Tierney—you two are made for each other," I exclaimed when we shook hands. With a moony-eyed glance at his bride, he shyly smirked in reply with a nod of agreement; the young man that I had known way back when was a basket case of problems—most of them due to a taste for vodka. It was painfully obvious to me that he needed someone—a woman—to smooth him over, Katharine had enough grit to her that expunged whatever ailed him, and he returned the favor with his steadfast manner to ease her troubled mind. The sense of harmony between them is uncanny in a magical awareness that seemed straight out of a fairy tale—a match made in heaven, and other such stuff only found in fables—or a romantic Eugene Riley film.

I considered the significance of reconnecting with this collection of people from my past; it's been almost like an episode from *This is Your Life.* I shrugged off the feeling, and just let whatever might happen to me happen. There are events that body and mind cannot control—*who am I to question it?* To examine the significance will only send me on a trip chasing my tail. I sat back, half-dozing while the dinner preparations commenced; no one seemed offended by my sleepiness as they talked around me. I could feel Millie examining me as I surrendered to sleep. *"He's asleep guys, the poor thing,"* I heard her observation as if from a million miles away. Their existence beyond the time I knew them during their youthful trials comforted me—it seemed all is right in the world and soon, any remaining loose ends will be connected. It was weird like a fever dream.

After dinner, Sammy called Sylvester to tell him of our whereabouts, although I backed off to give her privacy, my ear remained tuned in to her lilting voice as it chirped and sang about kittens and horses, grilled asparagus sandwiches, and dandelion wine. When she let him go, she reported to me that he said to enjoy our visit. It seemed like she felt torn about staying, so I remained cued to depart at a moment's notice. In time, she relaxed again, and spent the rest of the evening out on the screen porch quietly drawing. Katharine and Jonathan engaged her by taking up pencils and sketchpads of their own; between the two of them, they were able to entice her out of the natural shyness that settled upon her since dinner. When she began to explain about her decision to stop making copies of masterpieces for a living, a flood of tears fell from her eyes as she lamented her inability to create anything that satisfied her.

"I don't know what to do, all I do now is doodle!" she cried with tempered frustration. I massaged her thin shoulders; she slowly relaxed within my grasp, heaving a deep sigh.

"But Sam, these drawings are beautiful!" Jonathan exclaimed, taking up her sketchbook and turning through the pages. "The forms are well articulated—you have marvelous lines, they're very free, fluid—your use of pencil is gorgeous, such a delicate touch in shading—your technical skill is a natural talent—you'd be considered an artist's artist."

"I've tried telling her this, but she won't listen to me, like somebody else I know!" I grumbled, shaking my finger at him.

"Oh, Guthrie, I do listen to you," Sammy sighed.

"And so did I—" he laughed. "Listen, Sammy, there is something inspiring you to make these—do you understand what it is?" Jonathan inquired with a gentle persuasion so not to cause her to withdraw from him.

"I'm listening to Beethoven," she muttered, pointing at her head.

"Beethoven!" Katharine exclaimed with a curious smile, she caught my eye, and I smirked.

"I love Beethoven—his music is beautiful to me—see this one—this is the *Cavatina*," Sammy replied, as she turned through the pages to a particular sketch, her eyes fluttered as her face lit up with a bashful smile. "I drive Guthrie crazy with my Beethoven CD's."

"She ain't kiddin'," I expelled a long horse sigh that puttered through my lips with an amusing effect that caused laughter to sprinkle around the porch.

"I love to paint while listening to Beethoven—his music is the perfect medium for sensory inspiration—I see colors when I listen to his music," Katharine mused with an empathetic smile.

"You do?" Sammy turned to her with wide-eyed astonishment.

"I painted these long, rice paper scrolls with watercolors while listening to his symphonies—remember those, Guthrie? One night, I had pinned them up all over the figure drawing studio walls, just to look at them all together—it was the only place where I could display them undisturbed. I hadn't been sleeping well for several nights because I had spent all my time painting, and it caught up with me while I sat looking at them, so I fell asleep on the model stand. When I woke up the next morning, Guthrie was sitting on a stool sketching me," she laughed, her face reddened a little. I exchanged glances with Jonathan as if he knew about the awkwardness of that long ago moment—her initial outrage that rose up from the model stand and my profound apologies for invading her sleep. To top off my discomfort, Millie snickered with a sound of intimate knowledge—I felt foolish.

"Sometimes it's tough to find someone who will sit still long enough to draw—sleeping people are the best," I laughed with a modest shrug that advertised my unease—I feared all the embarrassing moments of my life were about to be revealed for fun at my expense.

"You do draw a lot while I'm sleeping," Sammy smiled, her hand squeezing mine; her acknowledgement of my habit defused my troubled mind.

"My sketchbooks are filled with you—I'm no different from you, we both draw what we love." As I said this, I let my finger travel to the top of the page in her sketchbook where I recognized Hayden's hands enclosed within a design that was vaguely heart shaped. As if understanding my meaning, she isolated the hands in a circle of her fingers and thumbs; and she looked at them with a loving smile—oddly enough, I felt no pangs over this, because it is right.

"Those scrolls you made were beautiful—very vivid and free—I wish Sammy could see one," I said, turning to Katharine.

"She gave *Für Elise* to me ages ago, it's hanging in my study, come see," Georgia exclaimed. She led Sammy and Katharine away to explore the poet's inner sanctum.

Eugene sat in a rocking chair with his loaf-shaped son sleeping on his chest, and Jonathan busied himself with sketching father and son. "Katharine and I are trying again," Jonathan mused with a smile. "The doctor gave her the go ahead."

"Maybe sooner than you think," Millie said as she very carefully bent over to kiss the baby's head without waking him. "I thought I noticed that *glow* today."

"Jeez, she just about glows in the dark, Jonathan—she's pregnant all right," Eugene laughed, teasing his friend.

"Shhh—you're going to disturb the baby," Jonathan blushed; his grin radiated with hope that his future paternity has been foretold by the physical evidence that others have noted.

"What do you think, Guthrie?" Millie asked as her hand fell upon my shoulder.

"I'm not an expert about these sort of things—I initially thought she's just simply glowing with happiness, but I'd put money on it that she's got a bun baking in the oven," I chuckled.

"Looks like we're all in agreement, Jono—you better get that nursery ready," Eugene whispered as he nuzzled the fuzzy head of his child.

"Shit, I just finished renovating the entire house; she's going to get pissed if I start taking apart another room, and kicking up more dust," he said with a mischievous grin.

A peaceful silence fell over the room; I watched the sleeping baby, and I beheld the pure innocence that belonged on such a face—yet there lay wisdom on his little brow—a knowledge we're all born with—it is inherent in our life's fabric—the knowledge of the soul.

"Oh, what a beautiful drawing of the wee one," Sammy murmured as she peered over Jonathan's shoulder.

"Thanks, Sammy," Jonathan said. "Come sit—I want you to tell me more about these drawings you've made—why don't you think these 'doodles' are important?" he asked, turning her attention back to her sketchbook where she left it at the table.

With a slight hesitation, she sat down beside him.

"Oh—I don't know—I've always made them, they're nothing," she finally said, her words came out soft and slow, her demeanor wavering on the line of shyness once again.

"I don't believe they're nothing—they mean a lot to you—or you wouldn't make them. This is the core of your vision—Guthrie's right, they come from things you love, they are the things that matter to you—this is where you need to start. It's going to be all right—this is a huge step that you're taking—it's like you're starting over—fresh—you need to forget all that you've learned and begin again. It will take time—you need to reprogram yourself, be patient and relax, and keep doing what you're doing in your sketchbooks, you can't force it—just let it happen. I can't tell you how many times I've been frustrated with my work. I used to paint figures without faces for years—Guthrie remembers those, right?"

I nodded that I did remember the faceless self-portraits; the damn things disturbed me.

"Then one day I put a face on a figure—it was my own, that's when things finally made sense again—and then Katharine came along, and I had another face to work with," he smiled at his wife, and she ruffled his hair with her hand. "Give it time, it will come—for now, you're your own worst enemy by trying to push too hard—do you know what I mean?"

"Yes," she nodded, her gaze studied him in that half-closed phase; I knew she soaked in his every word. She suddenly looked exhausted. "Guthrie, can you please bring in my bag? I'm very tired—Georgia showed me where I'll sleep tonight—it looked so nice, it's calling me to go to sleep." She looked ready to drop, I had been watching the shadow of sleep creeping into her face all evening, and knew that she was going down with the sun; this evening has been too much for her in spite of its medicinal wonders.

"Sure, sweetheart, come along," I rose from my seat and took her by the hand. After fetching her things from the car, I waited for her to change and wash up. Then I watched while she made things right around her before finally lying down. I tucked her into the soft feather bed, and kissed her brow. She muttered apologies for being tired and then told me *I love you*. Once I felt satisfied that she was comfortable and unafraid, I returned downstairs to rejoin the company of old friends.

With the setting sun showering the final golden light of day into the valley, Jonathan and Katharine went home murmuring about their hopeful suspicions regarding expectancy. Eugene and Georgia with little Natty went to bed early because of their life duty to the running of the farm. Then after a few rounds of playing cards, Alice stretched and yawned extravagantly; on her way out, she teased her mom about not staying up too late, and then she cast the smirky-face at me as she bid us goodnight. As her footsteps scurried up the stairs, I suspected that mention has been made to identify me as an old flame to hone the girl's attention on me, I looked to her mother, and she just rolled her eyes with a shrug on the false pretense that she had no idea what that was all about.

Left alone, Millie and I took a walk outside to enjoy the fine spring weather, and the quiet of the night alive with the chatter of frogs, bugs, and other small things scampering in the darkness. She led me to the teahouse in the garden; while she lit the oil-lamps with a match, I sat down at the table and leaned back in the cushioned wicker chair. The air of romance now made prevalent by the warm light caused me to wonder about Millie's intentions, although I hoped that she wasn't interested in me in that way, my hormones quivered with hopeful urges.

"This is the best I can do for tonight so we don't disturb the sleeping household. Eugene has promised to have a cottage constructed for me to live in—sooner or later—you see, I come and go, and when I'm here, I keep my own hours, they know better than to expect me to rise before dawn, put on Wellingtons to muck out stalls," she chuckled.

"You wearing Wellingtons would be a sight to see," I snorted.

"Not in this lifetime," she smiled from across the table. "I do have a papermaking studio in a shed—Eugene and Jonathan fixed it up so I can have a place to make the necessary mess. Lately, I've been enjoying the art of making natural dyes from the plants that Georgia grows around here—my art is taking a new direction by using things from a garden."

"New directions are always good," I acknowledged with a laugh, and carefully studied her heart-shaped face with rosy cheeks softened by the yellow flame of the oil-lamps—I couldn't read her; it seemed she was being cautious about revealing her feelings.

"So, you've been on a journey," she continued.

"Yes, quite the journey—I've been through four marriages, had three children, and I am still in love with one woman," I replied.

"I haven't forgotten—Lenore was a very important part of your life," she nodded. "So, what the fuck, Guthrie—are you sleeping with your step-sis?"

"Arrgghh! I had hoped you wouldn't jump to that conclusion," I grunted. "Listen, I do love Sammy—I will love her until the day I die—but I will not marry her."

"If you're in love with her, then why not? Don't give me any of that you're too old crap," she scoffed with a frown that knit her dark eyebrows into a straight line.

"No—there's more to it—but to make a long story short, she's in love with someone else and he's in love with her, but other influences have distracted them—it's up to me to see that they get together this time."

"Life tends to be too complicated—but once in a while it sorts itself out after everyone gets on the same page—it takes some doing, and some pain, but it eventually happens," she said in a near bitter manner that recalled her long ago musings about Georgia and Eugene from her perch on the edge of my bed.

"I'm hoping that once I get her home, they'll just—I don't know, maybe fuck like silly rabbits—but I doubt it, at least not with me hanging around."

"They'll need time."

"Time—yeah, we all need that."

"Patience," she smiled, tapping my hand with a finger. I watched her hand return to her side of the table and once again wondered about her agenda.

"All right, get this—she has a sketch of his bare ass hanging in the place of honor above her drafting table," I spoke randomly, hoping to lighten up the mood with a funny tidbit.

"Nice! I assume it's a good looking ass," Millie laughed. "Or is it idealized?"

"I couldn't tell you if his ass is nice—but aesthetically, I guess it is an anatomically well-proportioned male ass that is pleasing for a woman to look at as it's walking away," I shrugged with faux bewilderment regarding feminine preferences.

"Oh, shit, Guthrie, you are so funny!" she burst out laughing. "Maybe you should have her do a watercolor of his manhood to see if that gives her a jolt."

"That was such a great class!" I marked with a near shout of laughter, feeling nervous.

"Eugene was a mighty fine model," she commented with a sly smile.

"He was a good sport about the whole thing—it takes a set of balls to sprawl like that in front of a studio class of thirty college students the first day on the job—it was a helluva thing for a guy to do because he's smitten with a certain girl," I chuckled with a shake of my head.

"Georgia was mortified that he took the job—I thought it was sweet that he didn't want her drawing from some other naked dude!"

"It's amazing what a guy will do—umm—" I looked at her, noticing once again how pretty she is; the nagging urge to kiss her became too over-whelming, so I needed to redirect my attention to something else. "Tell me, what happened after you last saw me in New York—I know what I read about on the front pages of the gossip rags at the grocery store—but I'd rather hear it from the source."

"Well, initially, I planned to tell Eugene that I intended to raise the baby alone. I didn't want him to feel that he had to marry me, but when he proposed, I was scared not to marry him. Oh, we were so miserable—I mean really, what was I thinking? I knew that he was in love with Georgia all along—everything was a mess. After our divorce, I was pissed at myself, so I took it out on him by depriving him of Alice. To make a longer story short, Georgia and Eugene are finally together. Alice is with them full time, I come and go as I please; it's the way it should have been from the beginning—had things been different," she shrugged.

"Yes, if only things could have been different—so much would have changed—for all of us. But things happen for reasons—like this—our meeting again—does it mean something?" I asked with an earnestness that begged for an explanation of the foreshadowing that I have detected throughout this day. She tipped her head to one side and her dark eyebrows crowded together in thought.

"Perhaps," she smiled, taking my hand and turning up my palm as if to peer at the life displayed there, her fingers traced over the creases and tapped the calluses.

"I don't believe in any Divine intervention or mystical bullshit—we do what we do just because we can." I leaned over and kissed her, but she pulled back and scowled at me.

"Guthrie—your journey is far from over, it does not end here."

"I know—but I'm tired," I sighed. I felt ashamed to admit it, but I am tired.

"You can find rest here, but only for tonight—you must get Sammy home to take care of the things that are waiting—Hayden is waiting for her."

"I'll see what happens tomorrow—Sammy might get me up with the Sullivan-Riley duo to hit the road—I never know for sure how she's going to react in a situation," I yawned. "Excuse me—it's not the company."

"You are exhausted, Guthrie—you poor thing," she said, caressing my hand.

"Yes, I am—I'm not as young as I used to be," I grunted, rising to my feet, feeling like an old man. I internally laughed at the notion that I had considered banging Millie out here—I don't have the energy to do it.

"Come along—I can find our way back in the dark," she said, standing up, and she held out her hand to me, but I didn't want to take her hand, I feared that if I did I was vulnerable enough to do something I'll regret later. "I have no intentions toward you," she smiled as if sensing my thoughts. "We had a nice thing once, but now we can be just friends."

"I do love her—I love her very much," I whispered. Then I sagged, my entire body suddenly felt limp, and I gasped for air, my throat threaded tight with stitches made of tears.

"Guthrie?" Millie asked with mild panic as I staggered into the chair and began to cry—actually sobbing, my heart ached. I don't understand why I fell apart, but I grieved in a way I needed to for the feelings that I've had; the weeks of focus on Sammy never allowed me to cut loose. Millie had this affect on me years ago. It was her calm presence that had encouraged me to open up about Lenore's death—I had wept like a baby back then, and she carefully put my pieces back together again, an evenhanded source of comfort.

"Does she know how you feel?" she asked after I became calm again.

"Millie, I don't know for sure what it is that I am feeling—I'm feeling too many things at once," I muttered. "There is one thing that I do know for sure—she is in love with Hayden and he is in love with her—I am not going to be the one to keep them apart because of my selfishness. I can't stay with her after I bring them together—I know that it's going to be hard on her when I leave—but if I stay, he won't follow through."

"Well, it's true—two roosters can't share the same hen house." She lightened my burden with a touch of humor, and I laughed in reply. "Listen to me—we all make mistakes, Guthrie—it's time to stop beating ourselves up about them. Do what you have to do to get them together." She spoke with such conviction I could not deny how right she was for saying it. I looked at her in the soft yellow light of the teahouse; her face looked flushed and her eyes were brilliant in an odd way. She suddenly laughed. "Oh, Guthrie—you must think I'm a fool—a woman my age carrying on like a teenager over you—it's kind of sweet—I'm in love with you—I was back then, but I didn't dare tell you," she declared, placing her clasped hands to her mouth as if in prayer. "I never believed that I'd ever see you again to tell you that I love you."

"Don't be silly—" I groaned, but I couldn't help feeling somewhat flattered. "You know who I really love—" I laughed. "You'd only be a surrogate—it wouldn't be fair to you."

"I would never expect you to forget Lenore, but someday the hurt will fade if you'd let it," she said, holding my hand.

"Does it say so in my palm?" I turned my hand over for her to inspect again.

"I wish I could give you a certain future—but I can't—your future is in your hands in a manner of speaking," she said, curling my fingers closed. "You must do whatever is set before you—put your heart and soul into it. You love Sammy—see to it that she is happy."

"I'll do that—if it is the last thing I do." With that said, I stood up to go.

"Ohhh, Guthrie, just hearing you say that made me feel like someone just walked on my grave—please, I think you need to be careful," she shuddered, rising to meet me.

We leaned in and clutched one another; while I kissed her, my body felt like it was on fire. We swayed with uncertainty, tempted as our lips and tongues twisted with passion; then we parted with a sigh and a moan.

"It's for the best that we do nothing—why start something we can't finish?" she said, backing off, but her hand fumbled for mine, and our fingers grasped on as if for dear life.

"Someone else said that to me once—or did I say that to someone? I forget—it was only a few months ago, but it feels like another lifetime."

"You have changed a lot, Guthrie Ryder, at the same time you haven't changed a bit—something has happened to you since we last met—can I come see you sometime?"

"Do whatever you want to do, Millie," I growled, feeling pissed at myself for wanting her. "I haven't changed that much—I've just had my balls rattled a bit by a few women since we last met; I'm a little more sensitive than I used to be," I chomped into my words with sarcasm.

"I think you're just horny and can't stand yourself," she teased.

"I'm afraid there's more to it than that—if I was just horny, I could get into bed with Sammy—but I won't do that—never again." I shook my hand free of hers and stepped away from the edge where I teetered.

"Then what is it, Guthrie?"

"I feel like a dying man making his last request," I muttered and then laughed, surprised by my words.

"You are a strange man," she laughed, but her smile faded. She came closer and peered up at me. "Do you believe that something bad is going to happen to you?"

"Either that or I'm just saying any old bullshit just to get you to lift your skirt for me," I laughed, rubbing my face that felt sticky with tearstains.

She didn't say another word—she lifted her skirt above her knees with one raised eyebrow arched with mischief. After that, we went at it, but *it* was without bliss. Trying to fuck in that tiny one room shed was ridiculous, we're both too old for such nonsense as we uttered more sounds like *"Ow"*, *"Shit"* and *"Hey, watch it"* instead of passionate responses. We knew we'd be kidding ourselves if we pretended that we actually enjoyed what we were doing to each other, but horny desperation inspires creativity, so we made the best of it. After the deed was done, we tried laughing it off and then became hideously self-conscious in that *what have I done* indignity, and adjusted our clothing as if to cover up the evidence of our folly.

"I'm sorry," I muttered, capturing her hand as we walked back to the house through the after midnight dew-covered grass.

"I'm sorry too—sort of kind of—not really," she replied with a laugh. "I wish there was something I could say to make this all right for you—for us—but I'm completely at a loss for words—which as you know is a rare occasion!" she exclaimed with amusing animation that always instilled in me a sense of fellowship with her—she understands me, and I always liked that about her.

"I've got some words for ya—what the fuck just happened?" I groaned.

"We had sex for the sake of having sex—just so we can walk away and not feel like we missed something. We've been on this path since you walked through the door at Katharine's shop because there's a comfortable history between us. We've been treading water for so long, you and I both needed to feel solid ground beneath our feet, but we still can't touch bottom together."

"So was it worth it?" I asked her.

"Yes—it was worth it—I mean, thank goodness we won't have any *what if* bullshit hanging over our heads when we part ways," she snickered. I laughed with her.

"What if—" I snorted. "Yeah, I guess you're right—I suppose I'd rather kick myself for being an idiot than not knowing for sure—thanks, Millie." I paused, fearing that I sounded too bitter. "Really, thanks—you've always been a good friend to me."

"Sure—thanks back at ya—I do mean to keep in touch with you—if that's all right."

"That's fine—you can do that."

"Alice thinks there is hope for us," she giggled. "I don't know what to think, but I don't think it would hurt us to explore the possibility of something, right?"

"Honey, I'd love you just because you're such an optimist even in the face of disaster," I laughed with her. "Goodnight, Millie."

"Goodnight, Guthrie—I'll see you in the morning—or at least before you leave, don't go without saying goodbye," she said, giving me a hug that was more inspired by weary consolation rather than another upsurge of passion. "It'll work out between them—don't worry, it's in their hands once you bring them back together—if they love each other, nature will take its course," she said, giving me a pat of reassurance on the shoulder as we entered the house. I only nodded, not wishing to voice my hopes or my fears—I just wanted it done.

∾

Sammy had to go to the barn at least twice to bid farewell to various critters; then after much pleading, a yellow and white tiger kitten became a passenger. I took the tiny tot in my large hands, held it up to my face, and scowled at it. *"Look you—yeah, you, kitten—stop being cute and listen up—I expect you to behave yourself—no whining and complaining, you got that? Don't make me have to pull over!"* The newly christened *Crouching*

Tigger-Hidden Pooh placed his wee white paws on my cheeks and licked my nose, purring his little kitty head off—how could I say no?

For the first fifty miles, I agonized over my indiscretion with Millie last night—it disturbed me that Sammy seemed to know. What she knew—or how she came to know about it, I don't know exactly because she didn't say, but she knew that we had been intimate in some manner. *Did she see me kissing Millie goodbye in the pantry? Cripe, I wanted to fuck her eyeballs out right there and then, but she wouldn't lift her skirt.* I finally broke down to explain myself using delicate terms to clarify what happened between us in the past, and left it at that—in the past where it should have remained. Sammy smiled as if with understanding, but said nothing. *"All right, I fooled around with her last night—is that what you want me to say?"* I confessed. She looked at me with those black button eyes, and then with a snicker, she rolled them heavenward and covered her ears. *"La-la-la-la-la-la-la!"* she giggled maniacally. I grunted and kept my attention focused on the road; apparently, my paranoia caused me to misread her normal mode of operation as smug secrecy.

I pushed *Delta Dawn* hard because I was sick of being in the car, and I could tell that Sammy was weary of it too. There is nothing more defining in a relationship between a man and a woman than spending every blessed minute together in a car for days, weeks, now months. In spite of everything, we did all right; I never once wanted to kill her, because I do love her. I didn't know if there was ever a time she wanted to eat me alive because she never said so—her silence might be a sign of gratitude for my not throwing her off that cliff in Utah.

We arrived at the house by twilight. In the indigo of the descending night, she saw that the lights were on in the carriage house next door. Before I could stop her, she ran across the backyard and ducked through the leafy bushes to let Hayden know that we were back. Moments later, I watched her return with him by the hand; his white shirt stood out in the darkness, his lower half obscured in denim; Sammy beside him, dressed in black, only her face and hands were visible. They hugged while speaking in low, excited tones and a sharp cry came from her. Trying not to gawk at their reunion, I turned my attention to unpacking the car. I parked the kitten in the cat carrier just inside the kitchen door; it mewed plaintively to be let out.

"Hush, you," I muttered hoarsely.

When I turned on the porch light, Sammy and Hayden's conjoined figures traversing the backyard became obscured from my view until they stepped into the illuminated half circle at the foot of the porch steps—the light split them apart. I hung back, watching them through the screen door; they gaped at one another in that weird silence that they share.

"Howdy, Hayden, how ya doin'?" I called out as I pushed through the screen door.

"Fine—and yourself?" he inquired with a somewhat breathless rasp to his voice.

"I've been better—it's been a long trip." I thought that he looked much improved since the last time we saw him in Taos; his scars have faded considerably, his hair has grown longer, and the cast had come off his arm. I had to admit that his face even looked a bit moony from a slight weight gain that filled in the crevices that had been so gaunt before—it seemed our initial worries about him coping alone were for nothing, he looked to be holding his own. Their bodies leaned toward each other with anxious affection, and she hugged him again; his arms seemed eager to hold her as he cradled her head under his chin. He couldn't look me in the eye as I stared him down, daring him to look at me. *Damn it man, don't be such a coward, look at me so you will know that I don't care what you do!* But I knew damn well that if he looked at me right now he'd see that it did matter to me. I came down the stairs and maneuvered around the human knot to open the trunk.

"Guthrie," Sammy murmured; something about the tone in her voice stopped me cold.

"What is it?" I asked with caution; she pried her body away from his once again, and she turned a troubled gaze toward me.

"Sylvester says that Preston was let out of jail today."

"Jeezus K. Ryst—you've got to be fuckin' kidding me!" I bellowed, shaking my clenched fists at the sky, and brought one down onto the trunk lid with a bang, punching a dent into the surface. It was all I could do not to scream my eyeballs out as my sanity wavered on a thread thin line. "Sammy, you better tell Jack that if I see a sliver of that fucker's shadow coming around the corner a mile away, I'll kill him." After that was said, I clenched my teeth to contain the rest of my rage.

23

Home

I am home. It feels so good to be home. I had missed the salty ocean bathing the air with its tactile moisture—the scent of home. I had missed the placid sky and the melancholy ocean; I had missed how the sandy beach feels like silk beneath my feet. I returned home with a renewed respect for the verdant landscape and the elegant grace of trees. The harsh desert Southwest in its alien beauty offered only a temporary fascination—I could not relate to it because it wasn't home. Now I am home where everything is familiar, here I can move through my life with certainty. Out there, I felt lost. Although it is sad that nothing will ever be as it was before I went away, I have no regrets. The experience changed my life forever. I have changed—I have grown. My homecoming was an adjustment period that had been complicated by the shock of Preston's release from jail. I got through the difficult first few days with the helpful patience of the two men who love me. *I am home.*

I am free. It took many more weeks than I could stand, but I answered all of the questions asked of me, and with the collaborating testimony of people who know me well, those who demanded the answers were satisfied with my autonomy, consequently dispelling Preston's allegations that I am incompetent because of my handicap. My testimony proved without a doubt that in spite of my handicap, I am able to make sound decisions pertaining to the maintenance of a happy and healthy life, and there is no one manipulating me. At last, my divorce is final. *I am free.*

During the conclusion of the divorce proceedings, Preston complained with vehement noises that my infidelity and the influence of my meddling family had sabotaged our marriage from the beginning. He went on-and-on in spite of Jill's sleeve-tugging advice to drop it—I think he just wanted to hear himself talk.

Judge Davis cleared his throat, and firmly took control of the situation. *"Mr. Ackerman, I am not here to compare sins. It is a sad event for me to preside over a divorce, especially when the circumstances have been so disagreeable that forgiveness cannot fix what is wrong in a relationship. I have been very lenient with you because of your personal difficulties with drug addiction and clinical depression, but none of that excuses you from poor judgment or violence. It is my opinion that you, sir, crossed an unforgivable line during your marriage to Ms. Ryder, and she simply wants to move on with her life. Therefore, it is my duty to grant her that wish—it is time for you to move on as well—I recommend that you heed your lawyer's advice, let it go."*

Before we finished, Jack asked to keep the restraining order in place for an indefinite period of time, but the motion was denied. The judge determined that since Preston's successful rehabilitation and counseling he is no longer seen as a threat to my safety. Jill then informed us that he has taken a new job in North Carolina, and will be leaving the area the next day.

When we parted ways inside of Judge Davis's chamber, Preston shook my hand with rehearsed amiability. *"I'm sorry,"* he said, and before I could form a reply, he dropped my hand and left the room. I watched as he passed by Guthrie in the hallway; he gave him a wide berth, and said nothing. Guthrie glared after him; although he said nothing, his expression was worth a thousand words—most of them not too good, but I knew he would offer hours of entertainment if he chose to rant after a few beers set loose his tongue.

Preston is finally gone, I'll never have to think about him again—but I do. Weeks later, I still have my worries—worries that translate into nightmares based on the awful memories of what he had done to me, and then I have to rationalize their significance during my waking hours, analyzing the puzzle of Preston Ackerman. It'll take time for me to shed the lingering after effects—time and patience. In the meantime, I follow through with my new life.

It is another fine morning; I turned my face toward the filtered sun shimmering through maple leaves. The weather throughout the summer and so far this fall has been classic; the necessary rain fell late at night, and the clouds burned off into a shifting mist with the sunrise.

My kitten, Tiggy-Pooh, has grown quickly; I should have had a cat a long time ago, the responsibility for another life is a therapy that I would have benefited from while growing up. His persistent chirping and cooing demands attention; he is my surrogate infant to practice secret fantasies of having a real baby someday, and he is more than willing to be babied. With his tendency toward getting into everything, Tiggy has created a sense of chaos in the house that keeps me on my toes. My *baby* is now stalking Daisy in the Rose of Sharon hedge; she hissed at him and darted away with her tail crooked in that sassy manner so typical of her—Sylvester says she's teasing him—Tiggy followed her, making her hiss some more. I rolled my eyes from them to Sylvester seated across from me.

"Good grief, Daisy, it's not like you've never seen him before—get over yourself!" Sylvester called to her. "I'm sorry she's such a bitch to your kitty," he laughed at his naughty girl as he admired the daring of my little boy.

"He doesn't seem to care how bad she treats him—I think she likes him, but pretends not to just so you will make a bigger fuss over her," I giggled, pleased with his laughter—Tiggy has been a source of entertainment that has made Sylvester more cheerful.

The two cats ran up the maple tree and peered around the trunk at one another. Their play became a stalemate until one twitched the fur on his back and then the other her tail; they both dropped to the ground, dove into the hedge, and then went careening crazily around the perimeter of my backyard and sprinting into the blue hydrangeas causing the blooms to tremble.

Sharing my morning coffee with Sylvester is a routine that I've kept from my old life; this quality time spent alone with my dear friend is more precious than ever. Looking at him—trying not to stare—I absorb him from across the table. He is seated in his usual chair, dabbling a brush in watercolors; he's working on a moonlit memory from Deer Isle, while I am doodling lines and shades of no consequence in my sketchbook. We're relaxed as we sit in our quiet; occasional sparks of anecdotes and observations that have always enriched our companionship break through the pervading silence. I am thankful that our rapport has not changed in spite of all that has happened since winter; he is a passive structure in my life, and I know his unspoken love remains unchanged—but it is subtly evident that things are different between us. There has always been a secretive caution we have maintained to cloak our past relationship from the view of others, but now it seems we're at an emotional impasse that has caused us to hide our feelings from each other. *Guthrie says we need time.*

It had been especially difficult for him to see Helena when she came home to testify at my competency hearing. She stayed with me at the house, sleeping in her old room, leaving Sylvester truly alone in the carriage house. I don't know if he harbored any hope for her to reconsider, but as I viewed his discomfort whenever they confronted each other, it was obvious that he still suffered over their failed relationship. Although she was sympathetic to the awkwardness between them, the tension in her posture radiated a barricade beyond her normal border of personal space that specifically refused him access during their exchanges of pleasantries, warning him not to get too close. I can no longer draw them on the same page. Once she left, we relaxed again.

Sylvester still comes for dinner every night, and when he takes his place at the table, he wears his loneliness like a skin, much like he always has—even while living with Helena, he was lonely. At the end of each evening, I watch him go home from the back door window; he traverses the yard toward the gap in the hedge with his head bowed as if contemplating the dew-wet grass, his shadow cast by the back porch light hurries ahead of him as if anxious to get home—to get away—escape.

Guthrie watches him too. *"He loves you Sammy—you two will know when the time is right,"* he said last night. His hand reached across the space between us to touch my shoulder and gave it a gentle squeeze. He tries not to touch me anymore—*he's afraid to touch me because of how he feels.*

How I feel about Guthrie has not changed—but a change took place long before our return home. I sleep alone in my childhood bed now, feeling very content as I slumber; I'm never lonely or cold. The funny thing is I never minded his snoring while we slept in the same bed—or in the same room, but now that he's far away in his room down the hall, I have listened to his steady rattle and hum, and I lie awake in awe of the intense racket.

I'm very worried about him. He goes out every night to drink at smoke-filled local bars—two weeks ago, he got into a fistfight with a mouthy asshole who made a short career of getting on his nerves—it was nothing personal, he was just irritating—so, Guthrie cleaned his clock. Although most of the people who were there would agree that the guy had it coming, Guthrie was told by the owner never to come back to his bar again—he was the newcomer, the obnoxious-wonder was a regular cast member. The next night, he had to find a new hangout.

There have been nights in which I've sat sleepless in the dark thinking about everything and trying to think of nothing. From my bedroom window, I can see Sylvester's lights shining beyond the flowering hedge long into the night. I have noticed that he has allowed the hedge to grow taller, so now I cannot see into his backyard to spy on him when he is stargazing. Looking at the hedge from inside his yard, I suddenly realized that he didn't allow the hedge to grow tall on purpose—he couldn't trim it this past season because of his injuries. A sense of relief came over me once I remembered that Carrie's brother, Rick, has been clipping the hedge, and he is a full head and shoulders taller than Sylvester, if not more—he's even taller than Guthrie. I let out a gasp of laughter, feeling stupid for being paranoid.

"What?" Sylvester asked, smiling at me—his eyes gleaming with amusement.

"Oh—" I gestured at the hedge just as the cats burst through again.

"Oh, them—the silly fiends," he sighed, shaking his head.

I laughed with a meek nod, feeling embarrassed that I had to tell a white lie to cover-up my thinking about him purposefully obstructing my view of his backyard—*he knows there was a time when I did watch for him.* Biting my lip against further outbursts, I immersed myself in doodling, all the while conscious of his gaze upon me; I savored the sensation, and allowed him to continue watching me uninterrupted by my acknowledgement of him. *Does he know that I have spent all summer long looking for him, longing to see the glint of his glasses in the moonlight, but I didn't see his signal of loneliness—did he ever stand out there waiting for me?*

"You know, Samantha, I think you are amazing—" Sylvester suddenly spoke.

Startled from my thoughts, I looked up from the tangle of lines on the page, and found his gaze bright, tinged with an anxious glow, he appeared surprised that he had spoken aloud.

"Amazing?" I asked, curious about his observation that has gone beyond the safe topics of cats, gardening, the weather, his progress on Whitley's catalogue that Helena had abandoned, and our artwork—his prolific Deer Isle series stand contrary to my lack of production.

"You—you are amazing—you're so, I don't know, grown up, umm—" he nervously shook the words out of his mouth, his brow knotted as his face thoughtfully screwed up with dissatisfaction with his choice of words. "I guess that isn't what I mean—you've grown, but not in the way that a child grows into an adult—you've *'become more'*—more than who you were before you left," he paused to contemplate his meaning, once again uncertain. A murky tension enhanced his expression; his content mouth that had been smiling before this conversation started, suddenly turned grim while he reflected upon the questions that are praying on his mind. "I see it in your self-reliance—your acceptance of change is less traumatic—you're more grounded. In Taos, you seemed adrift—" Just then, color raced into his face. Seeing his blush made me wonder if his thoughts echoed mine as I instantly clasped onto the memory of kissing him in the Taos sunshine. Suddenly, he turned his face away and held up the sketch to squint at it, I thought maybe he regretted speaking.

"I felt lost," I laughed, feeling giddy that he wanted to talk to me about that mysterious period I spent on the edge of a Utah cliff. Since coming home, I've been returning to and from the dream-like time that I spent in Utah, trying to hide it, always fearing that if Preston found out about it, he would use it against me to prove to the world that I am incompetent.

I'll never let it happen again.

"The trip disrupted my routines and forced me to do without my normal structure—I had to rely on Helena and Guthrie to guide me, and then just Guthrie. There was a stretch of time when I didn't know anything for sure—other than the map in my lap and the meaning of road signs—it was very difficult being so far from home. I missed you terribly."

Sylvester laid his painting down on the table again; he examined me with a grave expression. I almost expected him to hold me up by the shoulders and squint at me like he did his watercolor a moment ago.

"What happened to you out there, Samantha? Guthrie called it an *'episode'* or a *'painting-trance'*. I've known you to obsess over your work, but I have the sense that what happened to you was different—something deeper."

"Deeper, yes—lost and adrift—I think withdrawn is a better description—after all that is part of my being autistic, which I think we all forget that I suffer from this—this affliction. It was something deeper—it was terrible and wonderful at the same time," I sighed with a shrug. "I was so focused on trying to find a way to express myself—trying to connect what I saw with what I felt about it—my concentration grew narrow because I felt scattered otherwise. Oh, Sylvester, it was so big out there—it was too much—I made Guthrie build bigger canvases to encompass it all, but they were never big enough. I couldn't see it very well, no matter how crystal clear the beauty was—sometimes seeing it through the windshield was easier—making it small—a limited view. It just wasn't mine to paint—it was not in here," I said, placing my hand over my heart.

With a sigh, I cast my gaze at the barn beyond the hedge. Guthrie is in there working; during the last few weeks, we have heard his occasional banging on something or the whine of a power tool, but I have discovered that none of the noises are associated with the creation of sculpture, just the organization of space—what he calls *puttering*. But it seems part of his puttering involves a significant quantity of beer—when he isn't puttering, he's sleeping off the sour results of a hangover.

"I'm sorry that I put him through such an awful ordeal—it really hurt him." Saying this saddened me. "I don't know why Guthrie didn't try to stop me."

Sylvester started to speak, but he stopped, I knew he didn't want to say anything against our mutual friend. I have sensed the silent competition between the two men; their friendship is strained, but civil. For a moment, I became afraid that he wanted to ask me about my relationship with Guthrie. Sylvester's silent discontent resounds when the three of us are together; his gaze wavering, as if he fears observing any hint of our affection at the same time that he seeks it to confirm his worst judgment of us.

"It isn't his fault—nothing I did satisfied me—I kept hoping the next one would be better," I blurted out to stop the query that has lain between us like a trip wire.

"When I visited the Kramer Gallery to see the first crate of work, I was stunned by their size—they were glorious—it made me feel so happy thinking that you were finally free," he said with hope in his voice, and then he sighed with a heavy expiration. "I was sorry to hear how you rejected them—how they seemed to upset you."

"I was not free—I was bad," I hesitated over the term that I chose to describe my unacceptable behavior. "They were lovely, my technique was impeccable, but I might as well have been copying from a Thomas Moran or a Georgia O'Keeffe, you know? They were never truly mine, no matter how hard I tried; I'd lay down the paint on paper or canvas and none of it was mine—I painted like a trained parrot talks; it was ridiculous. Guthrie should have known better—he should have made me stop," I finished my thought, and then my mind shifted to an anxious desire to speak with Guthrie. When I stood up, my sudden movement startled Sylvester, his eyes widened.

"What's wrong?" he asked.

"I must go talk to Guthrie—I should collect Tiggy-the-Pooh—" I stammered.

"No—no, he's fine, I'll watch him—they're having too much fun," he insisted; his uneasy gaze flickered from my face to the rustling bushes, and then a smile disguised his disappointment that I have chosen to leave now without finishing my coffee.

"Are you sure?" I asked, not wanting to impose on him.

"Yes," he nodded; the two furry fiends raced by, Daisy pitching a fresh hissy-fit. "Ah, the sound of fur flying—I forgot how much fun it is to have two cats—they're as bad as squabbling children—giggling one minute, crying the next—don't worry, I can handle it." He smiled at me with genuine pleasure that fleetingly forgot the distress troubling him. We paused in our connected gaze, teetering on the edge of something unspoken, but he looked away first, examining his painting as if he needed to ponder his next brushstroke.

"Don't overwork the watercolor or it'll turn into mud," I said.

"You know me too well," he chuckled.

"I'll be back." I let my hand touch his shoulder, and felt him raise it against my palm, not to shrug it off, but to accept my hand being there—allowing my palm to mold itself around the shoulder shape—it felt like a brief kiss. The mending ligaments in his shoulder continue their slow recovery from their trauma; it still gives him trouble because of the deceptive sense that it feels better, so he often re-injures the connective tissues whenever he goes fishing with Guthrie.

Guthrie. As good for me as Guthrie was when I was a child learning to overcome my disability, he did everything all wrong during the weeks we spent on the road—I became completely dependent on him, entrusting myself in his hands because of the unfamiliar territory all around us. He doted on me, spoiling me as if I were a child he had neglected; his love became crippling instead of nurturing, causing me to regress toward a careless oblivion that had potential to be detrimental to my autonomy. *I can't blame him.*

When I reached the barn, I paused in the doorway to watch him *puttering*; an almost spent cigarette dangled from his mouth as he pondered what to do next. I rapped my knuckles on the door, and he turned to greet me, removed the cigarette, and smiled as he crushed it into the ashtray on the workbench; his unsteady hand disturbed a line of empty beer bottles, they tinkled with glassy shouts of surprise because of his haste.

"Hey there, Sammy—I didn't hear you come in," he laughed, and then started to cough into his closed fist. "Have another cigarette, Guthrie—don't mind if I do," he chuckled, as he shook out another one from the pack and lit up. He's teasing me because he knows I don't like that he is smoking so much—his cough is getting worse, and he refuses to go to the doctor.

"Guthrie—why did you let me go?" I asked in earnest, ignoring his wayward attitude.

"Let you go—what are you talking about? Help me out here—I need a point of reference to work with." He scowled around the cigarette smoke that hung like blue tendrils of mist in the air around him.

The sunlight coming through the windows was golden and full of sparkling motes. I always loved this about the barn, seeing the dust—Guthrie in the dust, Whitley in the dust, and Sammy in the dust—my pony in the dust. I remember seeing Pony for the first time, standing in a morning sunshower of dust motes—she was a dust mote factory, every time she shook her mane or swished her tail, she created a shower of sparks. I could get lost for hours playing with them; I used to hold my hands out to try to capture the tiny particles, swirling them in air currents produced by a wave of my hand. I waved my hand through them now, and smiled at the memories that they conducted. Then I let my hand drop, and I looked at Guthrie. He stood scowling at me, waiting for me to explain my cryptic question; he quickly knocked back what was left in his beer bottle, and set it down in line with the rest.

"At the Island in the Sky—you let me get away—you know, withdraw," I fumbled, finding it hard to concentrate on my need to talk to him about what had happened out there; I feared hurting him.

"What was I supposed to do, Sammy, take you over my knee and spank you to make you mind?" he laughed, cracking open another beer that he pulled from the cardboard case on the floor, blowing into the neck at the fine mist swirling below the lip, making a low whistling noise.

I had feared that he wouldn't take me seriously, and his attitude marked his short-tempered demeanor. Ever since Millie came to spend a weekend with us several weeks ago, he has acted peculiar. He completely rejected Millie's desire to connect with him; she told me just before she left that she didn't want to force him into a relationship he didn't want. I tried to explain his obstinate nature, to which she whole-heartedly agreed— *"Guthrie Ryder's mode of operation is obstinate, but he's a big ole softy— especially when it comes to you. He'll never admit it, but he's afraid that I will take him away from you."* I made her promise to come again some-day. Although she agreed that she would, she was vague about when she planned to come back, she was going to Europe for a while *"To get away from it all."*

"Don't be silly, I'm serious! A good talkin' to would have done me some good—you shouldn't have let me go on for days like that, let alone two weeks. Oh, Guthrie—it's as if you wanted me to be dependent on you just like when I was little," I gasped, mortified that I said it out loud; the implied accusation had the potential to be explosive.

"Okay, I'm sorry—I fucked-up," he grumbled with exasperation.

"I am so grateful to you—you know that, don't you? I am grateful that you brought me home safely—"

"At least I did something right," he growled.

"But while we visited the farm, you fell to pieces because you are stuck in the past. You chased after Millie like you hoped to find something with her to replace me—like you had tried to replace Lenore with me."

"It wasn't like that, Sammy—" he sighed with a warning edge to his tone. "I'm sorry—I guess I—oh, fuck it—what can I say? I—" He chewed on his mustache in that way he does when he feels backed into a corner. "I never meant to hurt you—I tried—but I failed—I'm still failing you." He looked at me with abject fierceness, and I flinched from his wretched glare. "My being here is—"

"No, no, no—" I cried. I didn't want him to say anything about Sylvester; he keeps threatening to leave because of him. *We need time weneedtimeweneed—time.*

"I should leave. It seems like I am poison to you! The closer I came to you, you got worse—then when I pulled back, it was like I dropped you— ah, Buttons—I'm sorry," he groaned, he dropped his cigarette on the floor, stomped it out, and rubbed his face with his hand, briefly covering his eyes to hide the evidence of his pent-up emotions.

"I love you, Guthrie." I clasped one of his big hands inside of mine, and kissed the rough knuckles dinged with cuts and abrasions. "I wish there was something I could do to make you happier—Millie's afraid that you're about to self-destruct because of the way things are."

"I already have—at least, I did at the farm—she was there," he said softly, looking at our clasped hands. "I'm putting the pieces back together, but not very well," he sighed.

"We need time."

"I've been thinkin' it's time for me to head back to Cleveland—"

"Oh, Guthrie—must you go?"

"For a little while—"

"But you just started to work in your studio—I want you here." I fought back the tears that prickled in my eyes, and held his hand against my cheek.

"Sam—I haven't started anything, I'm just setting up for someday when I do—" he said, caressing the walnut panel he had brought home for the purpose of carving a relief he had in mind, and then his hand hesitantly pet my hair. "I should go back to sell Margie's house—I'll come back," he smiled. "I should go—especially since my presence here isn't encouraging Hayden to follow his heart through the hedge—I know if it were me, it would be killing me—it does kill me."

"Guthrie—don't say that," I whispered.

"It's true—believe me—it'll be for the best that I go."

I contemplated his figure in the sunlit dust motes. "Oh, Guthrie—I hate to have you leave us!" I cried, flinging myself against his body, hugging him. I could feel his heart pounding from the stress of our conversation; when he reluctantly enclosed his arms around me, I clutched him tighter.

"Sammy—Sammy—don't make this hard for me—I love you—but you are not, Lenore," he choked on his final words as I sobbed. "There now, don't cry, I won't leave right away—I need a few more days before I can even think about getting into a car again," he laughed in an effort to make a joke. "Shouldn't you be in the studio now? I made all those canvases for you—I thought for sure you would have covered every last square inch by now," he teased as he stepped away from my embrace; he bent down to fetch the cigarette butt from the floor and stomped on the dusty burn mark it made on the floorboard.

"I will—thank you for doing all of those canvases for me—thank you for everything," I said. My hand caressed the length of his arm—sinewy muscle with veins and coarse dark hair mixed with gray; my fingers tugged on his fingertips, but they failed to respond.

"You talk like I'm a soldier going off to war—I'm right here—I'm not going anywhere yet," he laughed with a wry smile.

"I know—but you seem—you seem so tragic—I hate thinking that I have caused this."

"No—I caused this—you have only brought me joy—there is no tragedy here."

"Our love was never wrong," I murmured, leaning against his chest, but he didn't hold me, his arms were no longer willing to offer comfort.

"I know—but the love of your life is sitting over there being terrorized by your kitten—and I bet you didn't even finish your coffee before you came running over here to harass me."

"Why do you avoid your feelings?" I fought back the tears painfully hooked in my eyes.

"It's what I do," he shrugged.

"Don't be afraid to love me—I will always love you."

"I will love you until the day I die—"

"Now you're talking like a soldier going off to war," I sighed, stepping back.

"A personal war, my love—it's just a personal war. Go to your studio, go paint—or doodle—it's getting past your time," he prodded.

I held his face in my hands and kissed him on the mouth. The moan that passed from him into my mouth reminded me of my wedding day when I had kissed Sylvester; he had moaned in the same way—as if I tortured him. I felt bad—I shouldn't have done it. As I pressed my fingers to his lips, I understood why he had to leave, and why Sylvester hasn't moved from the refuge of the carriage house in answer to my flirtation. I backed away from him; the sunshine through the barn windows caught the translucence of his deep-set eyes, the black fringe of lashes softened them with shadows. I whispered *I love you*; without replying, his steady gaze broke away and darted toward the window. I left him surrounded in a halo of dust motes.

❧

When I passed through the hedge again, I was happy to find Sylvester still seated at the table contemplating his painting, and I felt compelled to hug him. As I pulled him tight against my torso, I playfully kissed him where his hair is thinning in the eye of a hurricane from which it swirled; he made a mortified noise that echoed his unspoken annoyance with the aging process.

"My hair hasn't come back in that area since they shaved my head," he protested with a laugh as his hand covered the offensive spot that I have found intriguing.

"Oh, Sylvester, you've been thinning there a little at a time for years," I giggled as I playfully pulled aside his bashful hand to kiss him there again. "No matter, I still love you," I whispered, running my fingers through his shaggy hair before setting him free. He said nothing in reply; he only looked at me with a pensive expression while I collected my sketchbook.

After I coaxed Tiggy to come out of the Rose of Sharon bushes, I demurely bid Sylvester goodbye and went home, feeling his gaze on my back as I crossed through the worn gap in the hedge, I didn't dare peek into his private contemplation of my retreating posterior. I have once again flirted and run away, but what is stopping him from following me? He should catch me, stop me, he should say something like—*"What do you mean?"* Or even more directly, *"Do you really love me?"* My face radiated shame; I shouldn't tease him—it is unkind.

It is evident that Guthrie's intuition is right; our recent history as lovers and his continued presence in my house is a barrier that Sylvester will not cross—and the kiss in the barn only attests to the fact that I am still emotionally attached to Guthrie in a way that will always be a temptation to arouse suspicion.

Tiggy began to struggle in my arms on the porch, and as I manhandled him through the back door, I entered the house with an overwhelming angst that distressed me into a storm of emotion. As I leaned against the kitchen door sobbing, I hugged and kissed Tiggy's warm fur, and he licked at my salty tears with interest, purring as if to offer comfort; his sweetness eventually turned my tears away. As soon as I put him down, he trotted off to do kitten stuff; I blew my nose and wiped my eyes. *We need time.*

Time. It is time for me to go upstairs—time to begin work. Although I haven't painted anything, I've gone faithfully into the garret every day from nine to noon, and again from two to six; it is a different structure not having commissions clamoring for attention, and just like Guthrie, I go there to *putter*.

The studio seems so barren with the stacks of blank canvases primed and ready for me to begin my new life. But I feel snowed under by their whiteness; the only accomplishments so far are composed on the safe pages of my sketchbooks; within minutes of sitting down, I filled the last six pages of the most recent one with my prolific abstract inspirations, and I moved to find another in the flat file. While browsing, my fingers touched the spiral spine of a particular sketchbook that I have hidden from everyone—I have started to draw self-portraits. Lifting it out of its place in the drawer, I turned through the full pages; I have never examined myself before—always someone else—it is as if I am finally looking me in the eye and learning who I am—accepting who I am.

Since I was very young, everyone told me how much I look like Lenore—in a way I do—for as long as I remember it's been a thing for me to live up to—looking like Lenore, being like Lenore. Guthrie had put me on her pedestal in his heart—he still looks at me and sees Lenore. She is something I could never be. From these sketches, I see that I have a little bit of Whitley around my eyes and my mouth, but more importantly, I see me—just me. I am finally seeing what Sylvester sees because he never knew Lenore—never saw her—*never fell in love with her.*

I laid the sketchbook back in the drawer and slid it closed with a sigh. *Yes, time—we all need time—we'll know when the time is right.*

Sitting down in my chair in front of the easel, I took a deep breath and relaxed just like Jonathan had told me to do, clearing my mind of all that I've done before, letting go of the mimicry of styles. Jonathan had said that whatever self-expression I'm looking for is contained within my doodles. Without a concept to guide me, I took up a handful of my favorite brushes, filled the pallet with my favorite colors, and quickly covered the first pristine canvas with a rich patina of earthy green. Woven within modulations of the hue I found Guthrie, his deep-set eyes hooded by his stern brow, and his frowning mustache prominent in disguising his true feelings; my brush blended his features with marmoreal structures isolating his image—iconic, he stands alone, antediluvian in simplicity, a pillar in stature—grand and terrifying—mythical and godlike. With a sigh, my finger smoothed a rough patch on his cheek, the caress loving—longing.

Satisfied with this canvas, I put it aside, and picked up a second one; Sylvester rose to the surface of my heart, and he came into being within in a patch of pale blue comprised of ocean and sky. I paused and stepped back; I feared that I had made his image look too vulnerable in the gauzy surface—but that is how I perceived him, because he is still healing—and I want to nurture him, to love him—all I want to do is love him for the rest of my life. The brush caressed the canvas around the image of my beloved, creating an enclosure as if to protect him—to heal him; a yellow light caused tendrils of green to unfurl into the blue, weaving together into a hedge. I then made a large Rose of Sharon bloom, white with a deep magenta center. The maple tree's gnarled trunk and twisted branches spiraled upward to cradle the gabled roof of the house, and the twig fingers pointed to the night sky littered with stars and a fine crescent moon. I chose to paint the dark half a deep crimson, and as my brush swept over the suggested roundness, it created a fetal shaped blot that stopped my hand; I stared at it with awe—*Time—wait for the right time—it will come, we will know, we will know the right time.*

These last few weeks I have decided to forego Beethoven's influence to take in the sounds of home for inspiration. As I dabbled at this emotional oil on canvas sketch, I absorbed the ocean's soft sigh, the high-pitched cry of a seagull, and the guttural voice of a power tool from the barn where Guthrie has perhaps decided to carve a relief on the walnut panel after all. Below these familiar sounds, I detected the motion of a car crunching into the driveway, and I set aside my handful of loaded brushes to listen. *Who is here?* I recognized the sound of the engine. As if paralyzed with fear, I didn't dare go look, I remained in my chair and waited, listening, but the new intercom box on the wall didn't come alive with the request for admittance. I remembered with unease that the door at the bottom of the garret stairs is unlocked. When I heard the hall door open, I stood up and moved to stand behind the studio door while listening to the distinct footsteps on the stairs, my gaze watched the mirror across the room waiting to see who it is, but I already knew. *Oh, no, please no.*

"Samantha—yoooo hoooo, Samantha—your Mommy's calling you— she's waiting for you to come join her, Samantha, where are youuuuu?" Preston appeared at the top of the stairs bearing with him my nightmares. *He's got a gun.* "Well, there you are—Sammy in the looking glass—I never told you that I worked for Noah that summer—I know you saw me there— you came with *her* a couple of times—you never looked at me. I thought you were blind, but *she* said you saw everything—" *It's the revolver that Whitley kept in the nightstand by Lenore's bed.* "Noah was fucked-up in the head, you know?" *He had bought the gun a long time ago.* "Yes, I was there—I knew *her*—I was absolutely daffy about *her*—just like he was— my Uncle Noah. I sampled the little treat tied to the bed upstairs—oh, you know I just had to have me some of that—"*He told me never to touch it.* "Whenever Noah went out—I would go upstairs to fuck her—I helped myself to his pretty prize—he was so pissed when he caught me fucking her."

Whitley showed it to me so I knew where he kept it. "But the funny thing is, he blamed her for it—called her a cock-tease—" "*It's just a deterrent should anyone break in—it looks impressive enough to give anyone second thoughts about fucking with me—*" "—so he killed her." "*I don't know if it works, I only have six bullets for it in my dresser if I ever wanted to find out!*" "I saw him do it to her—" *Preston was always fooling around with it—scaring me. I never told him about the bullets.* "Man, he was fucked-up—I ran away fast—I got on the train and went back home to Boston—I never went back." *If anything were to happen, he instructed me to run away—use the fire escape.* "The cops questioned me, you know—I told them I knew nothing—I said I had quit my job because he was a weirdo—because he was fucked-up in the head—"

I quickly closed and locked the door between us.

"You're a bitch just like she was!" Preston shouted. Two gunshots splintered the door; one bullet hit the wall to my left and the other the window on my right, shattering the glass.

I released the fire escape ladder, and watched as it unfolded toward the ground like liquid silver; in a practiced move, I climbed through the open window overlooking the backyard. During all of the fire-drills of my childhood, I never minded dangling over the edge because it was easy-peasy, but today the reality of the situation caused me to freeze in the midst of my descent, the ladder kept swinging every time I moved—I nearly put my foot through my bedroom window. I cringed in place; I could hear Preston inside shouting, and then there was a loud crash. I screamed for Guthrie, but he didn't come—only the sound of a power tool squealing through wood answered. Then I screamed for Sylvester, and kept screaming until both Guthrie and Sylvester emerged from the barn in answer to my summons; their postures expressed their shock, and they both ran toward the house. Sylvester, being faster, reached me first, steadying the ladder to help me get down, but a shot from above brushed me off my perch, and it seemed as if Sylvester plucked me out of the air, softening the blow of my fall. As we tumbled together onto the grass, he forced us to roll toward the house. Guthrie arrived beside us gasping for air.

"Oh, fuck—he's got a gun," he growled. "That asshole shot at you—you've been hit!"

"Shit—" Sylvester sat up and plucked at my right arm just below the elbow; I gaped at it, too shocked to believe that it was actually my arm—my blood. Sylvester took off his painting shirt and tore at the ragged cotton sleeve to wrap my arm. I watched his face bent over his task; his brow shimmered with beads of sweat, his concentration toned with a flush of color that expressed his anguish over my wound.

"Listen, you're going to be all right, I think the bullet only grazed you." Although his tone was gentle, he met my gaze with a serious expression that tried to soothe, but its intensity frightened me instead.

"He was there when Mommy died—he was there, he saw her—he saw Noah kill her—Noah killed her because of what Preston did to her—Noah blamed her, so he killed her," I said after finding my voice. Guthrie and Sylvester stared at me as if shocked that I had spoken.

"What the fuck?" Guthrie asked, he held my head in his hands, his face nearly pressed against mine. "Oh-my-god, Sammy—what are you saying?"

"He worked for Noah at the gallery that summer—he found her upstairs where Noah kept her—Noah caught him doing bad things to her, and it made him mad, so he killed her because of Preston, because he said it was her fault," I sobbed.

Guthrie cursed vividly as his face glared with anger. "Get her out of here, Hayden!" he shouted as he scrambled to his feet and ran to the back door. I screamed for him to come back, but he didn't even look over his shoulder to acknowledge that he heard me.

"Come with me, Samantha—we'll go call for help," Sylvester said, taking me by the hand, he dragged me to my feet. As we crouched close to the side of the house, I saw that the Rose-of Sharon was in full bloom and beautiful.

❧

They're safe! I had last minute visions of them making a break for it across the backyard to their regular egress through the hedge and being gunned down in the process. It was almost comical to see Hayden shove her head-first through the nearest gap in the tight mesh of the hedge and then dive in after her; the rending of garments was very audible through the screen door. Suppressing the impulse to heave a sigh of relief, I listened to the quiet house. Not a sound.

For the moment, I sagged onto the kitchen counter and heaved a great sob for Lenore. When she first disappeared, Whitley and I had stopped at the Bearskin Neck gallery looking for her. There was a kid there, one of those nondescript Boston pretty boys with a summer job; he had an attitude problem when he went off in a huff to fetch Noah from the upstairs apartment. When Noah came down—he seemed normal, genuinely concerned. Considering his history with her, I should have insisted that we go upstairs to look around—but we didn't suspect him—he seemed all right. After they arrested him, Noah talked nonsense, the crazy fucker kept saying, *"She was mine—he didn't have any right to her."* We wrongly assumed that the *he* was Whitley because he had *stolen* her from him, as if Lenore had been a piece of property. They questioned the kid because the cops found his fingerprints in the apartment, but there was no evidence that he was involved. I had wondered if the kid knew about what his boss had tucked away upstairs, but he said he didn't know anything. What kind of sick fucker would find a missing woman tied to a bed, and not do something to help her? No, he contributed to her misery—her humiliation—what he did caused Noah to kill her. "I will make him pay, Lenore," I sighed, wiping my eyes.

So where is he? I really needed to know. I crept through the entire downstairs, until I felt satisfied that he was not lurking around; the planks under my feet made enough noise to wake the dead, and he isn't a lightweight either—he always tromped around the house like a pachyderm ballet dancing in the jungle so I was pretty sure he wasn't down here avoiding me. I contemplated the stairway, my hand caressing the rustic wooden beams barbed with potential slivers. Taking a deep breath, I ducked my head through the low, narrow entrance, and began to make the ascension, carefully placing my weight on each step, but the old wood cut loose farts of protest announcing my intentions; so if Preston still lingered upstairs, he already knew by now that I'm coming. I began to doubt that he was still in the house, and feared that he was next door already menacing Sammy and Hayden while I wasted time sneaking around inside an empty house—*that would be my kind of luck.*

The garret door stood open in the hallway; I put my foot on the bottom step and hesitated—*Sammy thought she was safe enough to leave it unlocked*—growling with seething anger, I felt bolder. "Yo, dick stain, are you up there?" I hollered through the narrow gap. No answer. *Merry fuckin' next Christmas—I'll knock him into the year after next when I find him!* A loud bang snuck up from behind me, its force smacked me in the back and knocked the breath out of me, and then a hard object popped out of my chest, and thunked into the stairs. "Son-of-a-fuck!" I exclaimed upon realizing that I've been shot in the back and the bullet went straight through my body—*I stand corrected, this is my kind of luck.* I slumped forward, pitching face first onto the unforgiving planks of the stairs, and then slipped back into the hallway. *Funny—what did I expect by coming in here to confront a psychopath with a gun?* Apparently, Preston thought it was funny because he was laughing—laughing real hard as if I had just told him the funniest joke he ever heard. I raised my head to take a good look at him gloating.

"Yeah, laugh it up, shithead," I taunted and laughed with him as I raised myself up onto my elbows; I gasped for air—*I can't get enough air.*

"I got you—I got you good, why are you still alive!" He stopped laughing and backed off as if in fear; he took aim and shot me again, this time drilling me in the head, knocking me flat. But the lights didn't go out yet, although I kept my eyes closed, I was aware; it amazed me that I could even think at a time like this. I began to doubt that the bullet hit me as I took a swipe at my brow where it felt like I had just been stung by a very large pissed-off bee above my right eye, and my hand came back warm and sticky with blood. I opened my eyes, but Preston was gone; I had hoped he would hang around to make sure I was dead—I had also hoped he would empty the gun into me instead of saving bullets for Sammy—or Hayden—God knows what he'll do to Sammy without the gun. I lay feeling helpless, struggling to catch my breath. I looked up through the gap in the garret floor at the peaked ceiling, the roughhewn beams, and old planks. I half expected to see Whitley looking down at me like he had dozens of times, beckoning for me to come up—*why not now since he's dead and I'm gonna die—is he waiting for me to join him on the other side? Nah, he wouldn't be hanging around.*

"Sammy?" I called, feeling confused. I struggled to sit up; my left side felt sluggish as I lurched to my feet. I'm not ready to die, not until I know she's safe.

❧

I screamed when I saw Preston running toward the carriage house; Sylvester grabbed my hands to stop their flailing, and pulled me away from the window.

"Samantha, shhhh-shhh, listen to me, everything is going to be all right, the police are on their way—I want you to hide in here," Sylvester said as he coaxed me into the coat closet under the stairs. "I'm locking the door—you're going to be safe—just be quiet, don't cry."

"What about you?"

"I'll be all right, I promise—this will be over soon," he faintly smiled and then closed the door between us locking me into darkness.

Clamping my hands over my mouth to force myself to be quiet, I hunkered down, deep into the corner next to his tall garden wellies and stared at the thin sliver of light coming through the bottom edge of the door; shadows of footsteps slipped in and out of the crack. I wanted to scream. I listened to the muffled growling voices of the two men as they confronted one another nearby.

"*Tell me where she is, Hayden, you fuck—why didn't I kill you the last time? I wasted two fucking bullets on that asshole, Guthrie—I should have saved one for you!*" Preston raged.

"*You are not going to hurt her anymore!*" Sylvester replied with unyielding courage as something crashed against the closet door.

Struggling to remain calm, I folded into a silent scream as fear and grief became trapped with me inside the claustrophobic darkness; the sliver of light a flickering beacon of hope—*Sylvester promised everything was going to be all right, it's going to be over soon.*

"*Look out, Hayden!*" Guthrie's voice shouted.

It was such a relief to hear his voice, I let out a cry with an effort that could have been joy, but pure terror inspired the sound that emerged from my gullet. Whimpering, I pressed my ear against the door; the wood absorbed the crash-bang noises of struggle. A gunshot rang out with finality, and then an unsettled calm filled with low murmurings and coughing followed.

Sitting quietly in the darkness, I watched the shadows flitting through the shaft of light on the floor, and I listened to the sudden bursts of some-one's quick motions moving back and forth, then stillness accompanied by renewed low murmurings. I waited. Fresh motion flickered as steps approached the closet door, a muffled gasp as the doorknob jiggled with curiosity.

"Shit," Sylvester groaned. "Samantha—it's only me—are you all right?"

"Yes, are you all right?" I cried with relief, sitting up, my hand searching for the doorknob, I gripped the cool brass surface turning it, but the door did not open.

"Fine—I'm fine. Please forgive me, dear heart, I can't find the key to open the door—I misplaced it somehow—as soon as the police get here, they will have to help me get you out," he said—then he laughed; it was a strained sound, close to a sob.

"Where's Preston?"

"He's dead—" he said the words without emotion. Then I heard flesh and fabric lean against the door and slide down the wooden surface.

"Where is Guthrie? I heard him warn you—is he all right?" I asked.

"He's here, but—oh, Samantha," he stopped, and said nothing more.

"I want out, Sylvester!" I cried. My inept fingers scratched at the dark-ness, seeking escape; I wanted to claw my way through the door—to com-fort Sylvester—to see Guthrie.

"Samantha—no, don't—please don't be afraid—don't cry—you're safe, Guthrie and I are with you," Sylvester's voice tried to soothe me through the wooden barrier between us.

"Please tell me he's all right!" I cried.

"It's okay, Sammy, don't be afraid," Guthrie called out. Although I heard his distinct voice, he didn't sound right; he seemed far away even though I knew that he was nearby. I envisioned him wounded, lying in a pool of blood—dying. *Preston said he shot him twice.*

I waited—sirens came, voices shouted, and then Sylvester's voice led them to where I sat hidden away. When I finally got out, Sylvester greeted me with news that Guthrie was already en route to the hospital. Preston lay covered by a sheet where he fell in the entry into the living room; there was a lot of blood everywhere—even on Sylvester, but he was uninjured—he said he tried to stop Guthrie's bleeding with dishtowels.

Sylvester came with me to the hospital so I could have my arm taken care of; the wound was just like a nasty burn, it stung mostly, and then throbbed. I barely paid attention to what they did to it as I fixed my gaze on Sylvester; I noticed his glasses had splatters of dried blood on them, and there was a faint smear on his forehead. His blue-gray eyes remained focused on me with an unreadable intensity that held my gaze; he didn't look away. As soon as the doctor finished taking care of me, we went to see about Guthrie's condition.

The long day became a long night, the attending physician said, *"It's just a matter of time, there's nothing more we can do for him."* Although Guthrie initially survived the gunshot wounds, and the operations to fix his collapsed lung and to remove the bullet in his head were successful, his condition deteriorated as uncontrollable intracranial pressure destroyed his awareness, and slowly shut down his body. I sat by his bed holding his hand while Sylvester remained beside me like a steadfast guardian through the night, and into the next morning. Neither of us slept.

Guthrie looked so tired; the emotional months we spent on the road had worn him out, but even if he had been stronger, it wouldn't have helped him recover. He lay immobile underneath the white sheet, his body much like a fallen tree; he was silent except for his breathing assisted by a machine. When I spoke to him, he blinked his clear blue eyes to acknowledge that he understood me—at least I wanted to believe that he understood me before he closed his eyes for the last time. He had protected me with his life just as he had promised to do when we set out on our journey. Although he had promised to love me until the day he died, I don't believe he will ever stop.

24

The End

I came back to Gloucester to tend to my grieving sister as she draped herself in black for Guthrie's funeral. She insisted on having the wake and funeral service held at home in the front parlor like we had done for Lenore and Whitley. Even with the closed casket, it still creeped me out having him lying there for two days while she held a private overnight vigil, but it seemed to please her as she piled plump feather pillows and a soft flannel blanket on the sofa.

I stayed with her for a little bit just to keep her company. While I read a book, her pencils busily scratched away in the sketchbook cradled on her lap. I peered over from time to time, taking note as the velvety blacks and delicate grays spilled across the white paper; her pencil marks fluid depictions of random motion—waves and swirls. I asked her what she was making—*"The ocean,"* she said; according to her, the more gritty marks made with the side of the pencil point were sand. If it were the ocean, it looked to me like a microscopic section of it—chances are it is something she saw in the waves, I've seen her on numerous occasions hunkered down on her haunches, practically sticking her nose in the water while it swirled around her feet.

Eventually, I left her alone and went to bed, feeling satisfied that in spite of everything, she seemed all right, always more resilient than people give her credit.

Sy had chosen not to partake in the overnight vigil after the last of our callers departed (which was good old Hank Pinkerton.) When he bid us good-night, he briefly hugged Sammy and planted a chaste peck on her cheek, but she hugged him a little harder and a little longer than his comfort could stand. No sooner had I left the room to give them privacy, I heard the back door click shut, he left. Sammy's very worried about him, and so am I.

Ever since *"it happened"*, he has become very strange. When he wasn't here doing his bit to help prepare for the funeral yesterday afternoon, he cloistered himself in the carriage house. I know it's how he deals with grief, but he's doing it almost too quietly. Thank god, he's not the type to go off his nut howling and beating his chest, but there is a grimness emanating from him that is disturbing. It seems he is having a hard time washing the blood from his mental hands—he told me that he feels responsible for what happened, which I can't figure out why he blames himself. He never touched the gun, nor did he touch Preston. Guthrie killed Preston, there was no doubt about that at all. The trail of blood had shown a single-minded determination as Guthrie ignored his grievous wounds, and dragged himself from the second floor of the house where Preston had left him for dead. He simply walked into the carriage house, plucked the gun from Preston's hand after a brief struggle, forced the barrel into Preston's mouth, and pulled the trigger. Sy told me that he thought no one would believe his account of what had happened, but the evidence speaks the truth, and justice decided to let the dead bury the dead. When the police arrived, he was covered in blood—blood from both men, his hands were stained by his vain attempts to stop Guthrie's bleeding with wads of dishtowels. He told me that Guthrie had waved him off, held a towel to his bleeding head, and went outside to smoke a cigarette to wait for the cops to arrive. *"He just didn't seem fazed by it at all, he kept saying, 'I'm fine'. He would not sit or lie down; the doctor told us it was adrenaline that kept him going."*

That crazy fight-or-flight shit—go figure.

I wish that I could tell Sy something to make him feel better; admittedly, I've never been very good with things like this—dealing with his depressions or his passions. I felt bad that he must have been miserable throughout our years together because of my inept abilities, but he denied his discomfort out of loyalty—or blind faith. All the wrong reasons had kept us together, and it's for all the wrong reasons that he has stayed away from Sammy since Guthrie's death. Her quiet distress this morning when he failed to meet her for coffee pissed me off—the jerk wouldn't answer the door. So I stepped through the gap in the hedge to set him straight, but apparently, he had come out from hiding because he sat at his computer; judging by the reflection on his glasses he was flipping through some mutated game of solitaire; I listened to him curse the foul game that frustrated him.

"So what's the object of this game—driving yourself crazy?" I asked when he finally noticed me at the screen door.

"I suppose—I don't usually have so much trouble with it," he groused in such a un-Sy-like manner that I found very queer, and realized that he felt embarrassed that I saw him like this. He was only wearing a t-shirt and boxers with his robe untied, the belt dangled at the sides; he looked as if he had just rolled out of bed—or worse, had not gone to bed at all because his eyes appeared burned and bleary, and he was unshaven. I've never seen him so disheveled at this time of day unless he's down with the flu; even during his darkest depressions, his sense of decency would never have allowed anyone to see him like this—he would have at least put on some sweatpants.

Without a direct invitation, I let myself in and glanced around at his desk, inspecting his breakfast with hungry curiosity.

"Mmmmilk and cookies—good deal, the breakfast of champions," I laughed, snagging a cookie and dunking it into his mug of milk. He glared at me and then smirked, but he didn't reply to my teasing accusation about his diet—he used to be so fastidious about eating properly; I'm also guessing that he hasn't gone for his morning run either. "Have you been smoking?" I sniffed the air, pretending not to notice the overflowing ashtray next to the mouse pad.

"I do now and then—you know that," he grumbled. "What do you want, Lena?" he asked with impatience, he clicked the mouse to restart the game; it seems as if he fully intends to keep playing this hand he's been dealt until he wins it—sometimes he's so obsessive its stupid.

"I want to bug you, for old time's sake," I teased.

"Oh, how kind of you," he grimaced. "Thanks for the sentimental thought, but don't you have pots to throw in New Mexico?"

"Are you trying to get rid of me?" I laughed, pretending he didn't hurt me with that comment; it did sting, but only a little—*my-oh-my, he wants to pick a fight!*

"Now why would I want to do that?" he sulked.

"All right—what the fuck, Sy—" I cried with exasperation. He's never been this difficult before—it is so out of character, now I'm worried.

"What the fuck what?" he grunted; yet another uncharacteristic noise—*has he lost it?*

"Sammy—she's grieving—so, where are you?" I prodded.

"I'm—I'm grieving too—he was my friend," he muttered. "Just in case you forgot, I had a front row seat watching him die—it's easy for you to come all the way out here to judge how I should feel and what I should be doing."

"That's not it—you're afraid to see her, why?" I stepped around to the other side of his desk to peer over the computer monitor at him.

"I'm not afraid," he protested, staggering out of the chair as if disgusted by my presence, and he self-consciously closed his robe.

"You are! I know how you are—you're moping around here being all pathetic and stupid. You're dying to go over there to do whatever you want with her, but you're all bent out of shape because she had an affair with Guthrie, and it's eating you up inside—that affair was over with—it was over before you got to Taos, he told me it was over!" The words bumbled out of my mouth in a mish-mash of whatever I could spit out to jolt him out of his funk.

"Helena—you're being irrationally weird—please go, and leave me alone," he sputtered, stalking off to the bathroom; but he didn't slam the door—he never slammed doors even when he was furious. The shower came on, so I settled at his desk for the duration of the siege. While I waited for him, I tried to figure out this fucked-up solitaire he's been playing and immediately started to curse the vile game for what it is. And I ate all of his cookies.

"Trick or treat smell my feet this is bullshit—" I slammed the mouse with irritation, and looked up when the bathroom door flew open and he glared out at me.

"You're still here?" he asked.

"I'm not done with you," I replied, scowling at him in return. The game put me in the mood to get mean; I wasn't going to take any shit from him until I made him roll over in submission.

"Cripe almighty, what now?" he groaned as if he were in pain; he turned his back on me, lit a cigarette and puffed a thick cloud of smoke around his head. This is an all too familiar scene from our past, his smoke screen while I nag him—*it's no wonder he didn't go ballistic and splatter my brains on the wall, how did he put up with me all those years? He loved you, numb-ass-dumb-skull, that's why*—or at least, he wanted to believe that he did. He would practically turn himself inside out to make me happy—as if making up for what he didn't feel because he really loved Sammy.

"I just want to help—I don't feel right about leaving here with the two of you like this. She needs you, Sy—really she does." My voice softened against my will, I couldn't fight with him if I wanted to—it seems as if throwing pots in New Mexico has mellowed me out too much.

"Don't you think I don't know that?" he snapped with vehemence as he cranked around to look at me, his face was nearly purple; I thought he was going to pop his cork.

"Chill out—look at you—you've cleaned up, you're dressed, and you even shaved—you look more like you—come on, let's go see her—please? She's very upset—she came over here this morning 'as scheduled', but you didn't answer the door, and she came back crying her eyes out—I can't believe you could be so cruel to her—your *dear heart*." My verbal dig into his weakness nearly caused him to fall over himself to get over there, but he stopped short at the sliding glass door, I almost slammed into him, but stepped aside in time to avoid contact—as if he had cooties.

"I didn't do it to hurt her," he murmured, leaning his forehead against the screen. "I had planned to see her today—I just needed time to think—I just—oh, forget it."

"What?" I asked, tugging on his sleeve.

"I was waiting for you to leave—I can't do this with you hanging around—or telling me what to do," he sighed heavily. I noticed that he fiddled with something in his hand.

"What's that—is that a ring?" I asked, grabbing his fiddling fingers. "I've seen it before—it's that diamond." I immediately recognized the oval-shaped diamond as the one I found in his underwear drawer whenever I put away his laundry. It's always been there like a permanent fixture resting inside the red velvet box with a white satin interior. I had never taken it out of the box, I was always too afraid to touch it. I figured the rock had to be at least a half a karat, if not more; now seeing it lying in the palm of his hand made me realize the special nature of it; the softness of the old gold had conformed to the shape of another finger that had worn it for years. A part of me wanted to cry because his sentimentality was always so touching. During our years together, he just about drove me crazy—I always accused him of being a woman because he was too softhearted about things.

"It's my mother's engagement ring—Jacob let me have it—I almost gave it to Samantha once—I came across it the other day while looking for something else," he blushed. It's funny how he's so private about things like his underwear.

"Good-gravy, if you do give it to her please don't tell her you've kept it in your underwear drawer for ten years," I chastised him with a grimace.

He smirked at me and shook his head. "Did you ever think it was for you?"

"Of course I did, you silly-boo," I giggled, recalling the elation I had once felt when I first found it, and then as the years progressed without a proposal—or even a suggestion of one, I shunned it—I nearly spit on it once out of spite.

"How did you feel when you thought that it was?" His voice carried a curious lilt.

"There was a time when I might have tumbled to the suggestion—but I mostly felt mortified by the thought—I'm sorry," I sighed, no longer wanting to berate him about the past.

"It's okay," he nodded, his expression unaffected.

"So why do you have it now—are you going to ask her to marry you?"

"Maybe I won't give this ring to her—it's from another time and place—I'll buy her a new ring—that is, if I ask her—maybe now is not the right time," he said, laying the ring down on his desk; it looked small and fragile like his mother did in the pictures on his desk. Sammy is made of tougher stuff; her inner strength is admirable, but right now, I feared that the loss of Guthrie weakened her resilient fabric.

"Of course," I agreed as I followed him out the door, feeling so pleased that I successfully dragged him out of his hovel to go see her. The two of us traveled through the hedge to the house, and we ascended into the garret where she sat working on her doodles in a sketchbook just as I had last seen her this morning. Her kitten lay asleep in her lap in a sprawl, his soft, white underbelly that she calls *"the hidden pooh"* exposed.

"Go," I laughed, giving the man a gentle push through the studio door, and he stepped up to peer over her shoulder. She did not turn to him just yet; her intense concentration seemed to make her deaf to our arrival. I heard him gasp when he saw his image repeated over every available space on the page, as if her pencil cried for him to be present. I left them alone. I have done what I came for; the rest is up to them.

∾

"Samantha," I whispered, my hand stroking her dark brown hair; its softness shimmered through my fingers. I could smell lavender.

"Sylvester," she replied, halting her work to turn around in her chair, her eyes focusing on me with cheerful clarity.

"I'm sorry about missing you for coffee this morning—please forgive me," I fumbled meekly, feeling so ashamed that I had hurt her. "I want to explain—"

"Oh, Sylvester—I figured you were just sleeping—or in the john, you did have a few drinks at the reception yesterday—I was worried that you might be sick," she smiled.

As I looked into her bright face, I realized that I've been set up—*but does it matter?*

"Tell me—I have wanted to ask you for a long time now—" I began to say just as my heart stubbed its big toe on memories that I have tried to bury, but the disturbance in the earth of my conscience has forced them to the surface; my stray thoughts always remind me of the treasure that love contains. "Why do you have a sketch of my ass above your drafting table?" I asked, pointing at the drawing that had caught my eye; its presence startled me once again in an amusing way that shakes me up inside.

"I drew it after the last time we made love—I thought it was funny to put it there—not that your ass is funny looking—I just like looking at it— and I like the way it makes me feel when I see it," she smiled, reaching out, she made a gesture as if to pinch it with her fingers.

"But why?" I started to laugh, bending down to nuzzle the perfectly combed part in the middle of her hair; I suddenly found myself unable to resist the temptation as I kissed the top of her head.

"I love it," she laughed, catching my left arm in her hands, she drew it around her, rubbing her cheek on my shirtsleeve, and then kissing my bared forearm below the rolled cuff.

"You love it?" I hugged her against my stomach, and she leaned her head against me.

"Yes, because it's yours," she giggled with a girlish sound that I always loved.

"Samantha—do you love me?" I asked, my voice quivering with strained emotions.

"Yes, I love you," she sang, her hands gripped my forearms as I hugged her tight. "I have always loved you, Sylvester!"

"I love you too, dear heart—I have loved you for a very long time." We silently contemplated our words for a moment; I listened to her quiet breathing, quick short breaths. "What are we going to do about this?" I exhaled once I realized that I had been holding my breath—but I was not really holding it, I was just not breathing at all.

"Guthrie said that we should get married," she whispered.

"He said that?" I asked, not really surprised. The last conversation I had with him took place on that dreadful morning. I confronted him in the barn after Sammy had left me because I needed to know what their arrangement was, I didn't care if I made a fool of myself. He stood in a halo of dust and sunshine weaving on his feet—he was drunk, he probably woke up drunk and intended to continue the buzz. *"Christ, what arrangement?"* Guthrie snarled, wiping his mouth after taking a swallow of beer. *"Hayden, don't be a fool—it is irrelevant how I feel about her—all that matters to me is how you and Sammy feel about each other! I know that she loves you—I was trying to tell you that in Taos—you, my friend, should get over there, and tell her that you love her!"* And then the last words he gasped as I stood beside him outside the carriage house—they were the last words I heard him speak in what remained of his life—*"She loves you—take care of her—love her."*

"I was so surprised—he just asked me one day—*"Do you love Hayden?"* and I told him, of course I did, and that I have loved you for a very long time. Then he said, *"We should see about getting you two married when we get back."* But when we got home, you were still so sad about Helena—he said that you and I will know when the time is right—do you think maybe now?"

~

Breathing—both of us—inhaling and exhaling, our lives intertwined once again. I could feel every breath he took, the gentle expansion and contraction of his ribs against my back, his every exhale whispered onto the top of my head. When his breath quickened, his arms gripped me tighter; I held my breath just so I could hear what he wanted to say. He took a deep breath.

"Samantha—I've been a fool—it was you I have loved, yet I had forsaken you for an old dream that I no longer believed in—but none of it matters—none of it matters now," he sighed, kissing my hair again. "You don't mind marrying an old fool like me?" he asked, laying his cheek on top of my head.

I let out my held breath and began to cry, feeling sorry for him—sorry for both of us—*we're so alone now.* "Are you sure that you want to marry me? My being the way I am—it's difficult, I know it is—I know that it was hard for Guthrie being alone with me while we were on the road. He couldn't do it—it was a relief to him to have you here to help him, but he's gone now, and now you will be alone—I don't want to be a burden to you," I sobbed. *I love this man—this manthismanthis man, who I love so much.*

"There, now, don't cry, Samantha—you have never been a burden to me. We will be fine—you and I alone—because we love each other," he said, petting my hair. "With you, I will never be alone—with you, dear heart, I have never felt alone."